Two Mothers, Twin Daughters

GRACE'S DILIMNA
BOOK ONE

MARILYN FRIESEN

Leaving England Behind

Grace staggered: extreme exhaustion caused her to slump against the rail of the ship, Tena-rae. The last few weeks had taken such a heavy toll on her both physically and emotionally. It made her heart ache even worse when arm in arm a group of girls leaned against the rail and crooned "The White Cliffs of Dover" as a tribute to their homeland. When the thick gloomy fog had thinned somewhat, she saw those white chalk cliffs rearing up in their entire splendor next to the choppy ocean. The girls had moved along, still singing, but Vera Lynn's words floated back to her:

'There'll be love and laughter
And peace ever after tomorrow
When the world is free.'

Like wisps of fog, vestiges of final moments with her mother stained her cheeks.

"Get out of my life! You are a disgrace! You are good for nothing!' Her mother's harsh shriek rang in her ears, crushing her spirit.

Grace's blue-gray eyes burned with unshed tears. Am I good for nothing, she mutely asked the wisps of fog floating by. If I am, then why was I born? If my heart were any heavier, it would sink like a stone in this vast gray expanse of ocean. She hated anyone to see her crying so bit her lip to steady it. The memories of her mother, Mrs. Adderley's, raging voice were harder to still.

"We taught you not to go to the bar! We told you not to get involved with those drunken Canadian soldiers!"

"But it wasn't a bar!" Grace protested. "It was at the community center and most of the soldiers drank very moderately."

It had felt hopeless trying to reason with her mother's rigid back turned towards her, so Grace faced the moisture streaked kitchen window instead. She stared unseeingly into the darkness to hide the teardrops that managed to trickle out between half-closed eyelids then mindlessly swished the dishes that her mother had left for her to do, through the sudsy water.

Grace was a thoughtful, respectful girl, perhaps a little shy, so it was a breathtaking day in her boring life when she and her friend first met those two Canadian soldiers. They, especially the auburn haired one, looked so sharp in their crisp, khaki uniform. She and her school chum, Betsy, had been walking home from school, arms laden with books. The sky had been a bright pretty blue, which was a luxury after so much rain and fog. In a few days, the academy would be close for the summer break, and they were walking along with light, brisk steps.

Then, stepping smartly, two soldiers pivoted around the corner, saluted, and offered to carry their books. Grace had caught her breath and stared. What could have been more flattering than having such incredibly good-looking privates salute them? She still marveled at how easy it had been to chat with those courteous strangers with intriguing Canadian accents.

Grace's lips curved upwards at the memory. *I am normally so reserved, yet I actually bantered and giggled with them even more than Betsy did! It would have astonished the schoolmaster, and probably most of the scholars.* Her smile faded, but it did feel like *the real me.*

Almost without noticing, their feet had carried them far beyond the Adderley's home street. Flustered, she had tried to take her books away from her companion, Randall Sutherland, but he just held on the tighter. "Not unless you come with me to the dance tonight," he teased with an easy grin.

The color drained from Grace's cheeks; she clearly remembered her reaction. *A dance? I've never gone to a dance in my life! Dances are wicked! I know that.* It was not dancing that tempted Grace, but the opportunity to get to know Randall better. *We wouldn't have to dance, would we? Maybe we could just, well... stroll around in the moonlight as they do in storybooks. Alternatively, maybe we could, uh, sit and visit or something.*

Looking back, Grace knew that it was then that she felt the first niggling pang of uneasiness, but she had been too busy laughing at Randall and the other private's nonsense to pay much attention. Grace's head lowered, shamefaced. The soldiers had teased and wheedled them, drawing attention to Grace's bouncy curls that were a shiny as a raven's wing'.

They praised her petal soft cheeks 'that an angel would envy' and teased Betsy about the cute up tilt of her freckled nose.

"Two such charming girls should not be allowed to shrivel up 'like dried old apples'," Randall had declared.

Finally, laughingly, Grace had given in, just as Randall unwrapped a sweet and popped it into her mouth.

"Just this once:" she sputtered, trying to speak sternly but had dissolved into giggles. She resorted to covering her mouth to keep from drooling!

Grace didn't recall where Betsy and the other soldier had wandered off. They had strolled away in a different direction while Grace happily trotted beside a soldier who was chivalrously carrying her books.

They had been strolling for a long time, Grace unconsciously detouring the streets where there was the most severe bomb damage. It had been easy to prattle lightly about many things, and forget the heavy cares of a war going on at least for the moment, then, feeling wonderfully weary; they collapsed on a sheltered bench in a common.

Randall unceremoniously dumped her books on the grass beside him and reached for her in, what struck her as a rather possessive manner, Grace shrank back alarmed, so he quickly released her, but left his arm resting on the back of the bench.

They chatted until Grace saw dusk creeping on and worried about not going directly home after school.

What if the air siren went off? Where would they go? She looked around for an air raid shelter. They were so far from the black, stuccoed cottage she called home. Will my parents be anxious? Grace hoped so but seriously doubted it. She was more concerned about her mother's fury. Even though it was her final year at the secondary school, her mother had many ironclad rules to keep her in line and her father half-heartedly submitted to them. Coming straight home was one of the ordinances. She knew there would be more waiting for her than gentle concern or even a stern reproof for not showing up promptly.

How was I supposed to have gotten out of this difficult situation?

"Oh well, the damage is done," Randall grinned mischievously. "If you're going to get into trouble anyway, you might as well make it worth their while. Why not go out for supper-- I mean High Tea with me? I'll treat you to steak, roast beef with Yorkshire pudding...kidney pie, or whatever your British appetite is craving."

Grace doubted that even the more swish restaurants could offer such swell fare in these hard times but her mouth watered at the prospect after so many months of unwelcome rationing.

"If you will allow me to ring up Mom from the pub you want to take me to," she bargained, "then I'll go. He nonchalantly agreed.

Thinking back, Grace could easily recall how her face flamed as her mother's strident voice carried over the wire. How many of those patrons heard the dressing-down I got?

The scene that occurred after the dance was one that she would rather blot from her memory. Even though she had hurried to do the dishes left for her, and make amends in other ways, it was impossible to appease them.

The anger! The mistrust! The accusations! Doesn't Mom have any faith in me at all? Why couldn't Dad have said just one word in my favor? I have never defied their wishes before! Had they not taught me to be uncommonly obedient? I even stammered out an apology that I really meant.

It was not well received. What a relief when she was able to slip off to her dreary attic bedroom. After she had washed the dishes, dried, and stacked them in the cupboards, her mother had turned to rail on Dad.

That night Grace felt like her vision cleared, since then she became increasingly impatient with her elderly parents' medieval ways.

Abruptly her thoughts switched channels. Oh, I wish Randall's gaiety didn't come from a bottle, so often. He is a wonderful young man, so charming and well mannered: her doesn't need drink to boost his morale!

A scene from one of their many times together floated into her memory: "Randall you had one drink, already, must you have another?" she had reached out to touch the cold glass.

"I'm fine, Sweet: no need to worry. I can hold my liquor. This will be the last. You should taste it. It's quite pleasant, in fact." She shuddered in refusal and he had never suggested it again.

Meeting Margaret

CHAPTER 2

Grace's physical distress tore her away from the unpleasant memories. Sighing despondently, she pressed her fingers against her throbbing temples and wished the ship could stop swaying. A wave of nausea reached her throat, making it sting. Almost before she knew what was happening, Grace was vomiting over the side of the ship. When she started to throw up, she couldn't seem to stop. Even after her stomach was relieved of all its contents, her reflexes were still heaving.

The slender girl collapsed to her knees while her red plaid dress swirled around her knees. Although she was grasping the rail with one hand, her chin sank against her chest.

Am I –truly worthless? Am I? She gazed at the heavy clouds on the horizon. We did get married; only at the courthouse, to be sure, but married nonetheless. Mom and Dad wouldn't put on a wedding, so we had to do it that way.

A snappy sea breeze quickly swept in and Grace shivered. She wrapped her hands around her arms to keep warm and leaned her head against the rail. A surprised look crossed her face as something pleasantly cozy settled around her shoulders.

"Why don't you sit down, Mrs. Sutherland," a fellow war bride invited, leading her to a deck chair.

Grace stared at her. "How did you know my name?"

"When I saw you chunder over the rail, I asked around." The woman explained while tucking the royal blue/sky blue and white blend shawl over her arms. "I'll ask a Red Cross nurse for something to settle your stomach. You stay right here."

The corner of Grace's mouth managed to tilt slightly upwards. As if, I have the strength to go anywhere else. She tucked her small, pale hands under the shawl. Who could this warm-hearted, gregarious young woman be? I feel so relaxed with her. Grace admired her fresh, country girl look, the chocolate colored eyes and gorgeous strawberry blond hair, but especially the light smattering of freckles across the bridge of her nose which made her look so much like a carefree country girl.

Grace's heart sank: which is exactly what I'm not these days.

"I'm sorry Mrs. Sutherland, I couldn't locate a nurse but here's a glass of water. To say you are looking greenish wouldn't be exactly complimentary but it's the truth!"

Grace smiled wryly, "If I feel this unwell now, what would it be like if a storm comes up?" She watched the white caps scurrying towards them.

"Don't worry about the weather, Grace, it may be just fine."

Grace managed to smile. "I thought you were going to 'Mrs. Sutherland' me all the way! I barely graduated; I'm too young for that!"

Grace caught the impish look in those gold-flecked brown eyes.

"I figured you would find being called 'Mrs. Sutherland' amusing" and you looked like you needed some cheering up. Let's get acquainted. I'm Margaret," she continued, and then pretended to curtsy, "Officially known as Mrs. David Seifert. I'm on my way to join my husband in Halifax. He's a soldier, but is on furlough now recuperating from a serious injury."

She stretched out on a vacant deck chair next to Grace whose stomach, thankfully, had settled somewhat.

"He's in a hurry to get back to the front and is as loyal to Canada, even though he was born elsewhere, as we are too merry old England."

Margaret leaned back in the deck chair and crossed her hands behind her head.

"It's a relief to be crossing the ocean. I got the jitterbugs from all those bombs whistling and all."

"Hopefully it's safer here."

A bevy of girls strolled towards them and stopped to chat. They seemed to know Margaret quite well, and were more her age, some with one or two children in tow. Grace felt so left out.

After they continued on their way, Margaret began reminiscing:

"It took ages and mountains of paperwork before I was approved for departure. By then David was calling me nearly every day to see if I was okay. You can imagine the frightful expense that was!

Here, let me tuck this shawl around you. There that's better. That wind is nippy.

"Do you know what? I'm going to have an instant family! David was a widower with two small children when I met him. I've never even seen the kiddies! I am so nervous! Oh, I do hope they will like me!"

"You'll make a good Mother," Grace said reassuringly. "How old are they?"

"Two and four: Sally turns three on August 22 and David Junior turns five on August 19 so they are two years apart."

A faraway look came into her eyes; "It must have been a sad, sad day for their family when their Mama Janet died of pneumonia. David wasn't even home at the time! He was on the battlefront."

Grace didn't know what to say. Hesitantly she stammered, "But, at least, they'll have you now."

"Thank you. Now tell me about yourself. Sorry for blathering so much. I can be such a jibber-jabber- once I get started," she turned slightly to face Grace," but I really do want to hear about you. Are you staying in Nova Scotia, also?"

The blast of a horn nearby made them gasp.

The Dunkirk Spirit

CHAPTER 3

"*Lifeboat* drill!" someone shouted. Hearing the officer barking orders was a nerve-wracking reminder of the seriousness of sailing during wartime.

Several hours later Grace and Margaret chanced to meet in the corridor.

"Why don't you come over to our cabin," Margaret invited, "The other girls are playing tennis so it will be quiet there for now."

Later, as she relaxed on her lower berth, she motioned for Grace to make herself comfortable on a nearby chair: as comfortable as she could under the crowded conditions.

"Where will you be living when you reach Canada?" Margaret asked.

Grace's face clouded over. Up until now, she had put up a good façade of being a carefree teenager, but if Margaret seemed so sincerely interested in her, her guard might slip.

She was dreading the strange unknown future that awaited her after they docked. It seemed easier to deal with by blocking it from her mind but hated to offend Margaret by not answering.

"I'm going inland." Her voice dragged. "I'll be taking the transcontinental out west to a place called Deer Flats. Somewhere way out in Alberta where ever that is, I can't even begin to imagine what it will look like over there."

Margaret looked at her keenly. *She looks too frail and forlorn to be on her own like this. I wonder how old she is.*

"How did you meet your husband?" she asked gently. "You seem so young."

Grace sat up stiffly. "I'm not young," she flared. "Everyone thinks I'm sixteen, or maybe even less because I'm tiny for my age, but I'm eighteen!"

She paused to let her temper cool. "We got acquainted...well mostly at a dance I guess. Or at least, that's how it started."

She stared gloomily at the narrow bunks opposite her. *It had been such a whirlwind romance. I was almost giddy with love from the first time we met, and thought he felt the same way towards me,*

Things had happened so fast, though, did we know each other well enough? Were we prepared to take such a big step during wartime?

She nervously twisted a curl around her finger. *What did Randall ever do to get deported? Was he dangerous? That is so very unusual. It's unheard of in fact. The only reason anyone is discharged honorably is if they are half dead, isn't it? But if he wasn't booted out, why in the world did they permit me to come, especially before the fighting is over?*

To make matters worse what little communication there had been between her and her parents had deteriorated severely. *Mom especially was very vocal in her disapproval of 'that bloke from a foreign country'.*

If only I wouldn't have been so desperate to get married, to flee the nest! If only --.Grace's cheeks flushed when she saw the worried look in Margaret's eyes, embarrassed that her mind had been wandering.

Grace stared down at the handkerchief twisted in her lap. She scrambled around in her thoughts to remember what they had been talking about then mumbled lamely: "Even though my parents were so opposed, we were sure we could make it work!"

"I guess most parents hate to see their children move so far away," Margaret suggested. "I know my Mom cried a lot, although she tried to be brave in my presence. At least, we were able to have several heart-to- heart visits before I left." She smiled sadly. "Those I will always cherish."

She rose and brushed out her long wavy hair then tucked it into a graceful chignon as a preparation for supper.

"They had so much they wanted to say—to share—to teach," she continued, unaware of the knife of jealousy she was twisting in Grace's heart. "It felt like we didn't have much time but Mom and Dad took the time, for which I am grateful. Dad graciously found out as much as he could about Canada and other things. That was a relief." She laughed. "It dispelled my fears of Indians with headdresses lurking behind every tree!"

Her eyes widened. "Oh dear, here I go again, doing all the talking! You must be so provoked with me!"

Grace's eyes flickered towards the woman beside her, then down at her lap. I wish you would just keep on, Margaret. It keeps my mind off my own troubles.

"Would you rather not talk?" Margaret leaned forward to catch Grace's reflection in the tiny, rectangular mirror." Am I being too inquisitive?"

Grace's eyes curved sideways. "I like listening to you," She responded evasively.

"Really? But I want to hear your story!"

"Someday…maybe… I'd like to hear more about your family. You seem like such a jolly sort."

A subdued quietness settled between them. Margaret hesitantly broke it.

"Yeah, I guess we did. I took it too much for granted especially when I was younger." She dabbed at her eyes. "I miss them…a lot…You're right, we were really close.

There were only the four of us: Mumsey, Dad and my brother Richard. He's in the air force somewhere."

She smiled "Just like a male, he doesn't keep in touch very good. Unless it's because…" her voice trailed off, then she abruptly changed the subject. "Why were your parents so opposed, Grace?"

"How can I know why? They wouldn't even speak to me after we were married! Literally." At least, Mom wouldn't, she amended to herself. Dad tried, but I was upset and gave him the cold shoulder.

"I was stuck living with them because Randall was stationed in France. They would have kicked me out if there was a place for me to go!"

Margaret looked aghast "Oh Grace, surely not! Was it that bad?"

"It was bad enough being so lonesome—and heartsick for Randall without any support from my parents," Grace responded grimly, "but there were other things. Remember the air raids? Of course, you do! They terrified me! Hearing those sirens was enough to make me sure I was going to die!

"I started panicking a couple years ago when Buckingham Palace and the Victoria Station were bombed. What was ever going to happen to our country? I know even Mother was upset because she practically idolized the Queen. She felt sorry for the poor, adorable princesses, knowing they must have been dreadfully frightened."

Grace grimaced; Mom cared more about the queen then her own frightened daughter.

Grace covered her face with her hands, unwilling to say what really bothered her about the air raids. If I could have snuggled close to my parents or held their hands, or even just felt their sympathy while in the bomb shelter, it wouldn't have been so awful! I had to sit alone in the dark with those horrible bombs going off—and not knowing where—let alone how—Randall was doing; it made me so apprehensive!

I'll never forget the time I scurried down the street to the sound of the air raid siren screaming in my ears and Mom not even meeting me at the door to see if I was all right! She was already in the shelter. Knitting, and leisurely sipping a cup of tea!

"It was because of all the bombings," Margaret explained, that David urged me to leave now; immediately; before the war was over. We were very worried when we heard on BBC radio that a shipload of children had sunk —the poor darlings- but my papers were completed by then," she lifted her hands expressively, "So here I am! I am nervous about being hit by a submarine, but David is convinced it would be more dangerous to stay in the British Isles. I hope, oh, I hope he's right! "She paused, then added thoughtfully. "We should be safe enough if it didn't leak out to the wrong people when we were leaving."

"Loose lips sink ships," Grace quoted.

After putting the light out, Grace peered fearfully at the heaving ocean through the small, round porthole. It was dark, but in the starlight, she could see the black hulks that formed the rest of the convoy. If just one desperate sailor would light up a cigarette on one of these boats, it could mean being destroyed by a submarine.

"Didn't it make you nervous that they told us to keep off the decks after life boat drill today?" Grace tucked the blackout cover securely around the window and switched the light on. "I wonder if they spotted something that they're not telling us about. After all, it isn't that windy."

"Where in England did you come from? London?"

Margaret shook her head. "No, we were from a coastal village close to the Scottish border, near Greenock: Lower Blossomby."

Grace shrugged her shoulders, "Never heard of the place."

"It was close enough to Glasgow," Margret explained, "to, to...not be safe."

"There was a lot of bomb damage done on some of the streets in our neighborhood," Grace continued, "many of the women were near beside themselves with fright. I'd see them talking in clusters at the street corners. The roof was blown right off a house not too far from our own."

"Randall was worried, also. He wanted to evacuate me weeks ago but..."

She sealed her lips, unwilling to voice the rest of the thought. He never could communicate peaceably with Mrs. Adderley, her mother, so there was sort of a deadlock.

Grace's shoulders sagged. All the fire of bitterness seemed to have gone out of her spirit, leaving a weary, discouraged look on her delicate features.

"Tell me about Randall," Margaret invited.

Grace smoothed down the hem of her brick red gingham skirt. Her thoughts were still on relationships. With an effort, she refocused. "Well, he's nice...and handsome..."

"Oh come on," Margaret teased, "He must have swept you off your feet by something more concrete than that! Maybe I should say the same things about David."

Grace looked at her blankly as if she wasn't sure what they had been talking about. Then she re-focused and her eyes grew soft.

"Yeah...you're right. Randall had such a charming way about him. I considered him by far the best-looking man in the community hall with his finely chiseled features and ..." Her voice trailed off.

"Soo?" Margaret made as if she would flits Grace's head. "What if I said the same about my man—that he is the best looking?"

"He has gorgeous auburn hair with highlights of gold."

"Ohh. So you married him for his hair!" Margaret pretended to be scandalized. "What if he goes bald?"

Grace gave her a playful punch, something she would have never done in her mother's presence. "Redheads never go bald," she retorted.

"Oh, is that so?" Margaret teased. "I don't think you have your facts straight. They might not go gray but I'm not so sure about the going bald part."

Grace didn't care, her solemn look returned. "We seemed so …meant…for each other,"

Margaret subconsciously shook her head. Married only a few months at the most and she's using the past tense!

They paused to listen as someone opened and closed a series of doors. When their favorite steward nodded, and playfully curtsied while inviting them for supper, they thanked him. The aroma of haddock and chips wafted up from the galley but they did not find it tantalizing.

The girls who shared the cabin with Margaret trouped in, chattering gaily. After washing their little ones' hands and sprucing themselves up, they left.

"Do you want to go right away, or wait for the second setting?" Margaret asked.

"I'll wait. I'm glad I stopped vomiting, for now, but sure don't feel like eating, although I don't know if I'll feel any better, later."

"I don't feel the best either," Margaret, admitted, she also looked a little queasy.

Grace glanced covertly at her newfound friend. She seems so kind. Can she really be as nice as she appears? Was Margaret shocked by anything I've said? Will she gossip? Dare I reveal more? Oh, I hope she is someone I can continue to share with, someone I can trust.

Laying there, with her ankles crossed, her hands locked behind her head, Margaret looked gentle and serene. She claimed she talked too much, but Grace didn't feel like it was loud meaningless chatter. Even the times they had nothing to say, Grace felt safe in her company.

Margaret was wearing a light green two-piece outfit. If she hadn't laid her hands across her abdomen, she wouldn't have showed. The joyful, yet tender look on her face revealed that she was very happy. Grace assumed that included being glad to be carrying David's child.

Grace had qualms about her own pregnant condition. It was difficult being in the family way when the baby's Daddy was not even around but it made it so much worse that her own mother was coldly aloof.

One of the many things she had to do on her own was to see a physician.

Her family doctor had peered at her from over the top of his glasses. "You think are pregnant, Grace? Hasn't your mother told you anything about the birds and the bees?"

Grace flushed. "But, but I am m-married,"

He shook his head and Grace hated the amused look on his face. "I'm sure it was not with your mother's consent."

Grace wanted to brace herself to keep from sliding under his desk.

"We will have to get a pregnancy test done, but I hope for your sake it isn't true."

His reaction made Grace feel fiercely protective of the little Unknown growing inside her. He scribbled something on a paper and handed it to her. She held it possessively against her stomach and fled the room.

Cautiously at first, then more freely, Grace shared what was on her heart. After they went down to eat, they chose a secluded table that was very private and far from most of the boisterous crowds.

"I can't believe it that I am sharing so much with you," Grace exclaimed, "This isn't like me at all."

"Lots of people are laying down their barriers 'during these trying times' and getting closer to others. I guess because we aren't feeling safe, so need each other more."

Grace nodded thoughtfully, "It's what people are calling the Dunkirk spirit."

Both of the girls were sober as they thought of the more than eight hundred boats of all shapes and sizes that had rushed to Dunkirk, France to aid in the rescuing of the trapped army. According to Winston Churchill, the best of the best officers, as well as other soldiers, had been surrounded and in danger of extermination so there had been an emergency evacuation.

Grace had a faraway look in her eyes. "I wonder how the French men and women felt when the Britishers left. Did they feel like we abandoned them?" She shuddered. "I'm glad Randall wasn't there."

Margaret reached out for both of Grace's hands and met her

eyes; "We Britishers know how to pull together when the need is greatest."

Grace nodded hesitantly.

The young women continued to visit long after someone cleared the supper dishes away. They had merely picked at their food but a considerate waiter provided them with a full pot of their favorite English beverage, tea, from which they replenished their cups from time to time.

"So how did you feel when you found out you were expecting with him not being around and all?" Margaret asked.

Grace hung her head and toyed with her spoon making Margaret wonder why the question was so difficult to answer.

"I was thrilled...at first. I was madly in love with Randall and thought it would be wonderful having a little boy just like him."

Margaret looked puzzled. She obviously couldn't figure out why Grace was talking as if it was all over when it was clear to everyone that she was crossing the ocean to be reunited with her husband.

"I hoped the babby would be adorably cute with auburn hair just like his Daddy. I could hardly wait until he—Randall, I mean, could have a weekend pass so I could share the wonderful news. It was all I could think of--all the time; the babby, and my Randall."

She unconsciously played with one of her dark curls falling over her slender shoulder. "It's lonely when he's gone," she concluded simply.

Margaret nodded.

Grace was quiet as if not sure whether to continue, then added hesitantly;" I'm still shocked by his reaction, 'A babby! So soon! Good grief, what were you thinking?"

He had been striding back and forth across the room when he said that, then stopped and stared into her eyes.

"Ohh-h, so you're gonna be a Mama, eh? That's what you really wanted! No more time for flirting with me, eh? "You just got married so you could have a baby, didn't you?

"I tried to insist that he would always have first place in my life, but he sneered and acted as if he didn't believe it. Then he took his beret and left! I'm just heartsick!"

He hadn't even kissed me goodbye, Grace thought secretly, but certainly wasn't about to tell anyone, not even Margaret!

"Maybe he was distraught. After all, a dreadful war is going on, and he couldn't be there to protect you especially while you are pregnant. Maybe he didn't want to tell you about the dangers lest you'd worry also so covered it up with a front."

Grace looked unconvinced.

"It was only eight -thirty!" Grace continued, "He didn't have to leave 'til the next morning! Why was he so upset about me getting pregnant? I thought he would be overjoyed! That got me...feeling...shattered."

Grace remembered flinging across the cot in the attic bedroom, wailing in despair. Dad had struggled up the narrow stairs to comfort her, but she had been inconsolable.

"I might have calmed down eventually if Mom hadn't come in right then and started scolding."

Margaret leaned forward, "Some people don't know how to show sympathy and caring."

Grace' twisted away. "That's not Mom's excuse."

She abruptly changed the subject in that impetuous way of hers. "I had all those piles of forms to fill out, and Mom refused to help. Not one bit: those papers from the government, y'know. I was so bewildered by it all, that I turned to a former schoolmarm for assistance."

Margaret nodded. "Yes, I got a stack too," she reminded Grace.

"I guess they wanted to know if we were worthy to be Canadian citizens,"

Margaret sighed: Grace was sounding bitter again.

"What really made me feel like crawling under the carpet was when they asked if I had to get married. At least I could honestly say 'no' ''.

She removed the quilted tea cozy and poured herself another cuppa, then slowly stirred in several teaspoons of sugar, obviously unaware of what she was doing.

"About those papers; I hardly knew if I should fill them in or not."

A waiter came around lighting the candles on the occupied tables. "We have to put out the electric lights soon," he explained.

Margaret smiled; they didn't really care. She took a taste of her lemony custard tart: should I tell Grace that I'm trusting God to carry us through? Why is it so hard for me to talk about Him?

She reminisced how her Heavenly Father miraculously caused her and David to meet seven months earlier. After Janet had died, his parents had attempted to care for their grandchildren, but when the elder Mrs. Seifert had a series of minor strokes, they knew that wasn't the solution.

Margaret met him in the flower shop where she worked evenings when she wasn't busy at the factory. He has been ordering flowers for his mother. When Margaret expressed her sympathy, she soon realized how easy he was to visit with.

The visits got longer and more intimate; before he left for some secret battlefront, her pastor- father blessed their marriage in a charming ceremony held in the flower-laden backyard of the parsonage.

Two months later Margaret was devastated when she heard he was critically injured and sent back to Canada to heal. Margaret's parents were so supportive during the time she was working through her grief, loneliness, and anxiety while preparing to join him in Nova Scotia.

Margaret tucked a straying strand of golden-russet hair back into place along with her memories and focused her attention on her young friend. I need to be the support to her that my parents were to me.

Grace glanced furtively around at the shadowy forms in the basically empty dining room, then dropped her voice to a whisper, "I began to wonder; what if he has deserted me?' I hadn't heard from him since he went back to France, not that that necessarily means anything during these dreadful times. When I learned that he was returned to Canada for some reason, I was appalled! It left me in quite a dither."

She clapped her hand over her mouth, "Oh, I shouldn't be telling you all this stuff," then shrugged her shoulders dismissively. "It's too late now to take it back!"

She paused to butter a piece of bread, and took a bite. "Eventually, he did send me the $200 required. You know about that?"

Margaret nodded. David had been glad to be able to help in that way.

Grace took a sip. "EHH, this tea is gross. I put way too much sugar in." She shoved it aside and took another bite of her slice of bread. "So I filled 'em out. What else could I do? He had better not mind when I land on his doorstep! "

"Are you pretty scared?" Margaret asked gently.

"Terrified," Grace's wide gray-blue eyes gave her away. With shiny raven black hair framing her pale, features, she looked far too fragile to face the harsh realities life had thrown her way.

Margaret longed to shield Grace from suffering yet It made her feel a little odd to be having such maternal feelings, except towards those two little darlings she would soon get to mother, so rose as if to leave.

However, Grace had so much bottled up trouble just wiggling to get out. She gripped the edge of the table, stark fear staring out of her eyes. Her face had gone ashen.

"Margaret! Did I tell you about the rumors?"

"No, what rumors?"

"That Randall is a 'lady's man'. That he's given to tippling! That he lived a wild life! How come I didn't find out sooner? Oh, Margaret, what if it's true?"

Margaret resumed her seat. "Then you'll just have to love him out of it." What a lame thing to say.

"But what if I can't?"

"You must try your hardest. Marriage is a commitment for life."

Once again, Margaret felt prompted to tell about Jesus, her Saviour who was such a big help with the difficult things in her own life. . She closed her eyes, took a deep breath, and then leaned forward.

"Grace, listen to me. Have you ever prayed to God? He can give you the strength to face these obstacles."

"God?" Grace lifted her hands in a helpless gesture, "What can God do?" She glanced at the blackout curtains on the portholes. "He has too much to think about as it is."

The big, black and white clock on the wall caught her attention. It was getting late. Almost twelve, but it felt much later. It was high time to go to bed.

The next morning Grace woke up feeling dull and despondent.

I've taken my heart and hung it on display for the entire world to gawk at. How can I ever feel comfortable around Margaret, again? She slunk past Margaret in the corridor, pretending to be fascinated by the tilt of a steward's jaunty white hat.

Margaret watched with amusement touched with pity. She's

humiliated about telling me so much. Oh, well, I'll just give her the space she needs until she's in the mood to talk again. That's what Mom would do.

What Grace hadn't realized, however, was that Margaret was more than just calm, caring young lady. Her father was pastoring in a small town church, and Margaret had learned much through observation and teaching about being gentle with the fragile feelings of others. She seemed to understand what Grace was going through, so gave her the space she required. Margaret was gracious if they chanced to meet, but did not impose herself on the troubled girl.

It was not long until Grace could feel her icy wall of reserve melting. She had no reason to suspect that Margaret was spreading ugly stories about her, even though with so many idle young women around it could have been a tempting opportunity to do so.

A couple days later Grace strolled up and down the corridors without anything better to do since she felt too reserved to get chummy with the other war brides. They seemed to all be older than she was. She made herself comfortable in a sitting area. Margaret was nearby chatting with some of the mothers lounging on the deck. Grace noticed how she would pay attention to the little ones, which caused both the mothers and children to warm towards her.

Grace was idly leafing through a magazine but looked up, startled when a ship officer strode over to her and asked if she knew where Mrs. David Seifert was. Grace pointed to the railing where Margaret was letting the breeze toss her floating hair. The uniformed worker went to her and they seemed to be conversing in low tones. Grace saw her eyes widen as she pressed her hands against the front of her skirt.

"Lower Blossomby, bombed! Are you sure?"

The man nodded.

"A radio message just came in. The Methodist church was hit during Wednesday night prayer meeting—"

Grace hurried over and clutched Margaret's arm since she looked ready to pass out.

"Oh, Grace! It was bombed! Our church was…"

Several hands reached out to lift Margaret as she collapsed to the floor. Grace hurried to follow the stretcher where Margaret lay, but an officer matched his steps with hers. "Are you a good friend of hers?"

Grace nodded.

"When she awakens tell her that someone wired for more information and there were seven casualties, including her parents." He paused, swallowed. "Break the news gently please."

Grace's eyes brimmed with tears. "I will," she replied, but her voice trembled.

The Death Angel's Visit

CHAPTER 4

*Grace*s pillow was flat, the bed hard. The darkness seemed to crowd in around her especially since the blackout curtains so snugly fitted into place. The even breathing of her roommates did nothing to soothe her: their presence was just a constant reminder that the air was stuffy, the swaying room crowded with bodies.

Unfortunately, there was more, much more than those mere trifles that were bothering her. She vividly recalled how Margaret had gasped doubled up in pain, when she heard that a bomb had destroyed their home church, and killed both of her parents. Margaret had taken to her bed immediately afterward, the door shut.

Brenda's little boy, Tommy, had a cold and was breathing loudly. Once he cried out in his sleep, and she was sure it would wake his mother. Whether Brenda heard him or not, Grace didn't know but she didn't go to him.

Soon Linda Lou, Nan's daughter, would wake for her midnight feeding. Grace wished with all her heart she could be sound asleep before then.

Then another sound assaulted her jaded senses and caused her heart to tighten. Why is there so much hurrying back and forth in the corridor at this hour of the night, why else if it isn't because of Margaret?

She heard low voices and a torch briefly created a beam of light beneath the closed door. Grace leaned on one elbow straining to hear the comments.

"Call...doctor..."

Her heart sped up. She debated whether to go to see if there was some way she could help, but the floor would be cold beneath her feet, besides she would be just in the way.

Grace clasped her hand over her mouth to keep from moaning aloud when she heard screams of anguish penetrating the thin walls and knew, just knew it was Margaret, dear, gentle Margaret who was suffering.

No God, no, please no.

Linda Lou whimpered and her mother was cradling her in an instant so Grace realized she was awake because of the unhappy commotion outside their doorway.

The disturbing sounds continued all night, and Grace sensed that the other women were listening. They talked in low voices, but Grace couldn't get herself to join in. She felt like her heart would break. No God, no, please no. she repeated in her mind.

Grace fumbled in the darkness for the ladder. Her dainty ruffled nightgown made descending awkward. She called softly to a passing nurse,

"How's Margaret?" she asked.

The nurse hurried past without answering.

Grace hesitated and looked both ways. Two torches were

illuminating the cabin next to hers. She stepped closer and looked in. Margaret's face was white, and Grace instinctively knew the cause was premature labor.

"Please, no!" Grace hadn't known she had cried out until the doctor looked up sharply.

"We have no need of onlookers!"

Margaret turned her head and gasped, "Grace!"

"She's a good friend," one of the other girl's retorted, but it wouldn't have been necessary. Grace fled to the bedside, and Margaret clung to her hand as if she would never let go.

"Please God, no, please God," Grace begged.

"If you can't shut up, leave!"

Grace wilted under the doctor's harsh words.

She leaned her cheek against Margaret's and was surprised how flushed it felt. Their tears mingled.

Grace's back hurt from being in such an uncomfortable position, but every time Margaret cried out her hand tightened around the younger girl's, so she knew there was no chance of moving to relieve her own pain. She was deathly afraid, not only for Margaret, but also for herself.

I have no reason to believe it, but I suspect I might be carrying not one babby, but two. This could happen to me also! It's not easy to carry twins to full term!

An hour later, the doctor turned away as if to hide the baby from the others in the room. Margaret sat up abruptly, her arms reaching out, "My baby, mine!" she cried.

"No," he said sharply. "You are too emotionally distraught---"

"But he's mine, mine!" Margaret broke down sobbing, "Let me hold him, please, please!"

The nurses stared at each other, the doctor, or Margret, transfixed.

"No! Cut your caterwauling! You need to rest, relax, and heal! There's a war going on. Act like a brave soldier and accept the pain!"

Doris, a spiky-haired passenger that Grace knew only by sight, leaped out of bed. "Give that infant to his mother, you, ----doctor!

Grace heard someone gasp, or maybe it was herself. She shrunk against the wall, saucer -eyed. The doctor shoved the baby into Doris' arms then stomped out angrily muttering his disapproval.

One of the nurses followed him to the door and soberly gazed after him. He is blond haired and blue eyed. Does that mean anything? How could he be so cruel? Could he be a spy? How was he hired to work on this ship? Who hired him?

Doris had transformed into an angel of gentleness as she knelt beside the bereft mother and offered her the tiny, little boy. Margaret cradled that miniature human being, no larger than a man's thumb while tears dampened every face in the room. The sympathy, the pain was greater because of the doctor's harshness.

Margaret hardly noticed when someone removed the chilled infant from her cupped hands. Then her eyes popped open.

"No, wait, wait!" she cried. On top of one of her suitcases was a miniature trunk of handkerchiefs and vials of perfume, some were treasured gifts. Right at the very bottom was a cute handkerchief of a little boy playing with a ball, a puppy at his heels. Grandma Wallace had given it to Richard but he had sold it to his sister for a tuppence since she was collecting them at the time. She tenderly wrapped the little body in the handkerchief, gave him one last lingering kiss on the forehead, and laid him in the hands of one of the nurses who promised to find a suitable container for burial.

Someone switched off one of the torches, and Felicity asked if she wanted a little light left on. Margaret mutely nodded. In her heart was such a deep ache she could hardly pray. She lay down, but not to sleep.

Grace crept out of the room. Margaret's broken-hearted sniffles followed her.

Grace tried to keep her own anguish muffled as she slipped back to her bunk but heads popped up all around her.

"How's Margaret?" several voices demanded.

"Fine, I guess," Grace answered woodenly, her eyes downcast, "Knackered out, of course."

"What about the baby?"

She shook her head unable to respond and swallowed a lump in her throat.

"How's the baby?" someone gently repeated.

"He-he didn't make it," Grace meant to whisper but it came out more like a sniffle.

A newborns' thin cry rent the air. His mother snatched up a light. The baby's bed was a wire net basket attached to the bunk. She picked him up, cuddling him close.

The crying awakened another infant. None of the brides dreamed of complaining about the disturbance. Mothers' clung to their own offspring, soothing and being soothed by the soft warmth of their own living children.

For a little while, Grace watched the mothers rocking their fretful children but it did nothing to soothe her nerves. She lay there, sleepless, cradling her swelling abdomen between her hands as waves of anxiety washed over her. She yearned to feel the reassuring kicks of her own little one, but it was too soon.

Morning inevitably came whether they were ready for it or not.

Grace yearned, possibly for the first time in her young life, for an inner strength to be a blessing. If only she had a handful of flowers to give Margaret. She had no idea how to comfort her. Sometimes flowers helped more than words. Didn't they?

She donned her white dressing gown, and after sashing it around the waist, ran a brush through her hair. Was she ready? No, oh, no, but she had to go see Margaret. She must.

The other women watched her with sad, thoughtful eyes but didn't have the courage to face Margaret's calamity, not yet.

Margaret appeared to be sleeping. Her face was pale and tear stained framed against her golden-brown locks that draped over the pillow. Grace hesitated at the door. Should I wake her?

Just then, Margaret's eyes fluttered open and she motioned languidly over to her young friend.

Frantically, Grace wondered if the sleepy girl had forgotten what had happened during the night. Then Margaret let in a deep intake of breath and jerked into the fetal position. Grace froze. Everyone else did also.

Up until then, one had been aimlessly pulling a comb through her short tresses, while the rest were listlessly going through various stages of getting ready for the day.

Grace pulled up a chair that was nearby, and shyly stroked back the thick, wavy hair that had fallen across Margaret's face.

What now?

"Thank you for coming," Margaret whispered.

Silence filled the room. Out of the corner of her eye, Grace noticed some of the other women were unobtrusively filing out.

"Hand me my Bible please." As she reached for it, Grace wondered if it was an automatic reaction from years of relying on God.

"Could you find John 14 for me?"

"First John or St. John?"

"St. John."

Grace scrabbled through the pages. I have no idea where it is. With a Mom, who is so pious and I've straggled along behind her to church all my life, yet I can't even find the book of John!

Then she remembered; it was in the New Testament. After that, it was but a moment until she found the right place.

"Read the first two verses out loud, Please. I need them."

Grace cast her an anxious look: is she going to start crying?

"Let not your heart be troubled. Ye believe in God, believe also in Me. In my Father's house are many mansions. If it were not so, I would have told you. I go to prepare a place for you. And if I go and prepare a place for you; I will come again and receive you unto myself; that where I am there ye may be also."

There was a momentary silence, and then Margaret turned to reach for Grace's hand.

"Thank you, "she murmured. "That was a balm to my soul. My baby is safe with Jesus," she continued. "I wanted so much to care for him, but Jesus knows what's best. He will do a much better a job than I could."

Doris cleared her throat rather loudly. Grace looked at her, startled and read the message in her eyes. Margaret is numb with shock. She has no idea what she will be going through.

Grace gently closed the Good Book and laid it on the shelf. She hesitated for an instant before tiptoeing out.

Doris linked her arm through hers.

"Let's get some breakfast before the kitchen is closed."

Grace didn't feel like talking to her, let alone eat.

A moment later a sleepy-eyed young woman kiddy -corner to Margaret's bunk hurried to catch up with them.

"You did well, talking to Margaret like that. I could have never done it."

Grace nodded. "Thanks."

Reaching Pier Twenty- One

CHAPTER 5

The ship docked at Pier 21, Halifax harbor, the following evening.

"Margaret probably wouldn't have lost her baby if we could have reached a hospital in time," Felicity remarked.

Several nodded in silent agreement, but Brenda said; "Yeah, but it's just one of those things that happen." The women looked downcast for a moment and then turned to prepare for disembarking.

Under different circumstances, Grace would have been eager to see the first glimpse of her new homeland.

Many of the young women crowded on the deck and craned their necks for the first dramatic view of the famous Peggy's Cove but were drolly told not to expect to sight it. Ships preferred to stay far away from that rocky shoreline.

Nevertheless, they eagerly pointed out to each other numerous Ocean Liners and smaller boats crowding the harbor. The many beams made bands of bright and dark against the leaden sea. The twinkling lights of the city were fascinating also, but Grace glanced wearily, almost indifferently at them. She wished she could enjoy it when she was more in the mood.

She trudged back to her compartment. After going to the loo that morning, Grace had panicked. Something was definitely wrong! She was spotting, and cramping!

She pulled a dress off a hanger then let it drop over her arm while staring blankly at the small round view of the ocean.

What shall I do, oh what shall I do? I'm gonna lose my babies just like Margaret did. Everyone is too busy, too distracted to assist me, and I have no idea where to turn for help. She folded garments and stuffed them into the worn brown suitcases practically confiscated from home.

The room was swimming around her, Grace felt nauseated. She pressed her fingers against her temples and leaned forward.

The others brushed past her, chattering enthusiastically, excited children in tow.

Grace fastened her baggage and dragged it behind her as she headed for the rail of the deck. The cramping had worsened as they crept slowly across the narrowing expanse of water.

The ship's bells were donging out the time, a grim reminder that this afternoon, this very afternoon; she was supposed to be on a train heading across the vast, empty continent of Canada. Was she fit enough to travel any further?

If only she could approach one of the Red Cross nurses and confide that she was experiencing what was called "Women's Troubles" in refined circles but her Victorian upbringing held her back. Besides, they rushed around doing Who Knows What.

She pressed her fingers against her eyelids, hoping it would ease vertigo. It didn't.

She glanced behind her. If only I could talk to Margaret but she's grieving, heartsick.

The last time Grace had peeked into her friend's berth, Margaret had been tenderly refolding all those tiny baby things her mother and friends had prepared for her, sprinkling them with scented baby powder. She was looking rather pale and hollow-eyed.

Grace took one last look around her own sleeping quarters and retrieved a sock from under a bed. She placed her hand on the chair to steady herself. A square-built cleaning girl carrying a bucket and mop came hurrying over to her.

"Grace, cheerios! I was hoping to see you before you were gone." She stopped and stared at her acquaintance.

"What's the matter? You look like you've seen a ghost!"

Grace brushed her hands feebly over her eyes. "I'm not feeling very well..."

"Here, sit down," Bertha hurried her over to a deck chair." I'm fetching a nurse."

"Oh, that's not necessary." Grace's voice trailed off. Bertha had already let the mop and pail land on the floor and was dodging through the crowds.

She did find a nurse and Grace was questioned in a quiet, professional manner which made her feel a little better. At least, my problems are in capable hands now.

Just then, Margaret appeared a look of concern on her face.

"Are you okay? What happened?"

Nurse White smiled, "Nothing serious...yet. We just want to keep it that way. She was informing me that her train will leave this afternoon, but it would be unwise for her to go any further, at the present."

Margaret looked concerned. "Will you need a place to stay?"

"I, I suppose. I hadn't thought that far."

"Why don't you stay with us here in Halifax?"

Grace cast the nurse a questioning glance.

"You may need respite for a long time, I'm afraid, "The nurse warned them, "Bed rest will be necessary since we aren't quite sure what is going on. There's another option...A home for unwed mothers in Chester."

"Oh, no, no," Margaret shook her head vigorously. "Grace would be most uncomfortable there. She is not an unwed mother. I'm sure David will welcome her to live with us. He's such a gentleman."

The nurses' professionalism cracked because of Margaret's effusiveness.

Grace reached for her luggage.

"No, you mustn't carry that," the nurse exclaimed just as the shrill voice of a frantic mother pierced through the babble.

"Austin! Austin! Where are you? My two-year-old 'run-about' has disappeared!"

The nurse hurried away, followed by several concerned mothers and a sailor or two. By the time, Austin had been returned to his mother's tearful embrace, Margaret and Grace had been swept along with the crowd, each struggling with baggage, that in their weakened condition, they shouldn't have been lugging.

Who Are Those Dapper Women?

CHAPTER 6

Not long after the gangplank was been lowered, they were crowded into the vast interior of Pier 21.

How strange it felt to be on solid ground once again. In fact, it didn't seem solid at all, but made them feel like they were wobbling, swaying, maybe. Bewildered, the girls looked around. Everything was so strange. They felt bombarded by all the bright lights and loud, cheerful voices. There was no hushed atmosphere, and certainly, no evidence of fearful suspicion of spies overhearing them or worse yet, bombs exploding. Nobody seemed to be afraid of anything. It made them feel strangely removed from the oppression of war.

Grace caught sight of some elegantly dressed ladies prancing past in their pointy high heels and chic fur stoles.

"Who are those dapper women?" she whispered, "They don't even speak English around here,"

Margaret followed their movement with her eyes. "Those are French Mademoiselles I believe. It sounds remotely related to the language they speak across the channel,"

Grace nudged her friend and eyed another group clad in bright yellow raincoats and rubber leggings of all things.
"There's some more queer fish. They don't speak the King's English, either. How they defame the language! What are they saying anyway?"

Margaret shrugged her shoulders. "Me thinks they're lobster fishermen looking for their sweet lassies from yonder bonny England, my, how they s-l-u-r-r!"

They moved along towards the immigration hall on second-floor observing, and being observed. Neither girl was feeling very hearty but did not want to be the first to admit to fear that they couldn't make it through the rest of the day without collapsing. Grace was relieved to have an older 'sister-friend' to lean on.

Margaret saw the drawn look on Grace's face and her heart constricted. I wonder how unwell she actually is. Oh, if only she could feel the comfort of the Holy Spirit like I do in spite of my deep pain. Father of Love; help me to portray it to her. May she accept Jesus as her Savior and Friend!

They were right in the muddle and confusion of an aimless throng; some of which were heading towards customs, while others were joyfully embracing loved ones. Since they was still a war going on, there were very few soldiers dressed in civilian clothes to greet their foreign-born wives, but hundreds of other people scanned the crowds for faces they recognized.

A shipload of evacuated children and another of European emigrants who managed to escape the war-torn countries arrived almost the same time as the Tena-Rae.

Off to the side, the girls heard the nervous, embarrassed giggle of a fellow Britisher whose Cockney accent confused and bewildered her new in-laws.

As Margaret looked on, she managed to forget her own heartache for the moment. Emotions were running high all around her. Uncertainty and fear marked many of the little faces disembarking the evacuee ship. She prayed, oh, she prayed, that they could find comfort and security in this strange, new land.

Meanwhile, Grace was watching those who had escaped with their families intact from besieged European countries. They were almost hysterical with joy and relief to be in a safe haven.

She looked around half expecting to see Randall there, but knowing better. Maybe everything would turn out all right if Randall could have—or is it, would have, been here. Before her spirits managed to plummet too deeply, she caught sight of a huddled group of immigrants who had obviously suffered for a long time.

"Look, Margaret," she whispered, "Some Hasidic Jews are sitting on that wooden bench, over there. I suppose they are waiting for their baggage to arrive: if they have any!"

Seeing them made their eyes pool. They were dressed very poorly in castoffs that someone must have given them, the children, no all of them, looking thin and scared as they huddled together.

"At least they are the lucky ones," Margaret's voice was thick with emotion," Everyone knows what really happened to many of the Jews that Hitler 'removed' to work camps."

At that moment a tall, broad-shouldered man appeared, waving to catch their attention. Margaret covered her mouth to keep from shrieking as she rushed towards him.

As they struggled to get closer to each other, his face lit up like a beacon: literally. With one small child clasping each of his big, strong ones, he excused his way through the horde; dropped their hands and put his own on Margaret's shoulders.

He breathed one word "Margaret."

Grace stepped back embarrassed.

"David!" Who knows how long they would have smiled into each other's eyes if his little daughter, Sally had not piped up.

"Ma-ma?" she cooed.

David lifted her up in his arms. "You remembered what I told you to say! Yes, this is Mama. Junior came meet your new Mama!"

With a solemn dignity that was amusing coming from a four-year-old, David Jr. shook Margaret's hand, then turned and offered his little paw to Grace.

Margaret reached out for Sally, "Oh, you sweet little, ducky! Hugs for Mommy?" Sally stared at her then turned to hide against her Daddy's neck.

David looked questioningly at Margaret's face, then down at her slim waist. Margaret flung herself into his arms and sobbed out her heartbreak.

Grace managed to coax the children over to a nearby bench that someone quickly vacated for her. She managed to distract them with hanky-games until Margaret was able to pull herself together and they gathered their little brood around them.

Grace looked on lonesomely.

Whisked Away in a Wheelchair

The crowd quickly parted to allow a nurse with a wheelchair to make a beeline for Grace,

"Oh, Grace," she said breathlessly, "I was so afraid we had lost you for sure, and I didn't want that on my records."

The doctor had caught up to her later and had given strict orders not to let Grace disembark. With an effort, the nurse pulled herself together to act more professional.

"Dr. Sauer requested that is an ambulance be waiting for you."

Grace's stomach clenched but the nurses' words kept tumbling out; "He recommends hospital care which will include complete bed rest. Since you will be monitored by a physician, everything will be just fine."

Grace doubted it, wasn't he the one who was at Margaret's bedside when she miscarried, could he really wish any good for anyone?

She turned beseechingly to her friend. "Oh, Margaret," she wailed; "I have to go to the hospital--in a strange land!"

Margaret reached out to comfort her. "Grace, we care! Surely, this is for the best. We'll pray for you."

"Oh...but please! Won't you come visit me too?"

"Of course!"

David looked from one woman to the other and admitted he wasn't the only one suffering on account of the war.

"We'll take care of your belongings," Margaret said compassionately, "until you are able to come home from the hospital."

Grace hardly had time to say goodbye before being whisked to the head of the line in a wheelchair. She got through customs quickly.

Meanwhile, as Margaret waited for her turn to go through immigration and pick up the luggage, she worried about leaving her friend alone in that big sterile, white hospital. Will she be all right? Is there someone I should inform? I don't even have any addresses for her loved ones!

Margaret's hand feebly stroked her forehead. What about me; how will I manage feeling so weak and feeble as I am? Will the children even like me? How will David feel about the miscarriage once he has more time to process it?

David sensed her anxiety.

"Don't worry, sweetheart," he said while opening the car door for her. "Remember today is ours! We haven't seen each other for over three months, so let's enjoy it!

A moment later, they came to a stop at a crosswalk and waited for the stocky, police officer to motion them on.

"I'll need to stop for gasoline," David informed her turning on the blinkers.

Margaret looked puzzled. "What's that?"

He cast her playful look;" Petrol," he explained, "And I just turned on my signal lights to indicate a right turn; signal; not flicker;" he grinned cockily; "Your suitcase is in the trunk of the car, not the boot." Need any more lessons on the English language, or do you think it will suffice for now?"

Margaret leaned back, relaxing, and rolled down the window. After she removed her second-best felt hat, the wind lifted her hair and cooled her neck. It felt good.

"It's you Canadians that need to learn to speak the King's English," she retorted with fake haughtiness. "Um, by the way, if you don't slow down the copper will be checking your number plate and will soon be blowing his hooter!"

David guffawed as he eased up on the gasoline. "The *policeman* will look at our *license* and *honk his horn*," he corrected.

Margaret looked distressed: "How am I ever going to manage?" She exclaimed.

David's look softened. "You'll manage, honey. A smart cookie like you will manage very well."

Margaret wasn't so sure.

Eventually, the lengthy route through the various streets ended as David pulled up in front of a tall house with gingerbread trimming.

Margaret's eyes lit up. Is this where we're going to live? This is just lovely! I didn't know David was that rich!
She admired the widow's walk and scalloping around the eaves, which are a truly Victorian style. Through the oval stained glass in the door, she could see plush maroon carpeting and a

winding wooden staircase-with a highly polished banister. Very
Impressive!

David came up beside her, lugging the suitcases. For some
reason, he looked embarrassed.
"Um, Margaret, we'll be expected to go in at the back."

She followed him around the house and up two steep, narrow
staircases to which Margaret assumed had been the servants'
quarters at one time. There was a small window in the kitchenette
overlooking a narrow alley and the backsides of other people's
houses, high fences, and rubbish bins. Therefore, we are just
renters! Oh, well, and neither am I Cinderella.

She leaned to look out the window. Here we live so near to the
sea, but not a patch of water in sight. That I will miss more than
anything, perhaps.
While she was gazing, the sun began slip behind the buildings
and to her great joy and relief, she saw God's great banner of love
flung across the sky. At least way up here, I will get a panoramic
view of the sunsets!

David stood uneasily in the doorway, one bulky suitcase in each
hand. "Do you like it?"
Margaret turned to him with a smile. "Just look at the sunset,"
she responded evasively. "We have a tremendous view."
She picked up little Sally and pointed out the colors to her then
took everything in the apartment in at a glance. It was tiny, very
tiny, to be sure, but they'd find a way. Why should I complain: at
least I have a good husband and we have a roof over our heads.
Many people live in crowded conditions similar to this because
of the war. She felt the color drain from her cheeks. In fact, even
now many are still refugees and who knows where my brother is.

Margaret was weary and overwrought; when they got to bed that night, her composure collapsed. She poured out her anguish of losing Baby Ricky and her parents so unexpectedly.

Although David tried to comfort her, he was struggling to block out his own terrible memories of experiences on battlefields. He didn't want Margaret to ever know, but scenes of atrocities were inked indelibly into his mind, the sooner he could get back and continue to seek retribution for the suffering his grandfather and others were facing, the better.

Grace's Misery

CHAPTER 8

Confined to a narrow white hospital cot, lying on her back with her hand tightly gripping the side rail was not Grace's cup of tea. The bed was hard; she was achy, hot and miserable from being in the same position far too long.

She stared up at the darkness, weary; despairing then leaned on her elbow to look around her. Katie, the mother-to-be in the bed kiddy-corner to her was stirring restlessly also.

"You awake?" Grace whispered.

"Ya," Katie sighed, "Have been for a long time. That noisy Big Ben makes it hard to sleep. When will this night ever end? It feels like the baby has its back against mine and has been squirming around continually. This is my fifth. We are both most uncomfortable." She paused, and then asked," How long have you been here?"

"How long? Four months, going on five: there's nothing to break the monotony."

"Four weeks! Whatever is the matter with you?"

Grace felt the colour come up into her cheeks as her Victorian upbringing cautioned her to be discrete.

"I, uh, it's something to do with the babby..."

"You mean the placenta, love? With one hand resting on her abdomen, Katie leaned over to speak to the younger girl. "Sometimes the placenta is beneath the babby and it can cause severe bleeding or even miscarriage if the mother isn't very careful."

Grace wasn't sure what the placenta was, but she did know what was causing her to stay in the hospital so long. It was more than just –that. They had managed to catch two heartbeats, which confirmed her earlier suspicions. She was carrying twins and 'they' were being exceedingly cautious.

"Yeah, that's my problem," she admitted looking down.

"Well, I was threatening to go into premature labour, " Katie fluffed up her pillow and straightened the blanket, "But it's settling down so I'll probably go home tomorrow. The kids will sure be glad to see me. And Jack."

Nancy awakened at the sound of their voices. "With so many leaving in here, wouldn't you be happier in a maternity home? The rest of us all get to go within two weeks of the babby's birth."

"Yeah, I've thought of that." Grace sighed. "There's a home in East Chester isn't there?"

Katie shot up with a yelp. "Grace, you would never want to go there!"

"Why not?" several voices cried out in unison.

"Well, first of all it's for," her voice dropped, "unwed mothers."

Two of the mother's-to-be looks plainly said: 'Well isn't she? We've never seen her husband come around.'

"And Grace is not--that. She's a war bride. Furthermore Ideal has a terrible reputation, haven't any of you heard of it?"

"I have," Patricia spoke up from the far corner of the ward. "I heard something on the radio about 'butter box babies."

"What in the world are you talking about?" Ruthann demanded.

Grace felt chilled and pulled the blanket over her shoulders. She didn't want to know.

Just then, the head nurse strode in and chided them sharply for being too noisy. After she left, the answer spread from cot to cot.

"Babies that aren't wanted because of their race, deformities or whatever are neglected until they die and butter boxes from the dairy became their coffins."

There was a collective gasp and unintelligible mutterings.

Grace reflexively hunched into the fetal position; when she did drift off, her slumbers laced with nightmares. By the time one especially gruesome nightmare jerked her awake, the first gray light of dawn appeared. She stopped trying to go back to sleep and stroked her rounded abdomen tenderly, yearning to have a more confiding nature towards God such as Margaret did. Fretful thoughts paraded through her weary mind. The future rolled out bleak and unremitting.

What am I doing here anyway? Just a few months ago, I was a carefree student, and now this! The radical change in my circumstances is –she searched her mind for the right word: abysmal.

She began counting the days since admittance but lost track since they flowed in a long unremitting stream. Even Sundays were similar to the rest of the week.

Late one rainy evening Grace stood by her window and watched the car lights flowing past in the city below her, her mind was not on the strangely colourful scene.

Sometimes it was embarrassing trying to understand the medical and cleaning staff. Some of their English, to say nothing of their accent, was like Double Dutch: incomprehensible!

"Hey, nurse, nurse," Grace called earlier that morning when her wheelchair wobbled. "I need help. I think this wheel is going to fall off."

Although the girl looked a little younger than she did, she was wearing a uniform, so must be a nurse of sorts!

"You're calling me a nurse!" The worker snickered and swept her hand over her dress. "I'm no nurse, I'm a Candy Striper. Get that, Englisher, I'm a plain ole Candy Striper. But yes, I'll get someone to tighten that bolt for you."

Even though the girl's amusement had caused Grace's cheeks to redden, she liked her. She was a mischievous, carrot-topped teenager. But being called a Candy Striper of all things was silly."

Yesterday a real nurse had wheeled her into the main room were all the new mothers, as well as a few mothers-to-be. They were gathering for a demonstration on how to fold diapers. Grace was totally flummoxed and more than a bit nervous. What in the world is a diaper? Is it a type of formula? Would they have to learn to measure and mix it? Would they have to use the stove? How would she be able to do that from the wheelchair? Oh, the instructor had used the word 'fold', so what does she mean?

The nurse who brought her to the instruction room noticed that Grace seemed nervous but she was inclined to be taciturn herself so didn't comment.

A pile of large white flannel squares were placed on Grace's lap since she couldn't possibly get close enough to the table to do this project, or so they claimed.

"What are these for?" she whispered to the girl on her right.

"What? Didn't they tell you we are going to learn to fold diapers?" Gail spoke loudly, causing Grace's ears to scorch. "Not that most of us don't know, anyway," she added.

Patricia leaned over the loudmouth.

"Diapers, Grace. You know to protect the babby's bottom."

Grace's puzzled look cleared, but her eyes stung. "Oh, we call them nappies."

Although some of the women laughed, those she knew best managed to look sympathetic in spite of their giggles.

Grace made sure she caught on quickly how to fold the...diapers.

Early the next morning, when Grace was still drifting in that delightful aura between sleep and wakefulness, a nurse breezed in to take her pulse and blood pressure and—at this she felt like pulling the sheet over her head-- asking disgustingly private questions. Why under Heaven's fair domain do they have to snoop into such personal areas of my life? I mean occasionally, sure, but daily? I never even shared with my mother such information.

Grace sighed, and struggled to change into a more comfortable position. She cupped her hands over her bulging tummy, and smiled wistfully, if I am carrying at least one little girl I want to have a warm, open relationship with her.

I wish I had just one jolly memory of Mother. Did she always have such a thin face and permanent frown lines around her mouth? Was her hair always streaked with gray and twisted into that tight, unbecoming bun? Oh, I hope not! Surely, I won't be turning gray early! What attracted Dad to her anyway? Has she always spent her spare time knitting?

Whom was Mom knitting for when I was young? Did she ever make me something pretty, or were all my babby blankets and tiny sweaters gray? She smirked at the thought.

Grace tried to remember what her mother knitted in earlier years. Since the war started, she always produced those eternal, and dreadfully ugly, black or gray socks and mittens for the soldiers that would end up covered with white lint she was sure. Grace wondered if anyone ever actually wore them. Maybe they left them behind for the enemy!

When her mother started making alternate brown and gray squares for army blankets, Grace suggested that the soldiers might appreciate something more cheerful than those scratchy old rags, as she secretly called them.

"These are more practical!" Heloise Adderley huffed while Dad sat nearby leisurely smoking a pipe.

Leisurely? Grace straightened at the memory. For the first time ever, she found herself wondering how relaxed he actually had been. Although his wife objected to him smoking so much, was that the way he coped with the tension in their home? Did it help him to feel as if he had control over at least one little thing?

How was it that she had never taken note of the quick frown of disapproval that would cross his normally placid features whenever Mother would go into a rant about something he could have thought was unreasonable?

Grace leaned her forehead against her hand, but why didn't he do something about it? She assumed he was trying to keep the peace, but didn't he know that in the long run there would always be an undercurrent of trouble if he didn't do something to remedy the situation?

The breakfast trolleys were clattering down the hallway and soon her favorite, smiling Candy Striper handed her a tray.

"Thanks, Elsie," she opened her mouth to say more, but the spunky girl beat her to it.

"Cheerios, Grace!" she said grinning roguishly. She turned as if to leave for someone else's' tray then added, "Oh, by the way, you got mail today. I'll get it after all these trays are handed out."

Grace's eyes widened in delight; "A post! For me! You mean something came in the po-mail for me!"

"Yes, Ma'am, and I think it is a card."

Grace could hardly eat; she was so excited. A card! Could it be from Randall? Did he get around to communicating with me after all this time? Maybe it's from Mom. Maybe she is actually getting lonely for me.

Ten minutes later Elsie dangled the card tantalizing just out of her reach, holding it in such a way that she could see only the British stamp. Grace leaned forward and snatched it with trembling fingers.

Everyone watched expectantly as she ripped the envelope open.

"Dear Grace, someone by the name of Margaret Seifert gave your mother your address and she in turn passed it on to me..."

Grace felt like screaming, she felt like ripping the card in two. Mother knew my address, but she never wrote. Why did I even bother giving it out? A nice, fat letter fell out. She would have recognised Betsy's large, sloppy writing anywhere if she had stopped to look.

"Is something the matter, Grace?" Elsie asked in a small voice.

Grace brushed a quick tear off her cheek. "I'm okay; it's just that, it's just that…"

She heard a low murmur of voices behind her, and when someone in the hall beckoned to Elsie, the Candy Striper seemed glad to escape.

After Grace had calmed down, she looked at the cheery get-well card. It had a proud mother duck strutting across the front and a string of yellow ducklings waddling behind her. Grace smirked. Is Betsy predicting something?

She snuggled down against her pillow and let her mind drift back to memories of war-torn Britain; the terror at the sound of air raid sirens, rationing that was far more severe than in Canada, and her not so distant school days.

Betsy talked of cheerful things, but Grace knew the history.

Inside the Ward

CHAPTER 9

Night fell once more as it had countless times before in that quietly, efficient hospital.

Grace's symptoms had taken a turn for the worse. I shouldn't have stayed out of bed so long; I shouldn't have walked to the end of the hall, and back—twice! She panicked and after jamming her finger against the little bell beside her bed, stammered into the intercom.

Several nurses entered and scurried around, changing her bedding and caring for her most competently.

Grace gripped the bedclothes. Have I made things difficult for the little ones? Will I lose them?

A nurse gave her a tiny white pill, but no one told her if it was to control symptoms or to help her relax and go to sleep. Maybe it was an iron pill!

After the others left, an older grandmotherly type pulled up a chair beside her and laid her hand on Grace's shoulder her head bowed as if in prayer. When she rose to leave, Grace stirred fretfully. The nurse noticed and stroked her hand. She bent over Grace and tenderly smoothed the hair off her cheeks.

"Don't worry, Grace. You overdid it yesterday, but after a day or two of rest you'll be okay." She squeezed her hand then pulled up a chair. "Do you feel like sleeping now?"

Grace shook her head. "It feels like all I ever do."

Nurse Browning chuckled, and Grace liked the sound of it: so pleasant and homey. "Once your little twins are home you will be longing for sleep."

Grace nodded.

The kindly caregiver pulled her chair closer. "I remember so well when my daughters were your age. That makes it easier to understand how hard it must be for you being that you are so far from home."

Grace didn't answer but her heart beseeched her to continue.

"It would have just grieved me to know my young daughter was laid up in a hospital somewhere all alone.

"Another telegram has been sent to your husband since there was no response to the first one. I hope you will hear from him shortly which at least would be something to look forward to."

Grace felt sad, uncertain. Would Randall be glad to see me or will being 'saddled down' with a wife and two babies be too much of an encumbrance? Why, oh why was he kicked out of the army? It must have been something horribly disgraceful. Why doesn't he want to be a daddy?

The nurse said something that she had missed.

"I beg your pardon?"

"I was just wondering; would you like me to inform your parents or did someone do that already?"

Grace sounded sad, "They know."

Since her patient was so unhappy, the nurse offered to pray with her. Prayer? What good was prayer? Mom was the most religious person I knew but did praying help her to be a more loving mother? Absolutely not!

"Go ahead if you want."

Nurse Browning laid her hand on Grace's shoulder then whispered a short, kindly prayer. Although it was just a few words, it warmed the girl's heart. Her 'god' and Margaret's seemed to be sympathetic Father figures: much different from the one her mother revered.

A bell rang somewhere down the hall so Nurse Browning trotted off to respond to its symptoms.

The monotonous hours plodded on. One day Grace boosted herself up on her elbow so she could see the clock ticking away. Only 6:30? I've been snoozing off and on for hours! How am I ever going to sleep tonight?

I've long finished all those Grace Livingstone Hill books that Margaret picked up the library for me, and I'm bored with those old, tattered magazines that the women pass from cot to cot.

She swung her legs over the side of the bed and looked around. Now that the room was empty, she was all alone: all the mother's-to-be that she had first become acquainted with had long since packed their bags and returned to their own abodes whether happy or sad.

Some had poked their heads in the door to proudly show off their newborns, but they were gone, and now she was restless.

Lizzie arrived recently and already her area was a cluttered mess of discarded cards, a handful of photos strewn across the bed top table, and clothes, even unmentionables in conspicuous places...Just then Yours Truly breezed in and tossed a fresh, new magazine Grace's way.

"I'm done with this," she announced. "The baby is long over-due and they are going to bring 'er on!"

"Good luck," Grace called but already her eyes were eagerly devouring the magazine; scanning the advertisements; coke, the drink that refreshes, and Aunt Jemimia's Buckwheat Pancakes being served to an eagerly awaiting family, etc. then settled down to savor a romance with a wartime flair. The heroine, who lived in some exotic, sea coast village, had a sailor -boyfriend who was a spy and she hadn't known it!

An hour later, she closed the periodical with a sigh. It was a pleasant escape, but so temporary. Her eyes rested on the cover. One of the four freedoms by Norman Rockwell graced it: a mother was gently tucking her little ones in while the father looked on, a newspaper in his hand emblazoned with a war headline. The picture made her heart heavy, but she couldn't tear her eyes away.

Did Mother ever tuck me in when I was worried and frightened? Did Dad? Will Randall be around to help me tuck in our little ones?

As she drank in the sweetness of the tender scene, she remembered seeing another "Freedom" picture somewhere. It was of people from many backgrounds bowing their heads in prayer.

Prayer: why do I keep thinking of it? Does it really help?

She studied the clock. Since this is Wednesday Mom is probably off to one of her everlasting prayer meetings while Dad sits all alone, so different from the idealized Norman Rockwell paintings. I wonder how Dad kept himself busy while Mom was pleading for him.

Hmm, doesn't he have a workroom or something, downstairs? She vaguely remembered him bringing her down there quite often when she was a wee, little girl. He was always building the most fascinating things.

A wave of homesickness hit her when she realized it was nowhere near 7:30 p.m. in Birmingham and, although she hadn't the slightest idea what time it was over there, her thoughts kept rolling down the same track.

She wondered about the girls from her form in school, the neighbours in their area. How were they doing? Were any of her friends married and starting families yet? In their somewhat shabby area of the city, most women never considered going to the hospital to have babies; the local midwife took care of them. Her brows knitted together, were the hospitals full to overflowing with war casualties?

Isn't it dangerous for Mom to walk the two blocks to the bus stop then ride over to the church? She recalled how suddenly Margaret's parents lost their lives. Have any churches in our area been bombed?

I'm glad that Betsy wrote, but there is so much that she probably didn't say, but what?

There was a conspicuous absence of newspapers in their ward or even the waiting rooms, and Grace wondered if the head nurse mandated it. Was it to keep them calm?

But they all heard things one way or another, and would exchange bits of news in hushed voices when the strident 'boss' as Lizzie mischievously called the head nurse, wasn't around.

Grace laid back and looked at the ceiling. She had always admired the royal princesses; they seemed so sweet and innocent in their full-skirted dresses. Will King George send Elizabeth and Margaret to a safe haven somewhere, or will they continue to be with their parents? Their mother is so caring; I do hope nothing happens to her, to them.

She shivered at the thought of a bomb landing on her parents' house, them killed, and her not finding out for days, maybe weeks later. Grace knew she would feel like she was sinking in a mud-filled black hole if they died without her ever being reconciled to them.

Only a week before she left, a roof was destroyed on one of the houses in the next street.

Her face lengthened as she continued to study the March 13th cover of the Saturday Evening Post, then her eyes lit up at the sound of a familiar voice at the door.

"Margaret! I'm so glad you came! Oh, I wish you could have brought the little duckies."

"Against hospital rules," David reminded her.

"They are with their grandparents, "Margaret rolled her eyes. "I hope they won't be too much for them."

"Dad will love it," her husband responded. "Without a doubt he has my fancy electric train on the floor by now, and they are on their knees having a swell time."

Margaret handed her a chocolate bar.

"A chocolate bar," Grace squealed. "Oh, it looks so yummy. Where did you ever find a chocolate bar? Thanks so much, I get so hungry for sweets sometimes."

Margaret laughed. "It was the only one left in the store."

Grace's look sobered. She had already torn off the wrapping and taken a bite, but stopped.

"Here you give it to the kiddies," she invited. "Tell them it's from Auntie Grace."

"No, oh, no," Margaret exclaimed, "it's for you."

"I already had one bite, and it's good, but I really do want them to have the rest. You can cut it up somehow so they won't know I took any. They probably don't even know what chocolate tastes like."

Margaret was reluctant and David refused at first, but when Margaret saw her friend's hurt look, she convinced her husband that they should take it.

After Margaret had tucked the treat into her purse, she asked when Grace would get out of the hospital.

"Maybe not too much longer: the doctor says if I am very,

very careful and promise to stay in bed as much as much as possible, I should be able to go soon."

They had a lovely visit and Grace convinced them that it was okay for her to walk slowly and carefully down the hall if they would assist her.

Discharged

CHAPTER 10

Several days later Margaret eagerly walked into the room and reached for one of the identical bundles lying on the bed. Having another woman to talk to would be nice.

After Grace donned the street clothes Margaret brought along, she stared at her reflection in a mirror. I am ghostly white except for these dark circles under my eyes. It looks like I am hiding a mammoth pumpkin beneath my shift. She shoved her dark hat on lower than necessary and was glad for the veil that would hide her sad eyes.

Margaret looked at her pityingly. Grace winced. She's probably praying for me. Please don't, she felt like muttering. It's just a waste of time.

"Are you ready to go?" David asked removing the car keys from his pocket and dangling them from his right hand.

Grace sighed heavily. "As ready as I'll ever be."

Margaret laid her hand on David's arm. "Why don't you carry her valise for her?"

David's rugged features reddened, but he picked up the suitcase and led the way to the door.

Grace glanced back one last time. Another chapter of her life had closed; what would be next?

Nancy had come in late last night, and was sleeping, Mary was moaning and groaning and obviously in a lot of pain. Grace waved but Mary was distracted.

Grace was relieved she had had the opportunity to go on an elevator a time or two back in Birmingham so it wasn't a completely new experience; still they made her nervous. She avoided looking at anyone as they sank downwards.

I feel so conspicuous with this huge bulge in front of me. It's obvious that I'm not that old either. She knew that her porcelain like skin was paler than ever from being indoors for so long, no blossoms in my cheeks for Randall to coo over, now. She sighed.

Margaret clasped her arm. "Are you okay, Grace?"

"Yeah." Good as can be expected, I guess.

"Just wait until we get you out into the spring sunshine, then you'll feel great!"

"Spring sunshine?"

"Yes, it's late May already Grace, and welcome to beautiful Nova Scotia in the spring of the year! Expect to see a few apple blossoms along the boulevards!"

"Here's the car," David announced a moment later.

Grace sank gratefully into the backseat while David dealt with her luggage; her eyes closed. She was oblivious to Margaret's happy voice extolling the virtues of seaside city in springtime and dosed off with her head against the small oblong window beside her.

Margaret's hushed voice mingled with her drowsy thoughts.

"They would have never let her come to our place if they knew about all the stairs we have to climb."

Quite a while late it was David's rumbly voice that awakened her just as the vehicle ground to a stop.

"Well, we're here."

She turned wide, appreciative eyes towards the newly painted Victorian mansion. What a contrast to the dull, shabby cottage and handkerchief-sized lawn where she had spent her growing up years. Oh, they were going up the back way.

Nobody had much to say as they struggled up the long sets of stairs.

Margaret hurried on ahead and opened the door. "Welcome to our humble abode," she said with a funny little curtsy.

Grace smiled slightly as she looked around, then asked; "Where are the children?"

"There's a pig tailed tomboy down the hall who's keeping an eye on them with the help of her grandmother. I'll get them. Just kick off your loafers and make yourself comfortable."

Grace nervously paced from window to settee then back again. It was obvious that the tiny apartment was too crowded even without her presence. I'll have to sleep on the sofa for sure, and how I hate lack of privacy. I wonder where the kiddies sleep. There were two doors. She cracked open one of them. It was a storage room with a little bed made up on the floor. This must be where Davey will have to sleep now that I booted him off the couch.

Grace glanced at David, at his glowering countenance. Oh, oh, I've gotten into his bad books already, probably with my snooping.

Feeling weak with exhaustion, she lowered herself on to the couch and her eyes drifted shut.

"I'll be leaving now--" David yanked the door shut behind him. He doesn't like me very much.

"Grace! Where is Auntie Grace?" Grace jumped and looked wildly around, then spotted Davey running in, a fat gingerbread cookie with raisin eyes in his hand.

Margaret's, "Shh don't wake Auntie Grace," fell on deaf ears.

Grace smiled when she saw the little children and reached out for them.

Davey chomped on his cookie and grinned at her but Sally pulled her Mommy's skirt over her eyes and hung back.

"Come on," Margaret urged, "Auntie Grace was lonesome for you. Can't you give her a hug?" Davey stiffened and drew back.

His chin jutted out. Everything about his body language declared that real men do not hug.

When Sally saw Grace's arms sink to her lap she came over slowly to pat Grace's knee and rest her head on 'auntie's' arm.

Disastrous News

CHAPTER 11

"*M*ail time!" David announced a couple weeks later when he came home for his noon break. He handed a sheaf of papers to his wife. Margaret sorted through the fliers, bills and such.

Oh, look, Grace," she exclaimed. "Here's a letter for you."

Grace's mouth dropped open as she reached for the lovely lilac-scented envelope. Who could be writing to me from Deer Flats after all this time? She studied the envelope closely and saw that it had been readdressed several times. Evidently, there were a number of Seifert families in the area. She wondered if any of them were related to David.

``Aren't you going to open it?" Davey demanded.

"Yes." Grace's fingers trembled as she slit the lilac-bordered envelope and pulled out matching stationary.

"My dear, dear Grace," surprised and puzzled at the unusually affectionate greeting, Grace glanced down at the signature.

"Your loving mother-in-law, Lily Sutherland."

"*My dear, dear Grace,*" she began again. "*This is the second letter I have written to you since the first one was eventually returned. I hope I have gotten the address right this time. I have longed to know you ever since Randall told me he had found a pretty little lass way off in England. He sounded so proud of you.*

"*How are you? It was such a disappointment to hear that you would not be able to come directly out here, but I certainly wouldn't want anything to happen to that precious baby you are carrying.*

Grace's hand trembled so badly she could hardly read. My mother in law! Lily! What a sweet name! What lovely writing. She seems so kind. She doesn't even know I am carrying twins. Why isn't Randall writing? What is this all about?

Margaret stared at her, fascinated.

"Shall I read it for you?" she asked.

Grace barely heard her. She sank into one of the sunny yellow kitchen chairs, her eyes glued to the page.

"I wish I could have dropped everything to come to you, but of course it is much too far, and perhaps you wouldn't have wanted me there.

"I heard you were in the hospital, but there is so much I do not know. Oh, I hope you are well and the baby is well."

Oh, she doesn`t even know I am carrying twins.

"Grace, I have such sorrowful news to break to you. I don't know how to share it gently enough so I'll just have to tell it the way it is. Randall got into serious trouble at a bar, and has been in jail all this time."

Grace looked stunned for an instant, but only an instant.

"No!" she screamed. "No! No! No! It can't be!" She stared at the paper but couldn't focus.

"In gaol! No! Not my Randall! What did he ever do to end up in gaol?"

Grace Goes to Pieces

CHAPTER 12

"Everything, absolutely everything goes wrong in my life!"

The confining walls of the apartment seemed to close in on her and Grace felt she had to escape before she screamed or do something even more drastic. She ripped the letter into quarters and stuffed them into the trashcan.

"Grace, what's wrong?" Margaret exclaimed, but the younger woman flung open the door and fled.

Margaret rushed to the entrance and looked out; she could hear Grace's feet pounding down the hall towards the stairs.

"Grace come back!" She called. She should never be running in her condition, especially down stairs. "Please be careful!"

Margaret wanted to rush after her but turned to look at the alarmed children. She stood there worried and confused. Grace will lose her babies for sure in her frenzied condition, but Sally is starting to wail. Oh, what should I do? She scooped Sally up in her arms and fell to her knees beside the dull burgundy couch.

"God," she cried, "Help Grace, help her, and please, please don't let her lose the babies.

Please God, put some sense into her head. Let her slow down, relax, and come back!"

A little hand pressed against her cheek to get her attention.

"Mommy, I'm hungry."

Scarcely aware of what she was doing, Margaret opened a tin of the newly popular mushroom soup, and while that was heating, spread some slices of homemade bread with a mayonnaise and tuna mixture. Every few minutes she would dash to the door, hoping and praying that Grace had returned.

she lifted Sally up to the sink to wash her hands while Junior got out his stool and sprinkled water over his own. Davey was being unusually obedient and she was vaguely aware of the concerned look on his face.

"Why did Auntie Grace run away?" he asked.

Margaret didn't know what to say so shrugged her shoulders then helped him dry his hands.

Although occupied with such mundane tasks, her stomach had knotted up with fear and anxiety.

They sat down and had their silent prayer, with which David was more comfortable. He hadn't said a word during all this tumult. Before the meal, already, he hide behind the newspaper, probably not knowing how to react.

After eating, Margaret mechanically squirted some washing liquid into the sink and added the utensils. She dropped what she was doing and hovered by the door every thought a prayer.

" I'd best be hiking back to work--" David took the short cut down the fire escape since Grace had clambered down the stairs.

Margaret tucked the children in for their naps. Davey was too scared to protest, Sally whimpered.

Because she was deeply concerned about Grace's reaction to the letter, Margaret did something even though it made her feel guilty. She took the torn up letter from the rubbish bin and pieced it together. After scanning it, she covered her face with her hands and groaned. This is really hard cheese. Lord, doesn't that girl have enough to worry about without this?

Fleeing to Nowhere

CHAPTER 13

But where was Grace?

She had floundered down the stairs, unlatched the gate to the high fence surrounding the back yard, and blundered into the alley, desperate to be alone.

A muscle spasm made her bend over in agony and in her weakened condition; she staggered over to a metal trashcan and sagged against it. She pressed her hands against her middle as waves of dizziness swirled around her.

After hurrying until she was about half way down the back alley, she paused, dismayed. What am I doing out here in my condition? She looked back at the sparkling white Victorian house behind her but was ashamed to return, besides her thoughts were too tumultuous. She plodded on, looking for a place to sit; there was none.

Well aware that her eyes had grown red and puffy from crying, which she couldn't seem to stop, Grace kept her head down and shuffled along. After coming to the end of the alley, she crossed to the next peaceful, suburban street. She was bushed and longed for a place to rest.

In the distance, she saw a bench: if only I can only get there. Waves of blackness made it hard to see, but she pushed one foot ahead of the other, hardly aware of what was before her.

A police officer's sharp whistle warned her not to cross right then, so she clung to a light pole beside her until he beckoned to her too.

He looked at her searchingly as she drew nearer. "Are you okay, ma'am?

Grace nodded not aware that all the color had washed from her face. "I. I just need to, sit down." She pointed numbly to the bench across the street.

Grace sensed that he wanted to escort her there but felt he shouldn't leave his post of duty.

"I'll ...be fine." she trudged off and eventually collapsed on the seat.

When someone else joined her, she focused enough to be aware that it was the same bus depot Margaret where children had waited with her that very morning so they could go shopping downtown. She still had her sweater on, and with that a few coins in her pocket. I'll take the bus.

It took an effort to climb the flimsy looking stairs but she managed, and even was able to find the right change before making her way to the very back. Someone, a man, she guessed, leaped up to give her his seat, but she barely acknowledged him as she sank down.

By the time the bus had merged into the traffic, Grace's face was deep into her hands and she was fighting the urge to vomit.

It's Too Soon!

CHAPTER 14

Grace spent hours huddled in the back seat of the lorry. People would come and go, the bus stopped and started, but the driver never noticed. There she was sometimes sleeping, often weeping, but never leaving.

She didn't know where to get off and was almost sick with worry about what her rash actions might do to the babies. She even prayed, begged God actually, to stop the labour pains that she was sure were gripping her.

In Grace's anguish and fear, she was terrified what might happen to the twins after they were born. Would she have to leave them in an orphanage—surely not Ideal—and work? Another pain knifed through her abdomen and she gripped both hands around her mouth so no one would hear her scream.

At times, the twins were kicking fiercely, but that just made her heart ache the more. It dawned upon her that she would have to eventually, get off the bus: the driver would go home, what would she do then?

She timed it so that several were leaving at the same time, and mingled with the crowd.

Two soldiers, on a short break from boot camp, eyed her with concern as she stumbled aimlessly down the darkening street.

One raised his hand as if to salute in respect to her obvious grief, but she hadn't even seen them.

She saw the lorry had discharged its load of passengers at a train station and wandered in. Now she discovered that things could get even worse. Just as she was sitting down, she soaked her undergarments, dress, the chair and a puddle was darkening the wooden plank floor.

Then she did scream and several women rushed over to her, anxious and concerned.

They babbled various things that Grace couldn't understand and took by the arm, moving her this way and that.

Grace couldn't help it, she felt hysterical.

A uniformed agent strode over and took things in hand.

Before she knew it, she was in an ambulance and given a sedative to calm her nerves.

Labor pains were upon her. "It's too early," Grace wailed, more anxious about the babies than her extreme pain.

She ended up in the same dreadfully familiar hospital.

"Calm down Grace," someone in white spoke sharply to her. "Calm down and relax. Relax. Relax, do you hear me? Relax! Lots of twins come early. It's normal. It's totally normal. I'm sure they will be fine."

Seven weeks! She should have been more careful! She should have been able to carry them much long longer….she screamed….

After that, she couldn't focus on anything but trying to get through the ordeal.

The next thing she knew, Margaret was beside her, soothing, comforting, and stroking her tangled hair off her face, love sparkling in her eyes.

"Margaret," Grace wailed. "Margaret, you came. "

"Of course I came, of course. They informed us soon after you were admitted. We are like David and Jonathan, you know."

Grace wasn't aware of how long Margaret stayed, but it didn't seem long enough. Soon three nurses and a doctor swarmed around her.

"Time to leave, doctor's orders:" That same head nurse. She has always been so brusque.

"Please," Grace begged, `Let her stay a little longer," but her pleas were brushed aside.

Margaret stooped to hug her. "You'll be fine, sis. I'll be praying –constantly- for you,"

"Oh please, please, do, "Grace squeezed her hand tightly just as the nurse took Margaret by the elbow and marched her out.

⁇

The Momentous Decision

CHAPTER 15

An idea had been tugging at Grace's heartstrings ever since the twins safely arrived. She remembered vividly the first time it had occurred.

It was while in the case room: bright lights and whiteness were all around. She was waiting with weary anticipation for that soul-stirring moment when the nurse would finish cleansing the squirmy, newborns; wrap them snugly in soft receiving blankets, then turn to place them one by one into her longing arms.

"They are fine, perfectly fine," the genial doctor reassured her when she fretted about how small they were. "Sure they are a bit tiny and will need extra care for the next two or three weeks but are strong and healthy. Congratulations, Mrs. Sutherland!"

Grace half arose on the bed, her arms reaching out, then she was cuddling them. For a long moment, she had eyes for nothing more than those incredibly beautiful, incredibly precious rosy-red bundles of humanity.

Finally, wonderfully convinced that they were healthy, her heart just melted.

To think they were hers, gloriously hers to love and to cherish as long as she lived. ! She felt a yearning protectiveness grip her as she gazed into those wide cloudy blue eyes, making an instant connection. A throb of joy filled her heart. I may seem young for such tremendous responsibility, but oh, I want to, I want to give them the best care possible.

Then, a darkly unwelcome thought slithered like an evil snake into her mind. Will Randall try to be a good father? He hadn't liked it when I got pregnant, and that was before I knew I was carrying twins! How well will he treat them? Can I trust him not to hurt these incredibly sweet treasures from Heaven?

"Mrs. Sutherland, are you alright?"

"W-what?"

"You seem pale: maybe I should put the babies back in their bassinets now."

Grace looked at the young nurse blankly then down at the babies in her arms. She wanted to protest but did feel faint.

She stared at the retreating figure almost numb with fear.

My own darling babies! What is going to happen to them? Will Randall be cruel or unfaithful? Before we were married, many young women prattled excitedly and made google eyes, as he'd stop to talk. What if he decides being tied down with a wife and two babies is to his liking?

What shall I do? Can I go to Deer Flats if he is gaol? Dare I? I refuse to leave the babies in an orphanage while I am a cashier at some dumpy department store and I can't leech off the Seifert's indefinitely!

Are there any doctors way out there in the wilderness? How can I care for the wee ones without any support?

No one in this world is more precious to me than they are! I will protect them with my life if needs be! How can I, if I am in a log cabin somewhere and he comes home sloshed?

A nurse came to check her pulse and temperature and insisted that she lay down.

Later, when the doctor went on his rounds, he and the nurse assumed she was asleep, Grace overheard them conversing in low tones.

"Worried... blood pressure too high...pulse racing...No word from husband..."

"He was a soldier, right? Was he discharged honorably?"

"No one knows for sure, not even Mrs. Sutherland."

"Something sure is suspicious. Everything is kept so hush, hush."

When the nurse spoke to her, Grace pretended to be just waking up, but she felt sick to the stomach.

The twins scheduled feedings were the highlight of the day for her and she begged the nursing staff to let her keep them with her all the time. They were kind but said it was against hospital policy, something about cross contamination and Grace needing her rest.

She said they were being given the best of care but it didn't reassure Grace.

I'd rest better if I they were close all the time. She pressed the little ones to her bosom. One of the infants was making tiny mewling sounds while searching for her fist.

Grace stroked her velvety cheek and pressed kisses into her bright, downy hair. She always pretended that it took longer to feed them than it actually did, the nurses were wise to her tactics but were indulgent with her.

I will need to name them without Randall's help or approval. Are there any names sweet enough for such darling twins?

She whispered name after name into the tiny ears wondering which ones would be perfect. When she had to fill out the forms for the birth certificate etc. she wrote her choices out in her loveliest cursive because they were the loveliest ones she could think of. Emily Margaret, Alice Grace.

Grace's strength was coming back. The twins weren't fragile preemies anymore. They are doing well. Soon she would be going home, or at least to David's. She must make a major decision. She must decide what was best for the children. Since Randall doesn't even know I have twins, can I, dare I give one little girl a chance for a happy, abuse free childhood and let Margaret care for her? After all, Randall thought I was only expecting one.

How could I have even thought about it? I could never, NEVER give up a child. Never!

But the thought persisted.

Don't you love your darlings enough to provide at least one with a safe, wholesome childhood no matter what the cost in personal joy?

That's an impossible decision! Life is asking too much of me! Her heart was wrung with anguish at the very thought. How much worse would the deed make me feel?

Then the question: which one? How could I ever choose one over the other? The thought made her nearly gag. Choose to give one happiness and the other pain? What an awful thought! Accept one and reject the other? That was even worse!

Margaret begged Grace to stay longer before heading west. She could tell that her young friend was distraught about something and tried to encourage Grace to unburden her heart, which she would do in an agitated, jumbled way.

Oh, how Margaret felt for her! Because of her own aching loss, she longed to adopt one of the twins, but prayed Seeing them made their eyes pool. They were dressed very poorly in castoffs that someone must have given them, the children, no all of them, looking thin and scared as they huddled together.

"At least they are the lucky ones," Margaret's voice was thick with emotion," Everyone knows what really happened to many of the Jews that Hitler 'removed' to work camps."

At that moment a tall, broad-shouldered man appeared, waving to catch their attention. Margaret covered her mouth to keep from shrieking as she rushed towards him.

As they struggled to get closer to each other, his face lit up like a beacon: literally. With one small child clasping each of his big, strong ones, he excused his way through the horde; dropped their hands and put his own on Margaret's shoulders.

He breathed one word "Margaret."

Grace stepped back embarrassed.

"David!" Who knows how long they would have smiled into each other's eyes if his little daughter, Sally had not piped up.

"Ma-ma?" she cooed.

David lifted her up in his arms. "You remembered what I told you to say! Yes, this is Mama. Junior came meet your new Mama!"

With a solemn dignity that was amusing coming from a four-year-old, David Jr. shook Margaret's hand, then turned and offered his little paw to Grace.

Margaret reached out for Sally, "Oh, you sweet little, ducky! Hugs for Mommy?" Sally stared at her then turned to hide against her Daddy's neck.

David looked questioningly at Margaret's face, then down at her slim waist. Margaret flung herself into his arms and sobbed out her heartbreak.

Grace managed to coax the children over to a nearby bench that someone quickly vacated for her. She managed to distract them with hanky-games until Margaret was able to pull herself together and they gathered their little brood around them.

Grace looked on lonesomely.

Whisked Away in a Wheelchair

CHAPTER 7

The crowd quickly parted to allow a nurse with a wheelchair to make a beeline for Grace,

"Oh, Grace," she said breathlessly, "I was so afraid we had lost you for sure, and I didn't want that on my records."

The doctor had caught up to her later and had given strict orders not to let Grace disembark. With an effort, the nurse pulled herself together to act more professional.

"Dr. Sauer requested that is an ambulance be waiting for you."

Grace's stomach clenched but the nurses' words kept tumbling out; "He recommends hospital care which will include complete bed rest. Since you will be monitored by a physician, everything will be just fine."

Grace doubted it, wasn't he the one who was at Margaret's bedside when she miscarried, could he really wish any good for anyone?

She turned beseechingly to her friend. "Oh, Margaret," she wailed; "I have to go to the hospital--in a strange land!"

Margaret reached out to comfort her. "Grace, we care! Surely, this is for the best. We'll pray for you."

"Oh...but please! Won't you come visit me too?"

"Of course!"

David looked from one woman to the other and admitted he wasn't the only one suffering on account of the war.
    "We'll take care of your belongings," Margaret said compassionately, "until you are able to come home from the hospital."
    Grace hardly had time to say goodbye before being whisked to the head of the line in a wheelchair. She got through customs quickly.

    Meanwhile, as Margaret waited for her turn to go through immigration and pick up the luggage, she worried about leaving her friend alone in that big sterile, white hospital. Will she be all right? Is there someone I should inform? I don't even have any addresses for her loved ones!

    Margaret's hand feebly stroked her forehead. What about me; how will I manage feeling so weak and feeble as I am? Will the children even like me? How will David feel about the miscarriage once he has more time to process it?

    David sensed her anxiety.

    "Don't worry, sweetheart," he said while opening the car door for her. "Remember today is ours! We haven't seen each other for over three months, so let's enjoy it!

    A moment later, they came to a stop at a crosswalk and waited for the stocky, police officer to motion them on.

    "I'll need to stop for gasoline," David informed her turning on the blinkers.

Margaret looked puzzled. "What's that?"

He cast her playful look;" Petrol," he explained, "And I just turned on my signal lights to indicate a right turn; signal; not flicker;" he grinned cockily; "Your suitcase is in the trunk of the car, not the boot." Need any more lessons on the English language, or do you think it will suffice for now?"

Margaret leaned back, relaxing, and rolled down the window. After she removed her second-best felt hat, the wind lifted her hair and cooled her neck. It felt good.

"It's you Canadians that need to learn to speak the King's English," she retorted with fake haughtiness. "Um, by the way, if you don't slow down the copper will be checking your number plate and will soon be blowing his hooter!"

David guffawed as he eased up on the gasoline. "The *policeman* will look at our *license* and *honk his horn,*" he corrected.

Margaret looked distressed: "How am I ever going to manage?" She exclaimed.

David's look softened. "You'll manage, honey. A smart cookie like you will manage very well."

Margaret wasn't so sure.

Eventually, the lengthy route through the various streets ended as David pulled up in front of a tall house with gingerbread trimming.

Margaret's eyes lit up. Is this where we're going to live? This is just lovely! I didn't know David was that rich!

She admired the widow's walk and scalloping around the eaves, which are a truly Victorian style. Through the oval stained glass in the door, she could see plush maroon carpeting and a winding wooden staircase-with a highly polished banister. Very Impressive!

David came up beside her, lugging the suitcases. For some reason, he looked embarrassed.
"Um, Margaret, we'll be expected to go in at the back."

She followed him around the house and up two steep, narrow staircases to which Margaret assumed had been the servants' quarters at one time. There was a small window in the kitchenette overlooking a narrow alley and the backsides of other people's houses, high fences, and rubbish bins. Therefore, we are just renters! Oh, well, and neither am I Cinderella.

She leaned to look out the window. Here we live so near to the sea, but not a patch of water in sight. That I will miss more than anything, perhaps.
While she was gazing, the sun began slip behind the buildings and to her great joy and relief, she saw God's great banner of love flung across the sky. At least way up here, I will get a panoramic view of the sunsets!

David stood uneasily in the doorway, one bulky suitcase in each hand. "Do you like it?"
Margaret turned to him with a smile. "Just look at the sunset," she responded evasively. "We have a tremendous view."
 She picked up little Sally and pointed out the colors to her then took everything in the apartment in at a glance. It was tiny, very tiny, to be sure, but they'd find a way. Why should I complain: at least I have a good husband and we have a roof over our heads.
Many people live in crowded conditions similar to this because of the war. She felt the color drain from her cheeks. In fact, even now many are still refugees and who knows where my brother is.

Margaret was weary and overwrought; when they got to bed that night, her composure collapsed. She poured out her anguish of losing Baby Ricky and her parents so unexpectedly.

Although David tried to comfort her, he was struggling to block out his own terrible memories of experiences on battlefields. He didn't want Margaret to ever know, but scenes of atrocities were inked indelibly into his mind, the sooner he could get back and continue to seek retribution for the suffering his grandfather and others were facing, the better.

Grace's Misery

CHAPTER 8

Confined to a narrow white hospital cot, lying on her back with her hand tightly gripping the side rail was not Grace's cup of tea. The bed was hard; she was achy, hot and miserable from being in the same position far too long.

She stared up at the darkness, weary; despairing then leaned on her elbow to look around her. Katie, the mother-to-be in the bed kiddy-corner to her was stirring restlessly also.

"You awake?" Grace whispered.

"Ya," Katie sighed, "Have been for a long time. That noisy Big Ben makes it hard to sleep. When will this night ever end? It feels like the baby has its back against mine and has been squirming around continually. This is my fifth. We are both most uncomfortable." She paused, and then asked," How long have you been here?"

"How long? Four months, going on five: there's nothing to break the monotony."

"Four weeks! Whatever is the matter with you?"

Grace felt the colour come up into her cheeks as her Victorian upbringing cautioned her to be discrete.

"I, uh, it's something to do with the babby..."

"You mean the placenta, love? With one hand resting on her abdomen, Katie leaned over to speak to the younger girl. "Sometimes the placenta is beneath the babby and it can cause severe bleeding or even miscarriage if the mother isn't very careful."

Grace wasn't sure what the placenta was, but she did know what was causing her to stay in the hospital so long. It was more than just –that. They had managed to catch two heartbeats, which confirmed her earlier suspicions. She was carrying twins and 'they' were being exceedingly cautious.

"Yeah, that's my problem," she admitted looking down.

"Well, I was threatening to go into premature labour, " Katie fluffed up her pillow and straightened the blanket, "But it's settling down so I'll probably go home tomorrow. The kids will sure be glad to see me. And Jack."

Nancy awakened at the sound of their voices. "With so many leaving in here, wouldn't you be happier in a maternity home? The rest of us all get to go within two weeks of the babby's birth."

"Yeah, I've thought of that." Grace sighed. "There's a home in East Chester isn't there?"

Katie shot up with a yelp. "Grace, you would never want to go there!"

"Why not?" several voices cried out in unison.

"Well, first of all it's for," her voice dropped, "unwed mothers."

Two of the mother's-to-be looks plainly said: 'Well isn't she? We've never seen her husband come around.'

"And Grace is not--that. She's a war bride. Furthermore Ideal has a terrible reputation, haven't any of you heard of it?"

"I have," Patricia spoke up from the far corner of the ward. "I heard something on the radio about 'butter box babies."

"What in the world are you talking about?" Ruthann demanded.

Grace felt chilled and pulled the blanket over her shoulders. She didn't want to know.

Just then, the head nurse strode in and chided them sharply for being too noisy. After she left, the answer spread from cot to cot.

"Babies that aren't wanted because of their race, deformities or whatever are neglected until they die and butter boxes from the dairy became their coffins."

There was a collective gasp and unintelligible mutterings.

Grace reflexively hunched into the fetal position; when she did drift off, her slumbers laced with nightmares. By the time one especially gruesome nightmare jerked her awake, the first gray light of dawn appeared. She stopped trying to go back to sleep and stroked her rounded abdomen tenderly, yearning to have a more confiding nature towards God such as Margaret did. Fretful thoughts paraded through her weary mind. The future rolled out bleak and unremitting.

What am I doing here anyway? Just a few months ago, I was a carefree student, and now this! The radical change in my circumstances is —she searched her mind for the right word: abysmal.

She began counting the days since admittance but lost track since they flowed in a long unremitting stream. Even Sundays were similar to the rest of the week.

Late one rainy evening Grace stood by her window and watched the car lights flowing past in the city below her, her mind was not on the strangely colourful scene.

Sometimes it was embarrassing trying to understand the medical and cleaning staff. Some of their English, to say nothing of their accent, was like Double Dutch: incomprehensible!

"Hey, nurse, nurse," Grace called earlier that morning when

her wheelchair wobbled. "I need help. I think this wheel is going to fall off."

Although the girl looked a little younger than she did, she was wearing a uniform, so must be a nurse of sorts!

"You're calling me a nurse!" The worker snickered and swept her hand over her dress. "I'm no nurse, I'm a Candy Striper. Get that, Englisher, I'm a plain ole Candy Striper. But yes, I'll get someone to tighten that bolt for you."

Even though the girl's amusement had caused Grace's cheeks to redden, she liked her. She was a mischievous, carrot-topped teenager. But being called a Candy Striper of all things was silly."

Yesterday a real nurse had wheeled her into the main room were all the new mothers, as well as a few mothers-to-be. They were gathering for a demonstration on how to fold diapers. Grace was totally flummoxed and more than a bit nervous. What in the world is a diaper? Is it a type of formula? Would they have to learn to measure and mix it? Would they have to use the stove? How would she be able to do that from the wheelchair? Oh, the instructor had used the word 'fold', so what does she mean?

The nurse who brought her to the instruction room noticed that Grace seemed nervous but she was inclined to be taciturn herself so didn't comment.

A pile of large white flannel squares were placed on Grace's lap since she couldn't possibly get close enough to the table to do this project, or so they claimed.

"What are these for?" she whispered to the girl on her right.

"What? Didn't they tell you we are going to learn to fold diapers?" Gail spoke loudly, causing Grace's ears to scorch. "Not that most of us don't know, anyway," she added.

Patricia leaned over the loudmouth.

"Diapers, Grace. You know to protect the babby's bottom."

Grace's puzzled look cleared, but her eyes stung. "Oh, we call them nappies."

Although some of the women laughed, those she knew best managed to look sympathetic in spite of their giggles.

Grace made sure she caught on quickly how to fold the...diapers.

Early the next morning, when Grace was still drifting in that delightful aura between sleep and wakefulness, a nurse breezed in to take her pulse and blood pressure and—at this she felt like pulling the sheet over her head-- asking disgustingly private questions. Why under Heaven's fair domain do they have to snoop into such personal areas of my life? I mean occasionally, sure, but daily? I never even shared with my mother such information.

Grace sighed, and struggled to change into a more comfortable position. She cupped her hands over her bulging tummy, and smiled wistfully, if I am carrying at least one little girl I want to have a warm, open relationship with her.

I wish I had just one jolly memory of Mother. Did she always have such a thin face and permanent frown lines around her mouth? Was her hair always streaked with gray and twisted into that tight, unbecoming bun? Oh, I hope not! Surely, I won't be turning gray early! What attracted Dad to her anyway? Has she always spent her spare time knitting?

Whom was Mom knitting for when I was young? Did she ever make me something pretty, or were all my babby blankets and tiny sweaters gray? She smirked at the thought.

Grace tried to remember what her mother knitted in earlier years. Since the war started, she always produced those eternal, and dreadfully ugly, black or gray socks and mittens for the soldiers that would end up covered with white lint she was sure. Grace wondered if anyone ever actually wore them. Maybe they left them behind for the enemy!

When her mother started making alternate brown and gray squares for army blankets, Grace suggested that the soldiers might appreciate something more cheerful than those scratchy old rags, as she secretly called them.

"These are more practical!" Heloise Adderley huffed while Dad sat nearby leisurely smoking a pipe.

Leisurely? Grace straightened at the memory. For the first time ever, she found herself wondering how relaxed he actually had been. Although his wife objected to him smoking so much, was that the way he coped with the tension in their home? Did it help him to feel as if he had control over at least one little thing?

How was it that she had never taken note of the quick frown of disapproval that would cross his normally placid features whenever Mother would go into a rant about something he could have thought was unreasonable?

Grace leaned her forehead against her hand, but why didn't he do something about it? She assumed he was trying to keep the peace, but didn't he know that in the long run there would always be an undercurrent of trouble if he didn't do something to remedy the situation?

The breakfast trolleys were clattering down the hallway and soon her favorite, smiling Candy Striper handed her a tray.

"Thanks, Elsie," she opened her mouth to say more, but the spunky girl beat her to it.

"Cheerios, Grace!" she said grinning roguishly. She turned as if to leave for someone else's' tray then added, "Oh, by the way, you got mail today. I'll get it after all these trays are handed out."

Grace's eyes widened in delight; "A post! For me! You mean something came in the po-mail for me!"

"Yes, Ma'am, and I think it is a card."

Grace could hardly eat; she was so excited. A card! Could it be from Randall? Did he get around to communicating with me after all this time? Maybe it's from Mom. Maybe she is actually getting lonely for me.

Ten minutes later Elsie dangled the card tantalizing just out of her reach, holding it in such a way that she could see only the British stamp. Grace leaned forward and snatched it with trembling fingers.

Everyone watched expectantly as she ripped the envelope open.

"Dear Grace, someone by the name of Margaret Seifert gave your mother your address and she in turn passed it on to me..."

Grace felt like screaming, she felt like ripping the card in two. Mother knew my address, but she never wrote. Why did I even bother giving it out? A nice, fat letter fell out. She would have recognised Betsy's large, sloppy writing anywhere if she had stopped to look.

"Is something the matter, Grace?" Elsie asked in a small voice.

Grace brushed a quick tear off her cheek. "I'm okay; it's just that, it's just that..."

She heard a low murmur of voices behind her, and when someone in the hall beckoned to Elsie, the Candy Striper seemed glad to escape.

After Grace had calmed down, she looked at the cheery get-well card. It had a proud mother duck strutting across the front and a string of yellow ducklings waddling behind her. Grace smirked. Is Betsy predicting something?

She snuggled down against her pillow and let her mind drift back to memories of war-torn Britain; the terror at the sound of air raid sirens, rationing that was far more severe than in Canada, and her not so distant school days.

Betsy talked of cheerful things, but Grace knew the history.

Inside the Ward

CHAPTER 9

Night fell once more as it had countless times before in that quietly, efficient hospital.

Grace's symptoms had taken a turn for the worse. I shouldn't have stayed out of bed so long; I shouldn't have walked to the end of the hall, and back—twice! She panicked and after jamming her finger against the little bell beside her bed, stammered into the intercom.

Several nurses entered and scurried around, changing her bedding and caring for her most competently.

Grace gripped the bedclothes. Have I made things difficult for the little ones? Will I lose them?

A nurse gave her a tiny white pill, but no one told her if it was to control symptoms or to help her relax and go to sleep. Maybe it was an iron pill!

After the others left, an older grandmotherly type pulled up a chair beside her and laid her hand on Grace's shoulder her head bowed as if in prayer. When she rose to leave, Grace stirred fretfully. The nurse noticed and stroked her hand. She bent over Grace and tenderly smoothed the hair off her cheeks.

"Don't worry, Grace. You overdid it yesterday, but after a day or two of rest you'll be okay." She squeezed her hand then pulled up a chair. "Do you feel like sleeping now?"

Grace shook her head. "It feels like all I ever do."

Nurse Browning chuckled, and Grace liked the sound of it: so pleasant and homey. "Once your little twins are home you will be longing for sleep."

Grace nodded.

The kindly caregiver pulled her chair closer. "I remember so well when my daughters were your age. That makes it easier to understand how hard it must be for you being that you are so far from home."

Grace didn't answer but her heart beseeched her to continue.

"It would have just grieved me to know my young daughter was laid up in a hospital somewhere all alone.

"Another telegram has been sent to your husband since there was no response to the first one. I hope you will hear from him shortly which at least would be something to look forward to."

Grace felt sad, uncertain. Would Randall be glad to see me or will being 'saddled down' with a wife and two babies be too much of an encumbrance? Why, oh why was he kicked out of the army? It must have been something horribly disgraceful. Why doesn't he want to be a daddy?

The nurse said something that she had missed.

"I beg your pardon?"

"I was just wondering; would you like me to inform your parents or did someone do that already?"

Grace sounded sad, "They know."

Since her patient was so unhappy, the nurse offered to pray with her. Prayer? What good was prayer? Mom was the most religious person I knew but did praying help her to be a more loving mother? Absolutely not!

"Go ahead if you want."

Nurse Browning laid her hand on Grace's shoulder then whispered a short, kindly prayer. Although it was just a few words, it warmed the girl's heart. Her 'god' and Margaret's seemed to be sympathetic Father figures: much different from the one her mother revered.

A bell rang somewhere down the hall so Nurse Browning trotted off to respond to its symptoms.

The monotonous hours plodded on. One day Grace boosted herself up on her elbow so she could see the clock ticking away. Only 6:30? I've been snoozing off and on for hours! How am I ever going to sleep tonight?

I've long finished all those Grace Livingstone Hill books that Margaret picked up the library for me, and I'm bored with those old, tattered magazines that the women pass from cot to cot.

She swung her legs over the side of the bed and looked around. Now that the room was empty, she was all alone: all the mother's-to-be that she had first become acquainted with had long since packed their bags and returned to their own abodes whether happy or sad.

Some had poked their heads in the door to proudly show off their newborns, but they were gone, and now she was restless.

Lizzie arrived recently and already her area was a cluttered mess of discarded cards, a handful of photos strewn across the bed top table, and clothes, even unmentionables in conspicuous places...Just then Yours Truly breezed in and tossed a fresh, new magazine Grace's way.

"I'm done with this," she announced. "The baby is long over-due and they are going to bring 'er on!"

"Good luck," Grace called but already her eyes were eagerly devouring the magazine; scanning the advertisements; coke, the drink that refreshes, and Aunt Jemimia's Buckwheat Pancakes being served to an eagerly awaiting family, etc. then settled down to savor a romance with a wartime flair. The heroine, who lived in some exotic, sea coast village, had a sailor -boyfriend who was a spy and she hadn't known it!

An hour later, she closed the periodical with a sigh. It was a pleasant escape, but so temporary. Her eyes rested on the cover. One of the four freedoms by Norman Rockwell graced it: a mother was gently tucking her little ones in while the father looked on, a newspaper in his hand emblazoned with a war headline. The picture made her heart heavy, but she couldn't tear her eyes away.

Did Mother ever tuck me in when I was worried and frightened? Did Dad? Will Randall be around to help me tuck in our little ones?

As she drank in the sweetness of the tender scene, she remembered seeing another "Freedom" picture somewhere. It was of people from many backgrounds bowing their heads in prayer.

Prayer: why do I keep thinking of it? Does it really help?

She studied the clock. Since this is Wednesday Mom is probably off to one of her everlasting prayer meetings while Dad sits all alone, so different from the idealized Norman Rockwell paintings. I wonder how Dad kept himself busy while Mom was pleading for him.

Hmm, doesn't he have a workroom or something, downstairs? She vaguely remembered him bringing her down there quite often when she was a wee, little girl. He was always building the most fascinating things.

A wave of homesickness hit her when she realized it was nowhere near 7:30 p.m. in Birmingham and, although she hadn't the slightest idea what time it was over there, her thoughts kept rolling down the same track.

She wondered about the girls from her form in school, the neighbours in their area. How were they doing? Were any of her friends married and starting families yet? In their somewhat shabby area of the city, most women never considered going to the hospital to have babies; the local midwife took care of them. Her brows knitted together, were the hospitals full to overflowing with war casualties?

Isn't it dangerous for Mom to walk the two blocks to the bus stop then ride over to the church? She recalled how suddenly Margaret's parents lost their lives. Have any churches in our area been bombed?

I'm glad that Betsy wrote, but there is so much that she probably didn't say, but what?

There was a conspicuous absence of newspapers in their ward or even the waiting rooms, and Grace wondered if the head nurse mandated it. Was it to keep them calm?

But they all heard things one way or another, and would exchange bits of news in hushed voices when the strident 'boss' as Lizzie mischievously called the head nurse, wasn't around.

Grace laid back and looked at the ceiling. She had always admired the royal princesses; they seemed so sweet and innocent in their full-skirted dresses. Will King George send Elizabeth and Margaret to a safe haven somewhere, or will they continue to be with their parents? Their mother is so caring; I do hope nothing happens to her, to them.

She shivered at the thought of a bomb landing on her parents' house, them killed, and her not finding out for days, maybe weeks later. Grace knew she would feel like she was sinking in a mud-filled black hole if they died without her ever being reconciled to them.

Only a week before she left, a roof was destroyed on one of the houses in the next street.

Her face lengthened as she continued to study the March 13th cover of the Saturday Evening Post, then her eyes lit up at the sound of a familiar voice at the door.

"Margaret! I'm so glad you came! Oh, I wish you could have brought the little duckies."

"Against hospital rules," David reminded her.

"They are with their grandparents, "Margaret rolled her eyes. "I hope they won't be too much for them."

"Dad will love it," her husband responded. "Without a doubt he has my fancy electric train on the floor by now, and they are on their knees having a swell time."

Margaret handed her a chocolate bar.

"A chocolate bar," Grace squealed. "Oh, it looks so yummy. Where did you ever find a chocolate bar? Thanks so much, I get so hungry for sweets sometimes."

Margaret laughed. "It was the only one left in the store."

Grace's look sobered. She had already torn off the wrapping and taken a bite, but stopped.

"Here you give it to the kiddies," she invited. "Tell them it's from Auntie Grace."

"No, oh, no," Margaret exclaimed, "it's for you."

"I already had one bite, and it's good, but I really do want them to have the rest. You can cut it up somehow so they won't know I took any. They probably don't even know what chocolate tastes like."

Margaret was reluctant and David refused at first, but when Margaret saw her friend's hurt look, she convinced her husband that they should take it.

After Margaret had tucked the treat into her purse, she asked when Grace would get out of the hospital.

"Maybe not too much longer: the doctor says if I am very, very careful and promise to stay in bed as much as much as possible, I should be able to go soon."

They had a lovely visit and Grace convinced them that it was okay for her to walk slowly and carefully down the hall if they would assist her.

Discharged

CHAPTER 10

*Several* days later Margaret eagerly walked into the room and reached for one of the identical bundles lying on the bed. Having another woman to talk to would be nice.

After Grace donned the street clothes Margaret brought along, she stared at her reflection in a mirror. I am ghostly white except for these dark circles under my eyes. It looks like I am hiding a mammoth pumpkin beneath my shift. She shoved her dark hat on lower than necessary and was glad for the veil that would hide her sad eyes.

Margaret looked at her pityingly. Grace winced. She's probably praying for me. Please don't, she felt like muttering. It's just a waste of time.

"Are you ready to go?" David asked removing the car keys from his pocket and dangling them from his right hand.

Grace sighed heavily. "As ready as I'll ever be."

Margaret laid her hand on David's arm. "Why don't you carry her valise for her?"

David's rugged features reddened, but he picked up the suitcase and led the way to the door.

Grace glanced back one last time. Another chapter of her life had closed; what would be next?

Nancy had come in late last night, and was sleeping, Mary was moaning and groaning and obviously in a lot of pain. Grace waved but Mary was distracted.

Grace was relieved she had had the opportunity to go on an elevator a time or two back in Birmingham so it wasn't a completely new experience; still they made her nervous. She avoided looking at anyone as they sank downwards.

I feel so conspicuous with this huge bulge in front of me. It's obvious that I'm not that old either. She knew that her porcelain like skin was paler than ever from being indoors for so long, no blossoms in my cheeks for Randall to coo over, now. She sighed.

Margaret clasped her arm. "Are you okay, Grace?"

"Yeah." Good as can be expected, I guess.

"Just wait until we get you out into the spring sunshine, then you'll feel great!"

"Spring sunshine?"

"Yes, it's late May already Grace, and welcome to beautiful Nova Scotia in the spring of the year! Expect to see a few apple blossoms along the boulevards!"

"Here's the car," David announced a moment later.

Grace sank gratefully into the backseat while David dealt with her luggage; her eyes closed. She was oblivious to Margaret's happy voice extolling the virtues of seaside city in springtime and dosed off with her head against the small oblong window beside her.

Margaret's hushed voice mingled with her drowsy thoughts.

"They would have never let her come to our place if they knew about all the stairs we have to climb."

Quite a while late it was David's rumbly voice that awakened her just as the vehicle ground to a stop.

"Well, we're here."

She turned wide, appreciative eyes towards the newly painted Victorian mansion. What a contrast to the dull, shabby cottage and handkerchief-sized lawn where she had spent her growing up years. Oh, they were going up the back way.

Nobody had much to say as they struggled up the long sets of stairs.

Margaret hurried on ahead and opened the door. "Welcome to our humble abode," she said with a funny little curtsy.

Grace smiled slightly as she looked around, then asked; "Where are the children?"

"There's a pig tailed tomboy down the hall who's keeping an eye on them with the help of her grandmother. I'll get them. Just kick off your loafers and make yourself comfortable."

Grace nervously paced from window to settee then back again. It was obvious that the tiny apartment was too crowded even without her presence. I'll have to sleep on the sofa for sure, and how I hate lack of privacy. I wonder where the kiddies sleep. There were two doors. She cracked open one of them. It was a storage room with a little bed made up on the floor. This must be where Davey will have to sleep now that I booted him off the couch.

Grace glanced at David, at his glowering countenance. Oh, oh, I've gotten into his bad books already, probably with my snooping.

Feeling weak with exhaustion, she lowered herself on to the couch and her eyes drifted shut.

"I'll be leaving now--" David yanked the door shut behind him. He doesn't like me very much.

"Grace! Where is Auntie Grace?" Grace jumped and looked wildly around, then spotted Davey running in, a fat gingerbread cookie with raisin eyes in his hand.

Margaret's, "Shh don't wake Auntie Grace," fell on deaf ears.

Grace smiled when she saw the little children and reached out for them.

Davey chomped on his cookie and grinned at her but Sally pulled her Mommy's skirt over her eyes and hung back.

"Come on," Margaret urged, "Auntie Grace was lonesome for you. Can't you give her a hug?" Davey stiffened and drew back.

His chin jutted out. Everything about his body language declared that real men do not hug.

When Sally saw Grace's arms sink to her lap she came over slowly to pat Grace's knee and rest her head on 'auntie's' arm.

Disastrous News

CHAPTER 11

"*Mail*time!" David announced a couple weeks later when he came home for his noon break. He handed a sheaf of papers to his wife. Margaret sorted through the fliers, bills and such.

Oh, look, Grace," she exclaimed. "Here's a letter for you."

Grace's mouth dropped open as she reached for the lovely lilac-scented envelope. Who could be writing to me from Deer Flats after all this time? She studied the envelope closely and saw that it had been readdressed several times. Evidently, there were a number of Seifert families in the area. She wondered if any of them were related to David.

``Aren't you going to open it?" Davey demanded.

"Yes." Grace's fingers trembled as she slit the lilac-bordered envelope and pulled out matching stationary.

"My dear, dear Grace," surprised and puzzled at the unusually affectionate greeting, Grace glanced down at the signature.

"Your loving mother-in-law, Lily Sutherland."

"*My dear, dear Grace*," she began again. "*This is the second letter I have written to you since the first one was eventually returned. I hope I have gotten the address right this time. I have longed to know you ever since Randall told me he had found a pretty-little lass way off in England. He sounded so proud of you.*

"*How are you? It was such a disappointment to hear that you would not be able to come directly out here, but I certainly wouldn't want anything to happen to that precious baby you are carrying.*

Grace's hand trembled so badly she could hardly read. My mother in law! Lily! What a sweet name! What lovely writing. She seems so kind. She doesn't even know I am carrying twins. Why isn't Randall writing? What is this all about?

Margaret stared at her, fascinated.

"Shall I read it for you?" she asked.

Grace barely heard her. She sank into one of the sunny yellow kitchen chairs, her eyes glued to the page.

"I wish I could have dropped everything to come to you, but of course it is much too far, and perhaps you wouldn't have wanted me there.

"I heard you were in the hospital, but there is so much I do not know. Oh, I hope you are well and the baby is well.

Oh, she doesn't even know I am carrying twins.

"Grace, I have such sorrowful news to break to you. I don't know how to share it gently enough so I'll just have to tell it the way it is. Randall got into serious trouble at a bar, and has been in jail all this time."

Grace looked stunned for an instant, but only an instant.

"No!" she screamed. "No! No! No! It can't be!" She stared at the paper but couldn't focus.

"In gaol! No! Not my Randall! What did he ever do to end up in gaol?"

Grace Goes to Pieces

CHAPTER 12

"*Everything,* absolutely everything goes wrong in my life!"

The confining walls of the apartment seemed to close in on her and Grace felt she had to escape before she screamed or do something even more drastic. She ripped the letter into quarters and stuffed them into the trashcan.

"Grace, what's wrong?" Margaret exclaimed, but the younger woman flung open the door and fled.

Margaret rushed to the entrance and looked out; she could hear Grace's feet pounding down the hall towards the stairs.

"Grace come back!" She called. She should never be running in her condition, especially down stairs. "Please be careful!"

Margaret wanted to rush after her but turned to look at the alarmed children. She stood there worried and confused. Grace will lose her babies for sure in her frenzied condition, but Sally is starting to wail. Oh, what should I do? She scooped Sally up in her arms and fell to her knees beside the dull burgundy couch.

"God," she cried, "Help Grace, help her, and please, please don't let her lose the babies.

Please God, put some sense into her head. Let her slow down, relax, and come back!"

A little hand pressed against her cheek to get her attention.

"Mommy, I'm hungry."

Scarcely aware of what she was doing, Margaret opened a tin of the newly popular mushroom soup, and while that was heating, spread some slices of homemade bread with a mayonnaise and tuna mixture. Every few minutes she would dash to the door, hoping and praying that Grace had returned.

she lifted Sally up to the sink to wash her hands while Junior got out his stool and sprinkled water over his own. Davey was being unusually obedient and she was vaguely aware of the concerned look on his face.

"Why did Auntie Grace run away?" he asked.

Margaret didn't know what to say so shrugged her shoulders then helped him dry his hands.

Although occupied with such mundane tasks, her stomach had knotted up with fear and anxiety.

They sat down and had their silent prayer, with which David was more comfortable. He hadn't said a word during all this tumult. Before the meal, already, he hide behind the newspaper, probably not knowing how to react.

After eating, Margaret mechanically squirted some washing liquid into the sink and added the utensils. She dropped what she was doing and hovered by the door every thought a prayer.

" I'd best be hiking back to work--" David took the short cut down the fire escape since Grace had clambered down the stairs.

Margaret tucked the children in for their naps. Davey was too scared to protest, Sally whimpered.

Because she was deeply concerned about Grace's reaction to the letter, Margaret did something even though it made her feel guilty. She took the torn up letter from the rubbish bin and pieced it together. After scanning it, she covered her face with her hands and groaned. This is really hard cheese. Lord, doesn't that girl have enough to worry about without this?

Fleeing to Nowhere

CHAPTER 13

But where was Grace?

She had floundered down the stairs, unlatched the gate to the high fence surrounding the back yard, and blundered into the alley, desperate to be alone.

A muscle spasm made her bend over in agony and in her weakened condition; she staggered over to a metal trashcan and sagged against it. She pressed her hands against her middle as waves of dizziness swirled around her.

After hurrying until she was about half way down the back alley, she paused, dismayed. What am I doing out here in my condition? She looked back at the sparkling white Victorian house behind her but was ashamed to return, besides her thoughts were too tumultuous. She plodded on, looking for a place to sit; there was none.

Well aware that her eyes had grown red and puffy from crying, which she couldn't seem to stop, Grace kept her head down and shuffled along. After coming to the end of the alley, she crossed to the next peaceful, suburban street. She was bushed and longed for a place to rest.

In the distance, she saw a bench: if only I can only get there. Waves of blackness made it hard to see, but she pushed one foot ahead of the other, hardly aware of what was before her.

A police officer's sharp whistle warned her not to cross right then, so she clung to a light pole beside her until he beckoned to her too.

He looked at her searchingly as she drew nearer. "Are you okay, ma'am?

Grace nodded not aware that all the color had washed from her face. "I. I just need to, sit down." She pointed numbly to the bench across the street.

Grace sensed that he wanted to escort her there but felt he shouldn't leave his post of duty.

"I'll ...be fine." she trudged off and eventually collapsed on the seat.

When someone else joined her, she focused enough to be aware that it was the same bus depot Margaret where children had waited with her that very morning so they could go shopping downtown. She still had her sweater on, and with that a few coins in her pocket. I'll take the bus.

It took an effort to climb the flimsy looking stairs but she managed, and even was able to find the right change before making her way to the very back. Someone, a man, she guessed, leaped up to give her his seat, but she barely acknowledged him as she sank down.

By the time the bus had merged into the traffic, Grace's face was deep into her hands and she was fighting the urge to vomit.

It's Too Soon!

CHAPTER 14

Grace spent hours huddled in the back seat of the lorry. People would come and go, the bus stopped and started, but the driver never noticed. There she was sometimes sleeping, often weeping, but never leaving.

She didn't know where to get off and was almost sick with worry about what her rash actions might do to the babies. She even prayed, begged God actually, to stop the labour pains that she was sure were gripping her.

In Grace's anguish and fear, she was terrified what might happen to the twins after they were born. Would she have to leave them in an orphanage—surely not Ideal—and work? Another pain knifed through her abdomen and she gripped both hands around her mouth so no one would hear her scream.

At times, the twins were kicking fiercely, but that just made her heart ache the more. It dawned upon her that she would have to eventually, get off the bus: the driver would go home, what would she do then?

She timed it so that several were leaving at the same time, and mingled with the crowd.

Two soldiers, on a short break from boot camp, eyed her with concern as she stumbled aimlessly down the darkening street.

One raised his hand as if to salute in respect to her obvious grief, but she hadn't even seen them.

She saw the lorry had discharged its load of passengers at a train station and wandered in. Now she discovered that things could get even worse. Just as she was sitting down, she soaked her undergarments, dress, the chair and a puddle was darkening the wooden plank floor.

Then she did scream and several women rushed over to her, anxious and concerned.

They babbled various things that Grace couldn't understand and took by the arm, moving her this way and that.

Grace couldn't help it, she felt hysterical.

A uniformed agent strode over and took things in hand.

Before she knew it, she was in an ambulance and given a sedative to calm her nerves.

Labor pains were upon her. "It's too early," Grace wailed, more anxious about the babies than her extreme pain.

She ended up in the same dreadfully familiar hospital.

"Calm down Grace," someone in white spoke sharply to her. "Calm down and relax. Relax. Relax, do you hear me? Relax! Lots of twins come early. It's normal. It's totally normal. I'm sure they will be fine."

Seven weeks! She should have been more careful! She should have been able to carry them much long longer….she screamed….

After that, she couldn't focus on anything but trying to get through the ordeal.

The next thing she knew, Margaret was beside her, soothing, comforting, and stroking her tangled hair off her face, love sparkling in her eyes.

"Margaret," Grace wailed. "Margaret, you came. "

"Of course I came, of course. They informed us soon after you were admitted. We are like David and Jonathan, you know."

Grace wasn't aware of how long Margaret stayed, but it didn't seem long enough. Soon three nurses and a doctor swarmed around her.

"Time to leave, doctor's orders:" That same head nurse. She has always been so brusque.

"Please," Grace begged, `Let her stay a little longer," but her pleas were brushed aside.

Margaret stooped to hug her. "You'll be fine, sis. I'll be praying –constantly- for you,"

"Oh please, please, do, "Grace squeezed her hand tightly just as the nurse took Margaret by the elbow and marched her out.

The Momentous Decision

CHAPTER 15

An idea had been tugging at Grace's heartstrings ever since the twins safely arrived. She remembered vividly the first time it had occurred.

It was while in the case room: bright lights and whiteness were all around. She was waiting with weary anticipation for that soul-stirring moment when the nurse would finish cleansing the squirmy, newborns; wrap them snugly in soft receiving blankets, then turn to place them one by one into her longing arms.

"They are fine, perfectly fine," the genial doctor reassured her when she fretted about how small they were. "Sure they are a bit tiny and will need extra care for the next two or three weeks but are strong and healthy. Congratulations, Mrs. Sutherland!"

Grace half arose on the bed, her arms reaching out, then she was cuddling them. For a long moment, she had eyes for nothing more than those incredibly beautiful, incredibly precious rosy-red bundles of humanity.

Finally, wonderfully convinced that they were healthy, her heart just melted.

To think they were hers, gloriously hers to love and to cherish as long as she lived. ! She felt a yearning protectiveness grip her as she gazed into those wide cloudy blue eyes, making an instant connection. A throb of joy filled her heart. I may seem young for such tremendous responsibility, but oh, I want to, I want to give them the best care possible.

Then, a darkly unwelcome thought slithered like an evil snake into her mind. Will Randall try to be a good father? He hadn't liked it when I got pregnant, and that was before I knew I was carrying twins! How well will he treat them? Can I trust him not to hurt these incredibly sweet treasures from Heaven?

"Mrs. Sutherland, are you alright?"

"W-what?"

"You seem pale: maybe I should put the babies back in their bassinets now."

Grace looked at the young nurse blankly then down at the babies in her arms. She wanted to protest but did feel faint.

She stared at the retreating figure almost numb with fear.

My own darling babies! What is going to happen to them? Will Randall be cruel or unfaithful? Before we were married, many young women prattled excitedly and made google eyes, as he'd stop to talk. What if he decides being tied down with a wife and two babies is to his liking?

What shall I do? Can I go to Deer Flats if he is gaol? Dare I? I refuse to leave the babies in an orphanage while I am a cashier at some dumpy department store and I can't leech off the Seifert's indefinitely!

Are there any doctors way out there in the wilderness? How can I care for the wee ones without any support?

No one in this world is more precious to me than they are! I will protect them with my life if needs be! How can I, if I am in a log cabin somewhere and he comes home sloshed?

A nurse came to check her pulse and temperature and insisted that she lay down.

Later, when the doctor went on his rounds, he and the nurse assumed she was asleep, Grace overheard them conversing in low tones.

"Worried... blood pressure too high...pulse racing...No word from husband..."

"He was a soldier, right? Was he discharged honorably?"

"No one knows for sure, not even Mrs. Sutherland."

"Something sure is suspicious. Everything is kept so hush, hush."

When the nurse spoke to her, Grace pretended to be just waking up, but she felt sick to the stomach.

The twins scheduled feedings were the highlight of the day for her and she begged the nursing staff to let her keep them with her all the time. They were kind but said it was against hospital policy, something about cross contamination and Grace needing her rest.

She said they were being given the best of care but it didn't reassure Grace.

I'd rest better if I they were close all the time. She pressed the little ones to her bosom. One of the infants was making tiny mewling sounds while searching for her fist.

Grace stroked her velvety cheek and pressed kisses into her bright, downy hair. She always pretended that it took longer to feed them than it actually did, the nurses were wise to her tactics but were indulgent with her.

I will need to name them without Randall's help or approval. Are there any names sweet enough for such darling twins?

She whispered name after name into the tiny ears wondering which ones would be perfect. When she had to fill out the forms for the birth certificate etc. she wrote her choices out in her loveliest cursive because they were the loveliest ones she could think of. Emily Margaret, Alice Grace.

Grace's strength was coming back. The twins weren't fragile preemies anymore. They are doing well. Soon she would be going home, or at least to David's. She must make a major decision. She must decide what was best for the children. Since Randall doesn't even know I have twins, can I, dare I give one little girl a chance for a happy, abuse free childhood and let Margaret care for her? After all, Randall thought I was only expecting one.

How could I have even thought about it? I could never, NEVER give up a child. Never!
But the thought persisted.
Don't you love your darlings enough to provide at least one with a safe, wholesome childhood no matter what the cost in personal joy?
That's an impossible decision! Life is asking too much of me! Her heart was wrung with anguish at the very thought. How much worse would the deed make me feel?
Then the question: which one? How could I ever choose one over the other? The thought made her nearly gag. Choose to give one happiness and the other pain? What an awful thought! Accept one and reject the other? That was even worse!
Margaret begged Grace to stay longer before heading west. She could tell that her young friend was distraught about something and tried to encourage Grace to unburden her heart, which she would do in an agitated, jumbled way.

Oh, how Margaret felt for her! Because of her own aching loss, she longed to adopt one of the twins, but prayed tearfully, sacrificially, that God would give her the grace not to influence Grace's decision, knowing that the new Mom was feeling both physically weak and emotionally vulnerable right then.

Shopping and so Much More

CHAPTER 16

The day arrived. Grace must leave all that was familiar to cross a vast wilderness and lonely prairie, alone. She could no longer hold off making a decision what to do with her babies. With her suitcases neatly packed, paper sacks bulging with nappies and baby clothes, clustered in the grass off to one side, she was ready to go: at least as ready as she ever would be. Margaret perceived that the clothes for the identical twins were separated into different bags. She held her tongue.

Grace hesitated for a long time on the front doorstep of the apartment.

Women wearing summer hats, with handbags slung over their shoulders, strolled by. Cars motored up and down the street. A gangly pup scampered past in pursuit of a cat. Beneath a shady maple, the twins were sleeping cozily together in the rickety old pram. Everything seemed so homey and idyllic but it wasn't.

She stood there, deep in thought, unaware of just how much God could help with the terrible pain in her breast.

David had been checking the oil. Now he came over to her, wiping his hands on a rag, and stowed her luggage in the boot of the second-hand, Ford.

Upstairs, Margaret was cleaning little faces, and tidying up. She made a big, perky bow in the back of Sally's pink seersucker dress and tucked Junior's shirt back into his pants for the second time.

Sally reached back and patted her bow, then strutted out the door, Margaret didn't notice her antics; she was well aware of Grace's unhappiness, however.

On chubby little legs, the children trotted ahead of Margaret down the stairs, and out the door. She walked around Grace to let the children into the car.

Grace's heart thudded and raced. The children's light-hearted prattle seemed discordantly loud: only a few seconds more to decide!

Margaret looked up at Grace with a pleasant smile.

"Ready?"

She had announced that they would go shopping before meeting the train but hadn't revealed what they were shopping for. That was her surprise!

Tears came to Grace's eyes. She pointed to the sleeping babies.

"Choose one," she blurted, "Will you cherish her for me?"

"Are you sure?" Margaret walked eagerly over to the pram.

Grace nodded. "I must let one have a chance. I could never let them both go. I dressed them identically today: deliberately. So I wouldn't know— immediately—which one—which one—you—"

She covered her face with her hands, and sobbing, ran over to the car.

Grace had noticed even Margaret didn't know which one she was holding unless she told her. She was the only one who could tell them apart and she declined to share her secret.

The children stared at their 'auntie`. She lowered her head, letting her shiny-black curls conceal her face.

David opened the side door and placed the other baby in her arms. Grace lifted the blanket flap. She felt slightly relieved. She was holding Emily Margaret. Emily had been only four pounds, two ounces at birth, and Grace still considered her slightly frailer than her sister, so needed her mother's milk the most. They drove several blocks before anyone, even the little ones, broke the silence.

"You have Alice Grace. To foster, if our circumstances ever change, I want her back. Please."

"Definitely," Margaret replied, while David nodded in agreement, although they both wondered how they could ever let her go once they were solely responsible for her care.

Grace asked for a paper and pen. She knew David's shirt pockets always bulged with such practical items. Margaret reached over and slipped a small notebook and pen out of his pocket.

While using her purse and Emily for a platform, Grace proceeded to write.

Sept. 23rd, 1945

I, Mrs. Randall Sutherland, (Grace) of Deer Flats, Alta. have entrusted my daughter, Alice Grace Sutherland to the care and keeping of Mr. and Mrs. David Seifert of Halifax, N. S. with the full assurance they will return her to me at my request whenever that may be.

Her writing was rather shaky because of the movement of the vehicle so she asked them to stop for a moment. They pulled off and parked on a side street gracefully lined with shady maples.

Grace handed Emily to David then rewrote the note. After carefully scripting it twice, and putting her signature on both, she solemnly handed the pieces of paper over the front seat. David and Margaret read them, and then wrote their names beneath Grace's.

None of them knew if they would be laughed out of court with those handwritten pieces of notebook paper, neither did they care.

To them, they were as binding as a formal document witnessed by an army of lawyers.

Maybe I should have made a third copy and filed it away with a lawyer or something. Grace mentally shook her head, no, I trust Margaret.

Margaret removed a mini pair of scissors, a needle and thread from her purse. She handed them to Grace. After carefully taking out several stitches from the bottom seam in the lining of her handbag, Grace folded her copy of the agreement, and squeezed it into the opening then sewed it together again with almost invisible stitches.

David handed Emily back to her mother, started the car and they were on their way once again. Some girls would have acted foolish and giddy to make it easier to ignore the pain, but Margaret and Grace were not that kind. They were quiet and serious, almost gentle with each other.

Ironically, they each cared for the other woman's baby for the rest of the afternoon, then switched just before they got to the train depot.

The pram stayed home.

Margaret insisted on loading Grace down with many wonderful but practical gifts. She had not forgotten that Grace had said once that her birthday was January 25, and although it was early autumn, she used that as an excuse for her extravagant generosity.

They were not wealthy, by any means, but she could not bear to think of Grace going into the cold northern wilderness without being warmly clad. After much searching, they managed to find a beautiful winter coat in a hideaway shop marked at 75% off because of the time of year. Margaret seized it immediately.

They took pleasure in choosing several matching outfits in various sizes for the twins. The smallest ones were ivory colored frocks for their first birthdays.

Grace chose the Swiss-dotted lemon yellow dresses for when they turned three or four, and Margaret picked the green plaid set with crisp pleats and piping around the collars and waists. The two moms pictured them worn on the twins first day of school.

After making the many purchases, David rolled his eyes, and shook his head, but paid for them without too much complaint. When Margaret suggested getting them each a matching teddy bear, he shook his head: no, this had to be enough. He hoped they wouldn't have to live on crackers and water for the next month or two.

They drove to a park to munch on their brought along peanut butter and jam sandwiches and apples.

It was hard to talk, and harder yet to swallow. Grace caressed the twins with her eyes. They were sleeping peacefully on a spare blanket between them and as they often did, were snuggling.

The corners of her mouth turned downwards. They don't have any idea how I am about to change their destiny, and I have no way of knowing if it's for their good or not.

Soon, far too soon, it was time to say their final good-byes.

The women clung to each other loath to part. While standing on the platform at the railroad station, they covered the babies with kisses. David shook Grace's hand then took care of her baggage. They silently watched the train fill up.

Grace, looking lonely and dejected, boarded the train with only one small baby in her arms.

Margaret's hand rested lightly on David's shoulder. She stood motionless, staring at the train as it rumbled farther and farther into the vast unknown.

She looked down at the sweetly sleeping little innocent in her arms. What have I done? Was it even right of me to accept Grace's baby?

Maybe I should have protested more. My own sorrow must have been too obvious; otherwise, she would have never suggested it. She will find it so hard to forgive herself-- or maybe even me!

Margaret eventually became aware of David's concerned eyes searching her face.

"What will people think if I show up with one of the babies? Maybe they will think I kidnapped her even! We went everywhere together!"

David laid his arm on her shoulder and let her talk. "But of course not, "he interrupted, "Everyone knew that we were good friends with Grace. If you share the story with a few that are closest to you, they will understand, and the truth will get around."

"Just live one day at a time, honey. We'll get into a real quandary if we try to imagine what people might be thinking."

By that time, Junior and Sally were horsing around in the car. Sally got the notion to sit on the horn. It was such a neat seat, and just her size, too! The noise startled her and she howled loudly.

While Margaret rushed to comfort her, David used his penknife to slit open an envelope that had come in the mail. He had gone to the post office while the young mothers were shopping.

There was something about the look in his eyes that Margaret couldn't quite discern.

"A letter arrived from headquarters," he announced while starting the car. "They are aware that my internal injuries should be healed by now. Since I am an officer and didn't accept an honorable discharge, I am supposed to return."

"Right now?" Margaret gasped her hand flying to her throat.

"But I thought the war was over!"

"In Europe, yes, but there will still many skirmishes here and there. I'm supposed to help tie up loose ends." He grinned wryly. "You know my reputation."

Margaret scarcely heard a word he was saying. David was leaving!

How could she ever survive if he left now of all times? In the back seat, the children were making a ruckus but no one heard them.

She felt pushed into a long scary tunnel. Movie-like pictures flashed before her eyes...feverish children tossing and turning...voices calling... Mommy! Mommy!

Grace running through a field, an ambulance's light flashing, a siren wailing...and, oh, no, was that David in a hospital bed?

She felt the color drain from her cheeks as her head sank into her hands.

David shook her hard. She didn't know how many seconds had passed but it felt like an age.

"Margaret, are you all right?"

"Y—yes, I think so."

"I thought you were having a seizure," he confessed. "Davey, you sit down and stop hanging around Mommy's neck like that."

Margaret pretended to laugh. "I've never had a seizure in my life." She drew a long shaky breath. "Are there some awful things in my future, or is it just my overwrought imagination?" She shared what she had just passed through with David; he looked thoughtful but didn't comment.

Lord, I want to commit the future into your hands, she prayed silently. Help me to trust in You. Thank you for the knowledge, the assurance that You will always be with us, no matter what happens.

She glanced at David. "It's going to be very difficult with you gone."

He nodded, "I'll write as often as possible."

"Oh if only Mom lived close by so I could rely on her if needs be," but they both knew that could never happen.

"Maybe you can call my mother."

Even if she hadn't heard the hesitancy in David's voice, Margaret wouldn't have considered it. The older Mrs. Seifert just wasn't the gentle, motherly type. "

Alice's sleepy stirring erupted into loud wailing.

"Oh, David, we have to buy formula: like right now. I totally forgot about it."

David groaned. He had reconciled himself to a diet of bread and milk, more or less, after the women splurged at the stores, but he hadn't thought about the additional cost of formula.

How could his war checks reach her in time to prevent undue hardships? He pondered that for a few blocks then decided reluctantly they would have to dip into the saving fund meant for the new house until his first check came.

Meanwhile, Margaret now understood why Grace had been giving the babies a bottle once a day even though they were still so very young.

Entering the Vast Unknown

CHAPTER 17

It was a good thing that the rocking motion of the train kept Emily sleeping. For many miles, her mother leaned against the window, shaking with sobs. Grace tried to get a grip on herself.

People will be wondering what's wrong, or think I'm mighty queer if I can't stop being so emotional. She managed to hold it in for about five seconds, then a sleepy movement of Emily's little fingers got her thinking about Alice and once again, the tear rolled down her cheeks.

When Emily woke up, she was acting restless and fussy. Grace stared at her; she had never acted so upset in quite that way before. Why does she twist her head from side to side like that and keep whimpering? Does she have an earache? Oh surely not! I have no idea how to soothe an earache, on a train at that.

Emily's whimpers turned into loud, lusty wails and just as she picked her up, it hit Grace like a rock. She's missing; and searching for her identical twin.

Worry lines puckered Grace's forehead: I thought it was only me that would suffer; look what I have done to my little girl!

While feeling agitated and guilty, it was impossible to calm the two-month-old. What can I do? Oh, what can I do? People are beginning to stare at me, I'm sure of it!

She felt the back of her neck and ears scorch from the real or imaginary disapproval of those around her. What would Margaret have done? She was always so calm, so tranquil with the crying babies while I would get frantic.

Oh, she often sang.

For a moment, Grace pictured Margaret in the old, scuffed up rocking chair singing sweetly to whichever baby was upset. The chair was in the corner of their bedroom because there was simply no other place for it, but the melodies would float through the small spaces especially on the darkest of nights.

Grace quickly realized how blessed she had been to have Margaret help her care for the newborns, especially since she was so young and inexperienced.

The songs were coming back to her, and as she crooned, her own spirit calmed.

"Jesus Saviour pilot me over life's tempestuous sing. Boisterous waves around me roll, hiding rock and treacherous shoal, "(Edward Hopper.)

She rocked harder as the wails grew louder, but Emily's crying wasn't affecting her quite the same anymore. She was thinking of the words. "As a mother stills her child, Thou canst hush the ocean wild." Ocean wild: that's exactly what my heart's been like for so long now.

That's the secret of Margaret's serenity. She lets Jesus hush the storms, the grief, and heartache in her own spirit. Margaret suffered much but she always was there for me because Jesus was there for her.

"Lord, I want what she has," she whispered.

A toddler hopped off the bench at his mother's side and stood in the aisle watching her.

Grace smiled at him.

"Baby," he said.

"Yes, she's just a babby. She's sleeping now."

He nodded. "Baby cry. Baby go nigh-night."

"Yes, Babby has gone 'night-night."

He seemed content to just stand there.

"What's your name, little boy?"

He didn't answer.

"The babby's name is Emily. Mine is Gra- Mrs. Sutherland. Can you say, Emily?"

"Mmm'ee: baby small."

"Yes, Emily is very small, yet, "

He put his hand on the top of head: it barely reached. "Me big boy. "

He watched Emily making little sucking noises. "Baby hun-gee."

"Babby will be fine for a little while. Are you hungry?"

The small chap nodded.

Oh dear, what have I gotten into?

Grace gently laid the baby beside her and reached into her purse. Margaret had slipped a small paper sack of cookies into her hand while they were at the train station.

She took one out and showed it to his Mom. "Is it okay if I give it to him?"

"Bobby, you aren't hungry, are you?"

"Hun'gee!"

"Oh well, just one then. It will tide you over 'til we reach Toronto, You should have a nap. What do you say?"

"Tang-too!" He made a beeline for his Mommy's lap and snuggled there while munching on his biscuit, completely oblivious to the crumbs his mother was patiently brushing off his shirt and her skirt.

By then Grace was singing another song.

"What a Friend we have in Jesus, all our sins and griefs to bear…" She looked at Bobby so sleepy in his mother's arms and wondered if she had ever felt safe and secure snuggled up close to her mother.

Oh, Lord, give me that feeling of security that comes from being close to you. I want to trust you with my whole life; she gave a little shudder, thinking of Randall in gaol, even the unknown future. She looked down at Emily again: especially the future.

When Emily woke up, and after she had gotten her little tummy filled, Grace arranged her new woolen coat on the floor with the satin side up. Emily seemed to enjoy being able to kick and stretch in the less confining space.

She looked so sweet in the cloud soft sweater set Margaret had knitted for her. Margaret had taught Grace how to make one also, and she felt a bit guilty for taking the better one. It was obvious that Margaret's was so much fluffier.

Grace stooped down to remove the light yellow bonnet from the tiny girl and was pleased to see that Emily's coppery red hair was definitely beginning to curl.
Emily smiled at her and cooed. Maybe she will get over the loss of her sister soon. Please, God

The Deep Dark Forest

CHAPTER 18

Traffic on the roads nearest the railroad tracks was much heavier long before the train rolled into Toronto.

Bobby practically catapulted into his father's arms just outside Grace's window; his mother also received a wholehearted welcome.

Supper aromas were hovering in the air, so Grace got out her bag lunch prepared in the Seifert's kitchen, two of the sandwiches were bologna and lettuce, the rest peanut butter and jelly. She chose one with bologna on it, and carefully rewrapped the rest for another day. After studying the three apples, Grace decided to wait to have one. Her lips twitched when she dug deep into the bottom of the bag and discovered a big fat gingerbread man cookie that Davey had hidden there. Although it was a bit dry Grace knew it was his way of saying thank you for all the times she read to the children.

How she missed them all. Margaret had been like a mother and sister to her and even David had tolerated her presence reasonably well. She took a sip out of the Beaver quart jar of lemon aide and knew she would treasure the container forever, possibly using it for flower bouquets.

They were entering a deep, dark forested area now. Although Emily was sleeping well on the floor, she felt a bit cool so Grace tucked a white shawl around her, and then cocooned her in the folds of the coat. Her eyes moistened: although the shawl belonged to Ricky, created by a great aunt, Margaret had urged her to keep it.

The pale colours of twilight made Grace feel sad, the future bleak and uncertain.

 Usually, the question about Randall's confinement lurked in the back of her mind, now it hammered for attention. Why did he return home? Why was he in gaol? Why was I permitted to come if he had been dishonorably discharged? Did I just slip through the cracks?

The first star came out soon followed by another and another. It looked so dark and lonesome. Grace was stiff and tired from sitting so much of the time. When would they ever get there? Was all of Canada one vast forest? No, she remembered next was an endless prairie she had to pass through and who knew what kind of wilderness was up north where the Sutherland's lived.

As they rounded a curve, she could see the silvery rails snaking ahead of them through the heavily timbered area.

She peered out of the window and felt cold. I wonder how many bears and wolves are out there?

Emily woke up fussy, Grace fed her, but she wouldn't settle. It's going to be another long night, she thought.

As the thin young mother paced up and down the dimly lit rail car, Emily's cries pierced the air and several passengers were beginning to get upset. Grace became desperate enough to quiet her colicky infant that shyly at first, then more confidently sang in a rich, strong, contralto. She had a baby to soothe, and the words to 'Margaret's hymns' comforted both her and her child.

She heard someone remark that she had a voice like Judy Garland but was raised in such a way that she had no idea who that was.

Emily fell asleep and Grace put her down then sank back unto the hard bench. She had nearly dozed off when a voice near her ear startled her.

An elderly man with a pointy silvery beard and white cane was bending over her.

"Don't let those grumpy folks bother you," he said in an intense whisper. "We all like it that you care for your baby so tenderly."

The next morning when Grace awoke she couldn't remember if she had dreamed up the wizened little man's visit or not.

They were skirting mostly around a small town. With its, well-tended yards profuse with late summer flowers, it reminded Grace of England.

I would be blissfully happy to walk into a little vine covered stone cottage nestled in beds of riotously beautiful flowers and call it home: Nothing, but nothing is sweeter and more lovely, than an English cottage garden, not that I ever lived near one.

She had heard about the labor of love Mrs. Henderson, Margaret's mother, had put into their parsonage gardens and imagined Margaret with an idyllic childhood.

Her thoughts rambled on: Mr. and Mrs. Sutherland. What were their first names? Oh dear, I can't even remember what Randall said the names of my parent-in-law are, and I'm going to be meeting them soon.

She thought long and hard. Ben was it: Ben and Lily? Yes, I think that is right. Oh, I hope I don't forget.

She tried to figure out what they might be like. Will they be grim and impossible? Somehow, I know he will be. Maybe it is from something Randall said.

But Lily; what would the mother of a criminal be like? She watched a cloud floating by and the sun was whitening it with all its glory. Lily; with a sweet name like that; who uses such pretty stationary and writes kindly letters, surely she can't be that bad. Maybe she is heartsick at what Randall has done.

As Grace changed the baby, Emily gurgled and cooed: there was something about her merry eyes that reminded her of Randall. How could he have changed so much? Sure, she conceded, maybe he had been anxious about being a father while a war was going on, but why did he have to leave?

He was impulsive by nature, and surely didn't mean it quite as it had sounded.

As Grace leaned her head back against the hard seat, she wished for Randall's shoulder to rest against. I hope that things would work out one we see each other again. He had been so goofy and fun when they were dating.

How could he had done something so awful as to—She wanted to refuse to finish the thought but the ugly words 'land in gaol' leaked through anyway, and why, oh why was he sent home from the army?

Just then, a little voice piped up loud and clear. "Daddy! I haveta go wee-wee."

Grace smirked along with several others yet wondered if Randall would ever help one of their children find the lavatory.

Her mind drifted to a slightly different angle. Why hasn't he ever written me, or called? Didn't his father give him my address? Or doesn't he care for me anymore? Oh, I wish I was heading back to England!

This trip is so long, and all I do is think, think, think, I need more to distract me!

She recalled the peace felt while singing earlier, but the train was reverberating through more heavily wooded country, and the quiet, loneliness made her melancholy.

Oh God, if Alice would have died, there would have been closure; eventually, at least, but this separation is such a raw wound!

The uncertainty of not knowing if I made the right decision to let her go is so depressing. I need her; she needs me: Oh God, protect her, please, please. My own sweet Alice, my own precious darling: I think I'll die if I don't ever see her again:

Lord, my arms just ache to hold my dear babby. I can hardly stand it. Oh, God protect her. I implore you to protect her and give her a happy life."

Grace stopped short in amazement. It was actually getting easier to talk to the Heavenly Father, as Margaret called Him.

"God," she continued shyly. "I made a dreadful mistake. No, two: I married a-an alcoholic, and I gave my own babby way. Lord, how can I ever live with the end-result? The future looks terribly bleak."

Two tiny thoughts slipped into her mind. You have no proof that he's an alcoholic just because he drinks. Why don't you just trust me with your decision to let David and Margaret foster Alice? She might be very happy in their home. Isn't that what you want?

By then Emily was crying again, which made her mother feel guilty, assuming she was missing her sister. It was raining so hard by then that Grace could hardly differentiate between the pouring rain, which made the gray waters of the Great Lakes heave, and the blur of her own tears.

Fortunately this time Emily was only hungry, so was easier to settle. After filling her tummy, Grace changed her nappy; glad she didn't have to use salt water to cleanse her, like they did on the ship which caused such nasty rashes.

She straightened out the baby blanket on the seat beside her for Emily to lie on. The baby happily kicked her feet and even cooed.

Although her baby was obviously enjoying the freedom of no confining blankets, Grace was convinced she hadn't forgotten her sister.

She picked up the child and kissed her, "Bless you darling," she murmured. "Oh, Lord," the cry was wrung from the bottom of her heart. "Bless her wee sister also. May Randall love his little daughter enough that I can bring the sisters back together. She has such a delicate beauty. May her beauty help to win his heart. She has his bright coppery, gold hair, (although his is darker now,) may that bind him to her if nothing else does! Please, Lord, don't let him be abusive! Don't let him ever come home drunk like Betsy's father did!"

The same elderly gentleman; who used his white cane to punctuate the narrow aisle like question marks, groped over to where she was sitting.

"I love the sound of your wee baby." The smile on his face was angelic. "Are you a new mammie?"

"Oh, yes," Grace nodded shyly at the spritely man. "I'm one of the war brides from England. I'm bringing my babby home so we can be with her Daddy."

"May I hold her a wee bit?" he asked, carefully groping around the seat.

Grace pushed her things out of the way then touched his elbow to help him find a place to sit beside her. After he settled, she carefully laid Emily in his arms, worrying if she would actually be comfortable with him.

Her fears were unfounded, though. He stroked Emily's face with his delicate, sensitive fingers. "She is a beautiful baby," he observed. Grace's heart warmed with maternal pride.

Soon he left her to resume his nap behind a black fedora.

Someone in a jaunty red hat overheard her talking about being a war bride. Since her sister-in-law was also one, she tripped over and struck up a conversation.

As the miles rumbled by, Grace's thoughts turned increasingly to what lay ahead. She had changed, soothed and nursed Emily countless times, now that her brought-along lunch was gone, went to the dining car to eat, but still the train rattled on.

the scenery changed gradually with quaint red barns and towering elevator a charming break from the green fields of grain and acreages of unbroken pastureland which seemed to reach from eternity to eternity.

She appreciated the changing sky, though. Once, while more or less dozing the afternoon away, the slanting sun kissed her eyelids. She woke up, yawned sleepily then her eyes opened wide. What a gorgeous sight! What a marvelous closing to the day! Although she had never considered herself an artist, she yearned to paint a likeness of it.

Grace marveled at the delicate peachy-pink clouds 'embroidered' in a scallop of the palest mauve and it lifted her spirits until the last hint of colour had merged with the darkness.

Waking up early, enough to enjoy the sunrise came with the ride, but she first had to rub her neck and shoulders to get the kinks out, and stretch to ease the aches in her back. At that hour, the sun was just a band of gold against a few silhouetted trees; fellow passengers were still slumbering in awkward positions.

When Emily awoke, she waved her little hands at the sight of her mother. There was a trace of a smile lingering on Grace`s face for many a mile after that. Maybe just maybe she`s beginning to accept that Alice isn`t here.

Later on in the day when the frail blind man tap-tapped his way off the train, he stopped to pat Grace`s arm.

"Bless you my child," he said in a quavering voice, "and bless the wee one. "He stroked Emily's downy hair then a porter helped him to manage the stairs.

She watched a modern looking car with a sharp paint job grind to a stop at the train station where the elderly grandpa tottered off.

Someone in a suit and hat hopped out of the luxury vehicle and briskly strode over to him. Grace watched him march off with the frail gent, his hand under his elbow. He swung the car door open and helped him to settle in the front seat, tossed the valise into the boot of the car, slammed it shut, and whizzed off.

"Bless you Grandpapa," Grace whispered as she watched them leave.

She looked on as families, couples, businessmen, and the elderly, arrived, rode for a while then get off again. No one seemed to be going as far as she was.

When the train stopped in Regina, the first influx of homecoming recruits poured in. They hadn't even reached the battlefields before V Day was announced, Grace got the feeling some of them were disappointed that they weren't involved in helping to "bash them good" as one would-be soldier had put it.

They were so exuberant and rowdy that Emily was frightened and wailed at the disturbance.

A slightly soaked aspiring private snatched the baby and tossed her into the air.

"Lizzen kiddo, yer s'posed to celebrate. That ole war is over. If me an' ma buddies had gotten a chance to go earlier, we woulda licked those Germans long ago. We woulda chased ole Hitler an' his gang right into the Baltic Sea."

"Give Emily to me," Grace begged.

"For shame, George," one of his more sober minded companions remonstrated. He vacated his seat and awkwardly handed the baby back to her mother.

Grace noticed that not all the soldiers that boarded where raw recruits. Some of them, she was sure, were not much older than she was, but they seemed to have matured beyond their years. By the look in their vacant eyes, tired features, and various injuries she knew they had seen too much suffering and atrocities; that going off to war wasn't the big adventure the younger boys had been anticipating.

Her throat filled when she saw one young man whose sleeve hung limp and empty at his side. Grace wondered about them all, and it helped her to forget her own misery. They had left, some up to five or more years before, fresh faced and hopeful, and were returning, with haunted eyes and bitter memories. Would Randall be whole, in one piece?

When night fell once again, she peered through the small window beside her at miles and miles of unending blackness lit only dimly by tall street lamps when the occasional small railroad station came into view, her heartbeat quickened knowing that soon it would be her new destiny that would be called out.

She had only seen a pin prick of light in the darkness when the conductor announced the awaited words; "Deer Flats."

Long before she was ready for it, she, her tiny baby and her belongings were deposited on an empty platform beside a narrow red building. The name of the settlement was painted in neat black letters on a narrow white board. The small clusters of buildings were practically invisible in the scanty starlight. She hoped, nay, prayed actually there would be more to Deer Flats once morning light illuminated it.

Grace looked around fearfully. No one seemed to be around. Hadn't the message gotten to her father-in-law when she would be arriving?

Just before the icy fingers of terror managed to strangle her, she made out the flickering glow of a dim light—a kerosene lamp, she assumed, and a heavy farm wagon lumbering her way.

A gloomy looking man hunched over the back of a massive black animal, the biggest horse she had ever seen, and he was holding a lantern. That must be Mr. Sutherland: who else would be at this desolate train station at such an unearthly hour?

She walked slowly towards him, the baby cradled in one arm while dragging her belongings with the other. Why doesn't he come and help me, or at least say something? Before the thought was even completed, he did, but it wasn't what she had expected. Or was it: she couldn't imagine what his response might be.

"Well, hurry up," he grumbled. "I ain't waitin' here all night!"

With what seemed like exaggerated reluctance and lack of ceremony he tossed her luggage in the back then took the baby while she clambered on-board. She studied him out of the corner of her eye while they were trudging down the empty, dirt road, and saw the most sullen face ever.

Her mother looked cheerful in comparison.

Her heart sank; surely, it was the shadows that made him look so morose. The horse plodded along for ten or fifteen minutes then they crested a small rise and Grace saw lights that indicated a settlement. A wooden sign announced they were entering the town of Russet. All Grace knew about Russet was that it was far north of Edmonton, and Edmonton seemed like the end of civilization yet here she was beyond it.

His voice startled her. "Well, I suppose you will be wanting to see Randall, seeing's you got him into all this trouble any ways."

Grace felt stunned. Trouble? What trouble? Whatever could he be talking about?

"The jailer said to come on down even though its late," Mr. Sutherland continued. "He knows you are from afar and that I ain't aiming to come to town more often than usual."

In Gaol!

CHAPTER 19

Grace took a deep breath, and bit her lip to still its trembling. She could do nothing about the nervous feeling in her stomach, however. Her feet dragged. Would Randall want to see her?

Soon she would see the man of her dreams, was he still that? Grace hardly knew. She used to be so upset with him but time, and perhaps the gentling influence of the Holy Spirit, had been causing her to realize there may be a reason for his actions, a reason she couldn't comprehend. Grace remembered how warm and happy she used to feel in his presence; besides they were married, she would have to make it work.

My, what a dark, grungy interior.

"Here we are," her guide announced, unlocking the cell. Grace didn't know whether to bring the baby in with her or not. Her father-in-law hadn't suggested that he take care of her, and she certainly didn't want to offer a baby, her baby, to the grizzled gaol-keeper, a stranger, to tend.

There were only three cells and in the last one was where Randall sat for reasons she still did not understand.

She recalled how much she used to love him. No one ever set my heart to dancing like Randall. No one cared about me as much as he did.

The door was opening, the gaoler stepped aside; she wished she knew how to pray!

What! Randall's head shaved and wearing black and white striped garments! For some reason Grace had never expected it.

The lock clicked grimly behind her. 'I'll be back in 15 minutes," She was standing in the shadows and Randall didn't even look her way.

"Hi Randall," she said, clinging to the bundle in her arms.

Randal's head jerked, his eyes widened. "Grace! You came!" He leaped to his feet, arms outstretched, then dropped them stiffly to his sides, "W-what took you so long?"

Grace's mouth dropped open. "What?"

"I was expecting you months ago. I was so worried, what could have happened? Maybe your boat had been torpedoed or something. Maybe you had never forgiven me for being so rash."

"Oh, Randall," she took a step closer. "And I was wondering why you didn't communicate."

She saw the look of anguish in his eyes.

"I couldn't. Dad refused to give me your address, he was that mad at me."

"For, for marrying me?"

Randall shook his head, "No, for ending up in jail. I haven't even seen Mom since—"

Just then, the baby awoke, arms flailing, and Grace laid her gently on the cot. She just hoped it was cleaner than it looked.

Grace turned to look at him staring so mutely at her and realized how deeply her love did go towards him. All the mixed up feelings of the last few months were only surface turmoil, deep down she knew they were meant for each other and that she adored him.

They locked eyes: "You mean you couldn't write?" she asked. Shock, anger and relief coursed through her veins. She was profoundly relieved to know Randall had wanted to get in touch, but what kind of man was his father anyway? Why would he punish his son by not giving him her address?

Randall cupped her head between his hands, "I'm sorry, Grace. I'm sorry I got mad at you, I'm sorry I ended up in here."

He enfolded her in his arms and Grace laid her head on his shoulder. She could feel all her fears melt away in the security of his strong embrace.

"Oh, Grace, I didn't mean to do this to you," he continued. "Will you forgive me? Please, please forgive me for the way I talked the last time we were together. I was overwrought--with worry. So much was going on in my mind, so much terrible stuff back in France, then the blow, which changed everything. I do love you."

"Yes, Randall, yes, of course; please, let's not talk about it."

"But I have to," he pursued. "It was that cursed drink, and the blow—.

Grace lovingly placed her finger against his lips. "Please, Randall. This is our first time together for a donkey's years. We have the rest of our life to discuss it. Let's just be cheerful tonight."

He stared at her uncertainly for an instant, then lowered himself on to the bunk beside Emily and watched her.

"Do you mean it, Grace? I truly am sorry for all the heartache I've caused."

Grace nodded mutely. Her heart ached; his voice was quiet and subdued so unlike the self-assured Randall of by gone days. She hoped she could bring out the carefree charmer again, someday.

"Randall, you're precious," she said, looking into his eyes.

As her heart overflowed with love and compassion, she understood a little better how God felt towards His erring children.

Randall, I'd give anything to see the mischievous sparkle dance back into your dull, gloomy eyes once again. I don't know what you did, but I forgive you with all my heart. We all make mistakes.

Randall saw Grace's eyes darken with concern, but since he was not able to understand her expression, he dropped his head into his hands and groaned.

"Are you terribly disappointed in me? You'd have a right to leave me, you know."

Grace lowered her eyes. *If I had known how hard this was on Randall, I'd never have left Alice with Margaret. Alice, my darling little girl!* Not wanting some forbidden message to flash to Randall, she whirled around and flung her arm over her eyes.

Aloud she said, "We're in this together, Honey. I married you for better or for worse," but her voice trembled and he didn't know why.

Randall looked at her searchingly, then down at the baby.

"Do you mind if I hold her?"

"Mind? She's your own daughter: Of course you may hold her."

She tried to keep her face composed so he would never know how torn her heart felt because she couldn't show off the other little daughter at the same time. *I'm hiding a deep, dark secret from him.*

He studied Emily. "No, I think I'd better not."

Grace stared at him.

"I didn't realize a baby could be so pure and innocent," he continued after a moment. "I feel too unclean to hold her, to be a Daddy."

Grace bit her trembling lip: she lifted the babe and placed her in Randall's arms. He gazed at the small, sweet face for a long time without uttering a word. Grace wondered what he was thinking.

"She has red hair like you," she offered.

Randall nodded but otherwise did not respond. He handed her back to Grace. As she pressed Emily's soft cheek against her own, a tear slipped out unbidden. *There is another baby, somewhere, that should be here also.*

Just then, a loud knock sounded at the door, startling them both.

"Times up!" a gruff voice announced.

After kissing her tenderly, Randall would have released her but Grace clung, she needed him.

At the end of the dark, quiet hall was a clock. It showed that they had been together much longer than 15 minutes. Why had the gaol keeper been so considerate?

"It's about time you came," Mr. Sutherland grumbled, swatting at a mosquito while she struggled up into the wagon seat.

He hauled the baby up so she could manage better. Grace leaned forward and pulled her coat around Emily to shelter her from the chilly night air: and the mosquitoes.

Emily was wide-awake, looking at Grace. She's resting so trustingly in my arms, her mother thought, why can't I trust the Father like that? God worked things out between Randall and me far better than I could have ever expected. Margaret also showed me by her life how wonderfully kind the Heavenly Father is. I wish I could commit my whole life to Him. You know what, I can and I will. There is no better time to start then right now.

There in a rustic farm wagon, on a lonely dark road in the middle of nowhere, Grace bowed her head and prayed. There, while the stars twinkled so high in the sky above her, and the occasional cow mooed in the distance, Grace surrendered her life totally to her Saviour and asked His to deliver her from her sins.

Mr. Sutherland wasn't very communicative, but she didn't care, she felt at peace with her Maker. She noticed the sweet scent in the country air and the beautiful sound of the horse's' feet rhythmically clip clopping on the road, the wheels on the gravel.

They turned a corner and traveled on for a while longer, with the baby calmly resting in her arms.

A Sweet Lily

CHAPTER 20

Up ahead a lantern was glowing cheerily from a front window even though the hour was late. Grace hoped it was where they were going. Yes! They were turning down the narrow lane leading to the sweet white cottage!

Was that a flower behind those daintily ruffled curtains: a bright red geranium, perhaps?

Even before Mr. Sutherland stopped the horse by the garden gate, the front door was flung open by a pleasantly plump little grandma-type with snowy white hair. She hustled towards them with wide-open arms.

"Grace!" she cried, giving her a warm embrace. She held her out at arm's length and looked deep into her eyes.

"I have been longing to comfort the girl Randall chose. I just knew any girl Randall loved I would love, too. You have had such a hard time the past few months, and, perhaps I can make it up for you in some way. "

Grace was shocked by the unexpectedly warm welcome.

Mrs. Sutherland tipped her chin with a finger. "Randall's little wife," she murmured shaking her head and smiling faintly. She is so lovely, yet sad looking.

"It grieves me that you had to know pain and suffering at your age. I hope you were able to share with your parents in spite of that awful war going on." (Grace winced.) "May I be like a second mother to you since yours is so far away?"

Grace nodded mutely, trying to swallow the lump in her throat. Like a mother? My own Mom never showed such tenderness to me. Randall's sweet-faced mother beckoned her to come into the kitchen.

There on the small square table, spread with a dazzling white cloth, a very English looking tea awaited them. Grace gasped in delighted surprise.

"I know it's late but thought you might be hungry after such a long trip. I even remembered to heat the milk that you Englishers' love to add to your very strong tea. I had to ask around about some of the other details, though. Perhaps you will like it just a little? I so hoped to make you feel a little more at home in our strange back woodsy country."

"Like it?" Grace gasped, "Oh, Mrs. Sutherland, I love it!" She impulsively gave her mother-in-law a heartfelt hug then stepped back, ashamed. Eighteen years had gone by and not once had she ever been tempted to hug her own mother.

"What's the matter, honey? Is something wrong?"

Grace numbly shook her head.

"Don't you like cream puffs? They are made from our own Jersey cream but perhaps don't look near as lovely as what your mother made. Grace winced again, fancy Mom ever making cream puffs, the richest thing she ever made was scones, and that only once!

"... Although I did make them just today-- it was such fun preparing for your arrival. That's all right if you don't like something; I want you to feel at home here, not anxious."

The kettle was whistling merrily so she filled the teapot.

"Or don't you care for cookies? I frosted them a little before your drove on the yard." When she smiled, her light blue eyes twinkled and a dimple lurked near the corner of her mouth.

Cookies, Grace looked around, puzzled, not knowing to what she was referring.

"I, I'm not sure what you are talking about," she confessed.

"Cookies? Do you not know what cookies are?"

"Do you mean this?" Grace pointed to the neatly arranged pile of iced sugar cookies on a pink plate.

As Lily nodded, Grace reddened. I have to remember that biscuits are 'cookies' here in Canada.

"But is everything all right? I hope it's not all too strange..."

"Oh, Mrs. Sutherland, it's not that—It's nothing like that at all. Everything is just wonderful, just...too, too...wonderful."

After thrusting Emily into her grandmother's unsuspecting arms, she buried her face in her hands and turned away.

At that moment, Ben slammed the back door. He had returned from caring for the horse and wagon.

"What's that woman crying about now?" he growled brushing a piece of straw off his gingham flannel shirt.

Lily looked bewildered: "I have no idea," then quickly at the girl and saw her shoulders stiffen. She touched her lightly.

"Try not to take your father-in-law's gruff ways too personally," she said in a low voice. "He is quit deaf in one ear and suffered from shell shock during the first war."

Grace's head jerked up. That's one possible explanation for his unfriendly behaviour I never thought of.

Mr. Sutherland dragged a mint green chair out from beside the table and helped himself to a couple of cookies.

To Grace's surprise, Lily leaned her hands on Ben's shoulders, massaging them, and then stroked his graying hair. She murmured something into his good ear, which he must have understood, because he nodded.

Grace stared. She isn't even afraid of him. Did she know how Ben had kept Randall from writing to her?

Lily soon sat down, however, and while they were sipping tea and munching on treats, gently encouraged her daughter-in-law to tell about the trip, her family and the war.

Grace's heart overflowed with love towards the gentle woman. She felt safer with her mother-in-law than with Margaret even. It was a healing balm to be sharing with her. Even her husband's features seemed to soften when he gazed at his wife.

"Just call me Mom, or Lily if you're more comfortable with that," Mrs. Sutherland invited after a while. "My husband's name is Ben, or perhaps you knew that already?"

Grace nodded. "How do, Ben," she said self-consciously. He grunted.

Inevitably, the talk turned to discussing Randall.

Ben's lips compressed into a tight line when his son was mentioned, his eyes hardened. Grace turned to look at Randall's Mom and saw that hers were troubled.

"We're sorry about Randall ending up in jail," Lily confided, "and I'm sure he is to. He can be so impulsive, but truly has a tender heart! Maybe you can help him—somehow..." She gestured helplessly with her hands.

Grace couldn't begin to guess what had had happened, yet It must have been most dreadful if he had to be imprisoned for it, she was too scared to ask.

Ben soon lumbered off to bed, but Grace and Lily shared into the wee small hours of the morning, which really wasn't that far away.

Why is it that God has blessed me with such wonderful people in my life if I am just a nobody?" Grace marveled while they were washing up the dainty tea dishes together.

"A nobody? My darling child, why would you call yourself that?"

Grace didn't answer directly but her mother-in-law gently drew her out, and soon she was confiding many seemingly insignificant details of her basically cheerless past. Lily's heart yearned to find ways to bring joy and comfort to the young girl.

Grace shared quite a lot about Margaret, and as the clock crept past the midnight hour, she shyly confided about praying while traveling through the long dark night.

"That's wonderful, simply wonderful!" Lily burbled, clasping Grace's hand. "I prayed and prayed that you would learn to know my Jesus if you didn't already.

That gives me more courage to believe that Randall might believe someday, also."

"Life isn't near so hard when you have a friend like Jesus to take your troubles to."

The two ladies had gone to sit in the tiny living room while visiting. Each had chosen a comfortable, floral print armchair on either side of the potbellied stove. Lily kept her hands busy knitting a pair of wool socks for her husband while Grace had the baby nestled in her arms.

Emily was in the dreamy borderland between sleep and wakefulness and was making sucking sounds with her lips although her tummy was warmed and filled.

The sweet little innocent caused stirrings of maternal tenderness in the young mother, but A second later, she bit her lip as a shadow clouded her brow. Lily noticed the change in her expression but could not comprehend why.

Eventually Lily saw that Grace's eyes were falling shut. She felt very badly for not realizing how tired she would be, and hastened to show her to her room. Ben had set the luggage just inside the door and Lily insisted on carrying it all by herself to Randall's old room, which would be Grace's for now.

"You have that precious darling to carry, and you're much too tired to carry anything else," Lily insisted.

"Not even my handbag?" Grace asked playfully.

"Well, maybe your purse," Lily conceded.

When Grace walked into Randall's old room, a wave of loneliness threatened to overpower her. There was a quilt on the bed made up of a mixture of solid and plaid squares of cotton material. Grace was sure the pieces were from Randall's shirts although she had never seen him in civilian clothes.

A row of books, much read, was on a short shelf next to the corner. Grace hurried over to them, eager to see what kinds of stories had interested her husband. There was Black Beauty with its setting partly in dear old London, and David Copperfield by Charles Dickens, but although most of the titles were unfamiliar, even the lingering scent in the room reminded her of her missing husband.

Lily had taken her granddaughter from Grace. Now she gently laid her on the bed in order to remove her wrappings. Emily stirred sleepily while Lily was diapering her but didn't awaken.

"My, she must be very tired," Lily remarked, a soft note of longing in her voice. "She makes me think of my own little twins,"

Grace's head jerked up; her mouth dropped open.

"W-what did you say?" she blurted.

"My own little twins: I guess Randall never told you." She sighed deeply while picking at the lace edging on the little bonnet in her hands.

"They both had lots of dark hair and were so very tiny... Born far too prematurely, so they didn't make it." She dabbed at her eyes with the eyelet bonnet.

"My heart still aches when I think of them and the joy they could have brought to our home: two sweet little angels, Rachel and Rhoda. Rachel was the stronger and larger of the two. We hoped she would make it at least. But when Rhoda's little heart gave out, Rachel, seemed to lose the will to live."

"I don't know why I'm talking to you about this. I haven't shared it with anyone for a long time. I guess because you feel so much like family, and you have a baby girl."

She searched her apron pocket for a hankie.

"We had them sleeping together in a softly padded wicker basket because they were premature. We placed it on the door of the oven to keep them warmer. They'd actually snuggle. You wouldn't believe it unless you saw it for yourself."

Grace did believe it, her own girls did the same, and now they were separated, forcibly: by their own mother.

Now Lily was looking into Emily's eyes and cradling her gently in her arms. "So when Rhoda died, Rachel got restless—in a few hours she turned blue—and we couldn't, we just couldn't revive her—I still don't know why she—they had to go to." For a moment, she couldn't continue. "

"It was the dead of winter, February, in fact, and the snow plow rarely comes out this far, so the doctor couldn't come."

Lily was vaguely aware of how white Grace had become, and how increasingly agitated, but hadn't thought about it until later.

Grace's hands fumbled as she searched for a nightgown for Emily and shook it out. Soon the new grandma was lovingly dressing the child.

"Losing the babies caused me to turn to my parent's faith for comfort and I began reading the Bible Mother had given me when we got married. I surrendered my life to Jesus and He's been healing my broken heart, but Ben, -Dad- turned the other way. He became so bitter—"

"I—I guess I'd better go to bed, now," Grace gasped.

Lily looked up in surprise. "Oh, I'm so sorry. Did I say something wrong? You must be extremely tired!"

"I'm all right," Grace stated flatly too shaken to realize just how rude it sounded. "I just want to go to bed."

"Oh, Grace," Randall's Mom gushed earnestly," I am so thoughtless! May I bring you something, an aspirin, perhaps? You'll be way too tired for a bath, I suppose?"

"I'll go to bed just like I am, tonight."

Lily kept apologising for keeping her up so late, but Grace was not listening. Lily got the distinct feeling Grace wanted to push her out of the room but was too polite to, so with a breaking heart, scurried away to their own bedroom.

Lily felt perplexed by the girl's actions. I thought we were getting along so nicely. What did I say that offended her? As she slid in quietly beside Ben, who was snoring intermittently, she prayed earnestly that God would help her to understand.

Nightmarish Images

CHAPTER 21

Grace held her breath while searching for any signs of blueness or fever in the baby. *Ours won't die just because Lily's did, unless God is going to punish me for not taking care of Alice.*

She hardly wanted to take her eyes off the baby long enough to fumble into her eyelet and ribbon-trimmed nightgown. "It's just a coincidence that we both had twins, a total coincidence. Mine are identical; identical twins are not inherited."

She crawled beneath the fluffy wool comforter then blew out the candle that Lily handed her just before they reached the stairwell. It had shocked Grace that they had no electricity.

Grace burrowed under the covers to hide from the oppressive darkness but it didn't keep her from feeling haunted by what Lily had told her as well as other scenarios that came crowding into her overstrained brain.

After living with blackouts for so long, Grace had appreciated the faint glow of streetlights while in Halifax, and now this depth of darkness, evoked memories of the terrifying air raids back in Birmingham.

Grace cowered under the covers until she realized she was unconsciously bracing herself for the eerie wail of an air raid siren. She tentatively poked her head out but now the tomb-like silence made her skin crawl: never had it been so quiet in either

Birmingham or Halifax. Even the frog's music, which she wouldn't have been familiar with either, was silent that night.

Then it happened: pictures of naked, death cold babies loomed before her eyes. *Are they Lily's twins or my own?* Sometimes they seemed to be dark haired, sometimes bright, sometimes both. *What, oh, what have I done to my children?*

I must be the meanest mother alive to give up my own babby! Will God take my two sweet rosebuds back to Heaven because I am not worthy of them?

Grace lay rigid, willing the haunting scenes to fade away. She felt too tyrannized to change positions until she remembered to try praying. She eventually dozed off, but not to a completely restful sleep.

A loud banging on her bedroom door awakened her with a start.

"Wake up, wake up," a stentorian voice boomed. At first, she was too startled to realize who it was.

"Coming," she murmured sleepily but as her head sank back on the pillow her eyes drifted shut.

Mr. Sutherland had informed her on the way back from Russet that, since she would be living with them, he wanted her to help milk the cows. She was very frightened of such huge beasts but didn't dare protest.

"Come now," the grumpy sounding voice rose. "The cows need to be milked!"

She slipped carefully out of the bed so as not to disturb Emily who was sleeping peacefully beside her.

As she donned her wrinkled and travel-soiled skirt and blouse from the night before, she could hear the older couple just outside her door.

Mr. Sutherland was saying something about "paying her keep" and "your arthritis is getting too bad to be out there in this sort of weather" with Lily replying that "his arthritis was just as bad, if not worse."

Grace had learned to deeply appreciate the changing beauty of the Canadian skies while traveling, but if it was a leaden gray that greeted her that morning, or brilliant with the hues of a glorious sunrise, she couldn't have said.

It took all she had just to get through the big barn door without crashing into it first.

Mr. Sutherland got her busy feeding the little calves, which was not what she had feared she would be doing first off, and in spite of her weariness, wasn`t too bad.

There was one delicate-boned Jersey cow among all those great hulking black and white beasts. Mr. Sutherland showed Grace how to wash the udder then strip the teats to get the milk to flow. The sweet-faced Jersey looked at her curiously through doe-like eyes but didn't kick her.

Grace knew Randall`s Dad would probably expect more of her in the future, but was surprised that he had given her such easy tasks for the first day.

He handed her a bucket of feed and asked her to dump it in the long narrow trough in the chicken house, which she even enjoyed doing, then allowed her to go back to the house. She knew enough about farming to realize there would be eggs to gather later on, and that would probably be her job.

After Grace staggered wearily in to the tiny, two story cottage framed by the blushing colors of sunrise, she found her mother-in-law sitting at the table trying to coax a smile from the baby while the morning sun slanted on the two of them.

Lily was robed in a pink chenille dressing gown that made her cheeks blossom like the daintiest of tea roses. Grace wondered if her hair was snow white because of losing her twins, but that was the least of her worries. She felt jealous that Emily was so happily cuddling in Someone Else's' arms.

A recently drained nursing bottle was nearby. Grace's brow furrowed: she's my babby. I don't want her on the bottle yet.

Lily torn her eyes away from her gurgling granddaughter and said, with laughter in her voice:

"Emily is the sweetest little girl, but shortly after you went out she cried as if she thought everyone had abandoned her. I couldn't bear to hear her sound so unhappy so hunted up a bottle. I hope you don't mind.

"Are you ready for breakfast, dear? Ben will soon be in."

Grace sagged against the doorframe and her eyes closed. She slowly shook her head.

"I'm too knackered out." She reached limply for Emily then let her arms sag.

A tantalizing aroma wafted through the air and she opened her eyes a crack. There was a tempting array of dishes neatly arranged on the table now spread with a red gingham cloth. Rashers were stacked on a white platter with a yellow trim and surrounded by fried eggs. Nearby were bowls of freshly cooked applesauce, a platter of light fluffy biscuits and coffee.

It all looked so appetizing but Grace didn't think she could even take one forkful.

When Lily suggested putting Randall's old crib in the corner of the dining room since it would be handier there than upstairs, she nodded but it barely registered.

Grace stumbled up to her room and flopped on the unmade bed and before she could have mumbled, 'Jiminy Crickets' was asleep.

The Good Old Summertime

CHAPTER 22

The door was quietly opening when Grace awoke. Lily came in carrying a tray decorated with sweet peas in a tiny vase as well as a cup of tea. A small plate held two bangers as well as tomato and lettuce sandwiches made with freshly baked homemade cobs. Grace looked up gratefully, feeling very hungry.

"Thank you," she smiled, "And thanks for letting me sleep. It's rotten trying to rest on a train, especially with a babby!

"Oh, look bangers: that's even yummier than the rashers you had on the table at breakfast time! I was so sorry to miss what you served this morning that the scrumptious looking food got into my dreams."

Lily quirked her eyebrows, "Bangers, what are you talking about, my girl?" Her eyes scanned the platter before she pointed to the sausage.

"Do you mean these?"

"Why yes! What do you call them?

"We call them Farmers Sausage. Several of us get together every fall to butcher pigs and make our own sausage and bacon,--is that what you called rashers? (Grace nodded. Well, they were sort of similar.) "-- pork chops and other good stuff".

Grace's lips twitched when she thought of a light-hearted rhyme Margaret had taught Davey while making dinner one night: "six silly sausages sizzling in the pan, one went pop and the other went bang', but she didn't feel like she knew Lily well enough, yet, to share it with her.

She tentatively took a bite. "They sure are good. I haven't tasted such delicious bangers; I mean sausages in years, if ever."

"Call them whatever you like," Lily said comfortably. "It wouldn't hurt us to learn a new word or two."

"I'll let you eat in peace now." She turned to leave.

Lily was just stepping out the door when Grace called her.

Lily turned back, a pleasant look on her round, smiley face.

Grace nervously twisted the napkin in her fingers.

"Lily, I, uh, I shouldn't have talked like that to you last night."

"That's okay dear. Later I realized how desperately tired you must have been. My, it was dark already when you got home and in summertime the sun sets really late this far north."

Grace opened the window and breathed deeply of the fresh woodsy- country smells that she enjoyed very much.

"If there's anything I can do for you," Lily continued, "please let me know. I want to make your adjustment to living here as easy as possible and I feel badly for keeping you up so late last night.

"You were so tired this morning that I gave Emily a bottle every time she was hungry." Lily hesitated then smirked sheepishly. "I even gave her a bath in the oval enamel tub I used to sponge Randall in, and then dressed her in one of his nighties. She doesn't seem to mind that it is blue!

"She's getting restless again so I'll bring her up as soon as you're done eating."

As Lily went back to put her fresh buns and bread into bags, her thoughts returned to what had been troubling her all day.

Ben came in right then and she offered him a piece of thickly sliced buttered bread.

"I told Grace about our twins, Ben, and she got really upset. She doesn't even know them. "

"She's an odd one, that girl," Ben reached for a jar of freshly made strawberry jam that was cooling on the far end of the table.

"Odd! Why would you say that?"

He shrugged then took a big bite of his melt-in-your-mouth - good snack. "Why else would that big oaf from the bar have said that?"

"Because he is a big oaf, that's why! How could you imply that Grace is odd? She's your daughter-in-law! We hardly even know her. That girl has a lot on her mind. I hope you never imply that she's to blame for, for you-know-what. You didn't, did you?"

"Nope." Ben averted his eyes when he washed it all down with a thick mug of milk.

Lily cleared and wiped the table more hurriedly than normal. "There's a lot of dangers and difficulties out here that I scarcely think of any more, but to a frail young person from a crowded city, they could seem overwhelming.

No wonder she is easily upset." She frowned:" but it's more than that; I'm sure, something way more than that is troubling her."

Ben pushed back his chair and shoved his feet into his gumboots. Lily watched him meander back to the barn, a prayer in her heart for both her husband and daughter-in-law.

When Grace came down, she opened the window beside her, causing the sheer Swiss dot curtains to flutter in the cool, bright sunshine. She had found it an ideal place to iron her badly wrinkled garments with starch Lily provided.

Later she decided to feed her little one on the back porch. There was a nicely painted white swing there, made by Randall invasion of the enemy.

He was acquainted with several boys who joined just for a chance to get away from home and have an adventure, but not he. He arrived in Canada at the tender age of nine from a small country in Europe so empathized deeply with the distress the natives were experiencing.

David had no personal grievance against the Germans in particular, he was of partial German descent himself, but truly believed in freedom. No one could be happier to be a Canadian than he was.

David also loved the Maritimes; he loved the tranquil yet in some places rugged shorelines, her forests and rivers. He loved the maple trees that blanketed the hillsides, which reminded him of mounds of blossoms every autumn. He loved the narrow winding roads with an intriguing view around each bend. Something about the quaint old-fashioned villages was vaguely reminiscent of his Liechtenstein heritage and that tugged at his heart.

The only thing he did not love was the lack of tall, rugged mountains such as he would have enjoyed in his homeland.

When he got a deep hankering to climb, nothing nearby sufficed but his pocketbook refused to allow him vacations in the Canadian Rockies, and for sure not in Liechtenstein.

However, it was more than Canada's beauty that appealed to him. David's hatred of Nazism equaled his loyalty for democracy.

It infuriated him that the Nazis had invaded first one country then another, but he had a more personal grievance. A friend, who was a reporter, smuggled out news from time to time about David's own tall, angular; intelligent grandfather.

Asadoor Seifert had been an active member of parliament before Hitler's time. What good had it done him? David had no illusions as to what happened to the stately Jewish former Member of Parliament; he was sure he was in a concentration camp somewhere if he hadn't been killed already.

David was glad to be back.

Evenly spaced around him David sensed, rather than heard the shuffling of fellow troop members as they crept towards their predetermined goal somewhere in the massive forest.

A faint line of gray dawn edged the horizon, giving enough light to see, but just barely.

"Qui va la?" (Who goes there), a trembling woman's voice shrilled: David froze. They were discovered! Only his eyes moved as they darted this way and that to find the location of the sound.

A humble, dry-vine covered cottage came into his line of vision but he saw no one.

The forest was growing lighter now. He could distinguish the shapes of towering trees and shadowy forms of fellow combatants who were as rigid as statues all around him. A full five minutes passed before anyone as much as twitched a shoulder.

A birdcall fell through the air. It was the signal to move ahead. David sidled within two feet of the cottage. His heart lurched: through the window, he glimpsed the white, terror-stricken face of a young woman with a baby clutched over her shoulder. What will happen to her—to them? Who failed to warn her that she must flee or was she part of the Resistance Movement and hadn't known where to go?

the unnatural silence exploded with the thunder of gunfire. In one swift practiced movement, he whirled and aimed.

German soldiers swarmed like hornets clambering over fallen logs and dodging tree branches as they pressed unrelentingly closer, guns ever at the ready. David fell to his knees on the icy ground and aimed. A thin stripling of a youth came into his viewfinder. He could see the shock of blond hair protruding from his helmet: and the terrified eyes.

His finger stiffened on the trigger.

DON'T SHOOT! David glanced swiftly around. Who spoke?

The young enemy soldier was scrambling closer. It's either him or me, David thought desperately, raising his gun to aim. Don't shoot, the low but urgent voice commanded. Don't shoot or you will send a soul to hell!

Bewildered and tense, David felt unreasonably indecisive. . Who was giving him such commands? The gray clad youth stumbled on the icy forest floor, grasping blindly for his weapon. Nearby a bullet screamed through the air almost drowning out the angry voice to his left.

"You idiot! Why didn't you fire? It was either him or you!"

David hardly comprehended the raging voice at his side. A searing pain tore through his abdomen as he stumbled through the scene of terror. All around was confusion. Something dark and sticky was oozing above his belt line. He nearly tripped over writhing or prostrate bodies.

Help the wounded, bring them to safety, rescue the perishing care for the dying... Where did that line come from? I feel so muddled.

A hand was waving aimlessly in the air; he lurched towards it while a chant of "water-water!" beat against his eardrums. I must help-must help-must—. A blanket of darkness descended over him.

As long as David was floating in and out of consciousness, he was unaware that he never made it back to the battlefront but had ended up in a military hospital with a severe case of influenza.

Nightmares of his former time were haunting his sleep, causing him to toss and turn restlessly, screaming in agony.

David had a high fever, but even when it lessened, he was feeling restless and disturbed.

Why am I back here only to end up in a hospital? Why are those nightmares haunting me again? They hadn't been so severe back home. Bitterness as thick as bile soured his throat. Why, or rather who told me not to shoot?

Such insanity, after all this is war! I may not have been so badly injured if I'd been more on the ball.

He soberly accepted a glass of water from a nurse on her rounds. Margaret didn't want me to return. She hates war. She was so thankful and relieved that I had been permitted to come back to Canada and didn't have to return to the battle front. Why did I return? Am I that full of hatred and revenge?

He sighed. If I had to get the flu, it would have been so much nicer back home with my lovely wife to care for me. The nurses and doctor always seemed to exchange glances when they were discussing his case and he wondered why.

Yet, in the back of his mind, he was always thinking, always troubled by the nightmare that was realistic to the finest detail because it was something he remembered!

The aroma of bacon and potato soup was making its way through the ward and David wondered what his grandfather, Asadoor Seifert, ate in the Concentration Camp. His jaw hardened; that's why I wanted to fight. He blew on a spoonful of steaming soup. Why did my conscience, or whatever it was have to kick in and tell me not to shoot?

Strange Advice from a Chaplain

CHAPTER 24

When the chaplain came around later that evening, he received special instructions to reason with David, to calm him down. This he endeavored to do.

David lay propped up in bed, still pale and weak, haunted by persistent memories, suspecting that his old internal injury had become inflamed which was why he had been so desperately ill.

The chaplain congratulated him for being brave as he fought in the Lord's army. "You got many medals, I have heard."

David nodded but his smile faded.

"The Lord's army?" he bantered, "What did God have to do with war?"

"Everything! Those of us who claim to be followers of Christ fought in the army of the Lord. We can be so proud of the fact the enemy was vanquished and freedom reigns!"

"But what about that verse in the Bible: Matt 5:44, I think, about loving your enemies?" David grimaced. Why am I playing the 'devil's advocate', or is it, just that Margaret's opinions are infiltrating my thoughts.

"You're an idealist, man! I can't believe you are feeling guilty after all the good you have done in the fight for freedom.

"That verse was only referring to our daily life: those little irksome ways our friends and neighbors have about them. The good Lord wants us to forgive their nuances. He can't possibly have meant dirty heathens like those Germans!"

"But—" David's fist tightened beneath the spread. Hey, wait a minute; he's calling German's dirty heathen? I grew up speaking only German until I was nine. We're humans, too.

"Come on, David, cheer up. This is different. That was a mighty evil we fought, and God gave us the victory!"

"But-but they are human, also! What if they believe they were in the right?"

David felt like clutching his head between his hands. Why did life have to be so complicated? He couldn't get the terrified eyes of the loping teenager out of his mind. That could have been my blonde haired blue-eyed Davey in a few years.

"Human? How can you call the followers of Hitler human? His policies were very evil you know that! They had to be stopped."

The chaplain's voice brought him back to the present with a start. "They are possessed with a spirit of cruelty that would destroy the world if we would have let them! Don't you know what they did to the Jews? You must not know what went on behind the scenes!"

David's face reddened but he managed not to explode.

"My grandfather was a Jew," he ground out. Grandfather had vanished like thousands of others, had he been imprisoned in as bad a place as Austerlitz? Probably, oh, if only I could have personally freed him. Thank God Grandmother, Agne Seifert had a heart attack soon after the invasion of Austria. She never lived to know the horrors that went on in the beautiful, sophisticated capital city where they had lived.

The chaplains' voice broke through his reverie, "I'm sorry to hear that.

"Listen, David. You have been seriously ill, I presume?"

David nodded his head sank back against the pillow.

"Rest up all you can. Find something relaxing to read. What do you enjoy the most: a mystery, an adventure? I think we might be able to scrounge up some old Reader's Digests. They may be rather dog-eared from much passing around but will give you a break from your weary thoughts. I think the last one has a mighty good story about a war hero just like you."

He squeezed David's knee. "By the way, do you know who came up with the idea of a reader's digest? You've probably heard the story. He was a soldier lying in an army hospital cot during the first War. A mighty good idea it is, too: my favorite magazine.

"Just stay away from the Bible for a few days, old chap. The good Lord knows you are too overwrought to get much out of such a deep book for anyway."

The chaplain squeezed David's bent knee once more, a habit David was beginning to find annoying.

"You're a fine young man, Seifert. The army is proud of such dedicated soldiers as you."

Now this is a strange twist; a man of the cloth is telling me not to read the Bible.

David was so tired he just let the smooth words of the parson drift over him. The chaplain waited for him to answer. When he didn't, he squeezed the young man's knee again.

"I can see you are suffering so will leave. Just rest up good, and soon you will be proud that you fought for the Cause which was right!"

David's eyes opened briefly.

"Sir?"

The chaplain had turned to go, but he waited at the end of the bed for David to continue." Do you believe everything you are saying?"

The chaplain looked startled. "Why of course, son," he exclaimed but David had seen the brief flicker of uncertainty in his eyes.

"Well, good night," The chaplain said with forced heartiness," And hope you get well soon."

David wondered if the vicar was avoiding him during the rest of his the stay in the hospital. It was just as well, David didn't want to think that all the fighting he had done could have possibly been wrong; the guilt would have been too oppressive.

At least I didn't kill that blue eyed chap, he thought defensively, "And he sure wounded me. Nevertheless, you maimed, and caused others to perish, his conscience nevertheless accused.

David was finding it hard to relax. He was uncomfortable enough as it was, and two of the patients were engaged in a gripe session.

"The service is poor," they muttered loudly, "and the food even worse."

"Why aren't 'they' putting forth more effort to control our pain and to get us out of here so we can go home?"

David pitied the injured, but felt even sorrier for the nurses. They looked so frazzled and were doing their level best to bring comfort and cheer to the suffering. No doubt, now that the war was technically over, he was sure they also were eager to leave.

He glared at the soldiers who were doing most of the complaining.

"Aren't you glad to be alive?" he demanded which lead to some strongly voiced opinions. He didn't blame them for complaining, not really. He also wished he could be with the wife and kids.

He reached for his cup of coffee and his hand tightened around it.

Margaret! How is she doing? Is she really okay? It gave me the heebee jeebees when she acted as if she was having a seizure or something. Did the first army check ever reach her?

She probably doesn't have any idea where I am right now. Here I lay right in London and she's probably imagining me in the thick of the action way off in Berlin or somewhere.

How are the children? It's a relief that they adjusted to a new mother as well as they did before I had to go back. We were expecting some peace and quiet now that Grace is gone. Seemed like there was always some kid crying or fussing, but Margaret was so patient and serene. She thrives in the mother role. Even more than Janet did.

I hope none of them is sick and that Junior is behaving himself. He can be so rambunctious.

Grace...poor kid...she sure has a lot on her shoulders...I could have been more patient with her.

Will I ever make it to Germany? Maybe I should just to be relieved of my duties. Would it work? Under the circumstances, most likely: no one could have guessed that I wasn't completely healed internally before influenza hit me.

David pressed his fingers against his temples remembering how Janet used to pass her hand wearily over her eyes when she watched David Jr. cavorting around.

"Where did he get all that energy?" she would exclaim, and David would respond, "From you!" Janet was the athletic type, far more than Margaret was and before they had kids, they used to love backpacking together in their homeland and even explored remote corners of the world. That was while he was still getting an excellent wage from his Dad, doing office work, a job that seemed as dry as dust.

With too much time on his mind, the restless patient fretted about how inadequate the apartment 'back home' was and how steep and narrow the steps were.

We will be set back by dipping into the savings now that I'm gone, so it will be that much longer before we can start to build out in the country, he fumed picturing the quiet, peaceful life Margaret had enjoyed as a pastor's daughter in the pretty little seaside village of Lower Blossomby.

David hadn't learned to pray as freely as Margaret did without the aid of a prayer book, but felt the desire to try.

'Holy Father look down in mercy upon Margaret," he clasped his hands awkwardly under the covers. "Give her strength to cope with the difficult circumstances she has been thrust into."

David was feeling in a more mellow, cheerful mood after that little chat with God, so the next time a nurse stopped at his bed to fluff up his pillow, then hand him a fresh glass of iced water, he accepted gratefully.

"Ah...nurse?" he said hesitantly.

"Scott," she supplied. "Trena Scott" (She reminded him so much of Janet because of her slender build and Swiss features.)

He nodded. "I just wanted to thank all of you for your compassionate, dedicated service."

Although she looked stunned, at first, her tired face lit up and he marveled at how the weary lines melted away.

"Oh, thank you," she beamed. "I'll pass it on to the others."

It was getting late and dark. Gradually the ward quieted, save for the moans and occasional screams of the sick and delirious. He tossed restlessly although relieved the uneasy stillness wasn't being shattered by guns going off in the distance or worse yet, bombs falling.

He folded his pillow and sympathizing with Grace for being so bored in the hospital. At least she was in a safe country. Well, I am to, now.

He wished he could get a proper night's sleep but it seemed impossible. He still hadn't come to terms with the killing-in-time-of-war issue.

Nothing in his past had prepared him for the thought of not being loyal to his country. Even his church had strongly advocated it.

Love your enemies, do good to them that despitefully use you and persecute you. It's amazing that I can remember that verse so well. I only went to vacation Bible school at the Baptist church that one summer, and look how those verses come back to me!

He wished those strange thoughts would quit plaguing him. He had always considered it an honor to serve in the Canadian army and firmly believed that such a wonderful land deserved his loyalty.

Hitler's egotistic and racist idealism rankled him. It had been right to stop it and if everyone refused to fight because of religious or other excuses what would have happened to the world?

Maybe he would just have to block it out of his mind.

Where Was Margaret?

CHAPTER 25

Margaret was down on her hands and knees scrubbing the very floor David was lamenting about. She found it difficult getting it clean where the top layer had worn off and the black showed through. The edges were cracking and she wished she knew how to prevent it from breaking even more.

Her long thick hair, twirled earlier into a graceful French roll, was drooping now and damp tendrils clung to her forehead.

Margaret sat back with a sigh and surveyed the now clean floor as well as the rest of the room. The apartment seemed empty without the large, cut-down box in the corner where the twins had cozily snoozed. Seeing the bare space made her heart ache.

It had been a quiet day doing mundane things such as washing floors and ironing mounds of little dresses, big dresses, shirts and pillowcases unfortunately giving her plenty of time to brood.

What a lonely place the maritime province was. It may be close to the sea but that was the only similarity to her hometown. Even being in a tiny apartment facing the back streets of the city was a far contrast to the sunny village street of her childhood.

If she was back home in England, right now, she would quite likely be working in one of the flower gardens, poking around to find stray weeds among the profusely blooming blossoms that she loved, and working the soil so that everything looked pretty.

Margaret studied her watch: it was two in the afternoon here, so if the weather was balmy in England, more than likely neighbours would be stopping by, some to chat from the pavement while a few could always be coaxed to come in for a spot of tea with her and Mumsey, Dad, to, if he happened to be around. If the air were unusually sweetly scented, they would likely be having their tea on the porch while watching the sun sinking in the west.

She stood up to stretch, pressing her hand against the small of her back and peered out of the small curtained window over the kitchen sink.

The sky looked forbidding because of all the storm clouds that were crowding the horizon. It only increased her loneliness.

I wonder if the bombs are going off near Blossomby tonight. Margaret gasped. Mumsey, Daddy! They're gone, gone! How could I have forgotten even for an instant?

Margaret fought to calm herself as she heard small feet shuffling into the room.

Junior woke up early from his nap, took a few steps, flopped unto the couch and—vomited! Almost before she had gotten the freshly washed floor, but not dry floor, wiped, Sally managed to crawl out of her cot and said:

"Mommy, owies here," and she too had troubles. Sally never brought up her dinner, but the mess was just as bad to clean up, since she had recently graduated to training panties.

While Margaret was carefully tucking a light blanket around Susie on the couch, Emily started to cry. Margaret hurried to pick her up, concerned that she, too, may have picked up the flu bug that was going around.

Davey took his naps in the master bedroom, since it was quieter there. However, he had been promoted back to the couch for night-time now that the Sutherland 'ladies' were gone, so was upset when he saw Sally lying in his place.

Usually Margaret thought of Grace every day but right now, she was too busy trying to keep the trio happy, except to fleetingly long for Grace's help. As she rushed from 'pillar to post' as it were tending the children she figured her Heavenly Father must have known she would have too much trouble with lonesomeness so allowed this to happen right now to distract her thoughts!

In a typical Margaret way, she even managed to tuck her earlier despondent feelings aside and hummed a little while filling the square metal tub with warm water to bathe the youngsters. After putting a clean nightgown on Sally, she refilled the vessel with clean water to wash the small stained garments.

Although Margaret had laid a blanket on the floor for the baby to lie on, and put a plastic rattle within grasping distance, Emily was fussing.

As her cries sharply increased in crescendo, Margaret made her own share of footprints across the still damp floor in order to warm a bottle for the howling infant.

As soon as it was warm enough, she shook a drop on to her wrist to test it.

"I'm coming Emily: I'm coming— oh, I mean Alice," Her heart sank: that's the second time I've done that! Grace would have never made the same mistake!

Alice kept crying and twisting in her arms, refusing the bottle as she tossed a clean shirt to Junior and told him to put it on, She settled down in the armchair with the baby on her lap. Junior stared vacantly at the shirt. Margaret had never seen him stand still so long.

"Come closer to Mommy, son. I'll help you with those buttons. Junior lifted his clean shirt, eyed it briefly then let it slip back between his fingers. He leaned weakly against Margaret's side while she helped him slip his arms into the fresh garment.

"Have you been feeling sick for a while?"

Junior shrugged his shoulder. "I dunno. Guess so, maybe."

Knowing her boy as she did, of course, he wouldn't think about it until he almost dropped.

Margaret propped the baby bottle up with a cushion then searched the medicine cabinet for baby aspirin but couldn't find any.

I wonder where Janet would have kept it. She discovered some in the kitchen behind rarely used spice tins. She poured a glass of water for her flushed little boy and coaxed him to take the pill. Just like his Dad, he hated swallowing even small tablets.

Alice whimpered, the bottle must have slipped out of her mouth, Margaret reasoned. She went to pick her up and sighed. The baby was limp and fretful. Margaret closed her eyes for a moment to get her bearings.

The next two days dragged on like this. The place reeked with the smells of sickness.

More than once Margaret caught Sally just seconds before she tumbled out of her crib and wished she could sit down and rest, but there was no time.

The beds needed stripping; the tub empting and loads of wash laundered down in the basement. They were running out of nappies since she had put Sally back into diapers for the duration of her illness. She changed Alice into almost the last one and wondered how she would manage to get the laundry done.

Margaret opened the window next to the kitchen sink and hoped a little breeze would find its way past all those city buildings and into their steamy, tight apartment.

When a train whistled far in the distance, she bit her lip. The moaning sound reminded her of Grace. How was her young friend doing? How badly was she grieving because her separated babies?

Margaret looked tenderly at Alice who was nestled between two pillows on the double bed. Alice sensed that her sister and mother were gone, and in her sickness that made her more fretful than ever.

When Alice woke up crying, Margaret swayed gently with the baby in her arms. Mountains of washing still waited to get done, the square metal tub hadn't been emptied last night when she had bathed the children—again, but the baby needed comforting: that was more important.

Junior fell asleep on the floor and Sally was wandering around with her thumb in her mouth. She loved them all dearly but right then wished she could pack them up and go home to Mumsey for a spell. While her mother happily cared for the babies, Margaret would catch up on much needed sleep.

Mom was gone. Even if she had lived right next door, Margaret would never again see her, sing with her, lean her head on her shoulder, or do any of the other homey things that had been so much a part of her life.

Margaret surveyed the disarray and kept rocking. "Lord, I'm counting on you to see me through. " She felt at peace because she knew He would, so sank wearily into the faded armchair with Sally snuggling down beside her.

It was out of the question to use the wringer washer downstairs with the children sick, so ended up washing nappies and all the rest of the laundry at night with an old scrub board of the her neighbours.'

Margaret toiled on alone as mothers do, while the children alternately slept and fretted. When everyone was finally asleep at the same time, she lugged the heavy loads of laundry out to the line in the back to dry since she desperately needed dry nappies as soon as possible.

It might have made her day a little brighter if she could have heard what the milkman said two hours after the last little pair of trousers was pegged on the line.

"That English woman must be sure virtuous," he told his cronies.

"Why, she had laundry on the line by the crack of dawn this morning. I don't know how she gets it all done with two young'uns clinging to her skirts, and another not off the bottle, yet.

It was one of the more difficult weeks in Margaret's storehouse of memories since it soon became apparent that the flu bug had also caught her. She hardly removed her heavy chenille housecoat all week because of feeling so chilled and achy. A constant headache and stomach cramps made it impossible to function above a sleepwalker level and yet she toiled on...

"Mommy, I'm hungry." Margaret looked up from the pair of little trousers she was patching and a weary smile caressed her features.

"I'm glad you're feeling better, sonny. What would you like to eat?"

"A steak!" Junior replied bouncing excitedly.

"A steak?"

"Yeah! I want a whole steak all to myself and I'm gonna eat it all gone. Let's go down to Arny's store right now, and buy some."

"Oh, I don't know," Margaret hedged. "I don't think Sally is well enough."

"I'm all better, now!" Sally chirped her head popping up from the pillow.

From the bedroom, the sweet cooing sounds of a baby could be heard and Margaret knew that a tiny pair of booted feet would begin to kick rhythmically.

"My, it looks like everyone is awake and jolly. Maybe we should take a nice little walk to the corner grocery."

"Yippee!" Junior shouted.

"Lippee!" Sally echoed.

"No you're not!" Margaret chuckled, but the little ones had no idea what she meant.

Junior made a dash for the door.

"Whoa, buddy! First we'll all have to get ready."

"Me ready," Sally lisped, patting her crumbled nightie to make it smooth. Margaret touched her tousled mop. "Not yet, honey. First we will all have baths."

Juniour shook his head vehemently, "I don't want a bath," "We've been bathing ALL the time."

"Sure seems like it," Margaret replied cheerfully as she pulled the square tub out from under the bed. She parked it between the small electric stove and high chair and filled it with warm water, before hanging up a sheet to give Junior the privacy he desired.

Margaret handed him a squirt bottle to play with then filled the large white kitchen sink with sudsy water.

Soon Sally was playing happily with her yellow ducky while Margaret sponged Alice in an oval metal basin next to her.

Fifteen minutes later the young mother gazed lovingly down at her little band.

The children looked so soft and angelic with their freshly pressed clothes and halos of clean fluffy hair. She couldn't have loved them more if they had been hers by birth, but felt a twinge of worry. How can I ever give up Alice if Grace would come to reclaim her? I'm afraid I would feel like hiding.

She tied Davey's shoes and tucked his shirt in. True, their clothes showed signs of being well worn and somewhat faded but they were neatly mended so she didn't let it bother her too much.

Junior eagerly pulled the pram out of the front closet and pushed Alice back and forth through the kitchen-sitting area while Margaret tried to put tiny braids in Sally's straight, silky hair.

"Run and fetch my purse, Junior, "Margaret said and the little fellow was off like a shot. Margaret fixed the bow on Sally's crisp calico print dress, refolded her bobby socks then planted a kiss smack on her wee button nose.

Margaret carefully counted her money, while Junior horsed around excitedly and Sally sat on the couch with her doll and gazed down at her with sweet brown eyes.

Margaret jotted a few items down on her list then looked at Davey.

"Sorry Junior, no steak tonight."

He hopped on to the couch and jumped backwards before sprawling out on the floor.

Margaret tucked the grocery list into her handbag then stood staring out the small kitchen window.

"What are you thinking, Mommy?" Junior asked his hands now poised in the air like an airplane.

"Tally-ho!" he shouted, while using his outstretched arms to guide him over to Margaret.

Margaret's voice was a little shaky. "I was thinking about Auntie Grace," she responded.

"How come she hid that paper in her purse?" Junior asked right out of the blue before soaring across the room.

"Oh, she just wanted to. Come let's be on our way."

Margaret wrapped a quilted blanket her mother had lovingly sewn for Ricky around Alice and tucked her into the pram. How nice it would be to see Mumsey poke her head in the door and call, "Hi, how's it going?" Why did such a special person have to go?

"How come," Junior repeated, as he crowded under her arm a few seconds later to help her push the baby carriage.

Margaret looked blankly at him, "How come, what?"

"How come she took those wee tiny scissors and cut her purse all up then hid that little paper inside?

"She didn't want it to get lost."

"But why," Junior shook her arm.

"It is a very important document."

Junior sighed, knowing he wouldn't get any more information out of her today.

Margaret felt stymied; how would she manage the flight of stairs. Usually David hiked down with the folded pram while she carried the baby.

How was she supposed to do it alone? Junior scampered on a head, but Sally clung to her skirt.

Slowly and with great caution, she bumped her way down the three flights of stairs, stopping to rearrange Alice at each landing because her head kept sliding forward to press against the front of the pram.

The landlord was leaning against the front door, with an amused expression on his face. "I was wondering what all that noise was about," he smirked. Margaret's face flamed. Why didn't you come to help me then? she wanted to retort, but was too ladylike to speak her mind.

"You can park it in the garage for twenty five cents a day," he offered.

Twenty-five cents a *day*! That was daylight robbery! How would I be able to buy the basic necessities like milk and eggs?

"No thanks," she replied stiffly. "We'll manage somehow." Maybe
I'll just quit using the pram, but she didn't know how she could handle three children without it either.

It was such a green and golden day and as she pushed the pram along the sidewalk, it seemed as if the last traces of sickness swept from her body with the invigorating breeze.

"Pretty, pretty," Sally cried as she tried to catch the fluttering leaves drifting lazily towards her.

"Maple leaves!" Margaret smiled happily as the ginger and orange triangles danced around her. "They' have nearly all turned color!"

"They are awesome:" she breathed.

"Ah-tum!" Sally echoed.

Meeting a Swell Gal

The door to a Victorian style house nearby opened and a pretty girl traipsed out. The young woman appeared to be dressed for an afternoon party. She was wearing a flower adorned straw hat and short, white velvet jacket over an azure dress with a swirly skirt.

"Hi! I'm Janiece," she trilled. You must be new in our neighborhood because I haven't seen you before, but then we just got back from our hols. My Dad, Laurence Mc Innis, is a high-ranking officer in the Canadian army. That's why we were still able to take a decent vacation."

She paused to remove a small vanity mirror from her purse and fluffed up her hair.

"This wind sure wreaks havoc to the best coiffed hair styles.

" It's okay to be back, I guess. Dad made sure Mom and we girls had a swell time in spite of all that tiresome fighting over there, but I wish we could have stayed longer. We were at our cottage by the sea.

"Have you noticed my stunning tan?"

Margaret stared at her in amazement.

"Weren't you afraid to be so near the ocean during war time?"

"Not a bit. River John is such a sleepy little town that I don't think those old Japs, or whoever it is that we are fighting, ever heard of it.

Nevertheless, it does have a lovely beach. This is Canada. We're very safe here. Oh, and haven't you heard? Officially, the war is over, at least with old Hitler."

Margaret would have been annoyed at the snooty girl's self-important attitude if she wasn't so dismayed.

"There is still a lot of tension, Janiece, hasn't anyone told you to be cautious what you say?"

"This is Canada," the teenager retorted. "We're very safe here."

Margaret's brow furrowed. Back home in Lower Blossomby, they had a lovely beach nearby, but the youngsters rarely dared to dash there to frolic and play.

Those brave souls that did would sneak away without an adults' permission: it was too near an army base.

She knew that some of the school age children thought war was a great adventure and wove it into their games, but older folks were more cautious because of all the aircraft activity they had observed and the continual warning to be careful with what they said. Janiece ought to know better than to talk so freely.

"Are you going for a walk?" Janiece interrupted her thoughts, "Mind if I join you? I'm heading for the bus stop and it looks like you are going that way."

Without waiting for a nod of consent, Janiece stepped up beside Margaret, the imitation straw shoulder bag swinging jauntily at her side.

"I'm awfully bored today," she confided. "Phyllis is embroidering something for her hope chest, and Annette is working on paint- by-number. Me, I'm more into tennis, swimming, and activities like that, so that's why I am out and about."

"Sure come along," Margaret invited unnecessarily while Davey tugged impatiently at her hand.

"My, you have adorable children. Say, you must be the new Mrs. David Seifert. I'd have recognized them in a minute but they have grown so much."

Janiece opened her mouth to say more but actually managed to catch herself, before adding that they had appeared rather frumpy looking when David had been batching. She crouched down in front of Sally and the whole possession came to a halt.

"Hi, Suzie, do you remember me?" Sally pulled Margaret's skirt in front of her eyes. She didn't like this big girl who called her by the wrong name. Besides that perfume stuff she was wearing didn't smell as pretty as what Mommy wore.

"Junior, do you remember me?"

"Course I do," he retorted nonchalantly. "Daddy useta go out with Phyllis after Mommy died."

Margaret's jaw dropped.

"Oh, don't worry," Janiece, giggled. "Phyllis didn't want to be saddled with someone else's kids. Me? I think they're adorable. But He wouldn't even look at me. Who would? I'm only sixteen," she sighed.

"Let's so on," Margaret suggested. Janiece chatted easily and after getting over her initial worries, Margaret found it enjoyable conversing with someone who wasn't just out of nappies for a change.

"Mr. Seifert used to take his family over there," Janiece pointed to a large stately looking church on a hill. "That's where nearly everyone in this neighbourhood go, us to, when we're around. Will you be going there?"

"I don't know. We haven't been able to get out much."

Life has been so stressful, Margaret thought, finding a good church home would be refreshing. She missed seeing her Daddy leaning on the pulpit while earnestly portraying a thought to the congregation.

136 Steps in the Gray Cell

CHAPTER 27

Randall Sutherland paced the whole length of the narrow, gray prison cell, swerved, strode back and started the same process all over again. It was desperately boring being in jail, so boring he was counting his steps.

It was also humiliating.

How did I ever get myself into such a terrible situation? he asked himself for the hundredth, nay, what felt more like the thousandth time.

He replayed the scene where it happened once again, wondering how he could have responded differently, more coolly to the knuckle-headed brute. The jute box had been playing so loudly that no one else had understood what Tom had said provoking Randall so severely. Every time he rehearsed the scenario, his dander got up and sometimes he even wished he had done more.

He leaped to his feet and strode around the room, fed up with prison and sick at himself for ending up behind bars--he should have stayed on the battlefront.

A slow red crept up his neck, over his collarless shirt: his removal from the army was a shameful thing. For some reason it felt like more of a disgrace than being kicked into the pen.

Randall gripped the bars and pressed his head against the cell wall as a new worry nibbled at his consciousness. In religious towns such as Russet, people who did time behind bars were not accepted. Why, with a population of maybe two thousand, there must be at least five churches and plenty of hoity-toity members to look down their long noses at me if I ever do get out. How can I face their stares and snide remarks?

 His throat tightened, it would soon happen. Last report was that the old guy had made a turn for the better: didn't look like he was going to die after all.

Wearily Randall slumped against the wall. His well of thoughts was ebbing low, and so were his spirits.

Later, he silently accepted the plate of food handed to him and picked at it. His thoughts churned on.

If only Grace could or would have visited more. He would welcome his Mom's preaching, even. Well, maybe. Most of his cronies were off fighting somewhere, and even if they weren't, they wouldn't want to be seen visiting him in jail.

With nothing else to do, Randall sank down on the skinny cot, hung his head between his hands, and tried to figure out how long it was since Grace's visit. 'It's been sixty-five days since I've last seen my beautiful wife. Has her faith in me completely vanished? I must, oh I must win it back! If I could only see her again, I'd know how she feels about me. She didn't have any idea of what we had been going through in France but I wish I hadn't taken it out on her!'

He jerked as hot anger against his father raged within him. I'm sure it's Dad's fault they never come. A piece of ugly liver slid across the plate and landed on the floor. He gave it a kick. 'Good riddance to bad rubbish', he muttered.

How can I bear facing Dad again? One look of stern rebuke--no make that condemnation, would make the most hardened criminal cower and I'm no hardened criminal! Is there life after prison?

Randall pushed the plate of food aside and lowered his face into his hands, feeling empty and spent. After flopping unto his stomach, he buried his head with his arms. When a different line of thought bombarded his senses, he flipped on to his back and stared at a cobweb in the corner of the ceiling.

Last time I saw Mom was when we were in the courthouse and she was watching me hauled off in handcuffs! Mom went through enough with the twins dying and Dad being so bitter and all, and now I've caused her more pain.

While in his teens, he had wanted to hurt Dad by being defiant and rebellious towards that stubborn, old hardliner. Unfortunately, Dad had suffered less than Mom.

Dad had gotten so angry and domineering: it had been a relief to run off and join the army. At least then, I got out from under his fat thumb.

What Was Boot Camp Really Like?

CHAPTER 28

Dad scowled, "Boot camp will be good for him, that's just what he needs."

Randall soon realized that the other fellows enjoyed being with him which really boosted his wounded self-confidence.

He rediscovered a latent gift for making others laugh which helped him forget the frustration and anger of the last few years at home. Yup, boot camp was tolerable for all his young cronies and himself mainly because of Randall's mischievous streak.

Training was not as bad as Dad had predicted. He had rather enjoyed his first jaunt away from the old home place but never admitted that all that 'harsh discipline' probably helped him to fit in quicker.

Randall never minded following orders long as there was no personal barbs. With his roguish nature, it was sometimes easy getting into scrapes but even if the big shots got severe with him, many of them could not help liking that happy-go-lucky redhead from off the farm.

Randall's thoughts wandered back to his stint in the army. Life had been great before they went overseas , before the gritty terror of combat, hiding and marching on French soil, before the shock and humiliation of deportation.

After handing his unfinished plate of food to a guard, who commanded him to crawl around on the floor in search of the errant piece of liver, he stared out the window.

As the grate clanged down behind him, a smile caressed Randall's features. Grace was such an innocent looking sweet, slip of a thing. And one of his very first impressions was that she needed to be cared for as gently as a beautifully crafted porcelain doll, or flower even. His smile deepened when he compared her with the bold dancers, their painted lips and giddy laughter such a huge contrast to her that he never even wanted to admit that he used to whirl 'that kind' around the dance floors. Grace was quieter than those other, more refined, and such a refreshing change.

He grinned; the walk to the park had been just what he needed.

Yes, they had later gone to the community hall where the dance was held, but there was something so pure and refined about the petite young lady at his side that he had not cared to drag her into that garish atmosphere.

Randall went through the milling crowds to fetch punch and a couple sandwiches with her almost on his heels, then they had slipped out through a side door to stroll through what Grace called a 'common' located across the street.

What a lovely night it had been and the heady fragrance of peonies or was it lilacs had wafted through the air. He would always associate that aroma with the day he met Grace. Randall had longed to hook his arm through hers as they walked, but she had such a quiet reserve about her that he refrained, and admired her more for how she held herself back.

He tugged at his hair in exasperation, why did I give her a hard time about getting pregnant? That really was stupid of me: immature, too. He felt like kicking himself but then beads of sweat dampened his neck as memories bombarded him.

There was a Gideon's Bible in the cell. A thick layer of dust covered it. Randall leafed through it the day after Grace came to visit but that was the last time. It had seemed as dry as the dust on the shelf.

Now he took it down again, holding it loosely between his hands.

The light was dim and he didn't pull the string for the one naked bulb over his head. It wouldn't do much more than create more weird shadows anyway.

Whose Footsteps Do I Hear?

CHAPTER 29

What's that sound? Footfalls? Randall raised his head, every muscle on high alert. No one ever walked down this long corridor unless they were slamming a disorderly drunk into one of the pens. He half rose from the lumpy cot. There were no loud, slurring voices or growled commands and something besides the deep heavy tread of the jailer's boots. There was, yes! There were women's voices and the light, quick footfall of...surely not, after all this time could it actually be---?

He gripped the side of the mattress, ready to leap up. His heart raced. They were coming closer and Randall unconsciously combed his fingers through his hair. Maybe just maybe someone has come to see me. He heard the rattle of the key and gazed past the warden's lined face.

"Mother! Where's Grace?"

Lily clasped her beloved child in her arms and pressed his head to her bosom.

He hugged her quickly but looked frantically towards the door: the shadows were so dark; surely, she would not have stayed home. "Mom, I'm sorry for disgracing you, I really am, but why didn't Grace come?

Dimly his mother's voice penetrated his consciousness; obviously, she was focused on only one thing, bringing a confession. "I should have been a better mother. I'm sorry for being such a failure."

Randall searched her face. "I know you tried your best, How did you manage to get away? And where is Grace?"

Lily turned.

"I hadn't seen you!" She was standing behind her mother-in-law and concealed by the shadows.

Randall stiffened, wishing to go to her, yet afraid. Will she still love me after all these endless months?

Grace handed the infant to Lily. She took a step forward, hands reaching out imploringly. Randall looks so pale. Is that spunkiness gone forever?

"Merry Christmas, Randall."

He looked stunned. "What? You mean it's that time of year already?"

Grace nodded and searched his eyes, "Almost."

He took a step closer. "Is it all--still the same?"

She nodded. "Till death do us two part."

He wrapped his arms gently around her, and she leaned her head on his shoulder.

After a few moments, he held her out at arm's reach. "You've changed Grace."

"Really?" she asked, "In what way?"

"You seem frailer; perhaps...thinner. Aren't you only eighteen? You seem to have aged. Has life been that hard on you?"

"Yeah, but I'll be nineteen next month."

He noticed her long, naturally curling eyelashes droop against her pale cheeks. Sighing, she added, "I'll be all right." Randall's arms went around her once again, he wasn't convinced.

"It's my fault," he murmured into her hair, "If I wouldn't have gotten into so much troutrouble--"

Grace shook her head and tried to laugh. "It's just that I'm afraid of the cows, the constant strain of having to milk them is what's wearing me out--."

Randall's head jerked up "Afraid of the cows? Do you mean to tell me that Dad expects a little city-girl like you to march out and milk those beasts?" He swore vehemently.

"No Randall, no," His wife and mother chorused.

"That won't help," Grace added. She stroked Randall's cheek gently. "It's just that-that he's getting so arthritic in his knees and back so can't do it alone."

"Humph! "This can't be. This just can't be. I won't allow it." He gripped her by the shoulders. "We'll get you off the farm, Grace. I promise. I want something better for you. The hard work will kill you!"

"I'm not that frail!" Grace laughed shakily.

"It's too much for you! No wife of mine is going to be hauling buckets of milk and pitching hay and..."

"But what will you do?" both women cried together.

His shoulders drooped." I don't know. Anything that's available, I guess. We can't stay in Deer Flats, that's for sure." He gave them a sidelong look, "There are other reasons you know."

"It might work."

He shook his head. "I'm afraid not." He searched Grace's blue-gray eyes hoping she would understand. She nodded almost imperceptibly as a light went on in her mind. Facing cold shoulders and scorn would--could almost break a man, any man, who wanted to change his life. Besides, he and his Dad were bound to clash eventually.

Lily decided to change the subject. "Would you like to hold your daughter?"

Randall reached out to her." My, she's grown!"

"She looks like you did when you were a baby," Lily volunteered.

Randall grinned wryly, "Yeah. I guess I did have two eyes, a nose, and a mouth. At least I was never told otherwise."

Grace wrinkled her dainty nose up at him.

Emily made strange, but both women quickly reassured him that it was normal and her mother took her back.

Grace cradled the infant against her shoulder, and patted her back, swaying gently.

What a beautiful Mama she is: Randall's look was admiring before his face lengthened. She needs a good daddy, too. He tugged at a loose thread on the sleeve of his striped coveralls.

All too soon, the jail keeper was rattling the keys once more.

Partying Sisters

CHAPTER TWENTY-NINE

"*Lily!* It's about time you got here!" Elizabeth gave her plumper sister a slap on the back then shook Grace's hand.

"It's nice to meet you, Grace. I've been hearing so much about you from Lily's letters. Thumbs up; it's all good stuff. She seems to think you are the sweetest little thing since perfume was invented!

Elizabeth strode into her cheery red and white kitchen and filled the kettle with fresh water before placing it on one of the gas burning elements.

"So how do you like my new stove?" she asked Lily while deftly slicing an angel food cake baked earlier. "It just got delivered by train last week. Dalen Kroeker, the head of the school board, went all the way to Edmonton to pick it up for me, but then he had to go out anyway."

"Well, "Lily's light blue eyes twinkled merrily, "Don't come crying to me, when you get tired of your bright red appliances!"

Elizabeth harrumphed and swatted her sister with the potholder she was holding. "You're so nineteen-thirtyish in your tastes. I love the pastel colors in your kitchen--those mint green chairs and white cupboards are charming--but not for me!"

Lily pretended to draw back and huddle within herself, "And me? Can you imagine me with bright red appliances? Ben would have thrown me out on my ear if I dragged one of those contraptions into our house."

Grace was largely forgotten, but she didn't mind. She thoroughly enjoyed the lively exchanges between the two sisters since she had never had a sibling or even a cousin in her life. She was fascinated with this new side of Lily, whom she had only thought of as motherly, that was showing up.

Elizabeth poured tea into their matching yellow cups then ladled strawberries over the slices of cake arranged on small plates.

She reached into the icebox and drew out a carton of ice cream.

"Sorry, old girl, this won't be as good as the homemade stuff you churn up, but it'll have to do!"

Lily's look sobered and she almost reverently held her plate up to accept a scoop of the cool, creamy treat.

"I suppose this is the first time you've been able to get any since the war."

Elizabeth nodded, her face averted. Lily was suspicious that Elizabeth had been 'up to something'. She tried to fish it out of her.

"So the reason the carton is half empty is because you decided it was high time to invite the little girls in your class to a tea party," she teased gently.

"Some--none of them-- had ever tasted ice cream before!" Elizabeth said defensively, and then grimaced; she was never one to brag about her exploits.

"And I'm sure you found some excuse to give the boys some too," her sister needled.

"Well, some kindling needed cutting and..." Elizabeth shrugged her shoulders, "Oh forget it. Grace would you like some sugar in your tea? What a luxury not to ration it anymore. Or would you prefer honey?"

"Yes, please," Grace, said in a small voice.

"Sugar or honey?"

"Sugar, please." She had never quite gotten used to the taste of Canadian honey.

The conversation switched to other things and Grace found herself sharing painful incidents from her bleak past that seemed to make the eyes of her hostess grow moist. Elizabeth hopped up and drew a hanky from the pocket of a paisley print apron hanging behind the pantry door.

"I must be coming down with a cold," she muttered, but Lily knew better.

"Your beds are ready for you," Elizabeth remarked a half-hour later. Since no one was interested, she got out the checkers game and Grace would always play the winner.

Even though the women's hands moved adeptly over the board, their conversation was warm and often full of teasing.

Grace's heart warmed towards her gentle, cheerful mother-in-law.

Just before handing them a candle to light their way to the guest room, Elizabeth and Lily got out some Christmas gifts that had been stowed away in secret spots.

Elizabeth presented each of her guest's with an embroidered hanky and scented talcum powder: Rose for Lily and Lily of the Valley for Grace. "I guess it should be the other way around," she joked to her sister, "Since your name is Lily."

"You know what kind of person I am and the scents I like."

"But I never gave anything to you!" Grace spluttered.

"That's okay," Lily smiled. "You're still new here, and we want to make you feel as welcome as possible."

Lily gave Elizabeth a bestseller called The Robe by Lloyd C. Douglas that she knew her sister would love. When she handed her daughter-in-law her gift, she watched Grace carefully unwrap it and her eyes sparkle. It was a thick, lined book, a journal perhaps. Lily had sewed many tiny pieces of fabric together to make a crazy-quilt cover and had appliqued Grace's name on the front. Grace had never ever caught her working on it!

When Grace got emotional, and Lily hastened to comfort her, Elizabeth busily cleared the tea dishes off the table pretending not to notice.

Dreading Developments

CHAPTER 30

The next morning Grace woke up shivering and found that the air was so fresh, clean ...and cold...because the window had been wide open all night. An extra quilt was resting on the hope chest at the foot of the bed. She pulled it over her and cuddled deep into the cozy warmth. Early dawn was lighting the sky, it was so comfy under the stack of quilts and such a luxury not to face those lumbering beasts in order to milk them so early in the day.

She must have drifted off because the aroma of coffee wafting from the kitchen got her stirring next.

A heavy atmosphere that obviously had nothing to do with the bright winter scene outdoors descended over the house while they slept.

Each of them drank their coffee and ate their Wheaties but mostly in silence.

Grace had no idea what was causing Aunt Elizabeth and Lily to be so subdued that morning, but worried that it was something she had said or done.

Later, after she had stepped into her felt lined goulashes and was pulling on her woolen mitts, Aunt Elizabeth quietly stepped up to her.

"Be brave, little niece." Her voice was low but Lily couldn't have heard anyway, she was beside the couch, busy tucking the cooing baby into her pink snowsuit.

"Randall is a fine young man. It's unfortunate about what happened so soon after being deported, but I promise you, he has a heart of gold, and someday things will seem more hopeful. Never give up on him, okay?"

Grace heart squeezed, but she promised soberly. She yearned to know why he was sent home, and ended up in gaol if he was such a nice person but didn't know Aunt Elizabeth well enough to ask. They probably assume I know.

As they rode on the wagon seat behind Ole Bill, since Lily was too scared to drive the car, neither of them talked much. Both were anxious about facing Ben.

Grace appeared distracted by Emily's antics, but it was just a cover up. How would he react to them leaving without his explicit permission? Sure, they had left a note and plenty of home-canned soup on the back burner; sure Lily had hinted broadly that she wanted to go. Ben had pretended to ignore her, but his disapproval had been evident.

Grace quietly renewed the sequence of events in her mind. Much to her surprise, nay astonishment, Lily had suggested they go see Randall. They had been folding freshly laundered towels, sheets and pillowcases and Grace had no idea what the older woman was mulling over in her mind on such a peaceful morning.

After putting the laundry away, Lily had continued talking, but the familiar wreath of smiles on her motherly countenance was missing.

"Dad has gone to the local machine shop to get the tractor worked on. Usually there are several men hanging out there so he will likely stay there until supper. "

Grace continued to listen wondering what she could possibly be getting at.

"I told Ben I wanted to go see Randall, so he won't be too surprized."

She opened the door to the little cubbyhole under the stairs and handed Grace a suitcase. So, this was a well thought out decision.

Lily hadn't said so, but it was unspoken knowledge Ben would never have said 'yes'. Lily longed to see her son after a year of enforced separation.

As they drove, Grace glanced sideways at Randall's Mom. That was all history and they had had a wonderful time with Lily's spinster-sister, but now what? She suspected the older woman was asking herself, also.

The rhythmic sound of the horses' feet on the snow packed road soothed Grace's spirits as she watched the wispy clouds.

Eventually the red barn loomed into view, and later the small white house. Grace bit her lip to still its' trembling.

Ben looked up from stoking the fire in the kitchen when they drove unto the yard.

He pulled on his boots and shrugged into a farm jacket before venturing into the wintery air.

Both women stared at him waiting for his reaction. He carefully helped his wife to the ground and she scurried to the other side to take the baby.

Grace clambered down by herself, her heart caught in her throat. This not saying anything was pure agony: if he's mad why doesn't he just say so and get it over with?

Ben unhitched the wagon and led the horse to the barn where he rubbed him down and gave him a small amount of oats. Grace had meekly followed him there knowing she had missed chores.

"Shall I do something?" She asked in a small voice.

"The chickens need feeding."

As she walked over to the small chicken coop she saw her mother-in-law carrying Emily to the house. The baby gurgled and waved excitedly when she saw Grace so Lily turned and smiled. The corners of her lips turned up, but Grace knew even from that distance it never reached her eyes.

When will this heavy atmosphere ever lighten?

Ben came in punctually at twelve as usual but they ate the rest of the turkey soup and some fresh, hot biscuits in silence, then without having his usually lie-down on the couch in the living room, he plodded out.

After the two women cleaned up the kitchen, Grace put Emily down for a nap and Lily, also, rested.

Grace decided to tackle the never-ending ironing, which was in a basket beside the wringer washer.

She was still working on it when Lily entered the living room with a different basket: this one brimming with mending.

"I wish I had little grandchildren to mend for," Lily said smiling whimsically, but her daughter-in-law was still worried about Ben.

Emily was sleeping, the cat was outside somewhere, and both of them were saying so little that the clock seemed to be ticking extra loudly. Grace could stand it no more.

"Is Ben mad at us?"

Lily sighed. "It's hard to know what he is thinking." She laid the mending aside. "Maybe I should make a batch of his favorite cookies; they're called Dusty Miller cookies."

A peace offering: would it even help?

Milking Madness

CHAPTER 31

Grace trudged over to the barn slowly and reluctantly that evening. She ended up working on the chores by herself because Ben had made himself scarce, presumably at the mechanics garage, but Lily was unconcerned about his whereabouts. Is he punishing me by making me do them by myself? She was familiar with the different personalities of the cows by now but they still made her nervous.

"Oh, Grace, you know I would help you," Lily lamented, "But it's just that I have supper to make, and there are cookies in the oven, and"—

"Don't worry, Mom," Grace had responded, "Emily is too young to be messing around in the barn, anyway. It will be soon enough that she will beg to come along."

Grace put on a cheerful face until Lily turned and walked away, but then she had to face tying the cows into their stanchions: alone. Grace could feel her face drain of color at the prospect.

She watched them plod in one by one and out of habit turn into their own stalls. She swallowed once, twice. She knew them all by name, by now, and knew their temperaments quite well. How well did they know her?

Did they know she was afraid? Bobby, Ella-Mae, Blackie, and Goldenrod, gave no trouble, but Huffy was next, Huffy and that slender girl from Birmingham, England never did see eye to eye.

Each time Grace reached for her chain, Huffy swung her head towards her, threatening to bunt. By the time she gave up and went to the next one, Grace was weeping, and could hardly see what she was doing.

Roxie, number twelve, was ornery also, but not nearly as bad as Huffy. By the time Grace had the rest tied in their stalls, she was exhausted, and there was still the milking to do.

Grace pulled up the stool beside cow Number One. She wore her hair, which had grown a lot by then, in two plaits for chores. They flopped over her shoulders but didn't hide her fear like a cascade of curls would.

The barn cat and her kittens moseyed around looking for a treat. Grace hardly noticed them. Her nerves were shot; totally frazzled, by then, but she must go on. Milking these huge beasts would never, ever become her favorite chore. She left Huffy her for the last.

Somehow, the number of un-milked cows diminished and the need to face the most ornery one in the lot grew closer. Her heart pounded.

 The brawny Holstein was surprisingly docile when she fastened her chain to the bar this time, but Grace's relief was short lived. When the bucket was half-filled, Huffy gave it a swift kick, the milk spilled all over the place and the kittens came running from every direction. To top it off the beast's filthy tail lashed right across Grace's cheek.

Grace flung the empty pail, hitting the 'sneering?' cow right in its blocky nose. She raced over to the ladder, scrambled quickly into the hayloft, and pounded the hay, wailing until she sank into a fitful slumber.

Two hours passed since Grace had left the house. Lily put on her farm jacket and tucked an old shawl around the fussing baby.

What was keeping Grace so long? She hurried to the barn calling her daughter-in-law's name.

Grace climbed down from the loft, straw in her hair, and tear stains on her cheeks. She had never seen Lily's face go red with anger before. Lily thrust Emily into her arms.

"You go to the house!" she yelled. "Ben has no excuse leaving you with the chores. I don't care how grumpy he is, he shouldn't have done this to you no matter how mad he is at me!"

Frightened, Emily stared at her beloved Grandma. Just then, the barn door opened.

"What's going on here?" Ben rumbled.

Lily lit into him like Manitoba lightning. Grace was amazed: was this Lily, Randall's gentle, placid mother screaming like that? Without waiting to see if Ben ever got a word in edgewise, she escaped to the house to refresh herself.

Her in-laws strolled in much later; Ben looked subdued with his head down, and they were holding hands!

The next morning Grace woke out of habit even though Ben hadn't banged raucously on the door, demanding her to get up! She bundled up warmly and crossed the icy yard, not knowing what to expect.

Once Ben had caught her crying while doing chores, since it had bothered him so much, she had tried hard never to let it happen again. Grace knew that when her nerves frazzled as they were now, she could easily end up going to pieces again.

It happened, while she was hunched over next to Hollyhock. Ben said something, Grace never could remember what, and she started weeping silently, he saw it. She quickly swiped her hand across her cheek then used the corner of her blue checked apron to dry her eyes.

Ben studied her for a moment before reaching into the pile of straw in the middle alley. Grace's eyes popped as he plucked out a tiny white kitten with gold stripes and handed it to Grace.

"Go show it to the baby; you've done enough for today."

Lily was amazed when she saw the kitten and Grace had explained why she had brought it in. Now it was mom-in-law's turn to dab her eyes with her apron.

"Ben's softening," she explained, "That's the first time in years that he has shown any sign of tenderness. Oh, if only you could have seen what he used to be like."

Grace reminded her of the long talk her folks-in-law had the night before.

"Maybe he is beginning to mend." Lily acknowledged. She had told Grace about the physical and emotional wounds inflicted during the Great War, and both women begged God to heal him.

Getting into the Spirit of Things

CHAPTER 32

Lily really got enthused when the Christmas season was underway. The roads were somewhat better this year than they often were. She appreciated it that they were neither icy nor covered with deep snow--at the moment-- and she was able to shop locally for most of the ingredients for her well-loved Christmas cake and sugar cookies.

"Here, Grace, don an apron, we're going to make cookies today!"

"Cookies," Grace looked blank as she tied the oversized apron around her slender waist. I thought we made cookies every couple of weeks.

"Oh, I mean, 'biscuits'." Lily tossed Emily in the air and nuzzled her. "I keep forgetting what you Britishers call cookies. We need to stock up on Christmas cookies."

Grace's face broke into a smile of anticipation. This sounded like fun.

"I suppose Randall loved 'helping' you when he was a wee chap."

Lily's round face beamed with happiness.

"Oh, he loved everything about cookie baking day: cutting them, smearing colored icing on, adding the (lopsided) faces to the gingerbread men, just everything."

She lifted Emily high in the air again and gave her a kiss on her face still sticky with breakfast Pablum. "But he loved sampling best of all.

"He would get one or two of his little friends over and there would be a royal mess—and lots of fun!"

Lily saw Grace's eyes cloud over as she cleared the table and stacked the dishes.

Although Lily seemed occupied with washing up the rosy-cheeked little lamb and cooing to her, she was troubled. Why does Grace so often have these lightning fast mood changes?

Grace forced herself not to take out her frustration and despair on the hapless melamine bowls and cups.

When did Mom ever let me have one of my little friends over? She said we would be too noisy and it would bring one of her dreadful headaches on. For that matter when did we ever do such a 'worldly' thing as baking Christmas cookies?

By the time, I was in my early teens I was too embarrassed by our grungy house to want them to come down anyway, really, why did it matter. Everyone in our neighbourhood was all in the same boat, but somehow it seemed like my mother was more standoffish than the others were. I suppose because she was a Londoner she looked down on Birmingham as just not as good as where she came from. Am I that way, too?

She worked faster, hoping to crowd out the unwanted thoughts.

After placing the last dish on a towel to drain, she turned to Lily with a half-smile. "I suppose you want these," she asked while reaching into the icebox for a wire basket of eggs and the small butter crock.

Lily removed Emily's homemade bib and draped it over the back of the highchair. She positioned the baby in front of the pots and pans cupboard and handed her a wooden spoon.

Grace rolled her eyes and Lily was glad to see her smile return.

"Oh, yes, yes, you can get out the milk too. This is the first time I'll be doing Christmas baking since the war! Rationing sure lasted long, didn't it?"

"I think we will make Christmas cake first. How did your mother do it? Did she soak the fruit in brandy or--"

Grace thumped the sugar canister on the oilcloth covering and turned abruptly. "I'm not up to baking. I, I have a terrible headache."

She scooped up Emily and ran for the stairs.

Lily stared after her a moment before quietly getting out the yellowed and stained notebook with many of her mother's favorite recipes. Lily absently thumbed the pages. Why do I seem to have a way of saying all the wrong things?

Lily left the baking supplies; she slipped into the master bedroom, dropped to her knees and buried her head in her arms against the white, chenille bedspread. Only God could hear and understand the cry of her heart.

Only God could hear and understand the cry of Grace's heart. As she looked out the east window of her bedroom towards the distant gleaming tracks, she longed with all her heart to see Alice just once more.

Not only that, she wished she could recall seeing her mother smile approvingly at her. Was I that bad? Why did she act as if nothing I did was ever good enough? I long to remember having mother and daughter chats such as so many girls do.

Randall was also an only child, I just thought of that now, but he had a good relationship with his parents, well, especially with his Mom, but also with Ben before he reached adolescence.

She continued to stare at those endless tracks would eventually lead to the very city where little Alice was growing up: without her. Without a doubt by now Alice had no recollection whatsoever of another Mommy who used to feed her and cuddle her, another Mommy who loved her very, very much.

The tracks seemed symbolic somehow of the vast distance in her relationship with her own mother. Will it ever be better? Will I ever feel close to her? How can I ever be a good mother when I feel so insecure myself?

Emily was getting restless in her arms so she drew back the lace curtain and pointed out the 'moo-moo's' to the little girl.

Ben staggered into view carrying two big pails of feed.

"Da-da!"

Grace turned away from the window. Emily still doesn't know her real 'da-da', would Alice ever?

She put the baby down on the floor and the bright-eyed girl leaned forward, wishing she could explore this interesting new territory.

There was a basin and white porcelain pitcher on a stand in the corner of the room. Grace poured some water and sudsed up a facecloth using Pears soap. After scrubbing her face, she felt a little better so scooped up Emily once again to go back to the kitchen to try to act like a grownup.

"Come, Grace," Lily coaxed, a week later, "Come to church with us, tomorrow. Even Dad goes at Christmas time."

Most of the time, except when the roads were impossibly rutted because of break-up, Lily caught a ride with the neighbours. Like many farmwomen, Lily avoided getting behind the steering wheel at all costs. It made her face shine with joy that Ben would take her this time.

Grace looked down. "I, I got a headache."

"Just take an aspirin and lay down for a while; I could bring you a wet washcloth to place on your forehead. You could easily be better by tomorrow.

"You've been working too hard getting this place ship-shape."

Grace shrugged her shoulders. She suspected Lily knew it was just an excuse. She was afraid to meet the Gossiping Committee because her husband was a 'gaol-bird' and dreaded facing their looks of curiosity or worse yet condemnation.

"I've bragged so much about my adorable granddaughter," Lily continued mischievously, "that people will think I made it up if you never show up in church."

"They see her at the store," Grace mumbled as she rubbed and rubbed the pie cabinet she was polishing.

Lily looked at her uncertainly then decided to push her luck. "What really is the matter, Grace?"

Grace looked wildly at her and cried, "I can't bear to see all those happy, gurgling babies!"

Lily gasped as her hand flew to her throat. As usual, Grace flung aside what she was doing and dashed for the stairs.

Lily went back to changing the linen on their bed and, eventually Ben lumbered over to her.

"What was that all about?"

"I have no idea!" Lily looked shaken.

"I think you better sit down a spell," Ben led her over to a chair and poured her a cup of tea. It was lukewarm, but Lily made no comment about that.

"Isn't it enough that I'm going to church? Can't you quit asking her?"

Lily cast him a hurt look but forced herself not to get defensive.

"She has her reasons, I'm sure," he continued.

"But not wanting to see the babies! That's –awful strange. That's, that's—outlandish!"

Ben pulled up a chair beside her. "She's hiding something, that woman, and it's making her awful unhappy."

Lily nodded; "But what could it be, what *could* it be?"

Ben pushed himself away from the table. "I guess we all have our secrets."

"I want you to share with me, I can take it." They both knew he was referring to trauma on the battlefront.

Ben hesitated for a moment, and then shook his head. "It's not necessary to burden you with my troubles."

Lily stepped into his arms, "I can take it," she repeated while smoothing his fading auburn hair.

"Someday, maybe," he parried.

"I'll take that as a promise. It would be easier to share your burdens than to be shut out," she complained.

He kissed her on the forehead, "I appreciate that, but it would be cruel," he said, and went out.

Grace felt like she had to go to church for Lily's sake, but kept her head down most of the time and barely heard the joyous Christmas singing. She cried so hard when the little ones trotted to the front to say or sing their little parts that she fled to the outhouse, even though it was cold out. She vowed never to darken a church doorway again.

Grace was relieved when the Christmas season with all its festivities and joy was over.

A Quilting Bee for Less Than Three

CHAPTER 33

After the holiday season, slower days were upon them.

Grace's eyes widened when Lily lugged a bulging feed sack down from the attic and emptied the contents on the extended dining room table.

"Quilting time is here, once more!" Lily announced.

"Oh, good, I've always longed to learn how to sew tops together." Grace sat down in front of the pile of colorful scraps and immediately began to sort them into coordinating piles.

"You have an eye for combining colors," Lily observed.

Grace looked up with a smile. A sweet yet painful memory flashed through her mind. Daddy had always had a way of knowing when she had colored nearly all the pictures in her coloring book or when the crayons needed replenishing. When she was still in the early grades at school, he would occasionally stand and watch her color, hardly saying a word, but Grace knew he liked what he saw.

Grace picked up a garish orange and purple scrap that came from who-knows-where and hid it under the heap of unsorted fabric.

She wished her memories of her mother's responses could have disappeared as easily. Heloise would harrumph when she saw Grace painstakingly working on a picture, but her comments were even more depressing.

"Have you swept the floor, yet?" or "Better run upstairs to see if your bed is made properly. Yesterday the counterpane was crooked."

Grace pushed the scraps away and stood up. "I might as well start peeling potatoes for dinner."

"It's only nine-thirty, Grace, there's no rush! Besides, I thought we could make sandwiches from the leftover roast beef we had on Sunday."

Grace sank back into her chair, not even trying to hide her dejected feelings.

Lily laid her scissors aside and leaned forward: "Why are you so troubled, Honey?"

Grace's eyes closed. Honey: she called me Honey! No one ever, ever called me something so sweet before. Grace pushed some of the tinier pieces into a pile. She bit her lip, oh, if only I could share with Mom, I mean Lily: my heart hurts so.

"I'm okay. I...I got a bit of a headache coming on. I think I'm inclined towards migraines like my mother."

She pushed her chair away and stood up but caught the look of disappointment in Lily's eyes so resumed her seat. I'm too inclined to run off. It's time I grow up and faced my problems.

But how?

"So, what color of quilt are you planning to make this time?" she asked.

"The pattern is called Blazing Star and I thought I would experiment with various shades of blues, silvers, and greens."

Lily picked up a pine green print and sized it up beside a turquoise blue. She laughed. "Blues and greens should never be seen, together except inside the washing machine!"

Grace's spirit often lifted when she saw the merry twinkle in Lily's eyes. Lily was so much fun to live with. Now if I could only forget the past and live in the present, but no that would mean forgetting Alice and that I refuse to do.

Grace had almost called the dear lady Mom more than once but had caught herself just in time. Why is it so hard to cross that hurdle? Is it because I would feel like I had given up on ever having 'that kind' of relationship with my own mother?

Once it slipped out, they would both know that a major wall of reserve was crumbling to the ground, but Grace was too shy to push at it.

Lily hovered near to show her how to mark the squares exactly with a very sharp pencil. For perfect results, the pieces must be marked and cut out accurately.

About mid-morning, Lily put the kettle on and prepared a plate of date squares.

"May I ask you something?" Grace paused before taking a sip of her honeyed tea.

"Sure, go right ahead." Lily beamed over her perched-on-her nose reading glasses.

Grace hesitated too long and just then, Ben burst in, the door slammed shut behind him.

"Oh, forget it," Grace mumbled. "It's kind of silly."

Grace felt sorry when she saw how disappointed the older women looked.

Lily left the table and headed to the door with the teapot in hand. Grace looked down; she would find it very hard run and help a husband like Ben!

"I just made a fresh pot of tea, would you like some?" Lily asked.

"What I need is good strong coffee right now," Ben replied, "Ok, I might as well, there's a driving wind out there: might be blizzardy by noon."

Grace ignored the two while she continued to pick out the blues and greens from the piles. Silver was harder to find. Maybe she's planning to use it only on the tips of the stars. She had been looking forward to opening her heart to the older woman--if she could get brave enough--and now the moment may have faded away.

Over the last few weeks, there had been occasional brief moments of sharing with Randall's mom. Those she cherished as they were like bright snippets in the quilt of her life, but she was feeling ready for more...maybe.

She glanced up at the older couple. Ben was hanging up his jacket, which Grace admitted he faithfully did all the time, Lily was pouring him a cup of tea and placing a date square on the saucer beside it.

"I'm so glad I thought of making Date Squares." Ben's wife dimpled, "I remembered you telling me you were fond of them as a boy."

"Well, yes, and that's the treat you served me when I came to visit you for the first time."

"You remember that?"

"I sure do."

Grace reached for the stiff cardboard template and outlined one of the pieces of material Lily had chosen.

She had long ago noticed that Ben rarely if ever spoke directly to his wife in a harsh manner. He did a lot of growling and complaining about the weather and anything else that did not suit his fancy, but those comments were not jabs at her personally.

This intrigued Grace and she had been feeling almost brave enough to ask about it that very morning.

Lily slipped the comb out of Ben's top pocket and gently ran it through his thinning, hair.

Grace's jaw tightened and she had a wild impulse to throw the scissors across the table. Would you be acting so sweet to him, if he had yelled at you this morning? A calf had bunted her pail of milk and it spilled it all over the place. Grace felt so ashamed of her fierce reaction. Please God, help me to me sorry.

Since it was a drafty day, Ben sank wearily into his favorite chair by the pot-bellied stove, and Lily tucked an afghan around his legs to keep them warm.

Grace felt sad: I'll never be as sweet and docile a wife as Mom, I mean Lily. How can Randall and I ever have a good marriage since we're both dragging along so much baggage?

While Ben snoozed in the armchair, Lily joined her at the table although Grace was in a quiet mood.

The morning sun lit up the red geranium on the windowsill and laid a glowing pool of light for the cat to snooze in.

Eventually, Emily's happy gurgles broke the companionable silence and after she 'called' to be picked up, Grace went to lift her out of the crib.

Lily stacked the coordinating pieces in boxes and the rest back into the bag. It was time for 'Little Miss Sunshine' to have her bath in the same white enamel tub with the red edge Randall had splashed in twenty years before.

Lily's benevolent kindness towards her husband continued to overflow and Grace marveled. Why did Ben have to act so bossy when he asked her a get the broom to brush the snow off his boots? Couldn't he at least say' please, show a little gratitude? Lily went to a lot of work to bundle up in her heavy winter coat and woolen kerchief when she brought him a thermos full of chicken noodle soup.

Ben didn't let on if he noticed the disapproval on Grace's face. Lily's good deed had happened earlier that evening like it often had before when he had to stay out with an ailing cow or a birthing heifer.

Grace squirmed uncomfortably. She knew a first-time heifer was laboring long and hard but had high-tailed it back to the house as soon as the last bucket was washed and hung to dry. She spent no more time than necessary with that grouchy old-old chap.

Her disgruntled thoughts were hard to stifle so tried to take them to the Lord in prayer. I wish he would at least say'thank you' when Mom drops whatever she's doing to bring him those soft moccasins that an Indian friend of Randall's made? Why does she molly-coddle him?

Grace watched as Lily unwound the scarf from her cold-chilled face and. blow on her fingers to warm them.

"Whew, is it ever chilly out there! I could barely see the barn from the house. Good thing Dad has the rope strung up between the two."

Grace knew she should ask if the heifer birthed successfully. She paced agitatedly between the table and entrance.

"Why are you always so nice to Ben?"

Lily looked startled at first then her face softened.

"I'm afraid you have no idea what your father-in-law has gone through," she replied a trifle sadly. "Ben suffers from severe burns on his legs since the first war and the cold makes them ache terribly. I feel sorry for him."

She removed her gloves and pinned them up to dry on the short line behind the stove, "I keep hoping, praying the old Ben will emerge again, he was so positive and strong. I love him , although others may see him as a cross old man."

They had laid the quilting project back on the table after supper, and now Lily pulled up a chair but her fingers were too cold to use the scissors.

After warming them against her cheeks, she shuffled through a mound of cloth scraps.

"There's a lot of dark in the 'quilt' of his life right now but I want to add enough brightness to make it beautiful, to make the pain he is going through endurable."

Grace marveled at the throb of longing in her voice but looked down quickly when she saw a tear tremble like a jewel on Lily's eyelash.

Spring thaws arrived at the homestead.

The whole driveway was deeply rutted but then the main road was not any better.

Grace felt so hemmed in by breakup that she struggled with loneliness for the clean, urban orderliness of the city.

Shortly after finishing the breakfast dishes, Grace worked at scraping the pile of limp and wilted carrots that she was going to add to the stew for supper, such faded reminders of the bright summertime were not good for anything but soup or stew!

She glanced out the window at the driving rain and wondered what it was like in Birmingham right now. Rain she was certainly familiar with, but not all this mud. She pictured the dockworkers at work. . Since Betsy's da worked on the docks, the girls would sometimes watch the men unloading ships. Grace never told her mother where she was and Heloise didn't ask. Grace was too afraid of her mother's disapproval to go more than once or twice but it was a pleasant memory.

She brushed a strand of hair off her forehead. The commons would be green and fragrant. It was fun wandering through them even when it was showering. Saturday mornings were especially nice when distant sounds were subdued and the nearby birds cheerily flitted from tree to tree.

She recalled that favorite, secluded place in the grove of May trees where she loved to relax but there was nothing like that here! Back in England, there was tarmac everywhere: no tromping around in gumbo like soil in rubber boots that caused a rash on the calves of her legs. The way the mud stuck to them it was no wonder Ben called them gumboots!

Grace rinsed off the last of the carrots she was planning to use and laid them aside. As she reached for one of the Spanish onions, the only type that not moldy yet, something outside the window caught her attention. She looked closely as a dimly outlined figure emerged from the trees.

Her mother-in-law obviously must have caught sight of 'him' also, because she hustled to the stove to put the kettle on. Lily spoke as if talking to herself, or continuing a conversation never quite ended.

"I try to give my level best to my husband," she said and Grace noted the sadness in her voice. "If Ben continues to go the way he's going, there will be no Heaven waiting for him at the end of the road, so I want to--I must--give him as much heaven on earth as I possibly can."

Grace hung her head; pretending it was the onion that made her cry. All winter her attitude towards Ben had been unkind. "Lord, help me to feel differently towards him," she prayed. "Help me to repent of my resistance."

Several minutes later Grace heard stomping at the backdoor when Ben came in, rain dripping off his hair and sliding in silvery rivulets down his raincoat.

"What------miserable weather," he growled. "That ----- -----cow has gone into hiding! Grace get your coat and help me look. This mud is obscuring all traces of footprints."

He looked down at the puddle surrounding his boots, and Lily hastened to get a floor rag. The cloth was soon sopping so Grace fetched the mop and pail.

"But Emily will be due a feeding soon!" His wife protested.

"Give her a bottle, then."

Lily and Grace cast each other silent glances. It had become increasingly evident that Emily's fussiness worsened when drinking cow's milk. They had tried Farmer's Wife brand formula, which Emily tolerated fairly well but had run out. It was only available in the city.

"What are you two conspiring for?" The statement was against both of them, but the malevolent glare focused on the younger woman.

"We aren't," Lily said gently. "It's just that Emily doesn't tolerate cow's milk, and if she gets too much during the day, her crying will disturb your badly needed sleep, tonight."

Ben looked disgruntled, "Oh, well then," He turned to go. At that moment, the kettle began to whistle.

"I'll have a cup of coffee ready for you in a minute." Lily hurried to prepare one. "Take your boots off and rest awhile," she encouraged. "You'll feel more like going back out after having something hot to drink."

.

Lily handed him the steaming mug after he sat down at the kitchen table. Grace did not miss the small smile they shared. After awakening
Emily in order to nurse her, Grace shared a few moments of sweet communion with the contented baby but twenty minutes later

discovered just how dreary and bone chilling the weather actually was.

She slogged behind the older, slightly stooped man in the plaid cap. The golden collie dog loping ahead of them was the only cheery stroke of color in the gloomy landscape.

Dixie stopped short, sniffed the air, and gave a sharp bark. They shuffled through last year's pasture grass to see what had interested her, sure enough, there on the sloping bank of the Linden Creek near a willow tree, was the missing Holstein standing guard over her calf.

"Oh what a darling babby," Grace said.

Ben moved in closer. The cow was ornery and mooed threateningly. Grace was terrified. Will I be attacked? Ella-Mae was pawing at the mud!

Grace's heart hammered; this is the reason I'm so afraid of cows.

She cut Ben a quick glance: he also seemed to be rigid, tense. What should I do? Where should I go? She retreated a few steps and Ella-Mae tossed her head. Grace's mouth went dry: Is she going to attack me?

Grace's movement caught the collie's attention. Dixie glanced at her, barked once, then lunged towards the Holstein, braced herself on her forefeet, barked loudly, did a few dance steps and repeated her actions. Grace quickly realized that Dixie was distracting the cow: not only that but she was veering her towards the barn!

She stared at the two of them then whirled around in time to see Ben hoist the calf over his shoulders and follow the dog back to the farmyard.

Ellie-Mae kept looking over her shoulder and lowing for her calf, but with a nippy dog hounding at her heels, she made no more attempts to be aggressive.

Grace trudged on behind until they were near the barn then struggled more quickly through the muck to drag open the big heavy door.

Ben lowered the calf into the hay, while Grace watched him. He seems so calm and gentle with the helpless beasts. I wish he would treat me just as civilly. Please God, help me to be charitable towards him. He has good reasons for being sullen.

Ben walked away to get something, so she crouched down beside the poor, shivering creature to stroke her nose. When Ben returned, he tossed Grace an old woolen blanket; she carefully rubbed the calf down.

Ben paused to watch her just like her Daddy used to when she was coloring, but Grace pretended not to notice. She was leery of Randall's cantankerous dad.

She returned to the house after the calf had latched on and was nursing contentedly on the colostrum, which is a cow's first milk. In a rare moment of communicativeness, Ben once told her it was important that calves got the super-beneficial colostrum before put on milk replacer.

Grace looked forward to the job of feeding this calf. Not only did it feel a little bit like her own, but also had a heart shaped white patch on her forehead. She asked Ben if they could call it Val and he agreed, but Grace secretly called her Valentine.

It was sure good to be back in the warm house. While she was changing out of her dripping garments, Lily added chunks of wood to the stove.

The flickering orange and blue flames looked cheery through the open stove door as Grace came into the sitting room.

After warming up beside the heater, she snuggled into one of the over-stuffed chairs with the cat purring on her lap and smiled reminiscently. Imagine a cat ever daring to cross the threshold of the house where I grew up in. At that time, it made no difference to Grace one way or another, but now she found it comforting to hear a cat purring in loud approval while she stroked it.

When my children are big enough, I am going to let them have pets! Lily heard a sharp intake of breath behind her and turned to stare at Grace. Why had her face gone ashen? Why was she holding the cat against her as if she was in need of comfort?

"Is something the matter, Grace?"

"I'll be okay."

The cat reached up to touch her cheek and snuggled up right under her chin.

What if Alice is crying; what if Alice is hurt? What if she is sick with a high fever and I don't even know about it?

She absently stroked the cat's soft fur, What if she feels like I abandoned her and is wounded forever because of my heartlessness.

Lily prayed that God would comfort the vulnerable girl. It would be so nice if she could keep from fleeing upstairs as she sometimes did when these moods hit her.

As Lily placed the quilting supplies on the table, she smiled, relieved.

Grace was getting in control of her emotions; she gently placed Puss on the floor, turned towards the window and dried her eyes with the hanky that was in the pocket of her dark blue skirt.

The two women placed blocks into a pattern while fragrant bean soup bubbled on the back of the kitchen stove, and the yeasty aroma of bread rising filled the air.

The peaceful atmosphere could be soothing and Lily wished it would encircle Grace's heart. She felt thoughtful; the younger woman loved the Lord, so why did such despair fill her soul from time to time?

After all these months of living under the same roof as her daughter-in-law, Lily still wondered what caused the girl such deep heartache. She was reasonably certain it was more than just the fact Randall was still in jail, so what could it be?

The little cottage was quiet save for the muted ticking of the clock or a log in the stove disintegrating from time to time..

Grace looked at the geranium that was blooming more profusely now that the days were longer. It added a friendly touch, so different from the dull, austere atmosphere where she had grown up.

I'm going to make home a cheery place for Emily, and she added firmly, inaudibly, Lord willing, for Alice to, as soon as possible.

Lily rose to put the nicely rounded loaves of rising bread into the preheated oven then continued to cut cloth pieces.

Grace picked up Emily who had finished her nap and was ready to play. She placed the baby on a folded blanket and handed her the string of colored spools that she delighted in. Grace watched her, a tender smile caressing her features. Lily noticed the faraway look in the girl's eyes.

"You've had a hard life," Grace observed quite unexpectedly. Maybe that is why her hair is snowy white!

Lily looked surprised. "Me? I have a good life! I enjoyed winter so much since I had a pleasant companion to keep me company, it went so fast."

Grace blushed but pressed on; "But you have," she insisted.

Lily's look softened, "It's not me that has had a hard life but Ben. I'm just the one that has been there for him all these years."

Grace would have protested but Lily looked like she wanted to continue so held her peace.

"Ben finds it difficult to share what happened during the war," Lily sighed and fiddled with a spool of thread. "If it wasn't for the horrendous nightmares I would have very little idea what went on during those dark years when he was gone. When he wakes up screaming and talking agitatedly then he will open up some."

She absently placed another spool on top of one on the table.

When the silence grew too long, Grace inserted a comment. "But you suffered too; you lost your--- babies."

Lily nodded and placed another squat, wooden spool on the pile. "It was my anguish that caused me to turn back to God, though. Sure I cried al lot, but I could tell it was healing tears."

She reached for a fourth spool and rearranged the setup. "He blamed himself for the babies dying; said he should have gone out before the storm closed in to fetch the doctor; said if he could have provided better, the babies would have survived...oh, all kinds of things."

Emily was fussy so Grace picked her up, and swayed back and forth while stroking the little one's back.

A heavenly radiance touched Lily's serene features. "It may seem like that to you: that I have suffered, but Jesus has been there for me. He has truly been a source of joy and comfort. I've been hoping you would find it like that, also. You seem to be carrying heavy burdens."

"Ya, I know I should pray more but it's just that I feel so guilty about—about--"

Grace clamped her mouth shut then leapt up to, to, what should I do, she noticed the pencil in her hand, so went to sharpen it with a kitchen knife. That was close! That was way too close for comfort! What would Lily have done if I blurted out that I left a baby in Halifax? What would she have said to me?

Grace shuffled the pieces of uncut fabric in an effort to keep her face averted. She spotted some cute pieces of flannel with fat elephants on it, and longed to make matching crib blankets for her two little girls. Oh, if only I could!

She imagined making one in secret while Lily slept or something, but knew that was impossible, because Lily would notice the missing cloth—as if there would even be enough for two covers!

She chose a piece of calico print left over scraps from an apron her mother-in-law still used.

It gave her a warm, fuzzy feeling to think of Lily wrapping it around small Randall's arms while saying their goodbyes to guests at the door.

Grace hoped anew that the conversation would drift in such a way that she could maybe open up just a little. As the silence grew longer, her heart beat faster.

Lily got up to put the sewing project away and laid out ingredients for making pies.

"Grace, would you mind if I asked you one little question?"

Grace's heart squeezed, but she nodded.

"I know you have accepted Jesus as your Saviour, but have you found Him to be your Comforter?

Grace blanched. Oh, this is the perfect opportunity to share. It's perfect, it's perfect...it's too perfect! I can't, I just can't! I might lose her friendship, her respect, her love even! They might kick me out!

"My Comforter? Not really. I am so troubled by things that happened in the past, but I can't share. I'm sorry, Mom, it's too awful; maybe someday but not yet." She had started working the lard into the flour mixture for making piecrusts, but her hands fell idle.

Lily reached out to wrap her arms around her, but Grace turned and stumbled to her room. The sound of her footfalls ended when a door shut.

Lily shook her head. *This is going on so long. Lord, please do something to help break her shell.* The startled baby wailed and Lily sought to give her the comfort she wished to bestow on the broken-hearted young mother.

As Lily rocked the baby back and forth in her arms, she went over the conversation in her mind.

Mom? Did she really call me Mom? This may seem like a setback, but the icy wall behind which Grace is trying to hide is slowly melting!

She plodded up the stairs and put the now sleeping baby beside Grace on the bed.

Grace was facing towards her when she entered the room, so Lily slipped a handkerchief out of her apron pocket and used it to brush the tears trickling down Grace's cheeks.

"Care to talk about it?"

"Oh, I wish I could. It's such a crushing burden I can hardly bear it any longer."

Lily sat down beside her and gently rubbed her back, but after Grace got herself more under control, she changed the subject.

"Mom, mind if I ask you something? Why was Randall put in gaol?"

Her mother-in-law's jaw dropped. "Do you mean you don't know?"

"You told me?'

"Why, yes, I definitely told you. Didn't you get my letter?"

Grace looked shamefaced. "You mean the one you sent me while I was in Nova Scotia? Yeah, I did, but I was too upset to finish reading it."

Lily's heart was in her eyes. She moved over to the dresser and picked up the gilded brush, a gift from Randall, and ran her hand over the soft bristles.

"Randall feels real bad about what happened. He was intoxicated. Did you know that?"

Grace hung her head, "I guessed as much. Did, does he drink much?"

Lily was silent for a moment, but then she sighed heavily. "He didn't used to...before the war..."

"But about what happened: I guess he never stopped to think that that a heavy beer stein could do so much damage."

Grace gasped:. "What happened?"

"He was angry--furious to be more exact at what this man said to him, so swung the mug at his head. The man just keeled over and collapsed to the floor. He was in a coma for several weeks before----"

Grace gasped; "He died?"

Lily shook her head, "--Before they knew if he would survive orsuffer brain damage. The jury thought it would serve Randall right if he stayed in the pen until Tom came out of his coma."

"Has he yet: what if he doesn't? What had this Tom fella said to make Randall so upset?"

Lily seemed focused on rearranging the things on Grace's dresser.

Grace leaned forward, "Please tell me."

Lily looked at her out of the corner of her eye before answering: "We don't want no crazy limey prostitutes around here'!"

Grace's face whitened. She clutched her pillow. "He said that? This, this Tom guy said--that?"

Lily nodded. "And Randall saw red. He was swinging mad: he wouldn't, to quote Randall, 'have anyone--let alone a slobbering drunk say bad things about my Grace'."

Grace looked overwhelmed with shock. Lily eyed her hesitantly for a moment then laid the brush down and headed back downstairs so as not to awaken the baby. Grace soon followed and collapsed into a kitchen chair.

"For me! He did that for me?" she looked horrified. "And I gave up my bab--" She clapped her hand over her mouth.

Lily gave her a keen look, which turned to frustration but didn't probe. Grace eased a circle of dough into a pie plate and with nervous haste tried to crimp it.

"Leave it, just leave it, if you need time to be alone," Lily soothed.

Grace groaned in anguish as she stepped into her boots, grabbed her chore jacket, and hurried outside.

Lily could see her quickly, agitatedly pacing down the rutted lane then cutting off into a field. It'll be hard trekking in all that mud. Her round, kindly face seemed troubled. Grace's whole life has been hard. Oh, if only she would share so I can help ease the burden. What can be so terrible that she absolutely refuses to get it off her chest? What did she mean by 'I gave up my bab...' baby? No, that's impossible. It was bab, not ba, besides Emily is right here sweetly sleeping with fluffy pillows tucked around her: which reminds me, I'll need to check if she is awake soon. She is old enough to tumble off the bed.

Lily mixed the sugar-cinnamon mixture with the apples in her favorite green bowl then spooned it into the crust. She covered it with another thin layer of dough.

Was she about to use some quaint British phrase? They really do have a hard-to-understand accent at times. Was she about to say 'I gave up my birthright: my boyfriend?

"Oh Heavenly Father, no, no not that," she cried in anguish. Did she have someone else who dearly loved her over in England, but jilted him because Randall charmed her off her feet? That would make the most sense of anything I've tried to figure out so far.

Is she bitterly regretting corning over to Canada--this primitive, lonely land—and being bound for life to a prisoner? I've never given it a thought! What shame and anguish it must be causing her.

Lily's eyes followed Grace's stumbling footsteps as long as she could. Please, God, may there be a breakthrough soon. This burden is too much for such a young girl to carry.

A Brave Decision

CHAPTER 34

"Dear Margaret, I have changed my mind."

Grace stared at the words then crossed them out. *No, that's too blunt; I can't just plunge in that way.*

She tore out another sheet of paper from her notebook. When it loosened other pages, she grimaced.

"Dear David and Margaret,
How are you all? I haven't heard from you in a long time." (Whew, that's better. *Now if I can only slow down my writing so it would be more legible.*)

She sat back and tapped on the ink blotter. *What can I write to make it seem I'm not as desperate as I really am?*

She leaned forward: How was your Christmas? Did you do anything special? I suppose you had a gala affair at David's folks. That must have been so exciting for the children.

She couldn't wait any longer to get to the point:

"It seems like it is high time to get my babby back." ('No that's not right, oh forget it, it is how I feel,' she left it.)

Please write as soon as possible to see what can be arranged.
I'll write later, when I can collect my thoughts better.
Love, Grace

P.S. This is my address for now:

Grace Sutherland
c/o Benjamin Sutherland
Rural Route 1
Russet, Alta

Should I put a phone number on? No, better not; who knows how many neighbours might be rubbernecking and then the gossip will explode.

She carefully folded it into thirds, and then because no one was looking pressed a single kiss on the stationary. It never occurred to her until much later that Margaret would worry that she hadn't written Mrs. Randall Sutherland on the envelop which was how most married women signed their names.

Lily noticed that Grace was scampering down the stairs like a colt or rather a happy-go-lucky teenage. She placed the iron to rest on its heel and waited expectantly to see what made the young lady so enthused.

"Mother, do you have a stamp and an envelope?"

"No dear, but you could ask Ben." She saw Grace's face cloud over. "We never keep extra stamps around. I don't know why: it's just Ben's way I guess."

Grace pressed her hand against her forehead; a*sk* Father? Ben? How could I? He's been griping and complaining a lot about the price of groceries as it is. He makes me feel like I eat too much, but I feel like I eat like a bird. I'm skinnier now than I was under rationing in England!

She walked out of the room. When Lily rang the dinner bell an hour and a half later, Grace waited apprehensively while Ben washed up at the enamel basin in the corner then found his place at the table.

"Uh, Ben I was wondering could I have a stamp, please."

"A stamp?" Ben's pale, shaggy eyebrows lowered. "Whatever do you need a stamp for? Are you planning to run off or something? I don't have any right now."

"She hasn't written her mother in a long time," Lily gently reminded her husband, but he kept on cutting his steak as if he had not heard her.

Grace fiddled with her fork. I haven't ever written her since coming to the farm. It's not her that I want to write, though, she doesn't care what happens to me. I wonder how Lily would react if I told her that? She would be so shocked!

Grace finished eating in silence and then went over to the window. It looked cold and bleak outside.

I need to get stamps. If it wasn't so far to town, I'd walk. It couldn't be more than five miles. I'll bundle up good. Grace was sorely tempted and for a several minutes considered it but reluctantly decided it would not be wise.

Grace was in a brown study for the rest of the day dreaming and scheming up ways to get to town and buy those all-important stamps but it seemed so futile.

Cutting Gossip

CHAPTER 35

Lily overheard a conversation at the country store that burdened her heart but she decided never to tell Grace. Not long afterwards, her loved ones noticed that she was quieter and the sparkle was gone from her eyes.

While in the store, she had been reaching for more spices, happily anticipating the response to her delicious Raisin Spice Cake, when loud voices from the next aisle caught her attention. When she heard Dorthea Witney's strident voice her hand paused in mid-air. *What could she be up to now?*

"Did you hear that Tom had taken a turn for the worse?"

"Tom, Tom---Who?"

"You know Tom Blacken, that big boulder of a fellow who got the Sutherland lad mad a while back."

"Oh, him: that red-haired fella that married a foreigner."

"Yes, from that Sutherland family. Tom has been in the hospital all these months now, but they don't think they can help him anymore. It's that strep thing that he got."

"Who would have ever thought a son of Lily Sutherland could have a temper like that! I wonder what ole Tom said anyway."

"No one knows for sure, but it was sure no excuse to hit Tom so hard."

Lily quietly put the tin of nutmeg back on the shelf and tried to slip off, but the voices followed her.

"Randall always was somewhat of a rascal. He was booted out of the army, remember? Nobody is ever kicked out without a very good reason. I wonder why he wasn't sent to the penitentiary long ago."

"Well, Tom's not lily-white either, it takes two make a fight."

Someone exaggerated the rumor about Tom taking a turn for the worse , but something strange *was* going on in room 209.

Last night Tom Blacken had been so agitated that the nurses put the sides up on his bed. He was also aggressive and rude so the doctor prescribed a sedative... after tying him down! For such a big, hulk of a man to be thrashing around and cursing, or whatever he was saying, in a semi-conscious state was disturbing, to say the least.

"He should be shipped off to a psychiatric ward," one of the younger nurses moaned. The nearest one was in Ponoka, more than a days' journey away: not a good option.

By hushed agreement no nurse went into his room alone to change him or his bedding, they always arrived in pairs. They were leery of those big, meaty fists and foul mouth.

"Vrrand! Vrrand!"

The nurses hung back, staring at each other, "What is he trying to say?"

"Vrrand, Vrrand'l, " he roared, and in his agitation, the blankets twisted around him or slid to the floor.

His big, heavyset dad lumbered over to him. "What do you want, boy?" The old man had been vigilant about showing his face but no one else did.

"Zee hain't no. Zee hain't no. Rand! Can ye ear me! Zee hain't nocrazylimeyprostitute!"

The young man's dilemma increased because no one understood his mutterings. Someone suggested he might be calling for Randall Sutherland.

"Get that Sutherland boy in," Hank Blacken suggested; "Let Tom get it off his chest whateber he is trying to say."

Looks of consternation crossed the circle of faces clustering near the door, but it didn't stop their tongues, not for long at least.

"But he's in jail! Won't that upset the patient more?"

"Sutherland is in shackles, that'll bring back angry memories"---

"Tom's um, mental state is quite fragile at this time"--

"Vrrand! Rand! Vrrandall!"

The doctor sighed. "Looks like if we want Blacken to calm down we will have to."

Hank Blacken nodded. "He ain't gonna settle if he can't get it off his chest whateber's bothering him."

He awkwardly pulled Tom's blanket straight. "Wish Mary was 'ere," he half-muttered. "She'd a-known how to calm the boy down." Mary had died ten years earlier.

The nurses looked sympathetically at him before filing silently out. The doctor and Tom's dad eyed each other.

"I'll see what I can do about making arrangements." The physician wrote something on his notepad before continuing his rounds.

Randall looked pale, thin and pathetic when he shuffled in two days later, heavily handcuffed. He kept his eyes to the floor certain that everyone was still blaming him for Tom's injury.

A look of relief broke across Tom's face when he recognized Randall. "She ain't nocrazylimeyprostitute." He slurred trying his hardest to make himself understood.

Randall's face softened. He had caught the patient's words, although everyone else looked blank. "Could you say it slower?"

With great effort, Tom ground out the words. "She- ain't-no-crazy-limey-prostitute."

Tom's dad looked pale. "What-who is he talking about?"

"My wife," Randall replied quietly, "my beautiful Grace."

More than one person looked sheepish.

"Flames o' hell," Tom panted, beads of sweat popping out on his forehead:"Lickin' at ma heels. Don't want that on ma conscience."

Two nurses straightened Tom's covers while another one offered him a drink.

Randall was marched out of the hospital room without any more ado. He wondered bleakly if the confession would even help shorten his sentence.

Spider Watching

CHAPTER 36

Randall sat with his elbows on his knees and watched a spider quickly, deftly spin a web against the corner of the wall. He was intrigued with its swift movements so rose to get a closer look.

Wow, that's amazing. That's really neat. How does she so quickly know where to put each thread? He wished he had a magnifying glass so he could see how she clamped the silken threads together to keep them from falling.

Randall paced, hands behind his back. Fearfully and wonderfully made, the words popped into his mind from somewhere; they sounded sort of Biblical.

He stopped mid-stride and swung back to check on the progress of the spider's web. It was developing rather close to the dusty, and thoroughly neglected Bible on the shelf so instinctively moved the Holy Word out of harms reach.

The Bible hung loosely between him hands while he sank back onto the cot without putting it down.

Fearfully and wonderfully made, why did that strange phrase lurk in his mind? He leafed aimlessly through the thin pages. That delicate web is a fantastic creation; maybe God feels the same way about me. Am I fearfully and wonderfully mad? His head sank into his hand as he pondered the next thought: if so, for what purpose?

Randall eyes focused on the beam of sunlight streaming through a high window. I wonder if He really thinks about me or if He just set me in motion like a wind-up toy then turned to focus on other more important things.

He rubbed his finger along the faded gold edge of the Bible then opened it. To his surprise, he found a page of topics right at the front with verses under each heading. After running his finger along the list, to see if anything would catch his attention, chose the one entitled salvation and looked up the references.

One especially impressed him. John 3:16 For God so loved the world that He gave His only begotten Son that whosoever believeth on Him should not perish but have everlasting life.

While keeping his finger on the page Randall decided to check on the spider once again. It had already captured an obviously panicking fly. That disturbed Randall although he refocused on the Bible. Deep in his heart, Randall felt like he also was in bondage like the fly and not just because he was in jail. He felt trapped and wondered if there was any way of escape.

Randall read the verse silently like a thirsty man trying to squeeze moisture from a sponge while in the arid desert. He repeated it aloud. His brow furrowed, there is a message in here for me, but what is it? He lay down on the rumpled cot and with his hands behind his head, stared at the water-blotched ceiling.

"Lord, help me to understand," he pleaded. He had the verse practically memorized by now so tried saying it by inserting his own name for the words 'the world'.

For God so loved Randall... For God so loved Randall Benjamin Sutherland that He gave His only begotten Son;-Why in the world would He do that... that whosoever believeth on Him shall not perish but have everlasting life.

Randall grimaced: I feel so dense. Why is it so hard to comprehend? Lord, help me to understand. Help me to believe. Believe what? His shoulders sagged as he carefully laid the Bible on the floor beside him.

That night he went to bed without any clear answers but a yearning to connect with God.

Stony Disapproval

CHAPTER 37

The familiar tread of the jail keeper plodding down the hall penetrated his consciousness but Randall chose to ignore it. He looked up when a key rattled in the hated lock.

"Your time is up, Sutherland," there was an unexpected note of gentleness in the prison officer's voice, "Try and keep out of trouble, son." Apparently, Thomas Blacken was home from the hospital.

Randall's hazel eyes widened. Does he think I guilty? If so, he never let on before today.

Randall looked around the familiar cell and panicked. How will I ever face the real world? Everyone will look down at me or walk on the other side of the street if they see me coming. How can I stand such coldness?

What about Grace: Surely, she will be ashamed of me. I have been in this 'cage' all these months and I'm no more ready to face the future than I was earlier.

Randall accepted the parcel of civilian clothes the jailer handed to him. He shook them out after the door closed behind him. My old familiar plaid shirt and Levis, he mused. He was dismayed at how limply the clothes hung around his thin, almost gaunt figure. Well, the food was nothing to write home about.

He sighed. To start with, I'll have to call someone for a ride. With my luck a half dozen people will be rubbernecking just when the phone rings. If even one person finds out, the whole community will know by nightfall that Randall Sutherland is out of jail.

Later Randall was surprized at how blinding the sun was; his eyes smarted.

On the dirt side road leading into town, he spotted a horse drawn wagon and soon recognized it as theirs..

Ben went in to purchase a few household items then without looking at his son, moved across the road to load chicken feed and a bag of milk replacer into the back of the wagon.

Randall leaned against the side of the Russet General store and idly watched him. Stony disapproval from Dad was nothing new. I wish I could have slipped home some other way without calling Dad. Maybe if I was just 'there' making myself useful he would not feel so annoyed with me.

A couple vehicles pulled up to the pumps and Randall recognized the drivers, they turned their faces away, or at least he supposed they had. He thought about joining the other men inside the store for a coffee while waiting, but hung back. He did not want to be recognized: not yet.

Twenty minute later Mr. Sutherland pulled up in front of the store. Randall had nothing at all to load up, so just hopped on the bench beside his father.

Neither of them said a word, not even 'howdy'. Without thinking, Randall's eyes strayed towards the two-story hotel as the horse plodded past.

Ben's hands tightened on the reins, "Don't even think of touching that filthy stuff again! Haven't you learned your lesson?

Randall clenched his jaw in an effort to hold back the fiery retort that leaped to his lips: No point in tangling with Dad if it can be avoided.

Mr. Sutherland had had plenty of time to mull over his disappointment with his one and only son. The lecture he had so often rehearsed leaped to his lips before they reached the outskirts of town.

Randall and his Dad were shouting at each other by the time they turned down the long farm lane. Randall's handsome face was white and taunt, his fists clenched; Ben's was red and his steely blue eyes flashed venom.

Grace ran to the door when she saw the horses through the window, but the fierceness of their anger stunned her. They brushed past her still fighting.

Emily was in her arms, arms and legs pumping frantically as her terrified wails pierced the air.

Lily took one look at her beloved men then slumped against the stove, groaning softly, the soup ladle dripping from her hand.

Randall whirled towards Grace. "Pack our bags, Grace! We're leaving!"

"NO!" The cry leaped from both women's lips.

"Please, Randall," Grace stepped closer, entreatingly, "Wait until you find a job, or at least until after dinner."

" No! I'm fed up. I can't take it anymore. We're going""

"I'm not having no————-under my roof!" Ben interrupted.

"But what about the baby," Lily pleaded. "It's cold out there, it's-"

Randall's look softened. "I'll take good care of her—of both of you—I promise!"

Ben laughed harshly: "As if that was possible!" He was too angry to stop to think how cruel that sounded.

Randall looked entreatingly at his wife then at his Mother. "See what I mean? I have to go!"

"But it's like winter out there! Where will you go? How will you go?"

"I'll ask Gary—"

"Gary?"

"Gary Palmer. You know. He didn't go to war because his father has heart trouble."

"Oh didn't you hear? His father died last summer and Dot went to live near her daughter in Toronto. Gary sold the farm and went into business which he always preferred anyway."

"Maybe I could borrow the wagon just to get to the Deer Flats train station."

"You'll do no such thing!" Ben growled. "Chances are you'd leave it in a broken down state beside the road somewhere!"

Which is ridiculous, Randall thought.

Grace felt dizzy from shock. Lily rescued the baby. They leaned against each other overwhelmed with dismay.

Ben took one look at them then stomped out the back door, mentally berating himself for making Lily so distressed, but too proud to admit it.

Emily's cries were subsiding. Grace took her from her grandmother and offered her some of the chicken noddle soup her they had been planning to eat. No one was hungry, not even the baby.

"Life is so awful," she said.

When Ben stomped out of the house slamming the door behind him, Lily brushed past Randall, snatched her shawl off the hook and rushed after him.

Grace stared at Randall, her mouth dry. What was happening to him? He seemed to be frozen to the spot, his eyes glazing over, "Randall, Randall," she called just as he fell convulsing on the floor.

Emily added her own screeches to the din. I can't handle that right now. Grace fled to the living room and thrust the screaming baby into the crib then fell to her knees beside the still writhing form of her husband,

"Randall," she yelled, "Stop it, stop it! You're going to hurt yourself!"

In an instant, Lily was at her side and forcing a six-inch ruler between his teeth to keep him from biting his tongue.

"He's having an epileptic seizure," Lily explained, "that's why he was sent home from the army."

They were so relieved when it stopped and without even seeing them, Randall stumbled over to the couch and fell into the sleep of the exhausted.

Grace sank back on her heels. "That was terrifying! What is epilepsy? I never saw a person with it before. When did he get it?"

Grace noticed that Lily was looking rather peaked herself. "I'm not used to it, either. It never happened when he was little. A concussion on the battlefield triggered the seizures so he was sent home."

"So he wasn't deported in disgrace."

"Oh, is that what you thought?

Lily sagged into one of the armchairs.. "No wonder you so often have a worried, faraway look in your eyes. Some think it is a disgrace," she continued speaking although her eyes had fallen shut. "That's why we never talk about it. Ben takes it very personally. He thinks he failed as a father that a son of his would have---that kind of a problem." The gold and white cat leaped on her lap and she absently stroked it.

Emily's cries were subsiding. Grace felt wrung out. Impulsively she pulled on her blue plaid woolen jacket and stepped into her gumboots.

Lily opened her eyes.

"Where are you going?"

"To talk to--Ben."

"I don't think that's a good idea."

Grace hesitated.

"But it's up to you." She got up to spoon the soup into glass quart jars and placed them in the icebox.

Grace closed the door behind her. It seemed like every step dragged as she slushed her way through the snow to the barn. The dog came and nuzzled her hand; she seemed to know something was wrong.

Ben was leaning against the pitchfork deep in thought.

Grace curled her fingers around one of the stanchions. The nearest cow swished its tail at her, she hardly noticed. Her favorite calf bawled out a greeting.

"I suppose you think it's all my fault."

Grace started. "What?"

Ben didn't repeat himself.

Grace stroked the dog's fur. "I don't know what to think."

Ben sighed and thrust the fork deeper into a pile of hay. "I'm not cut out for this 'Dad' business.

Grace bit her lip. *Is Randall?*

"Seems like everything I say rubs him the wrong way."

Grace agreed, she felt like yelling at him.

"Bet he thinks I don't like him."

"Well, do you?" Grace felt the color drain from her cheeks. *Did I really say that? That wasn't a Christ-like thing to say.*

Ben hung up the pitchfork and stomped off.

Grace looked around feeling helpless. *Are we really going to leave this, all of this because of a little spat?*

She remembered how difficult it had been tunneling through the wildernesses of Ontario just her and the baby and it looked like she would be launching out into the unknown once again this time with Randall. Would that be better—or worse? She sighed and murmured: for better or worse til death do us two part.

She trudged back to the house, the dog at her heels.

Randall was still sleeping. So was Emily. Lily was in the kitchen but looked sad.

Grace picked up the embroidery project she had been working on then laid it down. She leafed through a storybook borrowed from one of the neighbors. Why did I think this would be interesting? She went upstairs and lay on the bed, staring up at the ceiling and wondered what the future would hold, and then went downstairs to finish the ironing. I'm not packing until he insists.

When Randall roused, he appeared dazed and looked around, puzzled. Grace rested the iron on its heel and came over to the couch where he was laying. She knelt down and brushed the hair off his forehead.

"Welcome home, Randall."

A new look came into her husband's eyes. At first, there was a sparkle but then it faded. He leaned his head back against the armrest.

She continued caressing his stubbly chin. Emily was sitting on the floor nearby. She watched them intently, not knowing why Mommy seemed so interested in this stranger.

Randall sighed and swung his feet over the side of the sofa.

"Well, I guess we should be going."

"Randall please wait: talk it over with your Dad when you are both calmer. Give us a few days at least."

Randall's shoulders sagged, "This goes deep, Grace, really deep. I haven't been able to get along with him for years. I could never win his approval."

Grace's heart squeezed with she looked at the pain-lined face. He walked over to the window: "The snow is melting rapidly. Much of it should be gone by tomorrow."

"What will you do, what can you do?"

"Dad hates me." He got up and strode across the room, hands behind his back. "It would be better to go while the going is good. We never could see eye-to-eye. Maybe if I would get out from under his thumb--his prejudices against me--I could prove to him I'm not a piece of junk"—

It felt like a dozen protests sprung to Grace's lips but all she said was "You shouldn't be so impulsive," then found out instantly it was the wrong thing to say.

Anger flashed into his eyes. Without another word, he gave her an unyielding look while storming out of the small farmhouse.

Grace took that to mean he had made up his mind: they would have to go; they would have to leave the home where she had found so much security and contentment in the last several months.

She would have to leave all that was familiar and go with a stranger who already showed signs of being quick tempered and had the strange, unfamiliar disease of epilepsy.

What should she take? What could she take?' They were not prepared to start up housekeeping on their own.

Lily had gone to her bedroom to finish her nap. Now she came into the living room stifling a yawn. Their eyes connected and there was instant empathy.

"I will miss you," Grace said.

Lily put her arm around her shoulder. "We'll need to pray for each other. Prayer can change things."

"But will it?"

Lily nodded. She used the corner of her calico print apron to brush a tear off Grace's cheek before continuing.

"I have found Jesus to be completely trustworthy. And steady. I've gone through enough dark times in life to know He will always be near to help and comfort."

Grace nodded. It would be nice to have that kind of faith. Maybe I'll have it when I am at old as Mom.

"I want to believe," her voice trembled, "I feel so lonely and afraid already and we haven't even left. I don't know what I'd do without God."

"It needn't be too bad," Lily comforted. "Randall loves you, I know that, and Emily is such a sweet little thing. She will bring you much joy."

"You're still young, make it an adventure."

Grace nodded bleakly. "Well, I guess I had better start packing."

Grace assumed Lily would follow her upstairs into the bedroom, but she had other plans. She ducked into the shed nearby and came back with several slightly damaged but usable wooden crates.

"Oh, I won't need them!" Grace exclaimed. "I just have my suitcase to pack and the baby's things...and oh yes, Randall's clothes."

Lily looked at her sadly. "You have nothing, dear."

"What do you mean?"

"No bedding, no towels, not anything."

Grace's face fell. What would they do? Her throat tightened at the thought of Randall having an epilepsy spell in the middle of nowhere. How would she ever know what to do?

Lily placed a box on the table and reached into the china cabinet for a dainty teacup and matching saucer. Grace's eyes widened: it was the one with the pink roses on it.

Just last week when Grace had been murmuring about how lovely it was, Lily told her it used to belong to her grandmother. It was a treasured heirloom! Lily reached for another set and placed it on the table then added two neatly embroidered tea towels. They were made from bleached and hemmed flour sacks, but were so white Grace would have never guessed it if Lily would not have told her.

"Oh, Mother, what are you doing?"

Lily smiled then lifted a steaming loaf of bread out of the oven. When it was cool enough to pry out of the pan, she wrapped it in one of the tea towels and the two cups and saucers in the other one.

"Oh, Mother," Grace swallowed a lump in her throat, "You are giving your best."

However, Lily was not finished. She stacked the blue enamel dish set that they did not use anymore in the crate along with some extra cutlery in still another homemade tea towel then went into the woodshed for another box.

Grace stared as Lily tucked in two fat fluffy pillows and a matching sheet and pillowcase set. Lastly, she stuffed some of Grace's favorite recipes in the cracks around the edges. Gratitude shone in her eyes.

"You're being so good to me. How can I ever repay you?"

Lily's eyes were sad. "I wish I could do more, so much more."

She went into the living room and gathered up the partly finished quilt-top and, after pinning the unsewn pieces together, wrapped them into the finished part, .then lifted down an elegant covered casserole dish painted a soft rose and white and filled it with bars of fragrant soap that she and her sister Elizabeth had made. She added some wash clothes, and tucked towels and the quilt around the casserole dish. That should give it enough protection.

"You're sending stuff that's almost too pretty and delicate for the lifestyle we may be living," Grace demurred. "You should keep it for yourself."

"That's why you need it, Grace," Lily stated looking directly into her eyes. "Even if you just keep some of these things, like the teacups, on a shelf most of the time, just having them will bring you comfort: a women needs beauty surrounding her."

"After you have the quilt top pieced," she continued, "make yourself a cozy comforter, for you will surely need it. I will send a bag of wool and extra material along. You remember how to tie a comforter?"

Grace nodded. "You taught me well. How will I manage without a quilting frame?"

"Use it as an excuse to befriend some of the neighbours."

Just then, the back door slammed. "Grace, are you ready?"

Grace gazed at her mother-in-law with mute appeal. Randall saw the look and rested his hand on the hand pump, his eyes fixed on the pine in the middle of the yard.

Lily reached into her own hope chest and removed a blue checkered and white baby blanket lovingly created for a boy.

"Here, take this," she urged. "It was Randall's but I want you to have it."

Grace protested that she should keep it as a memory, but Lily said she had other things.

"Besides it's a chilly day and Emily will need it on the way." She happened to be passing a window just then and caught a glimpse of the naked trees whipped around by a cutting wind. "It might be wise to put her into her snowsuit--if it still fits--even if it is May already."

Grace nodded. "She's getting so active that it would be hard keeping a blanket tucked around her."

"How big will she be before I get to see her again?" Lily's voice trembled.

Randall quietly packed the boxes and suitcases into the back of the wagon while the two women watched.

The plan was to bring the wagon just to the train station. Ben agreed to come along to bring it back. Grace hoped the atmosphere between them would be less frigid than the weather.

She scanned the yard one the last time. In the kitchen window facing the driveway, the dear old Tango geranium was blooming as faithfully as ever just as it had been the first time she entered the yard so many months ago.

Lily only occasionally picked up the sleek gold and white cat, but now Grace noticed that she was cuddling it in her arms. She will find Puss a poor substitute for the cuddly, dimpled baby.

The snow was melting in places and bright green grass had appeared. Wish I could be here to help Mom put in a garden, or shell peas, and weed. Wish Emily could learn about the world in the freedom and security of a country home under my and her grandma's watchful eye, she added prayerfully; . Wish Alice could get to know her grandmother!

Dixie leaned against Grace's legs, when she did not pay any attention; he nuzzled her hand and whined softly. Grace dropped to one knee and buried her head in the collie's fluffy mane. Her arm wrapped around Dixie's neck. "Sorry dog, I'm leaving: who knows how long till I'll be back." Dear God, help me to cope.

"Are you ready to go, Grace?"

Grace looked up and saw that although Randall's face was kind, it also seemed sad. She turned to Ben what was he thinking? Then it shocked her: he appears haggard!

Randall had Emily in his arms and after Grace climbed up onto the wagon seat he handed the baby to her.

Grace partially unzipped the snowsuit and removed the hood. Emily would definitely be too hot by the time they reached the train station.

Lily let the cat go and reached out to her granddaughter for one last hug. Grace awkwardly clung to Lily from her high perch then turned silently away to dab her eyes. Randall climbed up beside her and Ben took the reins and clicked to the horses. Grace's heart sank: they were off.

For the first few miles, they stopped repeatedly to adjust the supplies in the back. Because the road was so rough, the boxes shifted around and the contents were in danger of damage. Eventually, Randall found a couple medium sized boulders that he used to keep the containers from crashing into each other.

Grace felt like she had parked beside a scowling stone statue in the middle of winter. Although Emily babbled excitedly and waved her little hands in excitement at all the cows in the nearby pasture, it was hard to concentrate on her joyful antics when her own heart was heavy.

After a while, Randall gave her a half smile and said, "She's a lively little thing, isn't she?"

Grace nodded but Ben cleared his throat. Her hand folded around the old, soft bound Bible that Lily had given her. It was another family treasure, but that was only one reason it would be precious to Grace. Lily had marked many meaningful scriptures throughout the years. Grace was grateful, they would help her to find direction when she needed it.

When they were waiting near the kitchen door, Lily had pointed one verse out and put an eyelet and ribbon bookmark in the place.' Lo, I am with you always, even unto the end of the world: Matt. 28:20 b. Grace knew she would read it until memorized.

When she glanced from one cold face to the other, her spirit faltered.

It seemed like a long time until Deer Flats came into view. They would be no stopping there because it was a one-horse town and the train they were leaving on would arrive in Russet. Grace's eyes caressed the steepled church and the post office as the horse trotted along.

She drank in the scene of the General Store where she had shyly exchanged greetings with the storekeeper and some of the customers on more than one occasion. Now there would be no more opportunities to work on her bashfulness there, and get to know some of the friendlier neighbours.

As the horse plodded onwards, Grace had plenty of time to think with Ben acting so sullen and Randall's face averted as if he had never seen the passing fields before.

She thought of one of the many things Lily had told her.

"You've been like a daughter to me,"God sent you to take the place of the little girls I lost."

Grace swallowed a lump in her throat. How would Mom react if she knew I had denied her the privilege of getting to know and hold one of her little granddaughters? She stared bleakly at the small clouds skittering past.

'I wonder if Randall will let me write Margaret. Of course, he will, but then her face clouded over.

We might have no fixed address for a while. How will Margaret and I manage to keep in touch? Grace never asked for stamps again after that first rebuff. Margaret slipped in postage when she wrote but Grace had lost courage to announce to her in-laws that she had deserted her daughter.

Now that Randall is home, I'm sure he will let me write. Her brow furrowed. I wonder how they are all doing. I hope baby Alice is okay. It's not a good time to get her now, though. She pushed at a pile of melting snow by her boot, In fact, could there be a worse time.

The hostile silence hovering like a cloud around the three adults was getting thick, tangible, and it was making Randall mad. Ten minutes later, after he marched into the train station with the last of their baggage, he strode over to Ben and faced him nose to nose.

"Make sure you treat Mom better than you treat me!"

Ben looked startled but then a mask quickly covered his face. He whipped the horse so sharply that Randall had to leap to get out of the way.

Grace and Randall watched the wagon disappear down the quiet, country road then they turned to look at each other.

Grace let out the breath of air she had been unconsciously holding. They were alone. It felt strange.

She looked around the small train station with its well-oiled wooden floors. When she had arrived in Deer Flats, she had never actually gone into the building, which was little more than a one-room house. Russet's train station was bigger but still considerably different from the vast, bustling one back in Halifax.

Grace put Emily on the floor and she managed to scoot off to explore the most distant corner of the main room in no time flat. Soon more passengers were milling around so the young mother scooped up her protesting daughter to show her what was out the window. Ah, a post office: now's the time to send Margaret a letter!

Randall was sitting on one of the benches lining the sides of the walls. His elbows were on his knees and his hands cupped his chin. He nodded when she asked for money to buy stamps and generously pulled out a crisp two-dollar bill. His eyes seemed sad, troubled, but she was too excited to notice.

With the baby bouncing on her hip, Grace hurried across the street to make her purchases. First, she went into the Drug Store and chose some pretty stationary with matching envelopes, which she would use later, then indulged in purchasing some sweetly scented talc for herself, since she had run out of special fragrances, except for what Elizabeth had given her, long ago. At the last moment, she added a round pink rattle with a handle to her small assortment of items. Hopefully this will given Emily entertained for a little while.

Then she hurried over to the post office. "Do you have any postcards?"

"Aiin't got nuthin' fancy," He apologized. "Jist these plain black an' white ones."

"That's okay." She squeezed in as many words as possible to Margaret before affixing a stamp. Here was her chance to ask about Alice without anyone reading over her shoulder.

Grace longed to be part of her other daughter's life and just writing to the little one's foster mother brought back many memories.

After mailing the card, and while she was heading back to the train station, she caught sight of Randall striding across the street straight to the 'no minors' entrance at the hotel.

"Randall!" she called.

"I'll be back in a sec!"

She hurried across the dirt street and clutched his arm, "Please Randall," she pleaded, "Stay away from there."

He paused, mid-stride, his features softening: "Grace, I won't get much. I promise, but I'm wound up like a top. I need something to relax me."

She reached out her hand imploringly, but he turned on his heel and was gone. Grace stared angrily after him. How could he do this to us? We haven't even started our new life together and he wants to nurse a bottle!"

The mournful whistle of the train far in the distance echoed the cry of her heart. I hope he hurries. What will we ever do if we miss the train? She trudged back, head down and hardly noticed the baby's fingers tangled in her hair.

Her outlook was as bleak as the lowering clouds. Looks like I'm stuck with both the 'worse' and 'poorer' part of the marriage vow, and it's 'til death do us two part.'

My old school chum, Betsy suffered at the hands of a drunk in the family; will I have to endure that kind of misery, also? She wandered from one end of the platform to the other, lugging the heavy toddler, searching for Randall. Will he get back in time? Did he even care if they missed the train? He is so irresponsible —oh God, help me not to think that!

She tried to pray: Oh, Father, I'm not nearly as sweet and forgiving as his mother is, help me to change. Help me to have a gracious attitude.

She saw the billowing plume of smoke of the coming train so headed back in to the railroad station.

Her heart squeezed with fear while staring out of a coal-dust speckled window while Emily leisurely explored around the boots and pumps of congenial passengers.

The train came chugging in from one direction while Randall dashed in from another. Although he helped to load all their baggage, she refused to look at him. She snatched up the baby with less patience than she had ever shown before and slumped into a seat in one of the narrow cars.

Randall stumbled slightly as he made his way down the aisle and sank down beside her. Yah, he stank like beer. She shrank back against the window, feeling guilty for doing so.

Oh God, what is happening to me? I have never been so hurt and bitter, so angry in my life: not even at my mother! Hot tears stung her eyes. Help me; please help me not to be this way. I long to have peace with God; please give it back to me.

However, the hurt,, the disappointment, or was it even hatred would not go away so easily.

The battle raged in her heart while Randall snored drunkenly beside her. As she peered out the window, she felt even more uneasy. Twilight gave her an eerie feeling, especially when she was far from home.

A verse from the Bible was niggling at her conscience but it took a while before the Spirit got through to her. 'He that hates his brother is a murderer'. Surely, I don't hate him. I hate what he does, but not him...surely not! I'm just upset that he's acting so, so irresponsible. Other, more forceful words wanted to crowd in but she repressed them.

It made her squirm uncomfortably, hatred sounded like such an ugly, nasty sin. He that hates his brother is a murderer! That's what the Bible says. But Randall is being so immature...so inconsiderate. Grace twisted the handkerchief in her hands beyond recognition. 'Lord I don't want to feel like this, but he is acting like a drunken scoundrel. He doesn't have a job but is dragging us to who-knows-where.

'He that hates his brother"— that still, small voice just wouldn't leave her alone. 'But Randall is being so..."

She turned to glance at him, but he was still sleeping, fedora pushed low over his forehead.
Grace's chin trembled. It wasn't doing any good to try to reason with God, to justify herself.

The words came once again so forcefully: he that hates his brother is a murderer. Grace sucked in her breath, eyes widening. Then I am no better than he! I'm as guilty as he is! Although the thought was shocking, at the same time it was a relief. The next time Grace looked at Randall, although his eyes were not open, she sensed that he was awake. He looked so, so what was it? Worn-down? Vulnerable? Oh, Lord I'm sorry for these unkind thoughts, this bitterness and unforgiveness. I want to repent; I want to be a support to him. He doesn't need to repent any more than I do.

Randall stirred and opened his eyes. "Got anything for a headache?" She adjusted the sleeping child in her arms and pointed towards her purse. Randall reached across her to get it and their arms touched. He looked uncertainly at her. Grace smiled. "Your mother sent a thermos of coffee along. It's in the overhead carrier." He tossed some aspirins into his mouth followed by the still warm coffee. When Randall got up to walk around, Emily woke so Grace asked him if he would hold her, she felt she needed a nap. She watched him with a renewed feeling of tenderness before drifting off to sleep.

In the middle of nowhere, they stopped at a town Grace had never heard of before. Before she could panic and wonder what they would ever do to make a living, Randall strode over to the counter to browse through train schedules.

Her heart sank; they would be getting on a westbound train instead of east, which meant they would be even further away from Baby Alice. What would it take to get her back?

Grace stared ahead of her as if willing her mind to conjure up an image of The Other Baby. 'Please God; I need to see my dear baby again. I need Alice, Emily deserves to know her twin sister, help me to know what to do to reunite them. Lord, it seems so impossible right now, but you can make it work: please, please work a miracle. I know you care about her, about us, and I want so much to be a happy, *united,* family.

Randall looked at her quizzically from time to time but didn't ask what she was on her mind.

They had been traveling through the mountains for a long time when the lights of a small town gleamed through the window.

"Golden B.C," the conductor called. Grace felt sad as they collected their belongings and clambered out. Does he think there will be golden opportunities here? While surveying the bleak landscape: the ice covered river: she hardly thought so. Why couldn't they have moved to Edmonton or some other city where there would be more job opportunities?

Emily chose that moment to wail her protest at the long and tiresome journey.

Grace cringed when she caught the stares of the dark-coated crowd milling around in the lamplight but tried her best to soothe the very cross infant.

The light dressing of snow left her feet feeling cold.

"We'll go to a hotel for tonight," Randall announced, leading the way to an awaiting taxi. The driver and Randall did all the unloading of their stuff. Most of it would remain at the station for the present. Fortunately, it was easy to find a hotel with a 'no vacancy' sign since it was early April.

Grace had her arms full with the screaming child.

After settling into their hotel room, Randall got out the pot of beans. It was barely warm but he ate hungrily. Grace was hungry, too, but she hardly had a chance to eat. The baby just wouldn't settle.

Randall threw his fork down and glared at them.

"Is that kid going to howl all night? I need to sleep."

"I'm trying the best I can," Grace tried to keep an edge out of her voice. "Her gum is very red and sore, so on top of everything else she's teething.

"I wish I would have thought to bring along the Wonder Oil."

Randall sighed. "Well, I guess we'll have to put up with her crying then. It's too late to pick up anything at the store. Is she still hungry?"

Grace looked down. "I don't think she's tolerating these beans very well. I can give her the other half of the banana if it's not too mushy by now and graham wafers soaked in formula, but then what will she have for breakfast?

"Well, I for one will try and get some sleep."

"WAAA! WAAAH!"

"If that's possible," He changed into his pajamas and pulled the blanket over his head.

The exhausted young mother tried to soothe the fretful child, but how her arms ached: and her head: and her back, but most of all her heart. Grace prayed a lot that night, although troubled she sensed the Lord's presence was near and it comforted her.

In the wee, small hours of the morning, she laid Emily on the bed they had made for her on the floor and crawled in beside Randall.

Just as she was drifting off to sleep, the baby began crying again so she tucked the warm little body close to her own then they both slept well- until Randall woke up screaming.

For the first time since Grace left Alice with Margaret, Grace admitted that it could have been a disaster if two babies had been screeching that night.

The next morning Grace gradually become aware that they weren't at the farmhouse anymore and someone else should be there. She didn't think much about it as she cuddled with Emily for a few minutes. After all, she was used to sleeping alone.

Oh, right, Randall was home, or rather back. Her eyes widened. Where was he? She was in a strange hotel room all alone: she had been abandoned!

After carefully slipping out of the bed, Grace flew to the window. Where was Randall? How long had he been gone? The sun was already visible behind the mountains!

The frightened young wife fell to her knees beside the bed and buried her head in her arms. 'Oh, God, oh God, help me, help me,' she begged.

Grace noticed her Bible lying on top of the folded clothes in her suitcase.

'Please God, please may there be something in here to comfort me, steady me.' The Bible fell open to where Lily had left the lovely croqueted bookmark: "lo I am with you always.' Always, even here? Even in Golden, B.C. With no means of support and no knowledge if or when my husband will come back? She read them repeatedly until the words stole into her heart, bringing comfort.

Grace laid the Bible aside, but with a continual prayer in her heart and with nothing else to do, shampooed her hair with the hotel provided shampoo.

Her watch stopped during the night but she was sure it was getting close to dismissal time. While her head was bent over the sink and her locks covered in suds, Emily woke up so Grace quickly finished what she was doing and changed the baby's nappy.

Although feeling very tense, Grace forced herself to comb her hair and freshen up. Soon she knew someone would come and tell her she must leave, but where would they go?

Someone knocked on the door: after unlocking it, she cautiously peered out.

She nearly collapsed. It was Randall. "Where have you been?" she demanded.

"Looking for work, of course! What did you think?"

"Take us with you," she begged, "They're going to kick us out soon!"

He turned on his heel. "Don't be so antsy. I just wanted to check on you but I gotta be going again. If I don't get back in time you can just, well...I will be back in time."

Grace grabbed his arm: "Why did you come to Golden of all places? There would have been far more opportunities in a city like Edmonton."

Had he really been looking for work, or was that just an excuse? Her eyes trailed after him as he swung off down the street. I never knew he would be so cold and abrupt with me. Does he even want me—us around? Our marriage relationship seems so strained. My premonition was right: two babies would have been a disaster.

She lifted her eyes to the mountains in the distance. It was a ruggedly beautiful setting, lonely but attractive. Although her lips barely moved, she vowed a vow: "I will make this marriage work; I will get the babies back together again even if it takes all I've got."

Grace stared a moment longer out the door: there was more snow here than on the plains.. She quietly packed the suitcases and stripped the bed while Emily crawled around investigating everything.

Her stomach growled, now on top of everything else both she and the baby were getting hungry. She opened the shoebox of lunch that Lily had packed and found only half of a dry sandwich remaining. Grace forced it down with a paper cupful of water from the lavatory. She gave Emily a bottle: at least the powdered formula would still be okay, but could she get the bottle clean enough? Randall came back, still jobless. He had to take them with him, but first they must haul the overnight supplies to the train station. On foot: there would be no hiring a cab this time.

They knocked on doors.

The car dealer gave Randall a piercing look while Grace cowered in the background.

"Why aren't you in the army?"

"I, I'm home already."

For some reason that made the man exceptionally angry. "Huh! Do you expect me to believe that? No soldiers have returned to our neck of the woods yet. Not a single one! The newspapers fill with stories of complaints and mini riots because of the slowness of demobilization.

"You never went, did you? You skulked out in some trapper's cabin to avoid the draft didn't you?"

Randall's cheeks flamed. "How dare you say that," he exploded. "You don't know a thing, you"---

Grace grabbed his arm, "Randall, please: don't cause a ruckus."

Randall whirled at her. "Keep out of this! I've been facing this all morning." He thrust his face close to the dealer's: "I was there," he ground out, "I got an honorable discharge."

"Honorable discharge? A young scamp like you? Whatever for?"

Randall hesitated. Grace prayed he wouldn't say why he was sent home, it would not be well accepted.

"Well you're sure ain't finding work here. Many of our boys are still gone, some never to return and we don't need loafers like you."

Randall tried to march bravely away with his head held high. Pity filled Grace's eyes.

Grace felt completely knackered out from holding an almost one year old. She asked Randall if he would carry her for a few blocks.

He acted distracted while taking the baby but let her ride on his shoulders. Although Emily chortled gleefully, her parents were too careworn to notice.

After an hour of tramping up and down wooden boardwalks, Grace offered to take the baby to the train station so that she could put her down for a nap. Randall barely nodded as she walked away. She did worry about getting lost and did wander down a couple wrong streets but her spirits lifted when the rambling, red station came into view.

Although the young mother was badly in need of a rest, her little girl wasn't, so Grace let her play around the basically empty room and promised herself she would keep an eye on her.

Fifteen minutes later a chunky woman wearing a heavy-duty apron tapped her on the shoulder. Grace jerked awake with the cry 'Emily!' on her lips.

The matron showed her the very grubby, but smiling child, relieved, Grace reached for her.

"She was crawling towards the men's washroom so I thought I should rescue her."

"Oh thank you, thank you, Mrs.—"

"Smallbones: my husband is in charge here at the station and I come around to do the cleaning and sell a few sandwiches to anyone that wants them.

"You seem awfully tired. Are you waiting for the train? One won't come through 'til five-thirty-five."

'"My husband is searching for work." Grace was trembling from exhaustion and struggled not get all weepy.

Emily wanted down so Grace opened her purse and took out a graham wafer, which she munched on happily. Her mother wished she had something more nutritious to offer her.

Mrs. Smallbones looked at Grace keenly. She probably hasn't eaten all day either.

"I made too many sandwiches for the passengers that boarded the 11:45, so I'll just fetch you're a couple. They're good, my own home-cured ham and fresh cheese."

Before Grace could protest, she had lumbered off and was soon back with a wrapped sandwich and tin cup of milk. She hung around while Grace ate, feeding some to the baby. "That husband of yours, is he a strong man? Husky and able bodied?"

Grace didn't know for sure, after all he had been in gaol for so long.

"Yeah…"

"The saw mill is always looking for workers. With so many men gone, they are worried about not filling the quota before spring break up. It will only be for a few weeks, but by then there will be farmers wanting help with planting--."

Just then, Randall walked in.

"Da-da!" Emily squealed. Randall's tired face lit up with a smile, Grace eagerly told him about the job opportunity with help from Mrs. Smallbones.

The cleaning woman and her broom disappeared when she saw the young husband take Grace in his arms.

Three Years Later

CHAPTER NINETEEN

Three years went by, and the twins were still separated.

Three years of loneliness, guilt and sometimes resignation on Grace's part, three of years of joy, quiet acceptance and slipping into the feeling of normalcy on Margaret's part.

Nevertheless, it was three whole years and time does change people, how did it affect the children?

Margaret listened; for once the children were quiet. It seemed they had settled down nicely for their naps, the two younger ones, that is, Davey Juniour wouldn't be released from school for another hour or so.

She reached for her Bible and took the latest letter from Grace. It was just inside the back cover. Faint worry lines touched her brow. How was it going with the girl? It seemed like every letter revealed new difficulties and this one was no exception.

Margaret looked sad as she closed her eyes and sighed an inaudible prayer.

"Dear Margaret,

I can't bear to tell my dear mother-in-law what we are going through so hope you can take it. I'd crack up if I couldn't share with someone!

Randall is out of work—again, has been for three months this time. In a way I am not sorry he lost this job but we are in desperate straits. He had an epileptic fit while on scaffolding and fell. The job wasn't waiting for him when his arm finally mended.

Sometimes I am at my wits end to know how to respond to him. We are hungry nearly all the time but I know he scrapes up enough cash from somewhere to spend on beer. We are both too ashamed to beg for social assistance, which is doled out so reluctantly, anyway, and is such a disgrace.

Oh, I wish I had the peace and simple trusting faith that you and Lily Sutherland wear like a shawl. I am such a worrier. Oh, Margaret, I have even snapped at my little darling! I'm sure you'd never screech at your brood! How can I be so cruel?

I must have my Mom's genes instead of Dad's patience. Oh, of course, I apologised all over the place and hugged her to bits but how can I ever forgive myself?

I am so anxious about our no job situation. I would offer to take in babysitting but our one room suite and half bath are far too crowded to entertain extra children.

Thank you so much for the gift of money you slipped in your last letter. It's a good thing Randall wasn't home when the mailman arrived. I bawled buckets and Emily was all over me trying to comfort me so I tried to tell her they were happy tears. I used it to buy eggs and butter and flour and a bit of yeast to bake some bread. Fortunately, Randall didn't seem to notice that I was able to do some baking again which I haven't done in a long time, but appreciated the wonderful aroma of fresh bread when he came into the house. I wanted to make some Toll House cookies, but ran out of sugar. Every little child should have the opportunity to help make cookies.

I hope I can someday repay you. I haven't used it (the money) all up yet but am doling it out slowly so he won't get suspicious and wonder where it came from. As it is, I have to hide it because he rifles through my purse in the vain hope I'd have some money stashed away.

This week I bought a small bag of oatmeal and some powdered milk with the money, and oh yes, a bag of carrots because they keep for a long time in the icebox. Thanks to you, we won't go hungry for a while.

Emily is healthy, for which I thank the Lord. Her sweetness and innocence helps me to trust our Heavenly Father more. I have much time on my hands so am learning to turn to Mom-in-law's Bible in time of need. I still worry a lot and get sharp way too often, but I'm glad I have Emily and I'm glad I have God.

Lots of love,

Grace

P. S. Sorry for being so full of myself: I really do want a long fully detailed letter about everything that's going on in your life and especially about Alice. (Sorry if it sounds selfish.)

P. S. 2. We are in Chilliwack, now, but I'm sure we will be moving again soon. Have you ever heard of the place? Right now it is as chilly as the name seems to imply.

Margaret refolded the letter then gently placed it back between the worn covers of the Bible. She sat lost in thought until her burdened heart caused her to slip to her knees in prayer. She laid her head on her arm.

"It's been so long, Lord. Grace is almost dearer to me that a flesh and blood sister might be. Please be with her. Keep her, comfort her, and help Randall to overcome his drinking habit. Thou knowest what awful memories are still gripping him, and we don't. Thou knowest the anxiety Grace faces: please help him to find a good job, and keep it. May Grace continue to call upon you when the floods threaten to overwhelm her—"

"Mommy, Alice spilled the milk on the floor!"

It was obvious that Sally would have got the milk out of the icebox because Alice was too young to handle the door. Alice was on her hands and knees scrubbing at the floor with a tea towel.

"Let's not use a tea towel to clean the floor next time, okay, Sweetie. Sally you fetch a rag from the rag bag."

"But she spilled it!"

"Just do as I tell you."

"Alice, wait for Mommy to pour your milk for you okay"— she almost called her 'Sweetie' again but then remembered it was too easy to favor the daughter of her troubled friend over the other two.

She donned an apron and dressed the little ones in matching pinafores that she had made. There was time to make a fresh batch of cookies before Juniour would walk in the door and once again be reminded not to toss his books on the floor.

David came home two hours later: Margaret was thankful that the man she married had a steady job as a mechanic. There were still far too many veterans drifting aimlessly through life, addicted to the bottle, and not coping well with their violent past. David seemed to be so steady in comparison.

Soon it was bedtime.

"Away in a manger no crib for a bed," Margaret sang not caring that it was still a long time until Christmas. Juniour and Sally waited patiently on the couch until it was their turn in the rocking chair with Mommy. With a little smile on her face, Alice closed her innocent, young eyes and was fast asleep.

Margaret didn't put her down right away though. She stroked the soft copper-colored tendrils and wondered if her twin still looked like a replica of her. She prayed: from the bottom of her heart, she prayed, that Emily could be as happy as Alice was then carried her to the lower bunk that David had made: twin sized on the bottom and single on the top. Now all three children slept in the former storage room.

Margaret opened her arms to Sally who jumped eagerly on to her lap.

"Jesus loves me this I know," she sang smiling at Davey Juniour. Soon, all too soon he wouldn't want to be rocked anymore, thinking he was a big boy now. Already he was worried that the Other Boys in grade one would Find Out but she assured him Mommy and Daddy would never tell and since he wouldn't either it was their special secret.

After the customary three or four songs for Sally, she tucked a light cover over the two girls and planted a kiss on each smooth, untroubled forehead, praying that her little ones could remain carefree for a long time.

Now it was Davey's turn. My, he's growing to look more and more like his Daddy. She hugged him close and sang: "Dare to Be a Daniel," which he loved. Sally looked a lot like her birth mother, Janet, who Margaret had never met. None of the three was bone of her bone and flesh of her flesh, but she loved them as dearly as if they were.

Her voice faltered while singing "This little light of mine, I'm gonna let it shine," but Junior didn't notice.

If little Ricky had lived he would be just a few months older than Emily and Alice, and he, too, would have had an opportunity to snuggle in her arms, something she achingly missed.

She tried not to let her voice quaver as she thought about the baby she had lost on the ship, and that there had been no little brother or sister forthcoming since.

Soon the children were fast asleep and as Margaret finished tidying up the kitchen she wondered how much longer it would be before David came in. He often spent his evenings at the shop repairing a customer's vehicle.

Sunday rolled around once again. Margaret knew that David would rather do other things than go to church but he preferred attending to facing the stern disapproval of his tall, angular mother.

Something had happened over in Europe, or Africa, or somewhere that made him resent the pastor's enthusiastic support for the war effort, but he got miserable with Margaret if she ever encouraged him to share what he went through.

"Davey come stand by me as I brush the dust off your little suit. My word, what were you doing, Little Man, that you got so dusty?"

"The ball rolled under the bunk, Mommy."

"And you went to fetch it, I see. I had forgotten to sweep under there lately! Well, you sit on the couch and look at a book. Come Alice, I will comb your hair."

Oh my, how the time has flown: when I first came to Halifax Sally was even younger than Alice is now. I wonder if Grace has a church that she loves.

After clipping a barrette in the bouncy tendrils, she plopped the little girl on her Daddy's lap. He smiled at Alice and tweaked her chin. Margaret knew he was fond of the little red-haired girl now, although it had often tried his patience when the apartment was so crowded with two squalling infants, and another couple of toddlers who found plenty of mischief to get into.

"Where can a man find a moment of peace and quiet around here," he used to frequently grumble before swinging out the back way and leaping off the fire escape. Margaret's brow puckered. What long walks he would go on, and how troubled, almost morose he had often been especially the first few months after returning from the battlefield.

Would she ever really know the inner turmoil of his heart? Would he ever share?

It had been good of him to put up with all those extra people in their crowded apartment when they were newlyweds at that but what really had gone on in his heart? Why do men have to be so uncommunicative?

Alice was prattling away with her babyish lisp and Margaret smiled at the cuteness of it, her smile disappeared. How will we ever be able to give up Alice if Grace decides to take her back?

Randall, Grace and the twins had been on her mind a lot lately: she wished David would pray with her for them; and other things as she had expected he would before they were married.

As she combed Sally's shiny, blond hair into two almost waist-length braids and fastened them with ribbons, her thoughts continue to be prayerful. Lord, what is going on in Grace's life? Please be with them if they are destitute. Help Randall to get his drinking under control.

Wandering Thoughts in a Formal Church

CHAPTER 38

"Margaret we will have to hurry in order to get to church on time."

Margaret's eyes roamed over the kitchen and she sighed. The dishes were stacked neatly beside the sink unwashed. Oh well, at least the children got the table cleared and wiped and she had managed to sweep the floor before changing into her sage green suit and hat.

Margaret dreaded Sundays because unexpectedly a wave of heartbreaking memories would sweep over her and she would end up weeping right inside that dark, formal church. Nobody but nobody burst into tears in that tabernacle!

Daddy: how he missed her father. He had been a warm-hearted preacher in northern England, but he, and Mumsey had died in such a tragic way.

Alice, who was sitting on her lap as they drove, was singing 'Running Over' a little children's chorus, and didn't notice when Margaret sniffled and discretely wiped away a tear. David did though, and his hand reached out to cover hers. She smiled bleakly at him.

The two in the back were making such a ruckus and not paying attention to the little exchange going on in front of them.

Later, the sermon seemed to drone on and on: oh, if only that was Daddy preaching! Sure, it had been embarrassing whenever he mentioned something that happened at home to explain a lesson, but now she yearned to hear the sound of his rich, warm voice and see his gentle smile. How she missed his sincerity, his deep compassion for the flock and his endearing way of weaving in stories so that even the younger ones would pay attention.

How she longed to see her brother, Richard sitting close to the front on the far side with a batch of boys his age. She remembered more than once his mischievousness would threaten to boil over and father would quell it with a stern look. Oh, dear, where is my hankie?

Worse than that, where was Richard? Last, she heard he was flying in formation with many other planes, dodging bullets and heading for Berlin; at least that is what was rumoureded, although she never found out for sure. Since then she had heard nothing. That absence of news was harder to bear than the most fearsome of stories. Once again, Margaret turned to her Heavenly Father and poured out her heart to Him.

Margaret found it hard to control her emotions never hearing a word of the sermon, David saw her grief and hated the preacher for expounding on patriotism---again!

After church, there was the usual gossip and idle chitchat, so Margaret put on a pleasant expression and pretended to be interested.

Their vivacious neighbour, Janiece, strolled by arm in arm with a cultured-looking young man from the states. Her sky blue drooping and flower adorned hat was the envy of the younger set...or was it the man she was with?

"Well Janiece sure got herself a fine catch. I wonder when the wedding will be."

"Oh, hadn't you heard? It's going to be a June wedding, next June, of course, and they will be honeymooning in France. Imagine! In our day France was a dreadful place to be."

The first speaker grimaced, "I'm glad the war is over. My cousin was the only one from our family, who served, and he told me more than I cared to hear about the aftermath."

"Why would they choose Paris of all places? I heard there was a lot of damage and even a year later there were still many people going hungry and looking for work."

"Her father pushed for it."

"Her father?"

"Yes."

Margaret's ears perked up. Hadn't Janiece's father been a general or something? Maybe he was hoping she would learn first-hand just a little how dreadful it still was 'over there'.

Margaret turned to gather up the children, feeling sad and desolate. She was so quiet on the way home that even Sally noticed. "What's the matter, Mommy?"

"I'm fine, Sally. Just a little under the weather.." She leaned her head back against the headrest and cranked down the window.

Margaret looked at her husband's lean, clean-shaven face. She knew her mind had been wandering and wanted to know what David had been thinking about.

"A ha-penny for your thoughts!" she said trying to sound cheery,

David shook his head in frustration and a troubled look darkened his brow. He hesitated and Margaret was afraid he wouldn't tell her—as usual—but after a moment, he did.

"Even since I had that flashback of being stopped short in that icy forest with a bullet, I haven't been the same," he admitted. "I just can't seem to identify with Reverend Weihlmann's patriotic sermons." He lowered his voice, after a swift glance towards the backseat, added, "There's nothing patriotic about the wake of destruction we left behind us! I hate to admit it, but his sermons make me ill."

Margaret's eyes widened, "But what about Hitler?" she whispered, "He needed to be stopped."

David's hands tightened around the steering wheel. "Soldiers are mere puppets on a political stage. We're made to believe whatever 'they' want us to believe. There would have been other ways to stop him."

A boyish voice piped up, "I want to be a soldier someday. Just like you, Daddy."

His parents glanced quickly at each other but neither answered. The silence hung heavily in the car and Margaret was relieved when they pulled up beside the spacious Victorian house and wended their way to the apartment in the back.

Margaret hooked her arm through his and gazed up into his face.

"I've wondered if Reverend Weihlmann would be so dogmatic in his beliefs if he had ever seen a soldier fall because of a bullet from his own gun."

David looked grim. "I asked him once, and do you know what, Margaret? He won many honors in World War One!" He went silent, and then turned to stare at her. "Do you know what that means?"

Margaret nodded.

David sighed and ran his fingers through his thinning blond hair.

"How can someone believe in going to war? How can a Christian kill his enemy if God's love is in his heart? I just don't see it!"

"Let's try another church, next Sunday."

David sighed. Margaret had suggested that before, but in spite of his frustrations, he still hesitated. He had grown up with this denomination; all of his closest friends and relatives, who worshipped anywhere, attended the same church he did; his parents' were proud, formal people who wouldn't take it lightly if he 'heedlessly flitted from one church to the next'.

Margaret understood his fears about his parents' opinion; she also found it difficult to relate to them. They lived on the far side of Halifax. David and Margaret would never consciously avoid them, but something usually came up that made it inconvenient to spend much time with them. It seemed too far for a man as busy as David was.

Margaret had her own secret fears that had nothing to do with distance or time. She was nervous that the children would do something wrong when they did go.

The children had to sit quietly, for at least a half an hour on straight-backed chairs during each visit without fidgeting or swinging their legs. That was especially hard on Alice who was a sparkly child by nature.

David and Margaret had lingered outside the apartment while visiting.

While watching the three children frolicking in the falling leaves in their back yard, Margaret's heart ached for the small children suffering across the ocean; little children as precious to someone as her own were to her, were going hungry day after day because of the aftermath of the war. Many little children, just the size of her own, were cold and frightened, and from their earliest memories had been hiding in cellars, and secret rooms or in hot stuffy attics and other dreadful places simply because of being born into the 'wrong' race.

Many, many children would not see their Mommy or Daddy again for various reasons, and what kind of life would they live? Nothing would erase the emotional scars for many of the sufferers.

Why must I be so helpless to do anything about it?

Margaret remembered hearing a story about soldiers handing out bread.

One mother ate none herself, but divided her portion among her children. The soldier assumed she wasn't hungry but a higher officer knew better.

"It's because she's a mother," he snapped. It may have happened during the First World War, the civil war or any other time of fighting, but Margaret knew that as long as there were mothers it could happen again.

What was Grace suffering? She is such a devoted mother.

Clinging to an Oak Tree

CHAPTER 39

"We've been gloomy long enough!" David exclaimed, swinging Alice into the air, "Look! The sun is coming out! Why don't you pack a lunch and let's have a picnic."

Margaret masked her look of astonishment that he would suggest something like that and eagerly agreed.

She had put in a roast for dinner that morning, so quickly slapped together some roast beef sandwiches, cut and packed the cake she baked yesterday afternoon, added a few carrot and celery sticks as well as Barnum Animal crackers for the children and closed the box.

Junior hurried out with thermoses of milk and coffee, Sally carried the bag of apples while Alice trotted behind with her teddy wearing a bib!

The children bounced excitedly in the back seat of the 1936 black Ford. It was still dependable due to David's mechanical abilities.

"A picnic! A picnic!" the girls shouted.

"A nit-pic a nit pic!" David Junior chanted back.

David and Margaret grinned at each other. It was good seeing the children so happy.

"We really ought to do this more often," they encouraged each other.

A wind sprung up while they were traveling across the city causing the leaves along the avenues to dance delightfully. As soon as they found their chosen spot in the park, they hurriedly unpacked their picnic supplies, laughing gaily while struggling to anchor down the billowing red and white checkered tablecloth with plates. The wind whipping through their clothes and hair felt exhilarating.

After they hungrily consumed their lunch, David pushed the children high on the swings while Margaret went for a walk. Sometimes it was pleasant not having little chatterboxes grabbing on to her skirts and claiming her attention.

Another teasing gust of wind sent a wave of fluttering red and gold leaves to swirl on the ground. She smiled as the children's voices drifted over to her. They were eagerly begging their Daddy to stop the swings so they could collect pretty leaves 'for Mommy'.

As she hurried along, feeling as if the wind was chasing her, she smiled at the memory of the children racing through the colorful leaves, arms outstretched. Such a carefree time of life was theirs.

The walk in the park caused Margaret to feel serene and refreshed. It was good being out in God's beautiful world with the leaves cavorting around her, her long skirts billowing, and the fresh earthy scent of autumn scenting the air.

At last, knowing that David might be running out of ideas as to how to entertain the children, she cheerfully turned back. She knew this time of communing with God and nature would sustain her for many days to come.

As she came nearer, she saw David playing a lively game of tag with the children. She drew closer. Their shouts and laughter bounced through the air and they seemed unconscious of the shower that had begun.

Junior tagged David and he froze in a funny position. He shook the hair out of his eyes and called, "Where's Alice?"

Margaret shrugged her shoulders. "Last time I saw her you were pumping her high on the swing."

"Didn't you see her following you?"

"Following me? No!"

"I was sure you had looked back just then and spotted her."

Margaret sounded distressed. "Why no, Last I saw her was when she was on the swing."

"Well, she's gone," he said flatly.

Margaret knees weakened. *Alice! Grace's girl! Their baby. Gone! Alice! Where could she be?*

Margaret stiffened also as did her older children. *At her instructions, everyone s*imultaneously turned and called; "AL-I-I-ICE!"

There was no response.

Even after shouting several times.

Shouting frantic instructions to each other, they scattered to look for the lost child. Very few people were at the park, but those that were, joined in the search.

Just then, the rain clouds that had been blowing in, burst, oh, dear, surely she couldn't be far away!

The school-age children headed towards some service buildings while their parents searched further afield.

They put about ten feet between them and headed in the direction Margaret had come from. Margaret hoped, oh how she hoped they would quickly find the missing girl. It was growing noticeably cooler. The clouds were thickening and the wind furious.

Her anxious eyes darted this way and that searching for a bright head with coppery curls, and a yellow, green and blue and peach dress. It seemed like forever before she saw a gay fragment of cloth whipping in the breeze.

Alice was clinging to an oak tree as if it were her big strong Daddy. How fortunate!

"Alice!" Margaret called, then as she came closer, again; "Alice! Whatever are you doing?"

Alice continued to cling to the tree although her arms couldn't nearly go around it." Her big blue eyes looked round and scared.

"I wan' my sis'ser. 1 wan' my sis'ser."

"Sally's looking for you," Margaret soothed. "We'll be together soon."

But Alice continued to whimper, "I wan' my sis'ser. She sad."

All the way home Alice's little nose was pressed against the rain streaked window pane and she had such a solemn face.

Whatever could be going on in that small, child's mind? Why did she keep asking for her sister? Why doesn't she snuggle up to Sally?

Finding Teddy's Brother

CHAPTER 40

Meanwhile, Grace was much happier than Margaret feared she would be. She was singing while unpacking at the logging camp where they had spent so many busy weeks the winter before.

The rest of the logging crew wouldn't arrive for a few days but she didn't mind. They were going to have a little vacation before work began.

Grace longed to hike over the crunchy softness of fallen leaves, and breathe deeply of the fragrant piney air, but that would have to wait. There were windows to restore to sparkling brightness, cobwebs to whisk away, clothes to unpack and dinner to get onto the wooden plank table. Later she would.

As she picked up her dust cloth, the ringing sound of an axe greeted her ears ad she knew Randall was already preparing kindling for the cook stove. She smiled, grateful that he was doing his part. That meant he was probably in a good mood.

Although it was hard in some ways, she enjoyed life in the lumber camps. The women were generally more sociable there than in the big cities and drink was not allowed on site. When Randall worked so desperately hard in the crisp, clean air, he rarely woke up from one of those devastating nightmares, which he incoherently would try to describe to her sometimes, leaving her feeling chilled.

Just then, a chickadee trilled merrily through the open window and she whistled back. The bird winged off with Grace's troubles and they fluttered away in the soft, balmy sunshine.

Three-year-old Emily, who had caught her mother's enthusiasm, was frolicking just outside the door. A thin veil of golden aspen leaves was floating softly to the ground.

Emily shuffled through them, watching as they mounded up on either side of her tiny feet. Oh how she delighted in the bright autumn colors!

Tall skinny poplars were springing up everywhere. In the distance massive cone-bearing trees sort of took over, crowding out the kinds of trees that gaily fluttered their buttery-yellow finery.

Emily skipped over to a nearby clapboard cottage so similar in appearance to theirs. She knocked at the door but there was no answer so looked in at the window but nobody was home. Not even the three bears invited her for tea.

Maybe after nighttime they'll come, Emily decided. "Everyone will come soon: for sure after nighttime.

She flung her arms out wide then twirled around a small sapling.

There was a small stuffed toy partly concealed in the falling leaves. While they were clambering out of the truck, It had fallen out.

"Teddy!" she cried, "My teddy!"

Grace smiled while listening to the joyful voice of her small daughter then went to the bedroom to unpack the bedding and clothes.

Meanwhile Emily fiercely hugged her plump teddy bear, then dragging it by one fuzzy brown leg trotted off into the woods, after a redwing blackbird who warbled merrily. Soon Emily's lilting voice was also singing.

"Teddy, Ted-dee you are mine you see Teddy... Ted-dee you are mine, you see."

A tiny leaf-covered footpath invited her to come deeper into the woods. After skipping along for a little while, she beheld a silvery-green brook. It was so sparkling and pretty that in seconds, Emily tossed her socks and shoes aside a and dangled her feet in the shining water.

The wee girl was happily unaware that a few yards farther on was a deep hole with a swift undercurrent and if she had fallen in...

Forgetting her socks and shoes but clutching the precious toy, Emily continued her little adventure.

She tiptoed across the rippling stream by stepping from one smooth flat stone to the next. "Eue, eue, that's cold!" she exclaimed every time her bare feet curled around another rock, but kept on going, not at all aware that Teddy's arm was trailing in the stream.

One forked trail lead to another, each more delightful than the last.

She trotted on, sometimes stooping to sniff a late blooming flower, sometimes picking a leaf the color of pure gold.

Up ahead partly concealed by the glowing trees, Emily spotted a partly- grown black bear.

"Oh Teddy," she exclaimed, nuzzling the fuzzy cheek of her stuffed toy, "There's your brudder!

"Here Teddy, here Teddy!" she trilled. The cub tossed his head and ambled away.

"Teddy! Wait for me!" She heard a low menacing grow, startled, she looked around. *Where did that big **GRRR** came from*? Emily hurried along calling "Teddy, Teddy!"

A huge bear lumbered out of the woods and swatted the cubs' behind. The baby stopped peering towards the human baby and scurried away from its mother's broad paw. Emily hurried after it, stumbling over twigs and roots in an effort to catch up. Her feet hurt badly but she so much wanted to say 'hi' to that baby teddy.

Lost Among Big and Little Bears

CHAPTER 40

Emily's parents were anxiously searching for her, and even farther away, in a large Maritime park, a girl who looked exactly like her was clinging to a large oak tree and crying.

After the bears disappeared from view, Emily sat down and rubbed her feet.

"They don't like me Teddy." she wailed.

Emily was very tired. She dragged her bear to a mossy spot that made a cozy nest beneath the trees, then snuggling into the leaves and using teddy for a pillow, drifted off to dreamland.

Dimly through her drowsiness, she heard her name called.

"Mommy." she murmured. Slumber's softest mantle cocooned her. Perhaps an angel in snow-white raiment hovered nearby while she slept.

Soon after Emily awoke, she spied some raspberry bushes. She knew what they were because her mother often picked wild raspberries for pies and canning.

After munching on a few mouthfuls, she remembered to feed Teddy and managed to get his face almost as smeared as her own before continuing on her way.

"Let's go back to Mommy," she said a few minutes later. She turned and trudged slowly down a little trail. Although her feet were summer hardened, they were protesting constantly now, so she sat down and tucked her skirt around them.

"Teddy. I really wanna go home. I wish Mommy would come and get me."

Teddy looked at her through sober brown eyes but said not a word.

After a while she continued. "My toesies are getting cold. Where my Mommy go?" She put her chin on teddy's head and gazed at nothing in particular. "I'm glad you're with me Teddy," she said at last, "But I want Mommy, too." A tear trailed down her grimy face.

A flat sun warmed rock invited her to curl up on its smooth surface so she did. She fell asleep once again with only the stuffed toy for comfort.

"Emily... Emily..." faintly she heard her name called.
She turned over and went back to sleep.

A long time later, she woke up while strong arms were lifting her and wondered why tears were coursing down the stranger's leathery cheeks. She saw her little brown shoe dangling from a doggies' mouth and chortled with delight while reaching for it. While perched on the old man's shoulders, she commented:

"The sun is all gone now."

It was minutes after Emily left that her mother noticed her disappearance. They lost much time by heading down the dirt road they had come in on, thinking that that was where Emily would have trotted.

A half-hour later Grace's heart sank when she caught sight of the tiny pairs of shoes and socks scattered next to the creek.

"Oh, Randall," she wailed.

At her cry of alarm, Randall rushed over and quickly assessed the situation. He struggled out of his heavy work boots then dove into the deep hole.

Grace clutched the tiny footwear and stared after him, bug-eyed with fear. When he surfaced he shook the hair out of his eyes and said grimly,

"Go look somewhere else."

Almost too numb to function, Grace moved off wandering aimlessly until she found herself in the general vicinity of an old hermit's shanty. A dogs' barking announced her arrival and Mr. Huber himself came around from out back carrying a battered tin bucket overflowing with berries.

"Our girl is lost!" Grace called.

"Quiet, Buster," Mr. Huber commanded then cupped his hand around his ear.

"What's that?" he bellowed

"Our girl has -has-" she couldn't get herself to say disappeared: "—is missing."

He trudged over to her and laid a bony hand on her shoulder.

"Don't worry missus. We'll find her. Just tell me how long she has been gone; which direction you think she took, and what she was wearing."

"She was wearing a thin calico," Grace explained tearfully, "just a thin brown calico with tiny yellow flowers and no sweater."

He nodded, then in his abrupt way asked;

"How big? Like so?" He measured with his hand. Grace nodded and handed Mr. Huber one of the shoes.

He got the dog to sniff it saying, "I don't know if this ole mutt remembers much about picking up trails, but we can try."

He tramped off after agreeing on a set signal.

Grace went back to the creek and crossed over. After walking a little way, she happened to see a spot where several raspberries were on the ground. Could Emily have been here? She called to the men in the distance knowing that Randall wouldn't have left off searching in the pond unless he was positive she wasn't there.

They hurried over to her and Mr. Huber examined the clue closely although Randall chose to look in a different direction.

Grace struggled through the underbrush, trying to follow faint trails as much as possible but always keeping within shouting distance of the others. When she was too beat to carry on, she went home and continued helping by sending entreaties up to God.

Hours later, Grace almost collapsed into Mr. Huber's arms when he came out of the already night dark timber pick-a-backing her daughter.

Emily's head had been resting on Mr. Huber's shaggy, gray one. Their silhouette contrasted with the colors of the dying sunset. When she saw Grace, she popped up and waved excitedly.

"Hi, Mommy, I saw a great big teddy and it could walk! It could talk, too. Will my teddy talk when he gets big?"

Grace sat in the rocking chair with Emily's tangled curls pressed into the curve of her shoulder. She rocked back and forth, back and forth, slowly, gently. How good it felt to have the soft, warm body of her little girl pressed against her own. How wonderful to be cuddling her once again. Her heart trembled to think how easily they could have lost her.

Emily had prattled on about a big teddy. Had she really seen a bear? Grace hoped not, yet this was the time of year they fattened up for hibernation.

The ground was so hard and dry that although they had searched, few footprints showed and it had taken a genuine woodsman to detect any trail markings; bent grass here, a broken twig there that only he could follow, he and that old dog who was half-blind

As she was crooning softly to her sleepy child, Grace wondered what experiences the little girl had actually gone through. Surely, angels had been watching over her.

It was well past midnight on the other side of the vast continent. A little girl near the Atlantic Ocean had fallen into a troubled sleep. Waking up, she called to her mother, and Margaret saw a sweet look in the innocent, young eyes.
. "What is it dear?"
"I dreamed," she shared. "Alwis is ah bedder now."
Margaret tucked her in more snugly, pressed a kiss on the smooth young brow and left the room feeling deeply perplexed.

A week later, when Margaret received Grace's letter about Emily's experience of being lost, she marveled, recalling how hard it had been for Alice to go to sleep that very night and even how she had clung to a tree earlier in the day. Should the twins be separate?

Meanwhile back in Alberta it was getting late and the dark shadows were creeping around mother and daughter, but Emily slept trustingly in Grace's arms. While she rocked gently, Grace was in a prayerful mood.
Randall swung open the door. "When's supper?"
"Oh Randall," Grace confessed, "I completely forgot about making a meal." She gently laid Emily on the bed then felt her way over to the stove.
He sighed heavily and went out into the darkness to do who-knows-what.

Grace fished a match out of her apron pocket, struck it on the stove then groped around for a kerosene lantern.

After lighting it, she used its faint illumination in order to open some home canned beans, a sealed jar of sausage and fry some potatoes for supper.

Soon delicious aromas were filling the cabin, and while she was setting the table, she called Randall in. What could he ever be doing out in the dark anyway?

Grace's brow furrowed, Ever since Emily wandered away, he had been in a sour mood. Is he secretly blaming me for Emily's disappearance? Randall ate in silence then went back outside. A couple of the single men had arrived earlier that evening, had he gone to visit with them?

While heating water in preparation for washing dishes, Grace watched him go to the pickup and by the light of a flashlight take something from under the front seat. Something she hadn't knownwas there.

He uncorked a narrow-necked bottle, took a swallow, then another, paused to look towards the dimly lighted house then took two more. He re-corked the dark bottle, closed the pick-up door then slipped off in the direction of the outhouse.

I wish he would throw it down the hole!

Grace mechanically finished cleaning up the kitchen and soon crawled into the dampish feeling bed beside her daughter.

Why, oh, why does he have to drink so often? Will he ever be happy-go-lucky again as he was when we were still courting?

She sat up and wrapped her arms around her knees, staring bleakly into the darkness. If it wasn't for Emily, life would be downright miserable... and we could have lost her.

Oh, God, please deliver Randall from the pain of the past, from his alcoholic addiction. She pressed her chin against her cupped hands and wished her prayer was more fervent. I've prayed so long for Randall to change that it hardly seems worth it to keep on but knew she wouldn't give up.

She heard a sound on the doorstep so quickly lay down and pretended to be asleep.

Randall scooped Emily up and laid her on a folded blanket on the floor then crawled in beside Grace. Yes, his breath smelled awful.

A couple hours later Randall woke up screaming and thrashing out at an unknown enemy, Grace lay stiffly on her side of the bed not knowing what to do. She timidly reached out and laid her hand on his arm.

"Randall, I'm here, now. You don't need to fear the demons from the past."

He kept staring at the door muttering "I'll get you yet, I'll get you yet," then rushed into the night, leaving the door to the shanty wide open.

The moonlight streamed in making a path across the wooden floor. Grace watched him pace quickly down the rutted trail they had come in on earlier. She knew it could be hours before he would return.

Please God, please.

Grace had no way of knowing what time Randall returned that night, but by breakfast, he was impatient to be on their way.

"I have no intentions of staying in the woods another day," he announced while cutting into his stack of sourdough pancakes."

Grace's eyes widened "Why ever not?"

"I'm not tramping all over these woods looking for a lost kid ever again! It reminds me too much of...of..." his voice trailed off and he refused to continue his thought.

"I'm sure she won't get lost again! I'll watch her closely."

"I'll stay wis Mommy," Emily piped up.

"You bet you will." Randall retorted. He turned to Grace, "You might as well start packing: I'll need to find a different job."

Grace eyed him strangely. "You can't be serious. The rest of the crew will be back by the end of the week at the latest."

She handed Randall his coffee.

Randall looked intently at her. "Does it bother you that much to be moving on?"

She nodded silently. "Randall, honey, we need to be more settled. We need the income; Emily needs a place to call home."

Randall tapped on his cup. "If only those nightmares wouldn't come and tear me apart," he mumbled. He sat quietly sipping his steaming beverage. "Well, then don't pack everything: just the essentials: if we don't find the perfect job we could always come back by the weekend."

Grace looked relieved.

Now she would not have to dwell on the dreadful ordeal of searching for another job, which would probably mean holing up in some dowdy quarters. Nothing better would fit their meager budget. I hope that we will end up coming back, or going to another sawmill.

Just one day at a time, she muttered while folding Randall's plaid flannel shirts into neat little squares. One day at a time.

She smiled humorlessly while inspecting one of Randall's wool socks that needed mending, One minute at a time, is all I can take some days.

"What did you say, Mommy?"

"Nothing much, Honey." She tweaked Emily under the chin. "Better find your teddy. You wouldn't want him to stay behind would you?"

"NO! He might go play wis the udder teddies then I won't find him no more!" With that, she tunneled under the bed and dragged him out.

Grace didn't want to believe it, but she was convinced that Emily had actually seen at least one bear. It made her sick just to think about it.

After they left, Randall put the pickup into gear and made his way down the autumny trail. At the corner, he shifted it into park and rested his hands on the steering wheel.

"What would you think of going to see my folks for a while?"

"Oh, Randall, do you mean it? Do you mean it? I'd love to! We haven't been back for months, and the last time was so brief."

Randall's eyes were soft as he glanced at Grace from time to time..

Ever since he had suggested they go to see his parents she had burst into song and had been singing off and on for the last several hours.

He looked thoughtful as he braked for a herd of deer crossing in front of them. Grace has rarely bubbled over into song, yet I know she enjoys singing, and has a good voice. Had she been a lot happier while living with his mother over at the farm?

 I've been thinking too much of my own woes and not focusing on how to make life easier for her.

Home Folks

Lily gently brushed a strand of dark shiny hair off Grace's forehead and tilted her chin with one finger. "It's so good to see you. How has it been going?"

"So-so." she replied.

Lily looked at her thoughtfully for a moment: "Has Randall been—-drinking?"

"Yeah."

"Oh that naughty boy," Lily sighed before turning to look out the window.

Grace didn't know if she was watching Randall remove the baggage from their Ford pickup or staring at nothing in particular.

Lily turned back towards her daughter in law.

"You look tired, honey. Why don't you sit down? Here, I'll take your hat. And don't you worry a bit about helping with supper."

"Granma! You haven't talked to me!"

Lily reached down and swooped the little girl up in her arms.

"My own little darling! How's my sunniest sunshine?"

"Oh, fine!" She struggled to get down, and ran to fetch teddy that was toppling over the suitcases beside the door.

"And I sawed Teddy's brudder. He was big-BIG!" She reached her arms up as high as they could go.

Lily raised a quizzical eyebrow. "What is she talking about?"

"I'll tell you later."

Grace leaned her head against the old familiar sofa.

"Will you be staying a couple of days?" Lily asked as she hurried to mix up a cake.

"I hope so. I'll ask Randall." She started to head over to where Randall was filling their green truck with petrol but stopped. He had just opened the toolbox in the back and was taking out an ugly brown bottle.

Her temper flared: Not again! Where does he ever get the stuff all the time? Did he buy some when we stopped for petrol; I mean gasoline, last night while I was sleeping? Maybe he had it all along without me knowing it, but why does he want it? Why now of all times?

Oh.

Ben. He doesn't get along well with his dad.

Grace's brow furrowed. I've prayed and prayed that I could love and forgive him for drinking on the sly all the time, but I just don't understand why he can't quit.. Is it something to do with being in the war? Grace dismissed the thought. It can't be that. Lots of men were soldiers but no one ever talks as if they are troubled by what happened.

Oh, Lord, help me to understand, accept and forgive.

Grace felt nauseous when she got closer and smelled the mixed odors of gasoline and liquor but resolved not to say anything about it.

"Randall, may we stay at your folks for a while?" she pleaded. Emily, who had tagged behind her, clung to her yellow and white striped skirt. Grace picked her up almost as protection against the refusal she more than half expected.

Randall glanced at her briefly before looking down.

"It depends," he muttered looking significantly towards the barn. Grace felt like she knew what he was thinking.

"Dad went to an auction sale near Leduc to check out some high bred heifers," she reminded him, "and won't be back for several days."

Randall nodded. He glanced at her again and Grace saw some of the old warmth kindled there. Her heart responded.

"We'll stay."

"Oh Randall thank you, thank you," Grace cried giving him a hug. Emily's mouth popped open. She had never seen her parents embrace.

"What are you doing?" she exclaimed. Randall patted her on the shoulder grinning at her expression, and shoved the brown bottle in his pocket.

Grace considered pleading with him not to drink, but decided she wouldn't press her luck. She swung Emily up in the air instead.

"Oh, Emily, we get to stay with Grandma for a while!"

Randall looked at the happy pair. I'd love to be different, but don't know how to tell them. I'm getting to be so much like my Dad, he thought morosely.

The girls deserve someone better. A whole lot better. He shoved the bottle deeper into his roomy jacket pocket.

After Grace returned to the house with Emily skipping beside her, Randall trudged over to the far side of the barn, removed the bottle from his pocket, and eyed it thoughtfully.

Yeah, really I do drink a lot: way too much in fact. You'd think I was a baby, or something, the way I cling to the bottle.

God, if you are up there somewhere, do you think you could help me stop: for Grace's sake at least. His face lengthened as he thought of the stricken look that came to her face when Emily repeated a bad word that her father had used. You know that I love her but I doubt she does. God I'm so knotted up in side I just can't cope. I crave this wicked stuff 'cause it gives me such a release. It'll be awful hard to quit.

"God help me," he moaned. "For their sake help me. " I'd love to see the sparkle come back to Grace's eyes. It felt like she had become just a shadow of the blithe girlish lady giggling in the park. "Just help me to stop drinking and I'll do the rest."

Randall didn't feel worthy to ask for peace and forgiveness for himself, after all the wrong he had done but hoped God would listen to him for Grace's sake

Through the kitchen window, Grace saw a dark object hurled through the air and land in to the dugout with a plop. She looked up from the carefully seasoned pieces of chicken she was frying and met Lily's eyes with a questioning look.

Lily had been washing some baking dishes at the sink. She also was observing Randall's actions.

"I think it was a bottle," she said in a low voice.

Grace looked so relieved.

"Have another piece of chicken, Randall," his mother invited. "I made it just the way you always loved it as a child."

"Thanks, Mom, but I'm stuffed," Randall replied, placing his hand on his full stomach. "I already had three pieces and want to save room for your delicious chocolate cake and whipping cream that you were making before supper..

"Come to think of it, why don't you send a jar of your wonderful seasoning mix along with us? Or better yet, give Grace the recipe?"

"I'll do both!" Lily beamed. She knew they probably couldn't afford the variety of spices it called for.

Grace glanced at Randall out of the corner of her eye but kept quiet. Didn't Randall think of it that they almost never ate meat because it was too expensive? They could only afford it when he was working at the lumber camp. Oh, well, it was great seeing him so upbeat..

Emily was nodding over her unfinished meal. It had been a long day's drive in the rickety pickup and she was sleepy. Grace scooped her up in her arms and carried her over to the crib mattress made into a bed in Randall's old room.

Lily's voice drifted after her.

"How is it going, Randall?" she heard her say.

Randall considered nonchalantly replying

"Oh. Fine, how about you?" For some reason he wasn't in the mood for such flippancy. His mother had always been genuinely concerned, so willing to listen and had tried to understand his problems.

He couldn't get himself toshrug off her question when he knew she sincerely wanted to know. He scraped some pieces of meat off the drumstick on his plate before replying.

"Mom, it's hard," he admitted." I feel like such a failure. Grace is a terrific gal, and I love her, but I don't think she could ever comprehend the burden of guilt I carry about, about...well, different things.

"I, I drink to drown out the memories, of, of well, you know what but I'm afraid it's making things worse."

Neither of them looked up when they heard the soft footfalls that reached the bottom of the stairs.

Randall paused. Lily waited for him to continue, her mother-heart yearning over him.

His face was in his hands now and Grace could hardly make out what he was saying. "I can't look anyone in the eye any more. They think it is so honorable to go to war and "save the country" but Mom...it's ...it's..." He couldn't seem to go on.

Many responses leaped to Lily's mind but she subdued them.

"I'm haunted by guilt night and day. And the memories, oh the memories… It makes me beastly with Grace and Emily."

It was several minutes before he could get himself to continue.

They waited quietly. Grace slid into a chair at the end of the table, unsure if she was welcome or not. Nobody seemed to mind.

"I'm sure Grace thinks I don't like the baby—Emily, I mean. I do. I just don't know how to be a good Dad. I feel so uncomfortable before-such and innocence."

"I can't…bear to see the…stricken…look on Emily's sweet face when she finds out what a wicked man her Daddy is."

He turned to look at Grace.

"You are so good to me," he said humbly. "I'm guilty of being too gruff with you."

Grace buried her head on her arms. Randall leaned closer to his mother and Grace could barely catch what he was saying.

"She was a gay little butterfly when we first met but she's changed. I don't know why she is so downcast, so burdened all the time."

Grace felt her ears grow hot. Why is he sharing with his mom and not me, I'm his wife!

Lily laid a warm arm over Grace's shoulder.

"You have a sweet little wife," she said. "Just be strong for her."

"And to think she has a drunken brute for a husband," he muttered.

Grace reached out in supplication to her Heavenly Father; Lily's heart also soared on wings of prayer.

"It doesn't have to be that way, son."

Randall didn't respond.

"Jesus will forgive you."

He kept quiet.

Grace looked at him with heartfelt sympathy, her eyes wet.

"Try praying."

"Will He listen? He said 'love thy neighbour, and I, I---" he groaned and clasped his hands around his forehead once again.

"Do: for Grace's sake and Emily's: they need a healed man, a whole man."

He moaned.

"God loves you.""

"Randall," Grace said softly, pleadingly, "Give your heart to God. He can work things out."

He stared gloomily at the sun dying in the west.

"I'll be praying for you, son."

"Me to," Grace added.

"Thanks," he said huskily.

Lily thought he would leave the room then, but he didn't.

He watched while she spooned creamed corn into a small jar and flipped the wire handle over the lid, then left.

They were disappointed that he hadn't made a decision to surrender his pain and heartache,—his whole life over to God, but were more encouraged than they had ever been before.

If only it could last...

Huddling in a Hovel

CHAPTER 42

Several weeks later Grace found herself huddling in the far corner of a lumpy double bed. She tried to get some warmth from the lovely, but somewhat grimy quilt and it brought back memories of when they had visited the farm for a few days. Already it felt like such a long time ago.

The blanket may have been offering physical or psychological warmth but Grace was too unhappy to notice. She stared bleakly at the dull gray cement brick walls. The joyful hours spent with Lily seemed unreal as if they had happened to someone else or in a dream.

This has to be the most miserable shelter, yet, she sighed. Oh, to return to some sun-dappled forest and hear the ringing of the axe and shriek of the sawmill. She missed the fragrant woodsy scent, the hearty shouts and laughter of the brawny but honest lumberjacks but they had never gone back. In this dreary neighborhood, Grace hardly ventured past the end of the walk because there were so many rowdies lurching about especially after dark.

In the pool of dusty sunlight from the small window high above their heads, Emily was playing with a limp rag doll Lily had made her long ago. It had gone through many a washing, but Emily still loved it, perhapsmore than ever. Grace suspected it was because she knew Grandma Sutherland had created it for her. I'm so glad Lily did. Emily has pitifully little to play with.

A one-room basement suite was all they could afford that winter.

Randall had been angry with her when he left on what would probably be another futile search for work that morning.

"We'll never better ourselves if you lay around doing nothing all day," he had yelled, glaring at the heap of dirty dishes.

She tried to stand. Why doesn't he notice how ill I'm feeling?

"If you'd at least apply for a job as a maid we might be able to get out of poverty!" he continued, "I'm sure lots of people wouldn't mind you taking a sweet little girl like Emily with you."

The words tumbled around in Grace's mind, as well as the slamming of the door. She let herself slump back on the bed as soon as his back was turned.

Does he have any idea what it is like to be in these dingy, damp basement rooms day after day without seeing anyone? Rooms? It would be more accurate to say they only had one room to call their own.

The rest were filled with junk belonging to the owner, and Grace was hard put keeping Emily from exploring and possibly hurting herself on the trash!

Grace hurried over to the enamel basin that served as a sink. After throwing up she carried the container outside and emptied it in the garden. As soon as she had backed away, a large black mongrel came and sniffed at it, making her stomach heave.

Why doesn't Randall worry about me vomiting so much? She was reluctant to tell him what was causing her misery if he didn't act more caring. No way do I want to announce that an innocent new baby is on the way in this awful hovel! Babies deserve better than this. Every baby is so precious, they deserve to be cradled in luxury, at least for the first two years. This is such a far cry from the kind of home I would like to raise our little ones in.

God, why couldn't you have waited a tad bit longer to send us another child?

She gazed sadly at Emily who was pretending to wash her 'baby' in a cracked plastic bowl. Then her eyes turned to the pile of old, worn clothing that used to serve as the little girl's bed and was relieved that Lily had insisted they take the crib mattress along.

.

Softly Emily began to croon to her dolly; "Away in a manger no crib for a bed, the wittle Lord Jesus lay down his sweet head."

Grace tried to do the dishes but ended up leaning against the cold hard wall, nearly overwhelmed with dizziness and nausea.

Did I really feel this miserable last time? I'm sure I didn't. Grace admitted her food had been healthier during her first pregnancy. Even on the ship, the meals were more nourishing than what she had to scrounge together, now.

It had been so different with Margaret, also. The motherly young woman was such a source of joy and warm fellowship. Those three crowded rooms were like a palace compared to this hovel. Grace remembered Margaret's little touches that prettied up the place; dried flowers in a vase, a picture of cherubic looking babies taped to the icebox door, ribbons used as tie backs on the gingham curtains...Margaret's apartment was always so clean. I simply don't have the energy to keep this place up.

She buried her head in a pillow, and let discouraged tears trail down her cheeks.

A tiny hand patted her arm. "Don't cry, Mommy. It'll get ah bedder."

"Oh, Emily," she cried, caressing her cheek. "You are my little sweetheart!" I need to be happy for her sake, but oh, I'm glad Alice doesn't have to endure this! She hugged her little daughter close, and rocking gently. Would it be easier for Emily if she had another little person to chatter with? In her innocence, she is so accepting of our circumstances. Grace stroked Emily's straggly hair out of her eyes. Her bangs need cutting. Maybe God is giving me another baby so that they can cheer each other up in these dire circumstances.

Her head fell: but I do have two babies.

Maybe I was playing God when I gave Alice away! The knife of guilt twisted in her heart. Was I just too lazy to care for twins? Being pregnant with all the emotions accompanying it revived dormant feelings and Grace found it hard to breathe.

She looked around her once again: these cement walls are making me feel trapped!
"Mommy, I'm hungry." Emily's plaintive voice penetrated her troubled thoughts. "Mommy, kin I eat now?"

"Yes, dear," Grace got out the last slice of bread and buttered it for Emily.

"Aren'tcha gonna eat Mommy?"

"I'm not hungry."

She knew she ought to have read the Bible and pray with Emily but felt too discouraged, wondering if it was really worth it.

"Aren't we gonna read the Bible, Mommy?" Emily asked around a bite of bread." I thought we always did before we'd eat in the mornin' -time."

Grace dragged the Bible off the windowsill and opened it at random.

"By the rivers of Babylon we sat down, yea we wept when we remembered Zion." Grace couldn't help but smile.. God sure must know what

I am going through. "We hanged our harps upon the willows in the midst thereof. For there they that carried us away captive required of us a song; and they that required of us mirth, saying sing unto us one of the songs of Zion. How shall we sing the Lord's song in a strange land?

Yes, Lord, how can I sing here in Edmonton when I am so far from my loved ones?

If I do not remember Thee oh, Jerusalem let my right hand forget her cunning. Psalm; 137.

Emily stirred restlessly. "I don't understand all those big words."

"That's Okay. God wanted to talk to Mommy this time."

The frail woman looked around wishing for a private corner to pray but there wasn't any, so knelt beside the unmade bed. "Dear Heavenly Father, I need you so. I've been feeling so discouraged far too long. Are you really my Heavenly Father? Please help me, if you will. Life is so difficult."

Her voice dropped to a whisper. "Lord we're going hungry. I only sent one measly piece of dry bread with Randall for his lunch. No wonder he is cranky. We don't even have enough money to pay the rent! How much longer will they carry us?"

She hardly noticed Emily get down beside her and clasp he dolly's hands together. "An' bess Mommy and Daddy,' she lisped softly. "Help dem buy food...Help Dolly to be good..." She hesitated then repeated the same words over again.

Grace reached over and drew the little girl close.
Only Emily really loves me. I suppose that is not true. It's just that we move so much Lily and Margaret probably don't even receive our change of address cards before we're gone again! I don't even know what to write them about without letting it leak out how hard up we are!

"Lord, she whispered. Please send us some true Christians for fellowship. If I wasn't alone so much of the time it would be easier to be happy."

She nestled Emily's bright curls against her bosom and reached for the Bible again. After flipping a few pages she drank in the words: '11 He shall feed his flock like a shepherd: he shall gather the lambs with his arm, and carry them in his bosom, and shall gently lead those that are with young.' Oh, Jesus, what a beautiful promise. Thank you.

Please, be my Good Shepherd, carry me, I need you.

"My child, do you care more about Emily than I do about you? Even if I don't send you a special blessing, I want you to trust in me. I want you to believe that I care about you even if the way is dark."

She lingered for a while longer in God's comforting presence, and then rose to tackle the dishes.

It was clouding over, so Grace pulled the drawstring attached to the one electric bulb hanging from the ceiling and sat down at the table to continue reading in the Bible. Soon she felt courageous enough to tend to the pile of wash with the use of a large old-fashioned scrub board.

That afternoon, while Emily napped, Grace noticed a few stitches had come out of the quilt so carefully sewed them up by hand. It was very important to her to keep that blanket in top-notch condition.

Damp wash was dangling from every available repository in the apartment when Randall burst in several hours later, bubbling over with boyish enthusiasm. His bouncing steps and twinkling eyes revealed the excitement he was feeling.

Grace had snuggled up beside Emily after draping the final sock over the headboard. She woke up rubbing sleep from her eyes and feeling bewildered by all the ruckus.

"I got a job!" Randall whooped. "Part of it's for you," he amended.

"What is it?" she asked guardedly.

Will This Job Work

CHAPTER 43

"*Janitor*work. At the airplane factory. The pay is good, but, um, the work is kind of hard."

"What about Emily?"

"Oh, she'll just come along. There's chairs in the main lobby. She's used to sleeping anywhere."

Grace nodded ruefully.

"When do we start?"

"Tonight at seven o'clock."

Tonight.

At seven o'clock.

Grace took a deep breathe to calm herself and pressed her palms against her abdomen. Lord, I don't know how I can handle it. I'm so weak and exhausted as it is.

"And I saved the best for the last. I'll be a security guard there, so it's like two jobs."

Grace gave him a weak smile.

"And to celebrate, I'm taking you out for supper. I was paid today."

"Oh, Randall," she demurred, "do you think we should?"

"We will." he said, grinning broadly.

Grace gently awakened Emily and straightened out the covers on the bed.

She led her sleepy daughter upstairs to the washroom located in the entrance so they could both freshen up.

Soon they were sitting over large plates of roast beef potpie. It was the tastiest looking food Grace had seen in a long time and how her mouth watered!

Grace noticing that the moment Randall had walked into the house, his irritability had disappeared.

He must have been under a tremendous pressure trying to find work to support us all.

Now as they lingered over wedges of hot apple pie with ice cream, Grace saw Randall's exuberance fading away as a thoughtful concern replaced it.

"You've been looking peaked. Is anything wrong?"

"No not really," she said straightening her cutlery.

"I thought getting you out of that dreadful dungeon would have perked you up, but you're all done in."

Grace was touched by his concern.

"Look Randall, I love it that you took us out for supper. It's been a very special time. It's just that...that," she paused, wondering how best to word her surprise, then slipped her hand into his," It's just that we're...we're going to have a baby."

Randall jaw dropped "Oh, Grace!"

"It'll be all right," she whispered, "I may look fragile, but I'm strong."

"But you can't do janitor work!" His voice had risen.

"The nausea is usually over by three months," she hastened to reassure him. "As long as you help, I'll manage." She 'twinkled' her eyes at him.

"I will help," he said grimly, glancing at his wristwatch. "It's time to go now:" he flicked one of her ebony locks, "Thanks for the supper."

"Thank you for the good, good supper and evening," Grace said clutching his arm.

"And Randall," she added softly as they headed towards the cashier to pay their bill, "Let's not let news of this, this baby coming spoil our evening."

"No way! Maybe now I'll have the boy I always wanted!" He grinned but Grace later saw the cloud of concern in his eyes as they drove the old beat up Ford toward the factory. Randall was gripping the steering wheel so hard that his knuckles gleamed white.
I wonder what's bothering him most?

They had driven a long ways down the empty highway before he spoke again. "Grace...I want to be a good father...but it is so difficult. I've been such a failure....Wish I could do better. "It's awful to think of us having another child unless I can straighten out my life. What can I do?"

He fell silent and Grace played with the gloves in her lap willing herself not to interfere with his thoughts, yet praying fervently.

"To start with," he continued, "I vow...by the grace of God ,not to touch a drop of liquor ever again. That's the least I can do for you and the babies." Under his breath, he muttered So help me God.

"Do you want me to pray for you?"

"Please do."

"I will Randall. And you pray to."

There was an obvious struggle going on in his mind. Does hethink it is too impossible to change? I know it is hard, really hard, but God can help him.

"Jesus can help you," Grace whispered.

He looked straight ahead without answering.

"We're praying for you," she continued softly, "Mom and I."

"I hope I can change," he muttered while guiding the truck into the large parking lot of the airplane factory. I have to."

"Do you think we could have a prayer before we go in?" Grace suggested. Randall agreed readily.

It felt strange yet thrilling to be uniting in prayer with her precious husband. She had waited such a long time for Randall to want to make a change for the better that doubts had come in that he ever would. To think God was working on him in spite of my doubts!

"Lord," he pleaded, "If you can save me from my sins and prove it by delivering me from the power of drink I will serve you forever."

"Dear Heavenly Father," Grace added, "Have mercy on Randall. Cleanse him from his sins for Jesus' sake, and give him peace."

There sat there for a log while gazing at nothing in particular.

Randall looked bewildered. "I was expecting a long drawn out struggle once I decided to change. Not such a quietness within so soon!"

Grace's voce was tender. "The battle isn't over but the good Shepherd will help you," And me also, she added humbly, I have too often had a lack of faith. "He will give you the grace to do what's right."

"And I think I'll start like this, "he said giving her a big hug and a kiss. Grace, I am truly sorry for being such a bad husband."

"Oh, but I knew you cared," she whispered.

Emily bounced up and down between them and clapped her hands joyfully. "Daddy kwissed Mommy!" she cheered. Grace felt a little self-conscious; nobody ever showed such a public display of affection but she kind of liked it.

"And Emily," he said, turning to her, "You've got a new Daddy!"

"Goodie, goodie gumdrops!" Emily crowed not really knowing why her parents were so happy but she didn't need to. Just knowing they were, made her all bubbly inside.

Randall and Grace entered the building holding hands while Emily skipped along ahead of them.

They were eager to start their new job at least after their very exacting instructor departed.

Randall spent several minutes out of every hour circling the buildings for anything suspicious but the rest of the time hovered over Grace like an over-protective mother hen. He insisted on filling and lifting the heavy pails and even decided wielding the enormous mops was too much for her and only allowed her to run the floor polisher after much pleading on her part.

Grace found lots to do anyways with all the desks and bookcases that needed dusting and polishing, papers to straighten up, dustbins to empty and so on.

With all the chattering and giggling that went on, t was a wonder as much got done as it did. One would of thought they were a couple of honeymooners the way they behaved!

"Don't get mad, Randall," Grace said teasingly as the hands of the clock approached midnight, "but you remind me of a fairy tale character."

"Who?" Randall instantly looked sober, "The beast in Beauty and the Beast?"

"What? "Grace yelped, "How did you guess?"

"Cause that's what I've been like."

"But after your beastly disguise fell off my, what a wonderful prince was revealed!" She was dashing away from him even before he charged her with a dripping mop.

Two armchairs pushed together front to front to made a cozy nest for their little daughter to snuggle up in. Feeling wonderfully weary, Grace soon stretched out on a sofa nearby while Randall continued his rounds until his shift was over and the replacement arrived.

The streets were almost empty when they cruised along them in the gray dawn. When they saw the flashing red lights of the saloon up ahead, Grace gripped Randall's arm. Will the fairy tale end when he starts craving liquor again?

"Please God." She closed her eyes, "Please help him to resist temptation."

Randall hadn't even turned his head to look.

Later she realized it might not have been a temptation so soon after giving his heart to God, but every evening as they drove past saloons, Grace would pray silently until the lights were behind them.

When the nausea stage was a thing of the past, Grace felt so much better that she really enjoyed working with Randall.

The combined income was good enough that they decided not to go back to the woods that winter. What a relief! Moving was such a hassle!

CHAPTER 44

"*What's* the matter, Randall," Grace greeted him late one afternoon when he came home from the part-time day job he had landed.

He quirked his eyebrow: "Why do you ask?"

"You don't coming bounding in the door like you used to yelling: "Hi, Honey, I'm home!"

The old familiar grin replaced the weary lines on his face. "Maybe I'm just growing up," he teased.

"It had better be," she said shaking a finger at him, "But I sure liked you the way you were."

He sank wearily on the bed then flopped over. Grace tiptoed around making a lunch for them to take to their evening job at the airport and hated to wake him a half hour later when it was time to go.

Grace wished she could stop worrying, but after the first flush of excitement about being born again and going to church, Randall's enthusiasm had worn off.

Oh, Lord, I want so much to walk in your footsteps. I'm concerned about my husband. He doesn't seem interested in going to church anymore and how can we grow as Christians if we don't fellowship with believers?

Thank you that he still supports praying together, thank you very much, but oh, Lord, shouldn't there be more?

Is there some tension at his other job that is getting him down, maybe even creating a 'need' for alcohol?

Oh worry, worry, worry! When will I stop being such a worrywart?

Soon they were chatting companionably as they swished brooms and picked up paper scraps in the airport lounge.

Emily! Be careful!"

Emily had placed her teddy on the boot rack and, pretending it was a real bear, taken her rag doll, and was running full speed down the hall to get away from the dangerous 'animal.'

She slipped on a wet spot and went sprawling. Grace leaped to her aid.

"She's fine, Grace, don't coddle her so much!"

"But she hurt herself!" Grace sputtered. She planted a kiss on the hurting knee and set her on her feet.. Immediately Emily scampered off to fetch the now friendly bear and was off on another imaginary pursuit.

Grace frowned as she followed Emily with her eyes and Randall frowned as he looked at Grace but no one knew what the other one was thinking.

The days rolled around, and getting two paychecks, a month was greatly encouraging. Randall always handed her the money which she divided into specified envelops to make it easier to budget.

"You know what, Honey bunch; we are going to the shops today!" Grace said to her little girl one day after tidying up their little cement-brick suite.

Earlier Randall and she had found a sturdy second hand cot and lamp, both of which he was able to repair. Now it was time to brighten them up.

Emily eagerly ran for her little coat and matching hat, which were getting a little too small for her and hopped from one foot to the other while she waited for Grace to comb her hair.

As Grace opened her handbag to check how much money she had to spare, she saw part of the seam at the bottom was fraying. When she tucked it back together as a temporary measure, the hidden paper felt stiff against her fingers.

An excited look crossed her face: With Randall's attitude improving, perhaps I can soon get Alice back.

"Hurry, Mommy, hurry!"

Grace snapped her purse shut and was soon locking the door behind her. Emily skipped along at her side and was chattering a mile a minute, but Grace was dreaming of two little girls frolicking beside her. What was Alice doing right this minute?

Coloring Patterns

CHAPTER 45

"**Look, Emily**," Grace said fifteen minutes later, "Here is the cutest pattern. "It is called Sunny Bonita, and I'm going to make a quilt for your bed."

"Can I color it?"

"It's not for coloring, honey, but for cutting."

"Can I cut it then?"

"Come, let's go over here and look at the pretty cloth. I think this pink and white calico would be lovely for the bonnet and the dress. And a matching shade of pink broadcloth would be just fine for the tie belt and lining of the bonnet..."

But Grace was talking to herself because Emily had skipped off to look at the brightly colored spools of thread.

Soon, with the help of a clerk, they had the right yardage measured and wrapped up in brown paper along with some thread and a pack of needles.

Mother and daughter hurried home to make the first of a series of improvements to the dreary hovel.

After cutting out the pieces for twelve Sunny Bonita appliques and the corresponding background pieces, Grace carefully started sewing them by hand while Emily had her afternoon nap.

By the time Randall was home, all evidence of her project had vanished under the bed, there was a smile on her face and supper was nearly ready.

If Grace seemed to shoo Randall out the door the next morning, he didn't notice, but he did realise she seemed extra happy and that was all that mattered to him.

Grace eyed the lampshade speculatively. Why they ever sold one so obviously scorched is a mystery, but at least they let it go for a song. She looked at it this way and that and then her face lit up.

Why, I can make it look like a woman's hoop skirt, with even a hint of a petticoat underneath with the left over fabric from the quilt and Emily's outgrown slip.

Grace was beaming with pleasure as she snipped around her self-made pattern and almost forgot to hide it before Emily, who was looking out the window, calling, "Daddy's home, Daddy's home!"

"Pancakes tonight!" she announced as she scurried around the kitchen while preparing the spur-of-the-moment meal.

The next morning she finished the dainty looking lampshade then decided to keep it in full view. I wonder what Randall will say when he sees it.

It was back to appliqueing the Sunny Bonita pieces after that, and Grace was okay with it being only cot sized and deeply grateful for the crib mattress they had borrowed from her in-laws. Doing one for their double bed would have taken much longer.

She shook out the gorgeous quilt Lily and her had finished together and smoothed it lovingly; *Such warm memories.*

Grace wanted to lay the pink and white blocks aside for a while and start cutting up some of their oldest clothes, the ones which had formerly been used for Emily's mattress, and make them into an oval rug.

She could almost hear Randall's reaction if she did that. 'Grace, you are a wonder! And where did you ever squirrel away enough pennies to buy such a beautiful rug?'

'I didn't," Grace would have responded, feeling almost shy," I made it from our old clothes and cast offs from the Salvation Army Thrift store.')

However, envisioning her mother's stern disapproval was more vivid: and Grace knew the mat she was eager to braid and place beside the bed would have to wait. After watching her mother making rugs for so many years, she knew the knack of getting them to lie flat; and could hardly wait to begin.

Will Randall Notice?

CHAPTER 46

Whether the days were sunny or stormy, Grace didn't really care, the wintery days sped by while she was happily working on various projects.

 Because the young mother slid the cardboard box filled with her undertakings way under the bed, Randall was unaware of the surprises she was planning other than the lampshade, of course, which he hadn't noticed until Emily crowed about it.

It was a sparkly day in December when Grace whimsically stitched "With love from Mommy" in one corner of the quilt and draped it smoothly over the child-sized cot. It will be so cozy now over the winter months.

Emily was so excited that she bounced up and down on it a few times, but Grace didn't have the heart to tell her not to...this time. The little girl propped up her scruffy teddy bear and Grandma-made ragdoll against the pillow then dragged a chair over to the window to see if Daddy was coming.

Since it was too early for him to be off work, and Emily could hardly wait, Grace bundled her up good against the nip in the air and they walked along the streets until they reached the bus stop.

Grace wasn't as warm as her daughter because her coat didn't close anymore.

 It brought forth a few smiles that wintry twilight when the bus doors folded open and Emily danced with impatience until her father climbed out.

"Daddy, Daddy!" Emily squealed, "We got a 'pize for you! We got a 'pize for you!"

She nearly dragged him back to the basement.

"Daddy look! Look what Mommy made for me!"

"WOW!" Randall whistled. "Did you really make that quilt?" Grace nodded modestly, but her eyes sparkled with joy.

"You're a wonder! Whatever are you going to come up with next?"

"As if I'd tell you!" she teased batting her eyelashes at him.
"But as busy as I've been, I haven't forgotten to make supper," she said, going over to their tiny gas stove.

She took the baked chicken and scalloped potatoes out of the oven where they were warming and placed the platter on the table along with a bowl of creamed peas and a carrot-Jell-O salad. After pouring the tea, they were ready to eat.
"Grace, how did you know I got a raise today? Randall teased. "You had the celebration supper ready before I even told you!"
Just as she looked up after prayer, Grace's happiness was dashed as if with cold water. She had the fleeting impression that a little girl, who looked exactly like Emily, was looking pensively through the window at the happy family.
Grace's hand shook as she removed the chicken from the bone on Emily's plate. I should tell Randall about Alice tonight. How will he respond? Oh, Lord how shall I word it? Help me to say it tactfully.
She went over to fill Randall's cup with tea and placed her hand on his shoulder.
"Randall, I..."
Just then, Emily stood up on her chair and reached for the pitcher of milk, her feet slipped, the milk spilled, and as she lay howling on the floor, the moment shattered.
"Grace, what were you about to say?" Randall asked after Emily was comforted and the mess cleaned up.
"Oh, it was nothing, nothing," Grace, stammered, not knowing that her husband had observed how pale and frightened she had become.

Grace reminded herself to hum while scooping ice-cream into three bowls and handing them out. It was a long time before her heart stopped pounding.

By the next day, Grace's mood was back to normal and she scurried around to clean up just as soon as Randall closed the door behind him.

"Come, Emily," she called cheerily. "We're going to the shops!"

You're trying to distract yourself with much activity, her conscience accused her, but she ignored it. They donned their hats and coats and hurried to catch the streetcar at the corner.
An hour later, they were on the way home again with a paper wrapped parcel of material. Grace was planning to make a forest green tablecloth with a sunflower border.

She knew she would be hard put to get it all hemmed before Randall arrived, but stitched furiously until it was time to put supper on, then raced back to her sewing while it cooked. Five-thirty rolled around. He would be in any minute!

She hastily spread it on the table and set the dishes around. That lovely green, yellow and brown tablecloth seemed the perfect finishing touch to their tiny apartment. Somehow, with all the hand-sewn improvements cozying up the place, it just didn't seem like a dingy basement cubicle anymore.

Emily was so beside herself with excitement that Grace walked down to the corner with her to meet Randall. The little-pigtailed girl danced up and down as she clung to her Daddy's hand.

"Mommy has a new 'prize for you, a new 'prize for you, a new 'prize for you!" she sang," I'm not goin' to tell you what it is but it's for the table."

When Randall opened the door, he made an exaggerated pretense of looking for the new item. He exclaimed all over again about the new lampshade, the cheery curtains, the rug, Emily's sweet little bedspread then threw his hands up in mock despair.

"There are so many new things around here! How can a mere man find them all?"

"It's the table cloth Daddy!"

Randall opened his arms wide and his two favorite girls ran into receive big hugs. "Grace, I'm not worthy of a wonderful wife like you," he whispered into her smooth, shiny hair. "Man can't go wrong with a devoted wife like you waiting at home for him."

Then with a wink and a salute, he turned on his heel and marched out the door.

"Where is he going, Mommy?" Emily asked. Grace grinned mischievously, "I don't know, but I think he'll be getting something nice for us. Meanwhile, I'm going to finish hemming this tablecloth!"

She gathered up the dishes and placed them on the counter then rapidly finished hemming the several inches that couldn't be seen from the door.

"He's coming! Daddy's coming!" Emily clapped her hands and danced up and down.

Grace flung it back on the table just as Randall stepped over the threshold. Randall eyebrows rose: "Why did you clear the table?"

"Why do you walk with your hands behind your back?" Grace retorted.

"Which hand? Which hand?" Emily cried.

"Hey, I'm supposed to say that!"

"That one! That one!"

"We'll let Mommy guess this time," Randall cupped Emily's chin with his free hand.

"Ha! I know which one now," Grace said, tugging at his other arm. He produced a beautiful blooming begonia. "There were mostly poinsettias at this time of year but I wanted to get you something you could plant outside in spring."

"Oh, Randall," she cried, "You don't know how much this means to me!"

With a flourish, Randall placed the flower in the center of the table, then they stepped back to admire the dazzling effect it had on the room.

Grace reset the table and even the chipped enamel plates and mismatched cutlery seemed more beautiful. As they filled their plates with cooked potatoes, boiled beets and fried hamburgers, it felt like a feast fit for a king.

Grace slipped her slim hand into Randall's brawny one and while still gazing at the plant, said; "Let's bloom where we're planted for God."

Randall gave her a quizzical look then thoughtfully nodded.

Grace's reflections were interrupted by Emily swirling about the room, her skirts sailing in a full circle and singing "Ever thing is just boo-tee-ful—boo=tee=ful—boo-tee-ful!"

The Mechanic Muses

CHAPTER 47

David lay on his back beneath a customers' slightly rusted yellow Studebaker and with his trusty wrench tightened the final bolt before turning on his side to push himself out. He was glad for the steady work as a mechanic and the reasonably good pay he was receiving but his mind was not on either.

My conscience is free, he muttered. As far as I know I never deliberately killed a man, and if I did, it was only in the name of duty. Why do I have to feel so condemned? Reverend Weihlmann preaches so passionately on the nobility of fighting for one's country. Why can't I be convinced?

He wiped his hands on a grease rag then used a cream cleanser to finish the job properly. Maybe I'm a yellow-bellied green gut. He smiled sardonically at the phrase his gang used to taunt each other with during school days but it didn't lighten his mood.

In spite of opposition from his folks, they had tried several different churches but nothing satisfied.

Someone entered the shop; David pasted a smile on his lips for the owner of the car he had just repaired.

"It's as good as new Mr. Fraser. I'll write up the bill and you can be on your way."

"Thank you, Mr. Seifert. I always come here because of your prompt, dependable service. I've been recommending you to my buddies whenever they gripe about car troubles."

"Well, thank you! No wonder I'm usually over-booked!"

His smile was genuine now.

"By the way, I heard your injuries had been rather severe: how are you managing?"

David didn't want to talk about it.

"I manage."

"Bet you regret V-day coming before you could get your revenge."

David could feel himself recoiling but tried to hide it.

"Naw, it's just a war. I have no personal feelings against the enemy.. They were mostly young fellas that thought : they were doing their duty..." His voice trailed off as he shuffled through some papers: "Now for the bill."

"No, I guess I couldn't get you to forget that," Mr. Fraser joked as he leaned against the counter.

A half hour later David looked at the fine watch that had beena graduation gift from his father: time for dinner. Soon he was clambering up the steep steps to their apartment and looking forward to being with his young family again.

Moments before he had seen three flat noses pressed against the steamed up window and had waved to the excited youngsters that he gratefully called his own.

Now, even before he was half way into the room, Alice flew into his arms.

"Daddy! Daddy!" she squealed.

Junior looked up while setting the table with a lop-sided grin. "Hi Dad,"

"You always hug Alice first!" Sally wailed.

She always runs to me first.

David's smile faded, why did she have to act so whiny, so unthankful? They didn't know how good they had it.

A flashback from the war had been bothering him. They had a way of coming at the oddest times. That girl; that young mother with her tiny baby, where is she now? Was she shot? He saw the cottage riddled with holes, but maybe just maybe, she had found refuge in a root cellar or something. That little kid would be pretty close to Alice's age.

Is she homeless, hungry, cold? Where was her Daddy? Had he been in a prison camp somewhere, or even Siberia? Perhaps one of his own men shot him!

"David!" Margaret exclaimed, seeing his pale set lips. "What's the matter?"

David looked distractedly at her and gently set Alice down between his knees. "A flashback, he reported in a low voice.

"I'll explain later," but then he thought, No, I have to put that all behind me: for the last time.

It wouldn't be that easy.

"What's a flashback," David Junior asked, then with an impish grin added. "Is it when you try to walk with the flashlight behind so you can see what's behind you?"

David ran his hands through his son's already mussed up hair. "Pretty close," he chuckled. "It's a memory. Now, let's eat."

"There'll be just enough time for my young men to comb their hair and wash their hands then I'll have everything ready," Margaret announced while carrying a white pitcher filled with a delicious vanilla sauce to the table.

David scooped up his son around the middle and carried him, legs dangling, over to the kitchen sink.

"Daddy, I'm too big for that," Junior protested, his face turning a bright red, but he was grinning sheepishly.

Soon the Seifert's were crowded around the too small table that they still used. "We're having waffles with peach sauce tonight!" Margaret announced as she carefully removed the cover from the steaming dish.

The waffle iron was a treasured gift from Janet's parents. David nodded.

"I helped bake the waffles!" Davey bragged.

"I helped make the sauce!" Sally chimed in."

"An'-an" I standed on a chair," Alice added. "an' tasted."

David smiled at the exuberant children, but it was evident that he was thinking about other things.

Because Margaret was looking at him, waiting for him to go on, he continued, "No wonder Mommy had time to make such a good meal with such wonderful helpers!"

He winked at Margaret who suppressed a grin. As soon as David slid into his chair, Alice crawled onto his lap. David held her soft warm hands and they bowed their heads for prayer.

Now that the children were older, David reluctantly agreed to pray aloud. Even though his prayers were by rote, Margaret did not complain. Surely, they were better thannothing, and he was good to her in other ways.

Nevertheless, this time she looked up in surprise: this was no memorized prayer.

"Dear Heavenly Father," his voice was husky so he cleared his throat then paused. Everyone waited.

"Dear Heavenly Father, "He began again." Thank you for my wonderful family," once again he needed to clear his throat,

"Thank you, Lord, for Junior, Sally, and Alice. Thank you most of all for Margaret who was willing to come all the way across the dangerous ocean to be our wife and mother. Thank you so much that we have sufficient to eat and a safe place to live. Amen."

Margaret and Sally stared at him. What a deviation from David's normal table grace!

Junior took the opportunity to lean across the table and grab the platter of waffles.

"Hey! You're supposed to let Daddy start first!" Sally protested. After that, everyone acted more normally.

While Margaret busied herself with cutting up waffles for the younger children and topping them with her delicious peach sauce, she cast David a quick, puzzled look: what prompted such a touching prayer? Why is he acting so mellow, so soft towards the children?

"Dad! We had a great game of baseball at school today."

David was focusing all of his attention on his son.

Usually, David looked distracted and barely heard his children unless the ruckus got unbearable.

"Tell me about it, Davey." he encouraged.

"Well, it was a tie for the largest time," Junior began "Henry was up to bat and Ron pitcher. All the bases were loaded. Everyone was tense wondering how he would do. We knew he had a terrific swing, but would Ron pitch him good ones..." and thus began a blow-by-blow account of the play.

"Mommy, Alice spilled her milk on my lap!"

Margaret was unbuttoning the back of Sally's dress and 'shooing' her off to change when Junior concluded his story with..."And boy, did our team cheer when Henry rounded the third base and slid home just as the bell rang!"

When the meal was over, the children stacked the dishes beside the sink and the table dropped back against the wall.

"It's Junior's turn to wash!" Sally said hurriedly, lest someone should suggest otherwise.

"Can't, I have to study for a History test."

He removed his books out of his school bag and flopped on the floor in front of the couch.

"Mommy, he has to do the dishes, doesn't he? He got out of them last time."

"There aren't many, son. You can be done in no time flat and still have plenty of time to study."

"Dishes are woman's work," Junior muttered.

"I know. But it wouldn't be fair for Sally to have more chores than you when she is younger."

Sally cast him a triumphant glance. David Jr. flipped his eraser at her. His aim was good. Too good.

"Ow!" Sally gave chase. He raced away.

David grabbed his arm in passing, "Slow down, son. There's not enough room for rough-housing." David felt sympathetic, however, as he recalled the children's reaction when they had stopped to talk to a janitor at an office building. They had torn up and down the halls, frisky as colts. They need more space, but that would come soon. The blueprints were already on the drawing board.

After finishing the dishes, Sally curled up in the corner of the living room couch with a storybook while David Jr. resumed his position on the floor. Margaret sat in the rocking chair to share a picture book with Alice. After David had retrieved his newspaper from just outside the door, he sank gratefully into his favorite, or rather the only, armchair.

There was a pensive look in Margaret's gentle brown eyes. What was bothering David when he came home for supper?

"Dad, where is Sarajevo? Davey looked up from his thick blue textbook.

"In Bosnia. What are you learning about, son?"

"World War one. Some guy ass—um- ass-assassinated some big shot—— Archduke Fernand I think his name was. Francis Ferdinand. Ferdin-and. I mean, and that caused the war to start."

Margaret sighed: Only in grade school and already they have to teach him that stuff.

David lowered his paper. He looked sober. "Son, this won't give you an A on your paper, I'm afraid, but all wars are rooted in hatred, greed, and envy."

Junior looked up in surprise. "Weren't you a soldier once, Dad? I thought it would be thrilling to be in the army!"

"Thrilling?" David gave a short laugh.

"Well, exciting then...or, or—noble, maybe?"

David shook his head, paused, and then shook it again.

"No son. Exciting wouldn't exactly be the right word. Not even thrilling. Tramping through half-frozen mud carrying a heavy rifle isn't a walk in the park.

"I am thankful to be a Canadian and once was convinced that joining the army was the noble thing to do." He fell silent. I don't believe many of our young men had gallant intentions when they joined the army, they were in it for the adventure, to escape the boredom of farm life for example.

David Jr. chewed on his lower lip. He really hadn't wanted to a listen to a sermon.

"It wasn't noble at all. The fact that we were shooting at fellow human beings sickened me and it still does. Davey, we were shooting at Daddy's who had little ones just like you and Sally and Alice.

They're also created in God's own image. It didn't seem right to cause them to suffer, or be killed."

He fell silent and hid behind the newspaper.

David Jr. doodled circles in the margin of his rough copy, and then looked up. "Um, Dad, where did you say Bosnia was?"

David was lost in thought.

"Let's look it up on the map," Margaret suggested.

There was a nice one in the big atlas stored under the couch and they hovered over it while Margaret leafed through the stiff pages to find Eastern Europe. David had retreated into a shell behind the paper.

David Jr. had fun trying to pronounce various strange sounding names and they got quite engrossed in a little history-geography lesson.

After a while, Margaret looked at the teapot shaped clock on the wall and suggested that they should have devotions.

Since David was always a silent listener, Margaret got out the Bible Story Book and read with two children snuggled up on either side of her and one on Daddy's lap.

"Before we pray," David interrupted, "I want to read the verse Mommy embroidered and hung on the wall: it's from Isaiah 39.

'He shall feed his flock like a Shepherd; he shall gather the lambs in his arms and carry them in his bosom. He shall gently lead those who are with young."

When Margaret met David's eyes, she saw Pain in them. Surely, this scripture has something to do with what was on David's mind when he came home tonight.

Three pairs of round sober eyes gazed at him.

"Some children are sad and lonely and are even going hungry. Tonight I want to pray for them."

After devotions were over, Sally stretched up on her tiptoes to put her arms around her David's neck. "I'm glad you are my Daddy and take such good care of us," she whispered.

Church Hunt

CHAPTER 48

The next mornings' mail brought the Sutherland's a flier welcoming them to attend services in one of the numerous city churches. Grace studied it thoughtfully then showed it to her husband. Randall merely glanced at it before tossing it on the table.

"Do you want to check it out sometime?"

Grace shrugged one shoulder. "Let's. We need to find food for the soul somewhere."

Grace was doing some serious fretting about the state of their wardrobes. Practically everything they owned was disgracefully shabby.

Then she gave a squeal of delight: Emily was four now. Could she possibly fit into that delightful lemon yellow frock Margaret had chosen for her so very long ago?

With eager, trembling hands, Grace unlocked the trunk and there it was in all its satiny glory. She lifted it high and shook out a few soft wrinkles.

"Emily, come here! I have something to show you!"

Emily skipped over, "Oh, it's pretty! Is it mine?"

"Yes, it is. Let's see if it fits you."

Emily was so excited to be getting something brand new that

Grace had difficulty pulling it over her head and tying the satiny bow at the back.

"Oh, how lovely," Grace exclaimed! "It was barely long enough but that could be remedied eventually since there was an ample hem. She tied the belt tighter; Emily was such a skinny twerp.

What will I wear, she mused. Oh, my maternity dresses! Of course! What perfect timing! She had packed them away when the twins were born they are in lovely condition. It will be a discreet way to announce that I am with-child.

, After gently passing over the red plaid skirt she had been wearing when Margaret first came into her life, Grace selected a two-piece dark blue outfit, which had three quarter length sleeves, embroidery on the cuffs and a scalloped neckline. It was the one she had been wearing while boarding the train but didn't want to think of that, now.

Grace was happy to discover the hatbox where her best hat and white Sunday gloves were stored and confident that she would feel appropriately dressed for the occasion.

What could Randall wear? She lifted up his dress uniform and gazed at it, smiling reflectively. This is what he was wearing when he swept me off my feet. It is still in perfect condition.

Would it be suitable for going to church, though? Oh, perhaps not….under the circumstances…. Who would know? It would be embarrassing if found out.

I wonder what is way down at the bottom of the trunk that Mama Lily may have packed and I don't even know about.

Here is a tan and beige sports sweater that I have never seen him wear. Oh and here is a white dress shirt. The collar is sort of frayed. I wonder if I would be able to turn it around so the good side shows. I'll have to try. These medium brown slacks will work just fine.

Grace sang as she mended the clothes and washed them in the sink. Emily caught her joyful spirit. Randall looked on fondly.. He loved to see her so happy. She seems like such a cheery butterfly these days. I can imagine how much like Emily she would have been as a little girl: if he only knew.

The clothes soon dangled from a line that strung across the room.

From time to time Grace ran over to the dripping garments to see if they were dry.

"They won't get dry any faster by you stroking them so fondly," Randall remarked drily.

"Oh, I know," she responded and he loved the soft pink of her blush.

After eating, Grace forgot about the slowly drying garments long enough to go for a walk with Randall and Emily.

There was a tiny park several blocks away. Emily was delighted with the merry-go-round, but they had to find something else for her to do when she began staggering drunkenly.

It was a lovely evening to take the streetcar downtown just to see the lights coming on all over the city.

"I will miss it when the street cars are a thing of the past,"

Grace remarked.

Randall nodded. "But so many people own cars nowadays that they aren't needed so much anymore."

When they got back, the clothes were dry enough to press!

"No one would ever guess how poor we are!" Grace exclaimed after they tried the garments on.

Randall's face clouded over.

Grace could have bit her tongue, what should I do to soothe his feelings?

"Oh, but we won't always be," she said. "With a wonderful provider like you at the helm, we'll go places!"

Randall's face relaxed into a relieved grin.

The next morning they took the trolley bus then walked the extra block or two to get to the church. Feeling just a mite self-conscious in their like new attire, they hesitated just inside the door until an usher nodded to them and showed them to a pew nearly half way up. Later when the offering plate came around Randall dug into his pocket and dropped in a dollar bill.

Grace frowned. Did they have to support a preacher they didn't even know? Oh, well, it's good that Randall cares enough about Christianity to want to do his part, and we are doing better since he's not spending his money on liquor.

The church service began with a stout woman beating out a tune on the piano. Grace cringed. It was an old familiar hymn, but she hit the wrong chords more than once, and each time it was on a high note!

The thin smattering of voices half -heartedly joining in on the singing did little to improve the sound. It brought back memories of going to church in Birmingham.

A young enthusiastic looking preacher strode to the pulpit and Grace soon forgot about looking around. With so much talent, how had he ended up in such plain surroundings? He would have kept them in stitches if it had not been such a sacred atmosphere. As it was, Grace saw teenagers snickering behind their hands. No doubt, he would be moving on to a loftier pulpit sooner rather than later.

After the service was over, Grace found it gratifying that's several worshippers came to shake hands with them. When the parishioners turned back to their own groups, Randall and Grace slipped out.

"Well that sure was enjoyable," Grace beamed as they headed home. Randall raised a quizzical eyebrow but did not make a comment.

"We'll go again, next Sunday, won't we?"

He shrugged and then nodded, "If we aren't too tired."

Grace agreed to that.

They went the next Sunday and the next, then continued until it began to feel like 'their' church. They made friends with another young couple who showed up about as often as they did.

Throughout the week, Grace sometimes found herself thinking about the funny stories that the preacher would so dramatically present. Obviously, his reputation was spreading because each Sunday more and more attendees showed up. His stories all had a good moral attached but Grace had a hard time remembering them later.

Randall became less enthused about attending church, and his excuses were numerous. It was too far, or he was too tired, Emily's has the sniffles so he didn't think they should take her out in the cold were some of his pretexts.

Dissatisfied and Longing for More

CHAPTER 49

After a few months, Grace decided not to suggest going unless he mentioned it first. He didn't, so they just stopped attending. Grace was disappointed that no one came around even after several weeks to ask them why they were not attending. Are we that unimportant?

Grace had been lacking the sweet communion with her Heavenly Father for quite some time and was missing it more lately. What had gone wrong, spiritually?

One Sunday afternoon when both Randall and Emily were napping, she got out Lily's dear old Bible, dusted it off and scanned all the underlined parts.

She yearned for the sweet camaraderie she had had first with Margaret and later with Lily. It would be nice to find others with whom the fellowship felt so warm and good. The chapel on 29th Street was okay but her heart had rarely felt warmed and filled there as it had with her dearest friends in bygone years.

She wondered if borrowing so many books from the local library had been making it difficult to appreciate the depth found in God's holy word.

Surely, the Grace Livingstone Hill books were beneficial at least. Weren't they? She thought regretfully of her newly acquired habit of choosing other bedtime stories for Emily and the Bible Storybook lay on the shelf forgotten. "Where is the blessedness I knew when first I found the Lord?" she sighed while gazing nowhere in particular.

The more she studied the word that Sunday afternoon, the more troubled she became. She looked up. Randall was drawing at the kitchen table, by then. It was a favorite pass time of his now that he was more relaxed and happy. Grace was amazed at his sketching ability.

"Randall, how do you really feel about the church we used to go to?"

Randall lightly erased a line before looking up. "I didn't know what to expect," he admitted." since church never was on my high priority list. But I hadn't been feeling as satisfied as I had expected to."

Grace's brow furrowed. "What do you think was the matter?"

Randall shook his head. "Who knows, what do you think?"

Grace shrugged her shoulders and closed the Bible but kept her thumb in it. "I read just now, about not forsaking the assembling of ourselves together but what if going to church can hardly be called a blessing?"

He kept drawing as if he had not heard her.

Grace studied his expression. "You'd rather not go back, right?"

Randall nodded. "I went because you seemed to enjoy it, and you are the older Christian. I thought maybe, just maybe I would get more out of it eventually, but it didn't work that way."

He lined up his pencil with the top of the page, and Emily who had also awakened took that as a sign that she could clamber up on his lap. He gently pressed her head against his chest and stroked her hair.

"But why don't we feel satisfied?" Grace was puzzled. "I know I've become rather indifferent to having my personal devotions and that scares me. Margaret always stressed the importance of daily communion with God. We don't want our Christian lives to go down the drain."

Randall picked up his pencil once again and sketched in the ear of a cougar. It was intently eyeing a herd of deer that appeared to be drifting closer to the rock overhang, the cougar concealed from their view.

"Yeah," Randall nodded, "We haven't been hungering and thirsting after righteousness like we ought".

Grace stared at him. "Where did you learn that verse?" She got up to lean her arm across his shoulder. He tweaked her nose.

"I'm not quite the heathen you think I am," he kidded.

"Sunday School was a habitual part of my life until my thirteenth birthday."

"Thirteen! Why did you quit at such a young age?"

Randall sighed as if reluctant to go on. "I loved nature and was pretty keen on hunting and trapping in those days." He continued sketching idly for a while without speaking. Grace sensed that he had more to say so did not interrupt his thoughts. He reached up to take her hand.

"The twins died when I was twelve. I guess nature walks were my way of coping with it.

"I got skilled at catching rabbits, squirrels, and martins, and even trapped the occasional weasel and wolverine. Mom was pretty happy about that because either a weasel or a martin was getting our chickens that year and that eliminated the problem.

"It was fun at the time, but looking back, I can see it never completely concealed the deep ache in my heart. That's when Dad and I started to drift apart.

"We took the finer looking hides to be tanned in Edmonton and all that spare cash made me feel pretty heady." He fiddled with an eraser for a moment before continuing. "It was years before Mom could look at a baby before tearing up. It made me pretty bitter to see her so unhappy but I tried not to think about it."

Grace was uneasily quiet.

"Eventually I had enough money to buy a fine hunting dog.

"One of my best buddies was a native Indian boy who was at a residential school much of the time but managed to teach me a lot about wildlife and nature when he was around."

Emily sat up straight. "What happened to the dog, Daddy?" They had not even known she was listening.

"It died." Was his voice getting husky on him? "It attacked a pack of wolves that was following us. The deer were elsewhere that winter, and the wolves appeared to be hungry."

"Oh, Randall!"

"Guess ole Champion thought he had to protect us from that pack of howlers. He didn't have a chance against so many, the poor guy, but he was sure fiercely loyal! Red Feather—I mean George had the presence of mind to shoot the leader of the wolves and the rest fled.

"I didn't have the heart to replace him. The dog, I mean, not the wolf!" He grinned lopsidedly.

"How old were you then?"

"Seventeen, maybe eighteen."

Grace quietly went to put the kettle on then later served tea and biscuits. "How did your mother feel about you not going to Sunday school?"

"I think she was pretty indifferent at first. She was taking it very hard that Rhoda and Rachel died and didn't go much herself, anymore. It wasn't until the pastor and his wife visited us fairly regularly and had us over for meals that she pulled out of it. Grandpa and Grandma—her folks, — came over more often then, and I think she got what you call converted. Dad couldn't give a—-"

"Randall!"

"Sorry. That was just a slip. Dad did not care whether I went or not. They were both hurting badly that God had taken my little sisters when they had waited so long for another child. "

Grace sipped her tea without a word. She didn't realize how ill she was looking. Randall did, however, his brows furrowed knowing that she often had nervous reactions to who-knows-what but also aware that she would refuse to talk about it.

Emily picked up a pencil and made her own picture in the corner of Randall's.

He quickly erased it and gave her another piece of paper to scribble on.

"So how are we going to respond to God?" Grace paused before adding, "How should we respond to Him? It seems like the church should tell us how to um, I think it's called grow in grace."

"Okay, let's admit it, "Randall drew a few final strokes on the sleek swishing tail of the cougar then laid his pencil down.

"If all we wanted from Church was entertainment we might as well go to the movies."

Grace gasped. "So what should we expect from a church?"

"Emily. Draw on your own paper. Please. This is Daddy's." He paused: "Inspiration? Direction? A sense of His presence? What do you think?"

"Something like that." She pushed her hair behind her ears. "More than anything, I'd like to have the assurance that we are on the right way to Heaven."

Grace stirred her tea thoughtfully.

"We sure don't want to miss Heaven's gate by being too casual."

Grace regarded him over her amber beverage: "So let's try another church."

Randal nodded.

"Tonight."

"Naw, this little kiddo-o needs to get to bed early. She's getting sleepy."

"I'm not sleepy, Daddy!"

Grace made a few sandwiches for them, and then after eating, fetched the Engermier's Bible storybook and read to Emily. She tried to teach her the song Jesus Loves Me. It was lovely listening to her warble in her clear high treble but knew it would be awhile before she could sing it all by herself. I wonder if Alice has learned that song.

Grace tugged at the string for the overhead light and sat down beside Randall at the kitchen table. They both prayerfully read in their Bibles while Emily played nearby. A peaceful silence reigned for about ten minutes.

Grace looked up. "I keep finding verses similar to this one in second Corinthians thirteen: 'Greet one another with a holy kiss," She looked at him almost shyly. "Doesn't it sound so loving? Do you think there are churches where that custom is practiced?"

"I hope so. It sounds so Biblical. I've been reading about Jesus' last days on earth. Part of it mentions how he washed the disciple's feet and instructed them to do likewise. I haven't been to any church, yet, where it is practiced. Can we really be Christians if we don't obey His teachings?"

"Or is it outdated?"

Randall frowned. "If those verses are outdated, then what is truth? What kind of Rock can we stand on?"

They discussed what they thought the church closest to the Bible should or would be like and visited several different ones but always left shaking their heads.

"I think we are just too fussy," Grace concluded.

Randall crossed the room and laid his hand on her shoulder. "Maybe the kind of church we are looking for won't be found in the city."

She looked at him questioningly.

"Country churches tend to cling to old fashioned values longer."

Grace walked over to the door and gazed at the thousands of stars in the sky. Her eyes focused on the two in the Dipper that always lined up with the North Star: "Oh to find a home for the soul!"

Randall followed her and looked where she looked. His resolve hardened. I must take the initiative in finding a spiritual home for my family.

Abe Wiens

CHAPTER 50

Good morning, sir, would you care for something to read?"

Randall looked quizzically at the older middle-aged man with his thick snow-frosted beard. This certainly wasn't the warmest time of year to be standing on the street handing out pamphlets.

Nearby some bells were chiming out the tune of 'Oh Little Town of Bethlehem', and it put him in a mellow mood.

"Sure." I'm not too busy anyways. "Which church are you affiliated with?"

The man told Randall then added. "It's a Mennonite church, but there aren't any in this city. The nearest one would be close to Russet, which is north of Edmonton.

Russet! Hey, he knew that place! His Aunt Sara lived there!

"Say, do you by any chance know Stanley Falkner?"

"Stanley? Sure, I went to high school with him!"

Randall scuffed his foot in the snow. "Happen to know how he is doing?"

"Haven't heard a word about him in a long time; do you know him?"

Randall nodded. "We spent our early years at the same one-room schoolhouse. Later I met him in Northern France and we fought in the same battles."

"Ohh."

Randall's newfound friend reached out his hand to passersby.

"Care to take a tract, sir?"

"Thank you."

He was kept busy sharing leaflets for a few minutes. Randall leaned against the brick wall of the old Town Hall building behind him, in no hurry to go anywhere. He skimmed through the small coloured pamphlet.

It was Saturday morning and Randall had been scouting around for work. He was tired of the foul language at his second job at the welding shop and hoped to find something different.

Although they enjoyed their janitorial duties at the airport, with Grace being in the family way, he wanted her at home to rest and take care of herself.

The tract was about salvation: how a person needed to admit their sins and repent in order to find peace within but it also mentioned finding a church home where the fellow believers also had new birth experiences and were trying to live the Bible way.

"Hey, this is right on! "Randall exclaimed.

"Are you a believer?"

"A-a what?"

"Uh, have you repented of your sins and accepted Jesus as your Savior?"

"I certainly have, but it's this part of a church that intrigues me. Tell, me, what does your church beliefs include?"

The tract worker packed the remainder of his tracks in his briefcase while saying, "Come. Let's go somewhere for coffee and get acquainted. I'll do what I can to answer your questions."

"There's a nice place south of here a block or two," Randall explained. "And the coffee's good."

They found a quiet table to sit at and introduced themselves.

"Okay. So what were you wondering about?"

"We are looking for a church home; my wife and I. Different things we have found mentioned in the Bible but are not in any church where we have gone. One is feet washing.

"I've been fighting in the war like so many other young men, and we've got to thinking that it doesn't seem like the Bible way: at least not the New Testament way.

"My wife and I are studying the book of Matthew and it doesn't sound like Jesus wanted his people to fight. I thought we read something about loving your enemies and doing good to those that despitefully use you.

"Something like that anyway. I don't remember the exact words."

Abe Wien's leafed through his little pocket Testament until he found the correct passage.

They leaned over the Good Book their heads nearly touching.

"Nonresistance," Abe explained, "Is one of our most basic doctrines. It goes far beyond just not going to war." He reached for the small pitcher on the table and stirred a little cream into his drink.

"The Bible says, "By this shall all men know that you are my disciples if ye have love for one another. That definitely includes greeting one another with the kiss of charity as you mentioned earlier. The fruit of the spirit is love, joy, peace, gentleness, meekness, long-suffering. Sorry, I can't remember them all off hand, but I think you get the picture.

"We really strive to be a humble, gentle people and love God with all our hearts as well as our neighbour as ourselves. This begins in the home, of course. If we aren't peaceable and forgiving at home, where it counts the most, we're really aren't nonresistant. We believe very strongly in loving our neighbors and that obviously includes not hurting them."

"Didn't any of your young men go to war? How did they get away with not going?"

Randall had visions of them thrown into prison camps but Mr. Wiens told them that many of them were able to serve as Conscientious Objectors doing other jobs. He looked troubled and Randall didn't know until much later that it was because those that hadn't truly been non-resistant in everyday life had been forced to become soldiers.

They talked for a long time, and then Abe looked at his watch. "I really must be going. It will be late before I get home and my wife will worry."

As the men rose to go, they shook hands.

"I want to learn more," Randall said, "Do you think we could meet again, sometime?"

"Actually I'm not in the city very often except on business. I'm foreman of the sawmill west of Russet and we keep pretty busy at this time of year. What do you do for a living?"

"Well... I'm mostly just looking for a different job, right now."

Abe seemed to be sizing him up.

"You look like a strong young man. Have you ever thought of working in a lumber camp?"

"Actually, I've done quite a lot of it."

"We can always use another man or two at the sawmill. Care to apply one of these days?"

"Sure. How far is Russet from here?"

"Sixty-five miles. We provide snug houses for the families and bunk houses for the unmarried.

"You did say you were married, didn't you? "

Randall nodded.

"We have a couple spare cottages right now. Well, I must be on my way. Stop in sometime if you're serious about working at the sawmill."

"You'll hear from me again!"

They each donned their cozy fur-lined caps, buttoned their woolen coats and braved the nippy north wind that had sprung up.

The temperature had fallen along with the night, but the cheery sounds of Christmas caroling drifted through the air.

"Shall I take you somewhere?" Abe asked. Randall hesitated.

"Well, it's pretty far from home," he admitted.

"I'll take you back."

Randall grinned to himself as they traveled. Russet was only three hours from Deer Flats, at 25 miles per hour. He knew how much Grace enjoyed visiting with his mother.

Maybe they would get to see his folks more often if he worked at the Russet sawmill.

"I wonder what is keeping him so long," Grace had just murmured when two white pools of light tunneled through the darkness. A moment later, she had her hands on Randall's shoulders—until she looked up and saw This Stranger standing behind him!

"Oh, hello... Sir... I didn't notice you come in." She reached out her hand and he shook it. "Would you care to have supper with us? I fed our little girl, but there is plenty left."

"Thank you, that sounds good."

Randall introduced his companion as a tract worker that he met over by the town hall.

"I had a wonderful visit with Mr. Wiens this afternoon and it got kind of late for him. He lives over by Russet."

"Oh, that's so far! Would you like to spend the night?" Grace looked helplessly around their wee abode. They had no place to put up a guest: not even on a sofa.

"I appreciate your offer. Thank you. Since it's too late to go home, anyway, I think I'll just stay at the Hotel. Isn't there a good one over on Jasper Avenue?

"I think so."

"I wonder if I could use your telephone."

"We don't have one but I'm sure the landlady would let you call from hers."

While he was using the telly, Grace scurried around picking up the crayons and scraps of paper Emily hadn't found before going to bed then set the table for the three of them.

A few minutes later, they sat down to bowls of hot, savory beef and noodle soup and homemade biscuits.

Grace was surprised when Randall asked Mr. Wiens to lead in a table prayer but it warmed her heart. The voices woke Emily and she crawled into her father's arms, but was soon back to sleep soothed by the gentle cadences.

Grace soon concluded that Abe was a genuinely humble Christian and felt little flutters of anticipation. Maybe he would have spiritual direction for them! Maybe the hunger in their souls would soon be satisfied!

It had not taken long before the conversation slipped from trivial things to meaningful.

"I have never met a couple so hungry for the word," Abe admitted as he poured brown sugar sauce over his piece of gingerbread. "It has been a real blessing to get to know you."

They talked long into the night and she knew before Mr. Wiens said his final farewells that they would be packing up for the tenth time in their married life and moving to another sawmill, but this time she didn't mind.

While the men were pouring over various scriptures, she heated water for doing dishes. Mentally she was already rearranging and storing belongings into boxes. She looked lovingly around the tiny apartment. The begonia on the table still looked healthy, even if it had become long and lanky and absent of blooms. She hoped it would survive transportation in such cold weather. Maybe in springtime, I can cut it down and coax it to bloom outside somewhere. I wonder if that would be possible.

The lovely bedspread, tablecloth, and lampshade would go with them of course. She wondered what Mr. Wiens thought of such beauty in a humble dwelling such as theirs but dismissed the thought as foolishness. Men didn't notice those things very quickly, did they? Except for Randall!

Her eyes were dry with weariness by the time Mr. Wiens shook her hand and ventured out into the swirling snow.

Randall and Grace stood in the open doorway to see him off, and then Grace hurried back in to tuck the blanket more securely around Emily's shoulder. The temperature was dropping!

The Cold Dark Wilderness

CHAPTER 51

Before too many days went by, they had packed all their belongings in to the trunk and handy wooden slat boxes Lily had provided. Over the years, they had accumulated more 'stuff' so Randall went out to get extra storage containers.

Mr. Wiens graciously offered to use his 1946 International three/quarter ton to haul their belongings. Randall' crawled along behind in their not so dependable dark blue Oldsmobile.

Grace chewed on her lip: "I do hope we'll get there without any trouble,"

"Don't count on it," Randall grinned just as the car sputtered and died. They were prepared for 'minor' emergencies but by the time he installed a new battery, the shiny red truck with its jaunty white plume of smoke trailing behind it was over a hill and far away. With the roads so hard packed, there was not even a track to follow.

"We'll catch up to him pretty soon," Randall, ever the optimist, announced. Grace was not so sure especially after snowflakes floated lazily down.

Soon Randall needed to switch on the windshield wipers and slowed down. "We're doing fine," he encouraged. "I'm sure we're on the right road. There hasn't been any turn off for miles."

"There's one ahead," his wife pointed. Just then, the wipers quit working.

Grace groaned. Randall stopped to fiddle with them while Emily stared out the back window, her arms wrapped tightly around her fat teddy.

"Grace, could you walk over to the turn-off and see which way the truck went?" Grace hurried through the blowing snow, clutching her collar close to her cheeks.

"It went to your left," she called on her way back, "But the tracks are blotting out pretty fast. Should we turn back?"

"Oh no, we'll be fine," he replied, trying once again to coax the wipers to start. He did not remind her that they were half ways there and did not have any home to turn back to.

With the doors, opening and closing so much Emily started, shivering and whimpering. The blanket covering her simply was not adequate for this kind of emergency. Grace looked worried: what should she do? The rest of the bedding was on the truck. She carefully removed some towels that were protecting the box of dishes on the floor and tucked them around her little girl. It only helped for a moment.

Emily wanted to sit up and see what was going on. She was scared of all the darkness around them and crying because of the cold. Grace was hard-put trying to keep her covered but being busy kept her own fears under control.

I wonder what the temperature is by now. I am so thankful that our unborn baby is still snug and warm.

The wipers started so Randall turned confidently down the

side road. Then had not gone ten miles when they encountered drifts so bad that Randall was not sure he would be able to plow through them.

"Grace see if we're still following the tracks,"

"I can't tell!"

"Well, we'll just have to keep on. I do not recall any turn-off do you?"

Grace shook her head uncertainly. The snow was so blinding it was hard to know.

They managed to plunge ahead for another mile or so then stalled in a snowdrift. Grace held Emily close. We are in the middle of nowhere, and how will anyone ever find us? She looked bleakly at the forest of snow-covered trees surrounding them, then leaned her head against the window and prayed, both hands protectively covering her abdomen.

Randall kicked the tires. Oh, if only I hadn't packed the snow shovel in the back of the truck, What was I ever thinking?

Grace put Emily down so they could try removing the snow in front of the vehicle, but she wailed loudly. It was obvious they would never get anywhere, using only their hands and feet so they carefully unpacked the crate of dishes. Randall admonished Emily not to play with them then used the box to scoop and dump the snow off the road in front of the car. It seems so useless because the snow was falling faster than ever.

When Grace shivered violently, he told her to get back into the vehicle and keep Emily warm. Icy tears froze on Emily's cheeks and Grace removed her frost-hardened mittens to warm the little girl's face, but she had to warm her own hands before she could do it. They eventually managed to get out of the drifted snow.

"Where there's a will there's away," Randall stated but not the upbeat attitude he had when they left the city.

The windshield wipers would not budge again so Randall had to drive along with the window wide open in order to see.

Grace worried about how bluish his neck was getting beneath his cap line. Emily was getting much too cold also even though Grace had crawled into the back seat to cuddle with her. She removed her coat to wrap it around their daughter and pulled the blanket around both of them.

After a few more miles, the car stalled, the engine died and Randall noticed how pale her face had become.

"Is it the battery again?"

Randall shook his head. "I don't think so. Too much snow got under the hood, I'm afraid."

Grace tightly clasped her hands. "Let's pray," she quavered.

Randall removed his cap. His copper-coloured hair fluffed up in the flurry and was quickly decorated with melting flakes before he cranked up the window. At least it was a trifle warmer with it closed.

She supposed.

With his hands gripping the steering wheel, he bowed his head and spoke a few terse entreaties ending with a quiet Amen. Randall got out and looked under the hood but did not have a clue what to do. As far as the eye could see, there was no one in sight on that little-traveled logging road.

What will happen to us? Grace wondered. Will we freeze to death?

Emily piped up. "Mommy, I'm hungry." Grace fumbled around in the dark for the basket of food and handed her some animal crackers and half a banana. Then she remembered the thermos of chocolate milk and poured her a cup. That will help to warm her on the insides.

Both Randall and Grace were silently praying. Nighttime came early in the North Country, and it was getting desperately cold in the car. There was not a light in sight or Randall would have walked to get help.

He was tucking his fur-lined gloves into his sleeves, anyway, and muffling his cheeks with a wool scarf to launch out on Mission Impossible when curved like a halo; a light glowed and gradually grew larger before separating into two distinct beams. Randall leaped out of the car and waved both arms wildly. He would not have needed to.

It was Abe Wiens. He rolled down his window and shouted:

"I thought you must have been having trouble when I couldn't see you behind me." He jumped out of the truck and searched for the snow shovel. "It was a long time before I found a place suitable to turn this big truck around."

The snow was flying vigorously off the top of the shovel while he spoke. When he stopped to rest on the handle, Randall took over. Grace looked down the long, empty road and at all the falling snowflakes lit up by the beams of the truck: "I am so glad you are here."

"Climb into my truck with your little girl where it is warmer and we'll see if we can get your car out."

He fastened a chain around a heavy-duty part under the car then got into his own truck to shift it into gear. With hardly any effort, it eased the smaller vehicle out of the snowbank. Abe jumped out of his rig to unfasten the chain and turned to leave, calling "I'll go slowly so you can stay close behind me."

Randall had other thoughts. "Could you wait a minute? I'm having trouble with my windshield wipers."

Abe, who was mechanically inclined, tinkered with them for a while then looked under the hood. "Something's broke," he announced. "You'll need to get a new motor for your wipers."

"That'll only be the second or third time," Randall grinned, as he ducked into the car to turn the key in the ignition.

"Ur, uh, I have another problem," he added. "The car won't start." Abe worked on it for a while but had no better success.

"Well, hop in with me. We'll get you home and bring the car tomorrow. BRRR that's if it isn't buried under a snow drift by then."

The truck cab was so deliciously warm and cozy that Emily stopped whimpering and fell sound asleep in her mother's arms. Grace dozed also with the aroma of old leather and shavings influencing her dreams.

She woke up when Mr. Wiens shifted into a lower gear and they entered the temporary settlement. It was a welcome sight to see the lights of the hamlet twinkling through the trees.

Tiny Cottage in a Snowbank

CHAPTER 52

*A*h, so this will be home for the next several months. The tiny, unlighted cottage seemed to be nestled into a snowdrift but Grace didn't care. At least it was home; at least it was a place to lay her tired head.

Or, was it? Would there even be any beds?

As soon as Grace peered in the door, she caught sight of the welcoming red-orange glow of a fire banked in the wood stove.

What blessed comfort, warmth, and cheer. While she sank down in front of the heater with Emily leaning against her, the men wrestled with the mattresses to put them on the built in cots and dumped the bedding on top. Grace left her cozy place beside the fire to straighten out the blankets and ice cold sheets. They crawled in, removing little more than their boots and belts.

Emily's teddy, which she had been clinging to all day, was not security enough anymore, so she ended up snuggling between Randall and Grace.

Sometime during the night, Randall got up to add more wood to the trusty stove but the others slept on. While he was doing it, he had long and tender thoughts about the deep responsibility to care for his dear family and prayed that he could do more than just an adequate job.

Grace woke up to the pleasant fragrance of a wood fire and was delighted with the little cottage by daylight.

"I'd love to stay here forever," Grace remarked.

Randall was sitting nearby searching for a suitable scripture to share with the family for morning devotions. He looked up in surprise.

"Why, so?" he asked.

Grace pointed out the main window displaying the silvery-pink colors of a bright new sunrise.

Young, delicate-looking willow trees were nearby and in the distance, she saw many fir trees weighed down with their burdens of heavy snow.

"Just look how beautiful it is." She walked over and stood behind his chair. "I have a good feeling about this place. Remember, Abe Wiens is being so kind to us. Did you notice how the houses were lit up last night? It was obvious that, in spite of the snow, people were socializing together. It looks like a friendly neighbourhood.

Grace stretched her arms then prepared to cook oatmeal on the wood stove while Randall brought the table and other things in. It was marvelous having more than just barely enough elbowroom!

As the porridge bubbled, she looked around happily. I love these varnished walls and the well built planed floor, it looks so clean and bright.

Just before they sat down to eat; she hurried to find the begonia in order to center it on the table. Unfortunately, it was only a forlorn shadow of its former self so she knew it would be discarded.

While they were eating, Randall offered to ask his mother for a cutting off her red geranium next time they saw her.

"Mom says geraniums are hardier than begonias," he explained, "and you would be able to start your own in early spring, or as soon as we can get cuttings."

While Grace was putting her crockery behind the curtained off cupboards, a neighbor by the name of Eva, popped in with a big pot of savory soup. Grace eagerly got out her lovely teacups from Lily and they shared a fragrant pot of Red Rose tea. They chatted amiably for over an hour before her visitor bundled up her youngsters and went back to her own cottage.

Emily had been shy at first of the two small overall-clad boys but soon the three of them were playing happily. Grace was delighted that her little girl would have small children with whom she could play.

"Why do those women wear those black thingies on their heads?" Grace asked as she buttered a piece of bread for Emily at dinner.

Randall tried to look sober but there was a twinkle in his eye. "That's to show that they are willing to submit to their husbands."

Grace pretended to shoo him off with her hand but was curious to know what it really meant so decided to see if there was any Scriptural basis for wearing a cap, head covering, or whatever it was called. She knew many women wore hats in public and especially to church and had assumed it was more of a fashion statement than anything. These head-coverings that were so uniform in color and style certainly didn't fit into the same category as hat, did they? Eventually, Grace found what she was searching for: in 1st Corinthians eleven. She read about wearing a head covering, and yes, it did mention submission but that was only one of the reasons.

Soon the Sutherlands were feeling very much at home with the sawmill crew.

"Randall, did you notice that most of these folks are from Mennonite families?" she asked several days later.

He nodded.

"I've never seen, let alone met Mennonites before so didn't know what to expect. They are nice people, aren't they?"

Randall agreed. "There's no cursing or swearing or dirty jokes spread among these fellows, which is such a relief." He yawned, stretched then swooped Emily up into his arms: "C'mon Little Pipsqueak, it's story time!"

"Oh, goodie, goodie. Can we read about the Three Bears?"

"Yes, but then we will read one from the Bible story book."

"Will it be about Baby Jesus?"

"Not this time." He couldn't remember exactly which one they had read last, but suspected it would more likely be about one of His miracles.

Grace sank into the well-worn but comfortable armchair someone had lent them and beamed affectionately at father and daughter so happily snuggling on the aging sofa they had discovered at a second-hand store.

Randall was fitting in well and Grace wondered if he ever even thought about drinking anymore. She enjoyed watching him stride towards the house, ruddy of complexion, fragrant with the scent of freshly sawed wood, and ravenously hungry.

"It sure feels good being with this crew," Randall remarked as he put his feet up on the ledge in front of the wood stove. 'In other work-gangs, I felt uncomfortable when coarse stories or curse words were shared." To say nothing of the anger and bitterness that sometimes leached out when former soldiers got to reminiscing.

Grace nodded sympathetically, "Careful that you don't melt holes in your boots," she cautioned. He ignored her until he was good-and-ready to remove his feet.   She picked up one of Emily's dresses and sewed a button back on. "So what would you think if I wore a head covering?"

He eyed her appraisingly, "Na, I like your hair just as it is. When you were a young bride you wore it curled under and it barely touched your shoulders. Now you don't curl it as often but I love it anyway."

"Even when it's so straight? I never have time to curl it anymore."

"--And shiny as a raven's wing," he winked. "I like it when you wear it in two braids dangling to your shoulders. It's cute."

"I only do that for dirty chores!" She gave him a little push.

He nudged her back, "Emily's hair is so totally unlike yours."

They both turned to smile fondly at their curly-haired daughter who was 'teaching' the teddy bear and doll to count to ten, not knowing that she still had a little learning to do herself.

Grace served hot chocolate and popcorn to everyone and soon after, they turned in because labouring in the woods is hard work.

Grace pondered that scripture in Corinthians silently after that, but eventually didn't feel comfortable praying without her head covered, so donned a kerchief when Randall wasn't around. He eventually found out but didn't comment.

Underneath the cheerful routine of daily living, both he and Grace had an undying longing to find Christians who shared the same convictions and concerns they did.

Did these Mennonite people have it? They seemed to be so at peace with themselves and each other.

"Grace, I think I'll eat dinner in the camp dining room if it's okay with you," Randall announced a week later while pulling on his lumberjack coat.

Grace nodded. She wasn't surprised. Quite often lately, he had been having some in-depth discussions with some of the fellow workers; Abe Wiens included, and assumed he wanted to continue with them today.

Secretly she was pleased. As her pregnancy was advancing she had been getting increasingly enthused about sewing for the little one, only problem is, it was taking so long to stitch everything by hand so was glad for the moments she didn't have to spend preparing a meal for her man. Emily and she could just a sandwich.

"Grace, what are you doing?" Grace looked up when her good friend Katharine Baerg knocked then peered in at the door.

Grace held up her tiny project. "Making baby nighties," she enthused.

"But by hand?" Katharine pressed her hand against her abdomen as she waddled through the door.

Grace's face clouded over. "I don't have a treadle machine," she admitted.

"Why don't you borrow mine?"

Katharine sighed as she sank heavily on the bench next to the table.

"Even since my ankles have been swelling so badly Justin has been so-o-o worried. We decided I'd better go back to the community with our little girl and live with my folks 'til the baby comes. That way I'd be closer to a doctor in case of emergency.

"I'm not up to doing any more sewing before this youngster arrives."

Now it was Grace's turn to look downcast. Their next-door neighbour, Beulah, Mrs. Abe Wiens, was nice, but she was old, well, older: she was probably at least fifty if not more.

Katharine and she had so much in common: they both had little girls and were expecting their second babies.

"Actually that's why I stopped in," Katharine stretched her legs out in front of her. "To tell you that Justin will be taking us back home. Mary Jane wanted to come in to play with Emily but I didn't think it would be a good idea: the parting would be too hard."

Grace missed Katharine after she left. Even though they hadn't spent much time together, both of them could tell theirs was the lasting kind of friendship. She often thought of Katharine while peddling away on the borrowed sewing machine, but it also reminded her of her dear mother-in-law whom she didn't see nearly as often as she wished.

Sometimes she would close her eyes and picture Lily busily piecing quilts at her gleaming black Singer treadle machine housed in its elegant wood cabinet and the miles between them would seem to diminish.

Have we even told them about the coming baby? I'm sure she would want to make something for him/ her if she knew. Grace felt her face redden at the thought of talking about it, especially over the telly. That would be embarrassing. Ah, well, Lily—Mom would understand.

It was a relief to her when she got to know another young woman close to her own age although she doubted it would ever become like the bonds she had already experienced three times in her life. That couldn't keep happening!

Henry and Eva Enns lived on the other side of the community so it had taken them longer to get close. . Grace quickly learned that Eva was a hearty, outdoorsy type and loved going for walks down logging trails. When Grace went along, Beulah's half-grown girls entertained Emily and Eva's sons.

"All this fresh air and exercise is doing wonders for me," Grace puffed as she tried to keep up with Eva.

Eva looked at her friend's rosy cheeks and realized she had been walking too briskly for the circumstances.

"Let's slow down a bit," she suggested. As their pace slacked off, Grace was relieved, she wasn't feeling so breathless.

"A little further on," Eva continued, "I have often feed chickadees; and if we are really quiet they might come around again."

A moment later, she took a piece of homemade bread out of her pocket and froze like a statue with her hand outstretched. Grace knew better than to talk, but took the opportunity to lean against a tree and press her hand over the small of her back.

It was enjoyable exploring the winter wonderland around the camp and they sometimes watched the sunrise and other times took a walk when the late afternoon colours were tinting the sky.

Eva pointed out various animal tracks; deer, raccoon, rabbit, mink, and even a bear, which should have been hibernating, and Grace was impressed at her knowledge.

Eva described the time she and Henry had sat out late one night and watched the beavers work and play. Grace wished she could have seen it too, but then decided the mosquitoes might have chased her right back into the house.

Once Grace invited Eva to bring her sewing over and they could work on projects together. It was a pleasant enough afternoon, but it soon became obvious that Eva enjoyed the outdoors to 'piddley' housework. When the sawmill was not in operation, she would more often than not, be working shoulder to shoulder with her husband around the farm.

Grace was glad Katharine lent her the sewing machine because now she didn't worry about getting her stack of two dozen extra nappies sewn as well as receiving blankets and a few nighties.

Eva put her finger to her lips, and Grace's drifting thoughts returned to the present. She followed Eva's pointing finger and smiled.

Not 500 yards away, a buck was staring at them, his face and shoulders framed by the lacy branches of a deciduous tree.

Sometimes, when the women were exceptionally quiet, they would see woodpeckers drumming away on a tree, or white rabbits flitting by. They enjoyed watching deer leaping gracefully at the edge of a snowy meadow.

"The woodland creatures are getting used to us," Eva said in a low voice. They don't run and hide so quickly."

"What an awe inspiring sight," Grace breathed later the same day as they watched eagles soar overhead.

The eagles soared out of sight, so she accepted a couple slices of dry bread from Eva and tossed some of the broken pieces on the crusty snow. After standing back, the birds swarmed around to feast on the delicacy. Chickadees were her favorite bird and both she and Eva were thrilled with how often the happy little birdies would land on their gloved hands, their shoulders, or even their heads! Until one day...

Someone is Coming!

CHAPTER 53

Once, while a chickadee was sampling the crumbs on Grace's out-stretched palm, while others were hovering close, awaiting their turn, Eva saw Grace's face turn ashen and she doubled over with pain.

"Eva," she gasped, as the birds scattered. "I've got to go home: now. It's three weeks early, but I don't think this baby is going to wait any longer."

Eva gave her a swift look of knowing comprehension and they hurried along through the sparkling woods. Never had it seemed so far, before.

Grace worried that there would be no time to fetch a doctor. She didn't even have time to panic as another contraction enveloped her, nearly bringing her to her knees as she squeezed through the door.

Eva sent a neighbour child to get Randall. "But you be careful," she warned shaking her finger at him. "This is no time for fooling around or watching the men at work. We need Uncle Randall to come back pronto."

Donny's eyes were wide and solemn as he bolted out and headed towards the sound of loud machinery.

Next, she hurried over to Mrs. Abe Wiens to ask if she could come over. Beulah had helped to deliver more than one baby in her day.

Emily, who had been playing there, crowded in close, her eyes wide with concern.

Beulah patted her bright little head and said, "You get to stay longer today: Dora and Beth play a game of London Bridges with the little ones."

Donny looked everywhere for Randall; his uncle spotted the boy and asked what he was doing so close to the dangerous machinery.

"I'm looking for 'Uncle' Randall," he said, tucking his mitten less hands up his sleeves. James swung him on his shoulder and headed 'out back' to where Randall and another man were working together to cut down a tree.

After James said a few words to Randall, he took the saw from the younger man, who bolted towards his cottage.

"Hey, take this little guy with you," James shouted.

Looking distracted, Randall hoisted Donny on his back then deposited him on his own doorstep without any further ado.

Randall flung open his own door, fearing the worse.

Grace was sitting, yes sitting, in the armchair. Randall had thought she would be in bed, hysterical perhaps.

"Oh, Randall, I'm in so much pain!"

He cradled her in his arms then tucked her gently into their homemade wooden bed. Beulah bustled around boiling water and doing what not all with Eva as her assistant, but Grace visibly relaxed and her eyes drifted shut as she clung to Randall's hand.

When her eyes flew open minutes later, Beulah wanted to shoo Randall out of the small cottage but Grace would have none of it, besides there was no time for argument: everything was happening too fast.

He hurried away to scrub his hands and throw on a clean shirt, tossing his sawdust covered jacket into the corner, and when he turned back the two women were blocking his vision. Later when Beulah handed him The Baby, Randall gazed down in deep adoration then a look of rapture lit up his face.

"My son," He breathed. Flesh of my flesh and bone of my bone: how could I have ever thought of not wanting to be a Daddy?

Beulah almost reverently took the scrawny, dark-haired baby from his father's arms so he would not chill. She sponged the newborn off and wrapped him snugly before tucking him up close to the serenely happy young mother who leaned over to caress the soft cheek and wrap the tiny fingers around one of her own.

Randall dropped to his knees beside Grace and gently stroked her pale cheek. "You did it, Grace. You delivered our beautiful second child into the world."

This isn't my second child, he's the third!

Randall missed the look of anguish deep in her eyes because his own had closed while he offered a prayer of praise and supplication to the benevolent Father of them all.

The news had a way of bouncing from one house to the next until by nightfall smiles were circling all around because of the new arrival. Although most knew better than to crowd in with gifts and congratulations, Beulah brought Emily over for a few minutes the next afternoon to be introduced to her sweet little brother. She hugged her Mommy and Daddy and after a reminder, kissed her baby brother, but at that moment was more interested in playing with the children next door.

Grace motioned towards the little red suitcase propped beside the door.

"Remember me saying that Auntie Beulah offered to take care of you for a few days after the baby was born?"

Emily nodded but seemed ready to bolt for the door. Dora and Beth had been helping her make cut outs from the Eaton's catalog and that was so much fun.

"Well tonight you will sleep with Beth in her bed, but you be a good girl for Auntie Beulah, okay."

"I will, Mommy, I will. Bye!"

Several hours later, Emily pressed her little nose against the frosted window after she had made a tiny peek hole with her finger.

"It's getting dark out."

"I know," Beulah said comfortably, "And soon we'll have some of that Green Bean Soup with sausages and those biscuits that you helped Dora to make."

"I don't want soup, I want my Mommy."

"She's probably sleeping, now."

"Emily," Dora called! "Come look while I take the biscuits out of the oven. See how nice and brown they are. Can you find the one shaped like a teddy that we made just for you? "

Emily pointed.

"I saw a real teddy once, but he wouldn't talk to me."

Dora and her mother exchanged glances. They had already heard the story about how Emily had been 'lost among big and little bears' and shivered at the thought.

Emily had had such a busy exciting day that she seemed almost too sleepy to finish her soup. Beth was going to help her with the bath since it was Dora's turn to wash dishes, but while the water was heating on the big wood stove Emily felt asleep on the couch with her ragdoll tucked in her arms.

"It's probably better that way," Beulah said in a low voice as she carefully slipped a nightgown over the drowsy girl's head.

Beth was disappointed but she didn't say anything.

"So the little girl is asleep?" Abe asked a few minutes later.

Beulah nodded.

"Well, that's sure better than her crying half the night for her mother. I thought you would have to rock her like you did our own children."

Beulah smiled: "I was hoping to."

Beth quietly picked up the paper scraps from their cut-out-doll project, then after a reminder went to dry the dishes. She sighed. "At least she'll sleep with me, tonight,"

"I get her tomorrow night," Dora retorted.

"She might wiggle so much she'll push you right off the bed," their brother Jack teased.

Beth stomped her foot at him.

When Tempers Soar

CHAPTER 54

Sally pushed Davey: "Get away from the table. I need all the room for my art project."

"But I always have to sit on the couch to do my homework. I'm sick of it."

"Do it on the floor, then."

"Can't. Alice will get into my stuff."

"Well, I sure can't. Alice will scatter all my pencil crayons to who knows where, if I got down there."
"No! I wouldn't!"
"Well, you'd beg to use them at least!"
Margaret gazed wearily at the squabbling children. This went on every night. The fact that they finally had enough money to build their own house did not help because they were still searching for the perfect location. They wanted a home in the country but not too far from school or David's job. At this rate, it would be ages before the project was completed.
David slammed the thick builder's manual onto the small stand beside him.
"Quit your belly-aching! Can't a fella have any peace and quiet around here for once?"
Alice looked frightened; her siblings fell silent.
David strode over to the door.

"Honey, your jacket," he ignored Margaret. His wife hurriedly got it for him. to. David hooked it over his elbow before scrambling down the fire escape and leaping. Margaret watched him stride away down the darkening streets. At least it's safer to take a walk at this hour than it would have been in Europe a few years back.

Alice had followed her down the narrow, dimly little hall which reeked of cigar fumes since that potbellied loafer had moved into the attic. Margaret had been sure their persnickety proprietor would have requested that he leave long before now but found out he was a shirttail relative.

"Why is Daddy mad?" Alice asked while lifting up her arms to be held.

"He's not 'mad', Alice just… irritated, I guess because we're so crowded and it …makes people fight too often."

Margaret swatted at a mosquito. She wished she could go for a long walk through the park with David, like in the carefree days before they were married. Carefree? She called those days carefree, with the war looming overhead and seemingly all around? When had she last been actually free from care: as a ten-year-old? She bowed her head: Lord, help me to lean on You.

She put Alice down and they walked hand in hand back to the stuffy apartment. Davey was reading a library book, now, but Sally wasn't finished her homework. She loved to draw.

Margaret had the children settled down for the night by the time David returned. Margaret wished they could kneel together before going to bed and pour out their troubles to their Heavenly Father. Was God even David's Heavenly Father? Margaret hardly knew anymore, but doubted if she should ask. Surely if they would pray together, their tension would ease.

There was another thing, though, that was making Margaret sorrowful. She had miscarried just last week: the children wouldn't be told, of course, and David refused to talk about it.

Two years ago, she had lost a baby at two and a half months and they had been so hopeful that this time it would be different.

'Father,' she whispered burying her head into the pillow. 'Thy will be done, and thank you so much for the children you have given us.'

Her eyes widened as she stared at the darkened ceiling. Randall is a Christian now; they have a stable home. How soon will it be before Grace asks to have Alice back? If she knew how crowded we still are in this apartment, would it be even sooner?

Coming Soon:

Emily & Alice